Robert W. Walker

author of *Blind Instinct* and *Cutting Edge*

Cold Edge

A KILLER ON THE EDGE.

A CITY FROZEN IN FEAR.

JOVE

$6.99 U.S.
$9.99 CAN

ISBN 0-515-12970-4

S > EAN

**Let Robert W. Walker take you to the edge of suspense
with the thrilling series featuring
Native American Police Detective Lucas Stonecoat...**

DOUBLE EDGE

*Stonecoat and Sanger face a new predator: the Snatcher,
a vicious psychopath targeting young teens...*

"A mesmerizing thriller. The return of Lucas, Sanger, and
others is well done and their latest case is brilliantly de-
veloped. *Double Edge* is superior ... a terse police proce-
dural. Mr. Walker quite simply snatches the reader's mind
for the entire book."
—Harriet Klausner

CUTTING EDGE

*Stonecoat and Sanger return to become entangled in a
literal Web of on-line intrigue, murder and mutilation...*

**"Just when you think there's nothing new to
be done with the serial killer novel"
(Ed Gorman, *Mystery Scene*)
along comes Robert W. Walker's *Instinct* novels featuring
brilliant FBI pathologist Dr. Jessica Coran...**

BLIND INSTINCT

*In Walker's newest, a crime spree of biblical proportions
plunges Jessica Coran into one of the most
unholy murder sprees in her career...*

EXTREME INSTINCT

*A satanic madman is drowning sinners in gasoline,
and cleansing them with flame. Only Jessica Coran
can stop him—by stepping into the fire...*

continued...

DARKEST INSTINCT

*The "Night Crawler" is loose. But are his ghastly crimes
the work of one killer, or two? Jessica Coran faces
double jeopardy . . .*

PURE INSTINCT

*New Orleans is the scene of the "Queen of Hearts" killer, and
one of Jessica Coran's most diabolical cases . . .*

"A world of suspense, thrills, and psychological games-
manship."   —*Daytona Beach News-Journal*

PRIMAL INSTINCT

*The psychotic "Trade Winds Killer" turns Hawaiian beaches
bloodred, challenging Jessica Coran to the death . . .*

"A bone-chilling page-turner."   —*Publishers Weekly*

"With *Primal Instinct*, Walker has arrived. A multilevel
novel packed with detective work."
                             —*Daytona Beach News-Journal*

FATAL INSTINCT

*Jessica Coran is summoned to New York City where a modern-
day Jack the Ripper has taken over the night . . .*

"A taut, dense thriller . . . an immensely entertaining novel
filled with surprises, clever twists, and wonderfully drawn
characters."   —*Daytona Beach News-Journal*

KILLER INSTINCT

*The blood-drinking "Vampire Killer" lures Jessica Coran
into the heartland of America . . .*

"Chilling and unflinching . . . technical without being
heavy-handed, and brutal without glorifying violence or
murder."   —*Fort Lauderdale Sun-Sentinel*

COLD EDGE

ROBERT W. WALKER

JOVE BOOKS, NEW YORK

This is a work of fiction. Names, characters, places and incidents are either the product of the author's imagination or are used fictitiously, and any resemblance to actual persons, living or dead, business establishments, events or locales is entirely coincidental.

COLD EDGE

A Jove Book / published by arrangement with
the author

PRINTING HISTORY
Jove edition / March 2001

The Penguin Putnam Inc. World Wide Web site address is
http://www.penguinputnam.com

ISBN: 0-515-12970-4

A JOVE BOOK®
Jove Books are published by The Berkley Publishing Group,
a division of Penguin Putnam Inc.,
375 Hudson Street, New York, New York 10014.
JOVE and the "J" design
are trademarks belonging to Penguin Putnam Inc.

PRINTED IN THE UNITED STATES OF AMERICA

10 9 8 7 6 5 4 3 2 1

PROLOGUE

Medicine man's eye: wise, vigilant

OFFICE OF PSYCHOTHERAPIST DR. THOMAS
   W. MORRISSEY
HOUSTON, TEXAS
JUNE 11, 2001

"Infaction, infactuation even, disin-crimination, drossen-tric, double-may-care, evolunacy, ignormality, grosso-nomics, micronausea . . ."

Sometimes the words pouring forth from the doctor sounded and resounded as a torrent of meaningless, mindless misinformation and drivel. The doctor of psychiatry said that he had written and published an entire book around the word *evolunacy*—discussing the evolving madness and lunacy in society; how it ebbs and flows throughout recorded history; how, like a pendulum, it continually proves that history repeats itself. The doctor's premise persuaded that mankind, like basic human personality, took one fixed and determined path, and as with each individual, whole nations and entire races had at birth a set of bedrock character traits that never really changed. The world, according to the doctor, was formed of a basic human-bestial foundation, at the cornerstone of which existed evil; and that trait, like the primitive brain, while wrapped in the gossamer of civilization, remained firmly rooted at the core of the human psyche.

The doctor had surmised that the true character of an individual or a nation—whether violent or inoffensive—never changed, despite outward appearances of change. Unable to keep it to himself, his revelation-summation had to be shared. The doctor shared as often as occasion allowed. He shared it with his patients in both private session and in group therapy—a thing he insisted upon for all his patients—waving a hardcover book with his likeness on the back like a victory flag.

This patient remained always filled with a murderous rage, a rage he could not rid himself of; it lived inside his brain and became his shadow—a powerful shadow. He fed on the bitterness, hatred, mindless fury. The patient knew the truth as well as the doctor. That proved Morrissey's message. The good doctor spoke of the medium as the message, the MO as the message. A bona fide serial killer, unable to help himself, obsessed to the point of repeatedly using the same medium, i.e., setting, victim, weapon, ritual, etc., for murder, set himself up for the fall and capture; and did so in a semiconscious state, desiring to be caught and punished. Like a bad boy who has done evil, a part of the culprit courts punishment for in the punishment comes affirmation, pride even, that others know what he has accomplished: evil to the tenth degree.

The patient hated the doctor, who represented one of *them*, even though Morrissey, more readily than anyone the patient had ever met, understood the killing need of the sociopathic personality. Still, Morrissey remained one of them—those who not only stood outside him but also against him—that army of other men marshaled against him. Men who stood for something, the so-called normal ones; men whose needs did not include the craving to kill in order to feel; men who were the opposite of the sociopathic creature shunned by all of society. Meanwhile, the sociopath, according to Dr. Morrissey, stood outside the grand, neon-lit world of "normal" society. The sociopath was forever looking in like the monster Grendel in *Beowulf*.

Suddenly, as often happened, the doctor started shouting at the patient, telling him that he had no idea of the possibilities to come from opening up to the greater human spirit; and since the patient could not see, feel, taste, smell or otherwise hear the bell that Dr. Thomas W. Morrissey rang, then he should go now.

"Come back when your mind is opened to your own salvation through self-discovery. To thine own self be true, my friend. Examine your true nature, and you will be first aghast and terrified, but you will deal with that. Move on, become whole. But you cannot heal a wound you do not see."

Fuck you and everyone in the system, the patient wanted to shout, but the last time he swore at the huge, hulking Dr. Morrissey, the man had literally thrown him bodily from the office.

Once again the patient was ordered away in a fit of impatience. "Out, out! Go back to your halfway hovel, you halfway man, afraid to take a step across that halfway line. I despise cowardice, mister!"

"I'm not a coward!" protested the patient.

Dr. Morrissey rose like a giant over the smaller man. "The hell you aren't!"

A long pause while the patient fingered the knife hidden within his coat, his thoughts turning to murder.

Morrissey let out an exasperated sigh, fell back into his chair and raised a dismissing hand and said, "Return in two days at your appointed time, but *only* if you have opened your eyes to your true nature, the inner self. Ugly as it may be."

"But the conditions of my parole say I gotta be here twice a week, Doc."

"Out, damn you. To hell with the conditions of your fucking parole. You're my patient now, not the state's. Your rehabilitation or lack of rehab is no longer their problem. It's mine. Your success or failure reflects back on me, son. So, now you damn well better just do as I tell you."

Morrissey, a big and intimidating man on the order of Thor and Zeus combined, bolted from his chair and chased the patient out the door, swearing after him. "Learn to do what the fuck I say, and you might, you just might save your body and soul in the bargain, and at the very least stay out of the pen!"

The doctor—holding tight to his most recently published book, the photo on the back showing all his teeth in a broad smile—slammed the door in the patient's bewildered face.

ONE

Ceremonial dance area

The scene of the crime proved brutally stark. The victim was a young woman named Marlee Balou, a known prostitute who worked the big hotels downtown. The victim lay minus her hands and scalp. Worse yet, the killer had actually scalped her while she remained alive according to the M.E., Dr. Leonard Chang, who could surmise this at a glance—something to do with the coloration of the wounded area, blood rising to meet the knife. Lucas knew that Dr. "Everready" Chang—as police referred to him, due to his tireless energy—would have to do his magic first, to be certain. Still, since Marlee was the second victim found in this circumstance—the other being a slightly older, homebound matronly thirty-five-year-old named Rae Chenoweth, who had lived on disability checks in another part of the city—Lucas guessed that Chang's confidence in his conjecture would likely prove true. Dangerous as assumptions might be, educated guesswork at a crime scene proved startlingly accurate among the well versed and experienced. Leonard Chang, though sporting the face and body of a young tennis pro, had been in the forensics field for seventeen years. As a result, Lucas felt confident that this victim, like the one before, had indeed been scalped while alive. The thought of it made the crown of his own head tingle with pain.

The removal of her hands, too, according to forensic fact, had come while she yet breathed. Chang surmised—as he had with Rae Chenoweth, a heavyset redhead—that Marlee Balou, a late-twenties brunette, likely had gone into a coma during the scalping, and that the removal of her hands, most likely went unfelt. Again Lucas felt the sympathy pains, but this time at each wrist. He unconsciously wrapped his left hand around his right wrist, fingered the connection there, and then massaged his left wrist with his right hand in the same fashion. The action didn't go unnoticed by Chang and other detectives in the room. Chang quipped, "Dooo you ever wonder what the old Chinese religious leader meant when he say to the boy, 'What is the sound of one hand clapping?' "

"Never gave it much thought."

"I figure it out sometime back at a football game."

"Really?"

"Then later with my child, my infant."

"Really? Then what is the sound of one hand clapping?"

"High five . . . It take two people to make the sound of one of our hand clapping, Detective. It mean, we work together, we get something out of the otherwise silent hand." Chang then lifted his hand for a high five over the dead body. Lucas, after a smile and a shake of his head, high-fived the M.E. Their hands came together and created a thunderous clap in the room.

Lucas stared at the victim a long while. He considered

the horror of the acts perpetrated on the two known victims of the maniac now terrorizing the city. Two women. Beaten into submission. Robbed of scalp and hands. Each victim had died an excruciating death via traumatic shock after an intruder had climbed through a second-story window.

Lucas was assigned to the case not because of his detective expertise or tracking ability, but because he was a Native American. Since Lucas was a Texas Cherokee, the thinking at top levels was that he might more easily track a Native American killer. The supposition went that if a killer is interested in the taking of scalps in a Texas city, then he must be the dreaded maniac red man of dime novels. Who better to track a red man than another red man, or so city hall thinking went.

The illogic of the brass never ceased to surprise or amaze. A background check of the original victim, the redheaded Chenoweth, turned up the fact that her ancestral tree held Native American and African-American branches—which explained the dark pigmentation of her skin. Like many black slaves in America, a brave forefather had escaped from Missouri not going North on the Underground Railroad but out West to Indian Territory. In her case, the Seminoles on an Oklahoma Indian reservation had taken in her great-great-grandfather, who then became a Seminole, accepting tribal life as his own. It happened a great deal more often than history recorded. Ms. Rae Chenoweth had kept meticulous family records, and she was the end of her line. It made her brutal death even more poignant, and for some, the discovery made it point even more to a Native-American perpetrator. . . .

Lucas didn't like the thinking, not for a moment. He had come to the case reluctantly, and the detectives already working the original discovery, didn't want his input. In fact, they took it as a slap in the face to be told they needed another set of eyes, ears, hands and feet on the case.

The first detectives to catch the Chenoweth case worked the 29th Precinct, and Lucas belonged to the 31st. Reason enough to dislike one another.

The 29th Precinct guys were Dave Harbough and Marc Damon. Harbough, near retirement age—holding on to the badge past his time, some said—stood six-four and weighed a good two-sixty or -seventy, while Damon, as tall but a decade younger, stood like a bean pole, the body of a marathon runner. Both men had clean records, and both were angry at their superiors, the circumstances, the killer, and now Lucas, who stood in the middle of the death room—a flophouse on Jupiter Street amid the squalid Oleander District that had once been a Spanish enclave but was now a black neighborhood. The run-down area and the squalor of the victim's surroundings told a pitiful story of a white woman prostitute living in a black ghetto. Lucas guessed that if it were not an election year, and if the two killings were not so dramatically and horrifyingly accomplished—the taking of scalps and hands painted a lurid picture in the press—then little notice would be taken of the deaths of an out-of-work, disabled alcoholic and a down-on-her-whore's-luck prostitute.

Tonight's victim, unlike the earlier one, had alabaster white on white skin that was almost porcelain to the touch now that rigor had set in. The differences between the two victims sparked some discussion.

"Yeah, but don't a killer normally kill within his own race? Not that cross-racial murder never happens. I mean since the MO appears the same, the usual assumptions maybe don't hold true here," Dave Harbough said aloud to anyone willing to listen.

"It's also true that usually a serial killer—if that's what we have here—preys on only one victim type. Here we have a slightly built brunette and a heavyset redhead with a considerable age difference as well," suggested Lucas, "not to mention their racial differences."

"The creep comes sneaking in here feeling no need to be selective. Young, old, prim or slutty, white, black, Seminole Indian . . . preferences would just slow him down," Harbough shot back.

Marc Damon's voice was muffled by a handkerchief he held over his nose to protect him from the odor of the days-old corpse. "Seems the only thing the two women had in common was their wounds."

"And the fact the killer sexually molested them both with a broom handle," added M.E. Chang. "Which he left, rammed far up into them like a pole, causing internal bleeding."

"Near forty years on the job," muttered Harbough, "seen a lot of shit—stuff that would curl a Mother Superior's pubic hair. But I swear, this taking of the hands and scalp while she was alive? And ramming a broom up her. Jeez, what the hell is this guy doing with the hands and scalps? You got any answers, Indian?"

Lucas looked Harbough straight in the eyes. "I know as much as you do at this point."

"Whataya make of the broom handle?" asked Damon.

Lucas only shrugged. "Reminds me of the Boston Strangler. He did the same to the old women he molested."

Harbough said, "There are marks on her arms and legs. Whataya make of them?"

Damon added, "Looks like he was making little pictures."

"A real artist, this guy. Really took his time over the body," Harbough commented. "Like to get my hands on the SOB, carve a few cool pictures into his flesh with *my* knife."

"Pictographs, archaeologists call them. Usually made by primitives," replied Lucas.

"Primitives?" queried Damon, his eyes squinting at Lucas.

"Primitive as in primitive peoples," Harbough explained to his younger partner.

Lucas leaned in closer to the victim and studied the carvings in her flesh that were nearly obliterated by the blood caked there. To truly see the pictures, they'd need M.E. Chang to clean the wounds, which he'd do for photo verification and evidence. In fact, photo identification of any fingerprints that might have been left on the body was now possible with the new technology available to Chang. However, since he had found only a few smudged prints on the previous body, Lucas held little hope the killer had gotten careless with his second victim.

Lucas dared take a handkerchief to one of the wounds, the one carved around the navel. "It's a snake, meaning cunning, wise or clever," suggested Lucas. "And this beside it is a lightning strike, meaning that he's not only cunning but fast, immediate, like a lightning strike. Of course, whether he's talking about himself or someone or something else, I don't know, but there you have it. Whoever he is, he doesn't know enough about Indian history to mark his prey correctly."

"Chang, can we get this broom outta her?" asked Harbough. "It's ruining my concentration."

"Sure, sure," agreed Chang, taking hold of the bristled end of the broom and sliding it from the body cavity. Fluids and blood that had been trapped by the smooth, plastic handle leaked out. Chang placed the broom in a large polyethylene bag, and tagged it as evidence. He'd scan it later for any prints.

"Whataya mean, 'mark his prey correctly'?" Harbough near whispered to Lucas, both men leaning in over the body now. Lucas stared intently at the pictographs carved into the flesh and then back to Harbough, who held an unlit pipe in his teeth.

"Tribal warfare among Native Americans left many fallen on the battlefield, and each kill was marked by the man who had done the killing, usually a distinctive slash, a series of lines, crosses, whatever, depending on your tribal sign. We did it to Custer's men, too," finished Lucas with a wry grin.

"According to the books I've read on Custer, he deserved a good carving up," replied Harbough.

"Sure got his jollies killing Indians," suggested Damon.

"To further his career, I think the man would have killed his sister," Lucas muttered. "Got his whole army and his kid brother killed at Little Bighorn."

"So, you think we should be looking in the Native American community for our killer?" asked Harbough.

"Look, this guy could just as well be a white man who wants us to suspect a Native American," replied Lucas, getting to his feet. "It's too early to be making assumptions about the killer's race. Especially since we have both a white victim and a mixed-blood Native American–black victim."

"I thought that's why you were brought in, Stonecoat," said Damon at Lucas's back.

"Trust me, Detectives, it wasn't my idea. I have enough on my hands with the COMIT program down at the Thirty-first. Last thing I wanted to catch was this shit."

"But you have caught it. Look, maybe we can help each other out here, Stonecoat. About those cold files. There's one I'd like you to dig out of the mothballs and look over, tell me what you think. Old case of mine. Some call it the Headless Horseman case. The weasel we put away for a series of beheadings?" Harbough left the question to hang in the air.

Marc Damon stood shaking his head, saying, "Oh, damn it, Dave, you're obsessing again over that Freeleng creep!"

"That creep is going to be set free in a couple of days, Marc. And as sure as the sun sets and the moon rises, he's going to go back to his old job, and this city's going to see a new rash of rape-murders involving missing heads. He'll make this hand and scalp guy look like a Boy Scout by comparison." Harbough turned back to Lucas. "Will you have a look at the case file—unsolved, lying in your Cold Room since this creep went up for attempted murder, rape and assault. The guy's name is Walter Karl Freeleng, and yeah, he's been a model prisoner and is taking a walk from Huntsville day after tomorrow. The system, as usual, sucks."

Lucas nodded. "Sure, I'll have a look. What can it hurt?"

"It's going to hurt somebody somewhere. You can bet on it, my friend."

Damon shrugged in Lucas's direction, saying, "My partner knows everything."

"Mark my words. Houston's going to see a new rash

of rape-murder-beheadings. You can take that to the bank."

"And if it comes true, you know you'll be the next in the box, being interrogated by IAD 'cause of your predictions. Everybody in the house knows you're—"

"Just you wait and see. . . ."

"At the moment, we've got our hands full with this crap," replied Damon, pointing to the handless, scalpless, lifeless prostitute.

"You ready to turn her over to No Waist?" asked Harbough of Lucas.

Leonard Chang, the medical examiner for the city of Houston was alternately referred to as "No Waste" and "No Waist," as well as "Everready," since he wasted nothing, and his waistline proved all but nonexistent. Lucas liked Chang, however, for his meticulous attention to detail and his thoroughness at both the crime scene and the lab. As a result, whenever possible, Lucas liked to have Chang cover his cases.

"It's still your call, Harbough," Lucas told the elder man. "I'm just here to assist."

Harbough nodded, accepting this. So far no one had relieved him of the duties of detective in charge, which fell to the first detective to take the call. Neither Harbough nor Lucas had ever met before today, but they each felt a good rapport building. "Look at that case file for me, Stonecoat, when you get a chance. But don't wait too late. I tell you, this Freeleng character is Satan incarnate."

Lucas watched Harbough limp off, no doubt a well-earned injury from previous days on the job. Maybe one day, Harbough would tell him about it, and Lucas could, in turn, tell the old veteran how he himself came by the flaming red scar that painted his own neck and upper chest.

Chang gave Lucas a quirky half grin, his big glasses bobbing as he said, "So, they got you on the case, Lucas. Maybe might be good idea."

"Maybe . . . might be . . . maybe not."

Lucas remained long enough to hear Chang tell him, "I can't tell you nothing new, but lab tests are likely to confirm it as the work of the same killer."

Lucas stepped away, found an exit with some breathable air, and promptly lit up a Marlboro Light. He'd taken up the habit only recently and was at the stage where he believed he could quit anytime—but this was hardly the time. He next located his car for the return trip to the precinct.

The drive back to the 31st gave Lucas time to think, time to recall just how he had gotten involved in the Scalper Killings. The press was extremely curious about the first killing and had already dubbed the killer, the Scalper. Meanwhile, top brass officials believed that the killer must surely be either Native or Mexican American, because of his penchant for pictographs carved into the skin. Lucas had remained skeptical on that score from day one. Tonight's newscast would only fan these assumptions.

As he drove the interstate across town, Lucas recalled the heated conversation he'd had with Dr. Meredyth Sanger—police psychiatrist—just previous to coming on the case after the discovery of the second scalping victim. It had been in Meredyth's office at the precinct; and it had gotten so loud that at one point, Randy Oglesby, her assistant, buzzed to ask if Meredyth needed to call in the troops.

Lucas and Meredyth had been arguing the relative merits of the Houston Rockets's starting lineup. He felt pleased when he could checkmate her with her own words, but now he had a far more serious bone to pick, and this matter would not be settled by a third party referee. He now pulled into the precinct's parking lot, entered the station house and went directly to the elevator and Meredyth's office. Once there, he barged past Randy Oglesby, and into the police shrink's office, shouting as he did so.

"Since when does the captain send orders through the house shrink?" Lucas demanded, nameplate and ID dangling from his shirt pocket.

"He called me a moment ago, from the mayor's office, Lucas. He . . . They want you on this case! What can I say? Some megalomaniac is carving people up and leaving clues cut into their flesh and finishing by scalping his victims and removing their hands. It's enough to strike terror into anyone, and who better than an . . . than you—"

"Who better than an *Indian* to understand a scalper? Is that what you were going for? You know, the American Indian didn't take scalps until white fur traders, trappers and settlers introduced the practice—when white government put a bounty on the scalps of red men, calling any red man who disagreed with them renegades, thieves and murderers."

"I seem to recall reading that someplace."

"Scalping began as a white thing, with such European traditions as economics, the push for trade, the Hudson Bay Company, sweetheart."

"Be that as it may, and as much as I'd love a history lesson right now, Lieutenant—"

"Men in white government cooked up the idea that you could pay a man a bounty on Indian scalps. The Indian retaliated in kind, counting *coup* for each white scalp collected. So, maybe what you really need here is a dyed-in-the-wool white cop who cares to know his own history?"

"We all know you're the man for this job, Lucas. Why fight it?"

"Why do you continually volunteer me, Meredyth?"

"I had input, but—"

"Ever occur to you that I might be busy with the COMIT project?" shouted Lucas. His tall, lanky Cherokee Indian frame paced like a trapped cougar before falling back into the chair in front of her desk. He leaned forward, forearms on knees, sitting silent a moment, taking council with himself, staring into Sanger's clear, intelligent eyes—eyes that spoke a world of knowledge about the well of the human soul.

He considered his next words with care, as he truly didn't wish to provoke the police psychiatrist's Irish. On more than one occasion, she had solicited Lucas's help. But somehow, as always when speaking to her, despite his explicitly sexual attraction for her and their mutual respect, words hurled themselves at her independent of his brain. So they came out ugly even when he wished otherwise. "Do whatever it takes, but find another boy! I'm not your protégé to be carted out before the mayor and the assistant deputy mayor and the press and your cronies at the country club or that exclusive gym you work out at. I'm not your solution to the world's problems, no more than I am your father confessor, Mere."

The tirade took its toll. She leaned back in her chair as if physically slapped, eyes blinking, cheek twitching, her strawberry-blond hair somehow raised. She simply responded, "You really do have a problem with the rich, don't you, dear? We should explore that sometime in a serious series of sessions, Lucas, really. It can only cloud your professional judgment when dealing with high-society crime, if you continually look at anyone with more coin jingling in pocket than you with . . . disdain."

Fuck you, he wanted to say, but held back. He only glared, sighed heavily and shook it off.

"Christ, Lucas, face it. *You* are *it*. The powers that be want you to take direction over the investigation."

"So no one else has to take responsibility should it prove unsolvable? So give it to the Cold Room file guy, because that's where it's headed anyway?"

"Nobody believes that, Lucas. Not even you."

He stonily seethed for a moment, thinking: *This maniacal killer is taking both their hands and their scalps!* Something many Native American Indian warriors did on the Plains during battle. The killer also carved Native American hieroglyphic impressions into their torsos, arms and legs; and so the killer might well be Native American. The killer might possibly be someone that Zachary "Three Hands" Roundpoint—himself a hired assassin—might help Lucas to corner.

What's this megalomaniac doing with their scalps and hands? Lucas wondered but stayed on his train of thought, shouting instead, "And for God's sake, Meredyth, at what time in our relationship did I become your protégé to be flaunted as some fucking miracle worker from here to the mayor's office in the first place?" Lucas shot up from his chair, realizing that he had begun to repeat himself. His frame loomed over the desk like the shadow of an angry bird of prey, displaying that trapped and cornered body language to her once more; but his body spoke guardedly in a mix of threat and sensual innuendo, and this made her smile in response.

"Don't use that tone with me, Lucas Stonecoat!" She hadn't shirked. Not so much as a flinch at his suddenly pouncing from his chair, his fierce eyes no less angry than those of a surprised mountain lion.

"All right," she finally admitted, "maybe it began with a *suggestion* from me, but now I have Captain Gordon J. Lincoln's full approval on this, Lucas. He wants us to work together on this case. There's a lunatic on the loose in Houston. Lincoln wants it this way, wants a quick end to it. I want it, the mayor supports it, hell the whole damned city of Houston wants it."

"All due to the success we had in the Coleson case?"

"You've created your own monster, Lucas. Face it. Since you've become such a celebrity, cracking the case of the century—"

"I had a great deal of help—including you, remember? And Dr. Desinor." The FBI psychic had been on loan for the case.

"In any event, you're now the mayor's man, my friend. Scream and bray at the moon all you like, man of the Wolf Clan. It won't change the fact that this is your baby, Lucas."

"You arranged this, Meredyth. I knew it."

"If it pleases you to think so. God, I wish I were half the manipulative bitch you credit me as being, Lucas, but it just isn't so. This is a PR problem you're having. You're more popular than you want to be, and I swear to you, the circumstances surrounding the situation inevitably led straight back to you, dear."

"I don't want this case."

"Think of it. The killer is using Native American pictographs carved into the flesh of his victims to tell his story of hatred and murder. He's killed a black-Seminole woman and now a white woman. It appears to be a clear case of revenge against society by some maniacal, blood-thirsty savage on some quest to fulfill some sort of prim-itive instinct. And how best to seek revenge on what the white man has done to his people than to kill women in so atrocious a fashion?"

"If he's Native, why would he kill Native if it's an act of hatred toward white society. And why black for that matter?"

"He likely didn't know the black woman was part Na-tive American."

"Damn it, Mere. Only a week ago we were arguing the fact that I don't care to baby-sit a squad of sniveling re-cruits, and you were telling me that it would only be a one-shot."

"Circumstances have changed, Lucas."

" 'See how it goes,' you said. 'It could save a life,' you said. Said, 'We all have a stake in helping up-and-coming rookies through the difficult transition of becoming street cops.' "

"That has to take a back burner to this, Lucas. Much as I planned on a comprehensive program—and sessions with you at its core—this madman on the loose changes everything. I could not have predicted these headlines any more than you."

"So, headlines are dictating this, huh? We're now being led by the nose by a bunch of reporters?"

"Fact of public life, Lucas."

"Meredyth, I'm just another cop. I have no secret pow-ers to bless every goddamn rookie that you counsel, and

I have no secret powers to catch this so-called savage of yours."

"Oh, please, is it that I've used the word 'savage' in connection with this guy that's troubling you? Well, sorry, but it's hardly a case of being politically incorrect at this stage. Damn it, Lucas, will you please just give it a try? You might actually enjoy working this case if—"

"Only if my captain directly orders it, and so far, he has not given me a direct order."

"Then I'll see to it that it becomes an order!" she shouted, losing control.

Lucas stormed out, half waving at Randy, the computer whiz, as he marched past.

Randy waved back, his eyes hardly leaving his computer screen. "Have a nice day. . . ." Randy's facetious words trailed Lucas through the door.

$\mathcal{T}$wo

Arrowhead: watchful

The last time that he'd looked at his gold shield, Lucas had reminded himself of the incredible struggle and journey of the soul he'd performed in regaining the position of Detective First Class. That had been his original, foremost goal, and it had had nothing to do with taking charge of the Cold Room files or the newly formed COMIT program. His original desire had been to be placed on active duty. That had been dramatically altered by his superiors, who felt it best to keep him tied to the routines of the office known variably as the Dungeon, the Cellar or the Cold Room—a room filled with the broken lives of dead people whose murders had gone unsolved.

Now they wanted him to ignore the very responsibilities they'd foisted upon him—to take time out to go after yet another maniac menacing the greater Houston area.

It felt good to be clear of Dr. Sanger and her office right now. He knew that if he'd stayed a moment longer, he would have really lost control and gone to a bad place. As he made his way through the labyrinth of the 31st

Precinct, Lucas surveyed the faces of men determinedly at work, combating forces as enormous as nature itself: crime, pestilence, poverty, stupidity, prejudice, hatred and all the social ills bred by modern life and society in a major American city.

He wondered at the prodigious effort lawmen took, all American law enforcement, and sometimes he wondered if it were not an impossibility to stem the growing tidal wave of crime and criminal activity flourishing just outside the glass and brick facade of the 31st.

He also gave some thought to the psychological effects of *The Job*, and the necessity for Meredyth and people like her. He privately thanked the fates for having her aboard at the 31st, as she was a far cry from some shrinks he'd known and hated. Aside from being beautiful and smart, she proved capable—extremely so. He could not fault her in that department. He knew that his attraction for her colored everything he said and did with respect to Meredyth; but he also knew that she stood as a faithful and stalwart ally, and that he'd been foolish just now to alienate her.

Meredyth proved her persuasive powers with the brass every day. She could be equally winning with Lucas, especially when she flashed those big doe eyes, and it felt great to have her plead for his help. Still, his recent bouts with insomnia, and the excessive workload already on him, convinced Lucas that adding more to his plate at this time could only prove a fool's quest. He could not possibly devote the time and attention required. He felt good about having remained firm on his stand against the assignment. Though he assumed it merely a temporary victory.

He now stood at the Coca-Cola machine, juggling

change for a drink, when beside him he realized that Randy Oglesby had come on the same errand—or had he? "Sounds like you two had a big powwow in her office," he said to Lucas. "Bad medicine?"

Lucas didn't mind the Indian idioms coming from Randy, as Randy had become prone to them early on in their relationship. No doubt the younger man thought them a kind of special language they shared. Coming from the kid who had helped Lucas in countless ways, through his computer wizardry over the course of two major cases, Lucas allowed for Randy's idiosyncratic ways and words. He knew that Randy harbored no ill will or ugly intention. Awkwardness and confusion about how to deal with Lucas were what led the young man into using such foolish language.

"Yeah, council meeting turned ugly."

"If there's anything I can do, you know, to help out, Lucas. You know I'm your man."

Lucas stood two heads taller than Randy. "Thanks, Randy. It's just that, damn it, I hate it that they assume this asshole doing the scalping is Native American, and that as such, I know more about him than the average detective might."

"Maybe you do, Lucas."

Lucas looked into the kid's sincere, shimmering eyes, half expecting to see a computer image imprinted there, as Randy spent more time before a computer than he did on meals, bedtime or sex. "Maybe I do, maybe I don't, but either way," Lucas replied, "the assumption on their part is racially motivated. Pisses me off."

"But Lucas, what in hell does a white man *really* know about, you know, the psychological makeup of a pissed off Native American?"

"Psychological effects of taking a woman's life?" he asked the kid. "Or are we talking again about the psychological effects of an officer doing his duty in taking a man down?" Lucas stepped away from Randy, but the shorter, younger man followed him to a table. "Look, Randy, either way, that's Meredyth's job. A cop starts thinking like a shrink in the field, he quick becomes tomorrow's worm meat."

"I know you didn't want to do that peer counseling thing she asked you to do, but this . . . this is different, Lucas. And you know, Lucas, Dr. Sanger's intentions are always good."

"And the road to hell is paved with good intentions. Like I have time to hold the hands of a bunch of recruits, or take on another case? She's gotta get real, Randy." Lucas realized that he sounded like a man confiding to another about a tiff between himself and his wife. The thought made him start. Had they evolved in a pair of grumpy old cop partners? Or was the fighting a ruse concocted of the strange chemistry between them—a formula for holding back out of a fear of intimacy.

Randy continued talking on another plane altogether, saying, "Still, Lucas, you know as well as I the power of peer modeling. That if a cop hears it from a shrink, he thinks *so what*, so much bullshit, right? But hearing the same conclusions from another cop in a tavern over beers turns the bullshit into hard-earned pearls of wisdom."

Lucas laughed. "Pearls of wisdom. Who talks like that?"

"Personally, I'm like you, Lucas," Randy said, disregarding the tall man's frown. "I hate pondering the gravest questions the job entails for all you guys who carry guns and badges. You know what I mean . . . how you handle taking a life."

"I have enough to do pondering that one for myself. Don't need to ponder it for others," Lucas said. "In situations of kill or be killed, what the hell is there to think about, when you come right down to it?"

"Meredyth's like, you know, Holden Caulfield in *The Catcher in the Rye.*"

"Never read it."

"She wants to save as many souls as she can, even knowing she can't save 'em all."

It had been one of Meredyth's pleas for Lucas's help that had first brought them together some years back, and he did treasure their friendship, their relationship, such as it remained. He had made no secret of his feelings for her, but she had kept him at arm's length while flirting with her other arm.

A part of him wondered if he hadn't reacted too rashly this day; perhaps Randy also thought the same, hence the kid running after him and sharing this Coca-Cola moment. They now sat at a plastic table on plastic chairs in the plastic world of the break room.

Randy spoke Lucas's thoughts aloud for him. "You must have some desire or, that is, you must like the possibility of, you know, working with Dr. Sanger more closely . . . you know, with her again." He fumbled and tripped over his last words, garbling them, unsure of Lucas's reaction.

"Pile on the misery and frustrations of unrequited love," he told Randy. "Is that it?" He smiled at the younger man and winked. "I gotta get out of here, back to my real work."

Randy nodded and lifted a hand Indian-fashion and said, "Until next time, my Cherokee friend. Good-bye and watch your back. She does, you know."

"She does what?"

"Whenever you storm out like you do, Lucas, she comes out to watch your backside as you depart. She's made it her life's work to watch your back, so to speak."

"Very funny, Randy. Good-bye and watch *your* back. And cut it out with all that Cherokee lingo crap."

"All right, all right . . ."

Lucas exited the plastic room, his drink only half finished, the can left sitting on the table.

As he made his way back to the Cold Room via the stairwell into the crypt below Precinct 31, he muttered about the seething thoughts prevailing now in his head. As he did so, he took no notice of the dark stairwell or the dungeonlike corridor of the ancient precinct building. He'd become so used to it. "Now they want me to ignore the very responsibilities I didn't want to begin with— responsibilities they heaved on me. Now the same *morons* want me to drop the cold files to go chasing after yet another maniac."

The stone walls all around had no answer for Lucas. But they felt cool like the inside of a cavern, and it remained as always quiet down in the Cold Room, which he now entered. He found his desk chair and dropped into its complaining embrace. At least it felt good, for the moment, to be clear of Dr. Sanger and her office, despite the verbal carnage he had wrought, like so many arrows sticking up from the corpses of soldiers in old black-and-white films, he thought. Still, he'd left the battlefield at just the right moment. He knew that if he'd stayed any longer, he would have really lost all control, and such a circumstance could come back in the form of choking regret.

31ST PRECINCT
THE FOLLOWING DAY

Lucas's tall frame filled the hallway, and his stride took him in three steps to the elevator, which he bypassed for the stairwell. He routinely took the stairwell up and down to the Cold Room to exercise a lingering, arthritic hip, a hangover from a near-death experience—one that had almost destroyed his future as a police detective, but one from which he had fought back. So, the stairwell represented steady exercise; besides, he thoroughly detested closed-in spaces such as modern elevators. He avoided them whenever possible—a genetic hang-up, he suspected.

He noisily pushed through the stairwell door, sending it into the wall. It was a habit that centered his aggressions on things hard and unfeeling, so that he might more readily control his anger.

He started up for his stairwell exercise, when he heard the familiar and peculiarly out of place sound of gunfire, a *pop-pop-pop* sound, not at all the ear-shattering explosion heard in Dolby Surround theaters.

Thoughts flooded Lucas's mind. Some maniac on the loose in the squad room above? Perhaps someone who'd grabbed hold of a cop's weapon? Or had some space cadet come crashing in off the street with guns blazing as in a Raymond Chandler novel? Or worse yet, had some cop suddenly lost it, opening fire and blasting away at his blue knight coworkers? Maybe one of Meredyth Sanger's pet psychiatry projects had gone horribly awry? A mental Grendel among the knights? She did, after all, have some fairly unusual patients who carried guns and worked out of the 31st Precinct.

The path Lucas now took, one he'd traversed hundreds of times before, had somehow become an enormously long tunnel filled with the unfamiliar. Up and around each half-landing he raced, silently asking, *What floor is this?* He'd never before noticed that the old building had no numbers in its stairwell to designate levels.

No signs to follow, no way to know, as he hurled himself up each stair and around each half-landing. With continuing gunfire coming from above in the squad room, he now saw every dead insect, every crevice and peeling piece of green paint like so much discarded snake flesh; every inch of his panting journey up the steps brought him new, different, fresher, sharper, clearer sights. It was as if the peyote he'd taken for his ongoing pain the night before continued its effect on him during this adrenaline rush.

He pulled up short, fairly certain he stood on the landing of the main floor. The gunshots now deafening, the gunman must lurk somewhere on the other side of the heavy stairwell door. Lucas heard screaming in what sounded to him like Italian, a number of colorful, American swear words interspersed among the Italian phrases. Screams came in reply, as victims of the mad shooter fell.

Bursting in on the gunman could get him killed. Instead, he lowered his 9mm Glock to his side and nonchalantly pushed through the door, as if deaf to the sound of the horror and offense taking place.

His eyes circled the room in a single glint before locking on target. Bringing his gun up, he fired as if on a shooting range, taking one of two gunmen down with a single shot to the brain, just above the eyes, center. A perfect shot, sending the thick-necked, swarthy-looking

Italian down so fast and hard he might as well have had a six-hundred-weight anvil dropped on him.

One part of Lucas's brain spoke academy training words of calm over and over, while another part of his brain sought the second shooter who'd dove for cover. The second hefty Italian-looking fellow had hit the wooden flooring almost as loudly as his dead coperpetrator friend. Suddenly there was an explosion across from Lucas, and he barely registered that the glass had shattered. A bullet meant for him—now lodged in the elevator door—had shattered the glass. Fourteen other cops, mostly uniformed men, lifted at once and each placed a bullet into the second shooter, whose body flailed fishlike until it hit a desk and careened over the messy desktop. The impact sent pencils, blotters, a lamp, files, framed photos and cups in every direction.

Silence. It felt like gold.

For a moment, Lucas wondered if there might not be a third shooter. But then with the stillness that comes after a confrontation of such intensity, it came clear that the moment Lucas had killed his partner, shooter number two had merely rolled to another position, lifted and fired, missing Lucas by millimeters. This action on the shooter's part had given bead to the other armed cops who had simultaneously opened fire on the bastard, taking him on a *bullet roll*.

For another millisecond, silence reigned. Everyone assessed his own person. Next came cheers. Men lifting their weapons in the age-old symbol for victory. Lucas pulled himself up and off the floor, someone asked if he'd been hit.

"I'm fine."

"Great . . . great decoy work, Injun!" shouted Kenny
Feidler, yelping and slapping dust from Lucas's now
wrinkled suit. "You Cherokees always did know how to
decoy an enemy."

Lucas gritted his teeth and said nothing in return.

Other cops began shouting his praise. "We were pinned
down by the two of them."

"They had semiautomatics," said another.

"Walked right in and opened fire."

"No warning."

"Likely on speed or crack."

Lucas only now realized that the two shooters had indeed used semiautomatic weapons, both guns had state-
of-the-art firepower. They had come prepared to wipe out
the entire station house. A pair of clowns mimicking movies like *The Terminator*, he supposed.

Other cops milled past to get a closer look at the man
Lucas had put down, some catcalling and whistling at the
size and position of the bullet hole to the forehead.

Lucas threw back his long, black and disheveled mane
and asked, "Anybody know who the fuck these guys are—
were? And what the fuck their beef might've been?"

"They had it in for Kirshner. Were trying to kill Kirshner," replied Fiedler. "Damn near did it, too, but they're—
that is, they were—morons. Liquored-up morons. Missed
killing Kirshner and opened fire on anything moving."

Lucas saw that Kirshner had lost a lot of blood. "Get
this man an ambulance!" he shouted.

Meredyth Sanger was now standing in the elevator
where the bullet had lodged. She'd come down, gun in
hand, to investigate the gunfire.

While it wasn't customary for police psychiatrists to go

about armed, Meredyth did. She had carried a piece ever since her encounter with the murdering on-line Web-site group that called itself Helsinger's Pit after a computer game—a group she, Lucas and Randy Oglesby had unmasked and brought to justice a few years before. Meredyth had since learned to shoot better, meeting Lucas on the firing range after hours. He often teased her, saying, "You're no Annie Oakley" and "If you want to ever work a case with me again, you damned well better learn how to hold and fire."

In cooperation with psychic FBI Detective Kim Desinor, Meredyth had also helped Lucas bring down the torture-killer of black teens the previous Christmas season when they had finally bagged the Snatcher. She also remained actively interested in Lucas's new COMIT program that meant to deal more efficiently with back-shelved, unsolved murders in Houston with the FBI's Houston Field Office's full cooperation. The program now had very nearly all the hard copy files eliminated and replaced with computer disks, leaving the old dungeon called the Cold Room, where Lucas's desk sat, with a great deal more space than when he had first taken on the office three years before.

Enlarged and modernized, the Cold Room now housed three detectives at three desks. Lucas had been placed over the unit as its chief detective. He truly liked the new title of "chief."

"Are you all right?" Meredyth asked first Lucas and then the room at large. "Everybody OK?"

With Captain Lincoln out somewhere ballyhooing with press, public and the mayor's office, and seeing that Sergeant of the Day, Hugh Price, had been one of the three men wounded, Lucas knew he had to take charge. "We've

got three wounded, one seriously. Get a 911 call for am-
bulances now!"

"Everyone remain calm," cautioned Meredyth in a
soothing, silky tone. "It's over now. Everyone take a moment to focus on breathing."

Lucas couldn't hold back, despite a sign from Randy
Ogelsby who stood shaking nearby. "Kirshner's been injured, probably a dead man. Two other men have bullets
lodged in them, and we have two dead perpetrators with
more holes drilled in them than the Texas shoreline. But
otherwise, it's been a picnic, so let's all do our breathing
exercises. Thanks," he finished with a furtive Jack Nich-
olson look that met her glare while the accumulated detectives and uniformed cops in the room broke out in a
raucous laughter.

Meredyth frowned that frown he so loved to bring out
in her, a nanosecond before she shouted in an officious
tone, "All right. So did anyone call for medics? This man
needs immediate attention." She finished by pointing at
Kirshner's prone body where Lucas was working his red
bandanna around the cellophane from a cigarette packet
into a bandage, tying it off as tightly as he could. Suddenly Everready Leonard Chang pushed Lucas aside to
apply a large bandage he'd come armed with.

Chang said, "This the new bandage everybody all talking about now. Has properties to make the wound clot.
More helpful than a cigarette packet, for sure."

Kirshner had been hit several times, but the wound that
might kill him came from a bullet that had gone into and
come out of his neck, severing a pulsating, bloodletting
artery there. Chang ministered to this wound exclusively.

"Sleep," muttered Jack Kirshner.

Meredyth kneeled closer to the injured officer. "No,

Jack, you want to keep awake, even if it is painful. No sleep right now, but later . . . sure."

Kirshner had lost a great deal of blood, and more towels were being pressed into his other wounds—three additional shots from the automatics to various parts of the upper body. Chang now worked to cover these with the new, high-tech bandages. "Too bad they don't got this technology in World War Two," he muttered. "Would save a lotta lives on battlefield."

Lucas doubted that Kirshner could possibly survive the trauma and shock, much less the ride to the hospital, high-tech bandaging in place or not. Kirshner, whom Lucas had only known for six months, had come in on a suspicious transfer, one that carried a great deal of gossip and speculation surrounding the word *womanizer*. Lucas had never questioned him on it, which is likely why the younger man liked Lucas. Still, a lot of questions revolved around Kirshner and hung on like forgotten clothes on a sagging laundry line.

Now the man's glazed eyes looked up into Lucas's own black orbs, as if reading the negative thoughts. Kirshner gasped. "A serpent."

"A serpent?" asked Lucas, thinking Kirshner wanted to confess something before dying.

"Good, keep him talking, Lucas," Meredyth continued to officiate at Lucas's side.

Lucas replied, "I'll do what I can."

"With the seriousness of his wounds, it could mean the difference between life and death. Trust me, don't let him sleep."

"I hope you're not suggesting that his life is in my hands."

"Just keep him talking, Lucas. He goes into a coma, and we could easily lose him."

Lucas sighed and turned his attention back to Jack Kirshner, whose flaxen hair lay damp around his head, and whose skin tone could now compete with the bleach-white underbelly of a fish. The man's features were drawn up in pain, and his body, likewise, found the fetal position.

"What serpent?" asked Lucas, holding Kirshner both by the hand and head. "Listen to me, Jack. Listen up. Dr. Sanger wants to hear all about that serpent, Jack." He finished by squeezing Kirshner's hand.

Kirshner, his usual ruddy handsomeness long gone, was hardly capable of breathing but managed a garbled reply. "Sleep serpent . . . lies dormant . . . ready to strike."

"Sleep is a dormant serpent?" asked Lucas.

"Separation . . . soul from body . . . separation journey . . . going out there all alone—" He paused to point to something over Lucas's shoulder—thin air. Then he continued, "A kind of . . . flirting . . . with emptiness . . . the abyss, the void. Preparing . . . for the big sleep . . . final resting place."

Oddly enough, this was precisely how Lucas Stonecoat viewed the act of sleeping, so perhaps insomnia—sleep's antithesis—for all its bad press, might simply be a noble form of struggle for life, a form of rebellion against the inevitable power of the gods who held sway—Morpheus being the most obvious.

Paramedics arrived and cleaned the squad room of the bloodied bodies like efficient ants, taking their cue from Chang all the while. Jack Kirshner, given the most attention, soon disappeared from view like the others. Lucas turned at one point and found himself standing alone among the blood pools that had been collectively created.

A wise and cunning old shaman had once told Lucas that he would spend a lifetime stalking death; a beautiful psychic had once told Lucas that death rode on his shoulder. He wondered if people who got too near him did not pay the ultimate price. He'd just begun to like Jack, and they'd shared a few beers together only the evening before. Jack had asked Lucas about the scalping cases, and he'd been pained and fully sympathetic toward the victims.

Now this . . .

THREE

Cactus flower: courtship

The parolee lay in bed, thinking—thinking hard and fast, his mind a swirl of images and information. He'd been examining and reexamining all day what precisely Dr. Thomas W. Morrissey had said and done in the shrink's office today; and how Morrissey had, by a feat of magic, made the patient *feel*. Amazing, for the patient had had no feelings, not one emotion, for years. Morrissey had returned him to his anger. He thought of the rage, focused on it, realized the nature of it—like a snake pit. The vipers inside his mind and gut and heart fed on themselves. He replayed every moment of the encounter in his mind now where he lay his head, attempting to find sleep and solace, knowing it would not soon come, for the mental video of the encounter with Dr. Morrissey proved too strong.

It must be that the doctor purely enjoyed making up words. The man invented words that the patient would go home and look up, words that weren't true words, words that had no standing in *Webster's* or the *American Heri-*

tage Dictionary or any other dictionary the patient could get his hands on. Words and phrases like *infactuate fact-ability* and *accountapliable, responsinicious*, and *affec-tiplicity*.

The patient had spoken to other of Morrissey's *parole-tients* and *parolkeys*, as he called his parolee patients; the patient had spoken to them all about this, and one or two of the other parole monkeys agreed with him, seeing it as a damnably irritating thing.

They'd talked it over after a group session one night. Another patient agreed that the white-bearded, Santa Claus–looking doctor with the barrel chest and the James Earl Jones voice used one of his fount of misnomers a great deal—factability. . . .

"It is a factability that you will improve your feeling of self-worthlionics once you put your nose to the grind-stone, son," he'd say again and again, a man not above using a cliché. In fact, his clichés proved more accurate than his usual gobbledygook. . . . His patients who knew his "language" to be nonsense laughed at him behind his back.

The parolee tried desperately to put it all out of his mind for now, to rest his brain. Morrissey hurt his head, he decided.

"Something-troubling-wrong, son?" Dr. Morrissey had asked in that other annoying habit of stringing words to-gether so fast that they took on a momentum and new meaning all their own, independent of understandable sound and sense. In fact, nearly every word spewing forth from Dr. Thomas W. Morrissey's mouth ran together like gushing mud over a growing delta of refuse. None of it was clear or separate or distinct.

The patient enunciated slowly, a kind of hint to the doctor that he ought to do the same, saying, "No, nothin' troubling or worrisome here." He smugly pointed to his head when he said it. Then he added, "No, and then again everythin'. Yes . . ." He then pointed to his heart. "Snafu, Doc . . . Situation Normal, you know? All. Fucked. Up. In here . . ."

"I understand heartache/break, my-boybut, please-tellme, whatever-else coulditbethat's bothering you-so?"

"Whole fuckin' world's going to hell in a handbasket, and you sit here in your plush leather chair with your Brooks Brothers suit and tie, and your Gucci leathers, and you—"

"No need for profanity or personal attacks, son," the doctor interjected. "That sort of thing's becoming a-chronic habit with you, my boy."

"And you ask me what's freakin' wrong? You don't even give a rat's ass, so why're we here, Doc?"

"Do you resent mebecauseyou believe I am onlyasking because it's my job to ask? That I'm your enemy because I'm one of them? That because I'm appointed-bythe court to help-inyour reentry intotheworld, son? Is that what's troubling you? If you'd like to go out back of the alley and do this *mano-y-mano*, I'm game, son."

"Man. I'm a man. . . . I'm nobody's son, least of all yours," countered the patient, ignoring the challenge.

"What's that?"

"I prefer not to be called 'son,' damn it."

"Really?" The doctor jotted a note. "And why's 'sat?"

"It's too much like 'boy.' "

"And if I refuse to call you a man? What will be your reaction, *son*? Unreasonable violence directed at me? Did your mommy or your daddy poke fun at your small weenie?"

"Shut up, damn you!"

"Did they call you 'boy' or 'son' in a way to make the words dirty?"

"I'll blow your goddamn head off with a nine milli-meter. Better yet, I'll cut your guts out with a fuckin' bowie knife, you fat weasel!"

"Your parole-prevents you fromcarrying-a-weapon ofany sort, much less using one, son. And as for threats, a single phone call, and—"

"Then I'll cut your fuckin' heart out with my bare hands before you make that goddamn call. How's that?"

"That might be wiser, son, but wouldn't it leave inde-fellible fingerprint umpressions? I think we're through for today, my friend."

"And I ain't your friend."

Morrissey put his hands together in steeple fashion, nodding, considering this. "Ain't that the truth, but I am your *head* doctor, and you realize that what is in your head, in your mind and thoughts, is also in your heart and soul, my boy. So, you want to take my advice, even if it's painful. Now, you want to go away from here and sit in a quiet place. . . . Contemplate what brings your rage boiling up so quickly, a simple word, a three-letter word: B-O-Y." He slowly enunciated the letters. "You are will-ing to kill someone over that? Look not at them, the ones you think are out to get you, my patient, but look inward at the guy inside you, the child inside you, so filled with murderous intent. Search out your problems and the so-lutions to your problems. Now get the fuck out of my office. Return at the appointed time."

The patient then thought about the group-therapy ses-

sions the old fart insisted upon. At first, it had been torturous, but after two sessions, the patient had become
actively involved, spilling his guts, explaining in detail
how he had killed in the past. He had actually thanked
the members of the group and Dr. Morrissey for having
had the opportunity to unburden himself. And how much
he had learned from the other group members as opposed
to the private sessions. He had Morrissey to thank for that
much. . . .

For a moment, Lucas felt so desperately tired that he did
not know where he lay: still at the hospital at Jack Kirshner's silent side, or was he home in bed? Then Lucas
rolled over, pillows flying with him; he found himself
wakeful with the dream that was no dream: Jack Kirshner
had not died, but he now lay in the sleep of death—coma.
Kirshner had gone comatose en route to Houston Memorial Hospital, and tonight he remained in critical condition, his life-threatening gunshot wounds attended to—
the best hospital personnel could do without surgery.
    Only the new biotech bandage that Chang had used,
with its blood-clotting properties, had saved Kirshner's
life.
    Problematic however. There was no anesthetizing a co-
matose man.
    Whether or not Kirshner pulled from the comatose
state, he could still die of his gunshot wounds, or complications arising. Lucas saw no upside to the situation.
    Lucas, having himself once been where Kirshner lay at
this moment, felt a great empathy with young Kirshner
who had celebrated his twenty-sixth birthday only a week
before with one Alena Collucci—sister to one of the Italian shooters, and the former girlfriend of other one.

Due to Kirshner's condition, his arms and legs had been restrained, coma or no coma, for if he suddenly came to and made the wrong move, one of the bullets still lodged inside could kill him. One of the bullets had lodged so near the heart that any movement might see Jack to his grave. Subconscious always being right, Lucas realized now that Jack's plea for sleep had a most practical, if unbelievable, origin.

Poor Benjamin John "Jack" Kirshner remained, at the moment, for all intent and purpose, like the Tarot card image of the hanging man, caught up in both invisible strands and his own limbs. Lucas related to this state, for he, too, had once been in a similar perdition, strung up by circumstances, hamstrung and dangling between life and death, decision and peace.

Feeling a kinship with the man in limbo, Lucas decided then and there to spend much of this night at the comatose cop's bedside. Others had filled him in on Kirshner's connection with the two who had stormed into the police station after him. The shooting had had nothing whatever to do with the job. The two gunmen, high on something Chang's lab would determine the exact nature of, had come seeking revenge on the white cop who dared soil their Italian flower. In fact, the young woman had lied to the men—she had told the men that Jack Kirshner had raped her. She'd since confessed to telling her brother and former lover this in order to "keep their respect."

The rape accusation had been nothing but a young woman's lie. Jack's closest friends on the force told a different story: The woman in question had been stalking Kirshner for some time now.

"Screwy world of Jerry Springer," Lucas had muttered

into Meredyth's ear on learning the cause of today's madness.

Lucas didn't fully understand it, but he felt connected to Kirshner in some strange, mystical fashion. *What was all that serpent talk just before he went into the coma?* Lucas wondered.

Meanwhile, Internal Affairs Division had quickly launched a full investigation into the shooting. They were stumped from the get-go, because in a normal cop shooting, you pulled the officer or officers' weapons, but how to do that with a complete squad room? The second of the two boozed up Italians had fourteen rounds placed in him from varying angles. So, what was IAD to do? Insist on having the firearm of every cop in the 31st Precinct?

IAD, being the assholes they were, did exactly that.

However, top brass, in response to having some dozen or so weapons turned in for tests to match each gunshot wound to its origin, in order to attribute individual responsibility for each bullet fired, issued fresh firearms to their army. This represented a solution that Captain Gordon J. Lincoln could live with. One of the guns being tested was the captain's, as the Sergeant of the Day had been cleaning the weapon for Lincoln when the first shots rang out, and he had instinctively used it. The sergeant, hospitalized but in fair condition, had just returned from the john when gunfire broke out amid the usual chaos of the squad room. The sergeant had hit the floor with the rest of the squad when Lucas had stepped through the door and opened fire on Shooter Number One. With his partner in crime dead, the shorter of the two Italians had been momentarily slack, confused. At that hesitation, the paraprofessional army of the HPD took full advantage. But by then the sergeant had been wounded.

Public outcry, especially from the Italian community, was already bogusly buttressed by phrases such as "excessive use of deadly force" and "excessive police response" and "foul play" and "overkill" and "racially motivated" and "police initiated hate-crime." Meanwhile, the two dead men had injured six civilian bystanders due to flying glass; one PD had broken his arm leaping down a flight of stairs to safety; a reporter for the *Union* had a busted nose; and four cops were shot down, one lying now in the arms of death in critical condition. Nine panes of glass, two watercoolers, and, of course, the intended target, were all taken out in a hailstorm of unleashed bullets. Meanwhile, the cops in the room, thinking of wives, children, the very blood pumping in their veins and ringing their ears, saw a defense of their stronghold as necessary, and not at all excessive. Not in this instance, not in this life. Lucas concurred.

Lucas had spent a large portion of the day with IAD. In fact, IAD questioned Lucas for the better part of the day both at headquarters and also later at the hospital.

Groaning deeply, wondering now if he were alone or if someone had come into his bed, Lucas once again felt the sheer drop off and abysmal depth of Kirshner's death-sleep, and the man's last lucid and communicative moments. Were they a presaging of his coma? A cry from deep within to not give up on him? Deep thoughts, those that delved into the nature of man during his sleep time, deep thoughts that proved hard to hold on to while under the influence of the sweetest, purest peyote Lucas had ever had. Lucas now went in search of his own coma.

Lucas had tried every other drug, legal and otherwise, to control his demonic-chronic pain, and now he'd turned to Native American remedies. Sometimes, he'd add a bit of acid—LSD—to the mix. Just enough to calm the demons of this world and introduce those of an altered state, he told himself. He often reassured himself that his drug use was not only medicinal in nature but also controllable. Amazing how clear everything appeared under the power of this newfound mix of drugs he'd been experimenting with. Even the ashen demons that visited him in the night now took on distinct features.

The LSD-peyote mix made him able to remember small and insignificant things, trivial information stored somewhere in his brain and never looked at again until now, such as things English teachers taught. He saw himself in a schoolroom in Hades, but in a moment, unaware how he had gotten from bed to bureau, he stared at himself, watching as he metamorphosed into his own spirit guide. His own features changed into those of a long snout, large yellow eyes and fierce teeth; his skin sprouted hair everywhere. He stood looking into the eyes of a salivating wolf, hungry and angry and filled with passionate lust.

In the mirror now, a woodland scene shows clearly. He is on four legs, in pursuit of a squirming, half-seen shadow creature. The creature is also on all fours. It is small and verminlike, sliding in and out of ground cover, its rodent tail coming visible, then an eye, then a shoulder, but never all at once. Lucas senses its movements prior to its actual appearance, and yes, there it appears just as his wolf's eye predicted. He pounces and the little creature squeals in horror and pain.

Lucas, as wolf, devours the squirming thing whole, never fully getting a fix on what exactly he's consuming.

Snow next came down in the mirror, covering the scene in whiteness.

An ancient Indian legend held that people like Lucas Stonecoat—people who defied death again and again— eventually came to terms with death, and that the old ones came a-visiting to tell this man among men that he must accompany them back to the land of the dead. Using the LSD-peyote mix, Lucas had found the land of the dead on many nights before this night; and he wondered if Kirshner, too, had found it in his comatose state.

Lucas had been surprised to learn that, in many instances, he enjoyed the company of the dead to that of the living. Certainly this held true in his current situation. *Peyote and LSD . . . what the fuck was I thinking?* he asked himself anew, wondering how many times he'd asked the same question—or if this were the first time. He wondered, too, how long the snow had been falling in his mirror and if the wolf had eaten a rat, a possum, a snake or what, and how many times that scene had been replayed tonight in his head. Time itself no longer existed—at least not for the moment; and so then, there was no moment, so words like moments couldn't exist, either. *No time words allowed,* he told his head, reminding himself with a smile. Stillness and timelessness, even spacelessness, none of it existed here inside him, inside his looking glass. So time did not matter. Nor for that matter did matter matter itself. . . . In conclusion, nothing carried weight, nothing mattered, hence nothing had meaning; life was not linear nor measurable, and was certainly not defined by a clock. It held no mass, and it could find no space.

Bodily fear, sweats, worry, stresses somehow insinuated themselves into the looking glass. Reality seeped in even here, on an LSD-peyote trip.

Lucas's new situation had him pulling a double shift

two nights a week. It had been an arrangement made for him, a kind of volunteerism in the wake of a loss of manpower at the precinct; a recent blue-flu epidemic calling for better wages and more overtime pay. The unofficial strike seemed petty now that Kirshner had been gunned down—for reasons having nothing to do with the job, other than that the infatuated female pursuing him had been obsessed with his uniform.

Lucas later heard ridiculously exaggerated stories of how the coroner had counted forty rounds in the body of the one Italian and half that in the other. The rounds had come from fifteen separate sources, all standard issue 9mm Glocks. The actual count was half that once all the caked blood had been washed away and the clean, wet body reflected back the burning overhead light, where it lay granitelike on the coroner's slab. Lucas recalled the surprised eyes when he had placed a single shot through the one man's brain. He vividly recalled the gaping hole directly between the eyes that stared back at him, eyes that had hesitated because Lucas—in plainclothes and with long Indian hair and features—had momentarily seemed to have flabbergasted the man. The gunman had in fact paused to squint at Lucas's long red scar that began just below the jawbone and continued to below his shirt collar at the neck on his left side. Lucas's disfigurement was a trophy from a near-death, high-speed chase and resulting crash and burn. The scar had become another badge for Lucas, one that alerted other men to the notion that he had come back from the land of the dead to talk about it.

Unfortunately Lucas's partner at the time, when Lucas had earned his flaming red flesh-badge, Lafayette Jackson, had not returned from the grave that day.

Lucas's burns had come as a result of having attempted to pull his unconscious partner from the flames of the car while under gunfire. Lucas took a near-fatal bullet in his attempt to save Jackson. After taking down the assailant, Lucas had gone into a coma; he'd come back, and he'd rehabilitated himself back to walking and talking like a man in control. Still, to this day, the incredible pain could only be controlled by drugs.

Lucas nowadays prayed to the gods of pain more so than any other. He now prayed that when tomorrow morning he awoke, the pain in his back, shoulders, hips and legs will have vanished—or at least abated. He continued to live with pain as a constant in his life, so constant that he often forgot its presence. And while the blackouts had lessened, possibly gone altogether, as he could not recall one now since January of the previous year, he had reason for hope—hope no doctor had ever offered, hope no doctor had foreseen and none had promised.

He had come a long way since that fiery night chase in Dallas that had robbed him of so much. While he could not change events leading up to the death of his partner, he could change any events that came afterward. Told he would never work as a cop again, he began the long task of rehabilitation, the greatest challenge and fear of his life. He had beaten all the odds, but the Dallas PD knew him too well, and they held him accountable for the death of his partner and several injuries incurred during the high-speed chase. It proved a ride that effectively ended his career in Dallas. His own police force, like his life force had turned against him; and his wife, after futile and soon halfhearted attempts, simply could no longer cope, and so the inevitable divorce followed.

This had all left Lucas penniless and without hope. Still he fought—literally did war with his own body, until it gave in somewhat, just enough to allow him to again walk upright and appear in control. That appearance of control that he had to maintain every day, had claimed him a place in the ranks of the Houston Police Academy. However, due to Lucas's injuries and past record, if Houston were interested at all, it must be by Houston's rule; and the collective *they*—Houston PD's controlling voice—although hard up for any cop who could stand a beat, insisted that Lucas reapply as a cadet. This meant he had to retake all necessary course work and the training any new recruit must go through.

Another in a long list of challenges Lucas, as a Native American, had faced all his life. Just another challenge. No one expected him to make it through the rigorous, physical demands of the police academy, given his medical history—a history of which *they* knew only the iceberg tip. Only he, Meredyth Sanger and his captain had ever seen the full medical file, for he had ordered his lawyer to expunge all copies save one, this after losing the lawsuit he'd filed against the Dallas Police Department.

His training officers, with a mandate to place a thousand more warm bodies on Houston streets within the year, in an effort to comply with Federal strings on Federal dollars, seemed little interested—three years ago—in digging into Lucas's past problems with Dallas. Lucas—plagued by Lafayette Jackson's death and the experience that had nearly taken his own life—kept a copy of his medical records in a bedside drawer, close at hand. He never hesitated to look it over again and again as a constant reminder of just how far he had come. Unable to sleep, he sat upright and dug out the medical file and read:

DALLAS MEMORIAL HOSPITAL
DALLAS, TEXAS

Date of admission July 12, 1991 **Date of discharge** June 2, 1992

Patient History: A twenty-seven-year-old American Indian male involved in automobile accident, also had alcohol in blood, admitted with multiple trauma—compound fracture of tibia and fibula, ruptured bladder, and multi-focal cerebral contusions, assorted abrasions, gunshot wound to upper left quadrant of chest.

In hospital for eleven months, initially comatose and encephalopathic. At time of leaving hospital, patient was fully conscious, alert, quite full of complaints. Further, patient understood that a Hoffman device was in place on his left leg, and that he must be careful in this regard to not place any undo weight on this area. He was to be given primary care by his aunt, uncle and grandparents, all of whom seemed most concerned for his well-being, each being attentive to doctor's directives. Arrangements were made with in-home health care providers to help with the suprapubic cystostomy as well as the pin care of the Hoffman device.

Dr. Rhymer, operating orthopedic surgeon, made plans for all follow-up care to be provided by Dallas Memorial. Arrangements were made for Mr. Stonecoat to be seen by Dr. Karl Wilkerson, urology, who performed the bladder operation and left the suprapubic cystostomy in place.

During Mr. Stonecoat's eleven-month stay, he underwent a tracheostomy as well as a hip replacement (left), a debridement of the compound infected leg and many consultations with Dr. Sanders on loan from the Veteran's Administration Hospital. Dr. Sanders was also involved in his rehabilitation efforts.

Final Diagnosis:
1. Severe chest injury—gunshot wound left, upper
2. Severe closed head injury
3. Compound tibia-fibula fracture—left
4. Wound infection, tibia-fibula
5. Crushed hip; replacement—left
6. Partial paralysis, right side arm, hand
7. Acute respiratory distress syndrome
8. Conjunctivitis

Operation:
1. Chest wound and closure
2. Tracheostomy
3. Swan-Ganz placement
4. Laparotomy
5. Hip replacement—left
6. Bladder repair
7. Suprapubic cystostomy
8. Arm, shoulder and forehead lacerations

Daniel Garvey, M.D.

TLT-219 #4314
D: 6/6/92
T: 02/07/52

Stonecoat, Lucas   Daniel Garvey, M.D.
368–58–7899   Discharge Summary

The shrilling ring of the phone jolted Lucas back into
the moment, its bansheelike cry causing him to curse,
"Who the fuck calls at such an ungodly hour?" His digital
clock blinked its way toward 2 A.M.

"Yeah, hello?" he barked into the phone, actually glad
for the disturbance.

A long-forgotten female voice replied, calling him by
his Indian name, "Moon Wolf, it is Tsalie. . . ."

He almost choked on his own breath as he first grasped
then gasped the name, repeating it aloud, "Tsalie?"

ℱOUR

Butterfly: infinite life

Lucas sat upright on the edge of the bed, still amazed at hearing Tsalie's beautiful voice after so many years.

"Are you there, Lucas? You haven't forgotten me, have you?" she asked needlessly. "It is your once ago friend, Jessie Starre," she added as if he didn't know, as if she still wore the soft mantle of innocence he had always associated with her.

"Tsalie, my sweet one. You are ever in my thoughts."

"But everything—even you—has kept us apart," she muttered, shyly, as if she regretted saying it.

Lucas found a deep breath of air to swallow. "Tsalie? How . . . how are you? Where are you? Where are you calling from? Are you in trouble?" The simple questions sounded so foolish, so mundane. He had loved her all these years, even after losing her.

"My uncle's house, only phone on the reservation that hasn't been shut off. Your grandfather would not have one. I have . . . I bring you bad news, Lucas, and for that I am sorry."

"What is it?"

"It's your grandfather, Keeowskowee."

"What about Grandfather?"

"I'm sorry to be bearer of bad news, Lucas, but the old one, he is dying."

"Again?"

"Again, yes, but this time it appears he will not remain. No more reruns . . ."

Lucas divided up the situation into two possibilities: Leave it to his grandfather to find a way to get the two of them—Lucas and Tsalie—back together, which meant that the old man's so-called deathbed acrobatics merely represented yet another ploy for attention, but this time with an unusually benevolent ulterior motive perhaps. Or the old man really was dying. Something in Tsalie's tone sounded a certain bell in Lucas's head.

"You're sure that this time Grandfather's actually leaving us? That this time is . . . different?"

"This time, we think—the family thinks—it's the real thing, Lucas. And he has asked for you to come home."

Home, Lucas thought. The word simply didn't apply to that wretched, pitted, stony, sunbaked plot of reservation land where only lizards and snakes found solace amid the rocks that grew as plentiful as weeds. Home . . . the word hardly applied to Lucas, who believed himself to be a modern-day man without a country. "I'll have to make arrangements. Tell him I'll be there ASAP."

"You're beginning to sound like a white man, Lucas. 'ASAP.' Just get home. He needs to see and speak to you while he can. He loves you beyond all things."

"I'll be there."

"Don't take too long, Lucas. He's failing fast." Even

with such dire words, her voice sounded lilting, an instrument like a flute.

"Tsalie, Jessie . . . Wind of Stars," he called her by her American name and then by the endearment that still meant so much to him, "tell me, is he in any pain?"

"We're keeping him happy with peyote, but yes, he hides the pain well. He is . . . like someone else I know."

"A brave man, my mother's father."

"Yes, he is a brave old man," she replied. Lucas imagined a tear coursing along her cheek. Imagined her long, flowing black hair, the hair he had once so often caressed, the smooth contour of her cheek, her wide forehead, eyebrows like bird wings, her butterfly eyelashes, lips large and moist and inviting.

"I'll be there. Tell him, I'll be there." Even as he said this, he knew he wanted more to be with her than to watch the old man die. The old man had had enough of this world, and Lucas knew this. Keeowskowee, the old man's tribal name, had died many times over in this life, had faced many battles. Time he was allowed to lose one, Lucas thought.

Hanging up, Lucas shook his head and held back tears, holding himself in check. Too many times now his grandfather had died; and on the brink of death, he had come back to hearty health, once sitting up on his deathbed and shouting orders at those around him to fetch his pipe and tobacco. Another time, his dying had all to do with gaining the affections of a woman. The old crafty shaman knew how to get people moving on his behalf.

Tsalie's voice had come as such a surprise. She'd moved long ago from the Huntsville, Texas, reservation and had gone north to live in Nebraska with her new husband chasing after work—some truck-driving school or other scheme Lucas had little understanding of. Now, after suddenly hearing her voice after all this time, Lucas felt as if a bird were let loose in his stomach. She still had the ability, even through the wires of a telephone, using only her voice, to turn him to a sniveling preteen. She made him feel like a would-be, *wanna-be* brave, somewhere in the neighborhood of twelve years of age with jelly for arms and legs, pudding for torso.

He sat stunned for a moment, got up and found the shower. He soon stood under the hot spray, thinking about her as he rubbed and lathered himself with the bar soap. He hadn't heard from her or seen her in years, not since high school when they were sweethearts. When he had left the reservation, years ago—to seek his place in the wider, white world, to become a detective—Tsalie had tearfully, and with anger, bid him farewell and good hunting. They spoke of a future together, but she didn't believe in it. He promised that once he had gotten his shield, he would send for her. But time passed and Tsalie— tired, perhaps fearful of the waiting—had married another man, a man named Billy Wild Hawk, Lucas's cousin.

She was now Tsalie Hawk, even if she still called herself Starre. Her family name of Starre spoke of a lurid, even sordid ancestry, a great-granddaughter to the infamous Belle Starr and the outlaw Starr brothers who terrorized Oklahoma territory in the late-1800s. The history only added to her mystique, Lucas felt.

Lucas looked forward to seeing her again, but the feeling came in the company of a taloned trepidation: Suppose his grandfather's condition was actually as bad as reported? If Tsalie thought it bad, it must be, for she was privy to the wily, cunning old shaman's games.

Lucas next considered Tsalie's jibe about his becoming

too white for his own good, using terms such as "ASAP." But after all, he did now have the responsibilities of a white man in a white profession in a white world. He had to consider the complications of dropping out of sight at this moment; the ramifications, who would be affected, how and for how long? He had serious responsibilities toward the department, his captain, even Meredyth, as well as his COMIT program detectives. After all, he headed up the program in the new and improved facilities created for his Cold Room files. They had already done a fantastic job of placing nearly two-thirds of all the ancient files on disks via computer scanning. Captain Lincoln had applauded the pace, but without Lucas closely overseeing matters, he knew that the pace would slacken. He could not lightly or easily step away, not even for a few days. He'd have to inform Lincoln, get Lincoln up to speed on this. "Up to speed, damn! How preppy *whiteboy-slang* is that?" he asked himself aloud as he turned off the shower. "Damn, Tsalie's already got me talking to myself and examining just how much white has rubbed off on me."

Stepping from the shower and examining his tall, lean and muscular frame, Lucas felt good that his daily regimen of alternating exercise and swims at the gym had paid off. His bronze skin pulled tight across a washboard stomach. But again, his mind wandered back to the old man for whom he maintained a great love and respect. No one on Earth was more important to Lucas than his grandfather—the man who had raised him and had made him keep to the old ways even as he rebelled and sought the new. Out of his struggles with Grandfather Keeowskowee, Lucas had finally opened the old shaman's eyes to Lucas's reasoning and all that lay behind the defiance; meanwhile, from the same loving struggle, Lucas had learned to value his grandfather above all things.

The old man's influence had led directly to Lucas's chosen path. Without Grandfather Keeowskowee's insight, and him caring enough to grapple with his grandson, Lucas feared what he might have become: another xenophobic, shiftless, spiritless reservation soul without goals, without passion, without direction—save the direction to the nearest watering hole.

All this, Lucas now confided in Meredyth, whom he had awakened with his call. He'd been unable to get hold of Captain Lincoln, something about an out-of-town engagement, according to Lincoln's housekeeper. More and more, Lincoln found his job to be one of a politician rather than a cop. As result, Lucas had next telephoned Meredyth.

"You must go to your mother's father, putting aside all other considerations," Meredyth assured him. "If your grandfather's time has come, you must be on hand to help him in the transition."

" 'Transition,' " he repeated. "Spoken like a true psychiatrist. And yes, I know . . ." Lucas thought how much he feared a life without his grandfather in it. "Death couldn't have come at a worse time, what with all I have to do, all the commitments and this new Scalper case falling on me." He lamented his situation for only a second, however, realizing aloud, "Hey, it wasn't so long ago that I lay in a hospital bed with so much time on my hands that I thought my mind would explode from the boredom. And my beautiful old grandfather came to me with his magic and medicine and prayed over me. He strengthened my spirit and resolve then, traveling to Dallas each weekend to see me when everyone else had deserted me."

Meredyth had met the old man. She spoke of the time

they had spent together, adding, "When we spoke, whatever we touched on, Lucas, he always brought it all back around to you, Moon Wolf, as he called you. He loves you, dearly."

"Death seeks a warrior, and Keeowskowee was a warrior. No magic that old man knows can choose his time of going," he told her.

Meredyth replied, "True . . . true enough."

"As every Cherokee knows, death comes like the wolf or the eagle. You don't know it has you in its teeth or talons until it wants you to know. Death arrives at its leisure, not that of the living."

"Make arrangements. Put this Houston life on hold. It will be a final act of love and devotion to the one man who has cared and nurtured you, Lucas, my friend. It's really all you can do. I'll talk to Lincoln, and I'll see what I can do to cover for you elsewhere as well."

"Thanks, Mere."

"Never mind that. Just go to him."

Lucas again thanked Meredyth for being a friend before he disconnected. Placing the receiver back onto its cradle, he felt an insistent twinge of guilt at having found his desire for Tsalie rekindled, heightened even this night— amid all the sorrow—and having found Meredyth merely a strong ally and faithful friend. He thought how easily he could fall in love all over again with Tsalie if she were single, if she wanted him. At the same moment, he dismissed the notion as foolish, childish behavior. Meredyth, while not his lover, appealed to him far more, despite the stiff-armed resistance she showed him. Still, this hands-off friendship had always been exactly what Mere wanted, and so be it. So he consoled himself, accepting his feelings for Tsalie. At the same time, he wondered if it were not more his memories of Tsalie that he desired.

Lucas's thoughts returned anew to his grandfather, and he asked himself again, *Whatever will this world be like if I do not have the old man for prattle, to harangue, to gossip with and chatter at?* The old man kept Lucas tied to reservation life, represented, in fact, his final tie to that life, providing Lucas with the latest stories out of school on everyone on the res. Lucas had maintained few other ties with the traditional Cherokee life.

A tear found its way to one corner of one eye where Lucas now sat on the edge of his bed, still fully nude and feeling vulnerable. Lucas thought of the abysmal emptiness the old man's stepping from this life would leave inside.

On hearing of his grandfather's condition, Lucas gave up any pretense of reaching REM sleep that night. Instead, he got up, laid out a fresh cadre of pain-numbing items and went to the latest Cold Room file that had caught his attention—thanks to Dave Harbough's pushiness.

He'd read of the release of a man whose name had come up in the cross-referencing of several rape murders in which the victims had been beheaded, but the creep had never been convicted of the crimes—not enough evidence. He'd been put away for attempted rape and attempted murder and possible attempted beheading, but after he'd been incarcerated, the sudden rash of rape-murder-beheadings ceased. Coincidence or common sense?

Lucas poured himself a whiskey over rocks and spent a couple of hours browsing case file #825764, relating to a woman murdered in her bed by a lust murdering possible headhunter—someone who took the victim's head away with him. Dave Harbough's notes theorized that the victim's heads were, most likely and most disgustedly, used later as a sex object.

Lucas now heated coffee and, while it perked, he buttered some toast at his small dinette.

In reviewing the file, he had found other, like victims, all done the same violence: rape, murder and beheading—in that order—within the confines of Houston, Texas, over a matter of eleven years until the killings had suddenly come to an abrupt halt. Each killing was marked by the exact same patterns, down to the serrations on the knife used for the beheadings, the positioning of the bodies on the beds, even the pattern of blood spatters to some degree, so attached to—so "into"—his ritual was the headhunter.

At about the same time that the killings ended, one Walter Karl Freeleng—an avowed white supremacist and neo-Nazi sympathizer, who was of questionable heritage himself and trying desperately to live it down or to overcompensate—had been imprisoned for attempted forcible rape with a deadly weapon.

Freeleng, who espoused the importance of the purity of the races, had climbed through a window in a tenement house to rape a young black girl he accosted in her sleep. However, while so engaged in terrorizing thirteen-year-old Celine Worth, Celine's grandmother, with whom she lived—after hearing unusual noises and after calling 911—placed a shotgun to Freeleng's ear. Then, hearing Celine's death rattle and seeing Celine's bloodied throat, Grandmother Worth knocked Freeleng into unconsciousness with the butt of her shotgun.

She then saved Celine's life by tying off the neck wound with the girl's discarded nightgown, effectively cutting off the blood flow. Grandmother Worth had been an ER nurse all her working life. She had also come from old pioneer Irish, Negro slave and Cherokee stock—what white supremacists called a mongrel.

Unfortunately, the knife he used could not be matched to the previous rapes, and Freeleng stood trial for only the single attempted-rape charge. In Freeleng's apartment, nothing whatever could be found to link him with the earlier killings, certainly no heads in the refrigerator, and although the arresting officers worked day and night to prove him guilty of what had become known as the Headless Horseman murders, Freeleng remained untouched on that score. Furthermore, the victims' heads, all eleven of them, were never discovered.

David Harbough's concern over this single case file had touched something in Lucas. Lucas had read of Freeleng's imminent release to early parole. He imagined the extraordinary struggle that Celine Worth had put up against her attacker. All the victims before Celine had, according to autopsy reports, submitted without a fight, but Celine Durrant Worth had smashed the lamp onto her assailant's head—had nearly escaped him—after she'd been forcibly raped. She had also struck Freeleng twice with a Louisville slugger she'd kept under her bed, alerting her grandmother.

Lucas admired both Celine and her grandmother, who had marked the attacker well. Celine had shown a great deal of grit, and she proved herself unlike the others who had believed the killer's lies up until the moment he had slit their throats on his way to beheading them—that is, if Freeleng were the Horseman.

Celine had been lucky in the end when the cold barrel of her grandmother's shotgun had created an indentation in Freeleng's scalp. The grandmother's alert had brought paramedics just in time to stem the tide of Celine's death. The story graced the front of the case file, but the case file was not about Celine, since her attack was not an unsolved murder. The true victims of the Horseman made up the bulk of the case file found in the Cold Room. It proved an amalgam of information amassed by a pair of hardworking detectives from some years ago, and Celine's case file information had been copied and added to the file on the series of other women near her age who had not survived similar attacks.

Seeing that the clock nearby read 6 A.M., Lucas knew he had to rush if he wanted to be on hand to meet Walter Karl Freeleng in the flesh at 8 A.M. at the appointed time of his release from the prison in Huntsville, Texas.

The clock struck 8 A.M., and Walter Karl Freeleng stepped through the prison door and stood bathed in freedom and sunlight outside Huntsville, Texas—a stone's throw to the Indian reservation where Lucas's grandfather lay dying. Determined to stop at the prison on his way to the res- ervation, Lucas felt a morbid fascination with Freeleng now. Besides, it felt like a legitimate reason for delaying the inevitable bedside vigil of the man he most loved in the world.

Freeleng likely expected no one to be on hand for his "graduation," that no one cared after so long. He probably expected a quiet release by the sovereign state of Texas today, because he stood today a "changed" man, a man the system might point to for better public relations.

Lucas, having never before seen the man, except in newspaper photos of the days following his arrest some thirteen years ago, now stood outside the prison gate and watched Freeleng as the convicted rapist breathed in the morning's dew-laden air. Lucas marked the man, and let the man know he'd marked him.

Another cop also stood nearby, one of the team who had put Freeleng away. Dave Harbough shouted at Freeleng, telling him in a controlled, level tone, "Hey, bastard. Enjoy your freedom while you can, because it won't be for long, you lousy piece of shit. My God shoulda killed you at birth, you slimy, worthless motherfuckingmurderingasswipe."

A third party climbed from a waiting car, a large white sedan, and waved Freeleng over to him. Lucas guessed the snowy-haired, large man to be Freeleng's parole officer, but the man, although huge in stature and girth, looked too ancient for the work of parole officer. After an exchange of words and a handshake, Freeleng, a tall, gaunt, giant of a man himself, climbed into the waiting car. The car quickly disappeared, chased by a hailstorm of verbal abuse from Harbough.

Lucas stepped over to say good morning to gruff, old Dave. A man another cop could both depend upon and learn from—a detective's detective. Lucas again sized Harbough up even as Harbough did the same with Lucas.

"Earring on a Native looks natural," muttered Harbough, his eyes squinting in the morning sun. "Me, personally . . . I don't care for 'em on every kid with a chip on his shoulder. No more than I care to see children wearing the U.S. flag on their backsides or the uniform of a foot soldier. But on you, the earring looks natural, Stonecoat."

Lucas caught a glimpse of himself reflected in Harbough's windshield, the earring and long, flowing black hair could not be hidden by the trench coat collar.

"You still have your eye on Freeleng for the Horseman murders. I got that loud and clear."

Harbough's chin rose and his eyes sparked with a new fire. "You read the file?"

"I did."

"So, what do you think?"

"I think you may well be right."

Harbough dropped his gaze to the ground, then raised it to the sky, and he walked about in a small circle. Finally the heavyset man said, "Thank you. I can't tell you how many times I've been told I'm a fool, that I should drop it. A guy begins to think he really is crazy after a while."

"He bears watching, this character."

"Retirement'll kill me as it is, but going into it knowing Freeleng—the Headless Horseman—is walking free . . . and I know it and everybody knows me knows it," he replied, snatching a More cigarette from his pocket and lighting up, offering Lucas one. Lucas took it and the light.

"Where's your old partner, Jim Wade? Expected to see him here with you," said Lucas, puffing on the cigarette.

They needed to smoke some sort of peace pipe between them, and each man sensed this. "Jim's long dead. Bought the farm in ninety-four."

"Sorry to hear it."

"Least Wade didn't eat his gun. Was a good man, Wade. Big C got him." He then asked, "How come you climbed outta bed to come all the way out here from Houston? I know why I'm here, but why are you here?"

"Let's just say it was on my way."

"On your way? To where?"

"Coushatta."

"The reservation, sure."

"Let's get some coffee, and I'll fill you in on my interest."

"So, you got an itch for my boy Freeleng? You read his jacket?"

"I read the Horseman file you and Wade put together, but no, haven't yet read Freeleng's file. Still, you had enough in the Horseman file on Freeleng . . . feel as if I have."

"Ahhh, yeah, the case file on the unsolved Headless Horseman's work. What'd you think of Celine Worth and her granny?" He laughed a warm laugh, as if seeing Freeleng in pain.

"How 'bout that coffee and we talk? Parlay what we know and what we think we know?" suggested Lucas.

"Ain't got any official help from no quarter, so what do I have to lose. Sure, let's talk, hombre."

Lucas recognized Harbough as the misplaced, misbegotten Jew that he was, a Texas cowboy Jew. As far from orthodox as a Jew roamed, Harbough wore a string tie and boots, probably enjoyed line dancing when not on the job, and no doubt spent a great deal of his spare time with horses in barns and women in bars. He likely thought himself to be more Texan than Jewish or anything else for that matter.

Together they walked across the street to a waiting storefront restaurant that reminded Lucas of a place he'd eaten at once in New Orleans on the fringe of the French Quarter. Size of a large postage stamp, he thought while staring at the unlit neon bulbs that snaked out a message: *Village Cafe.*

Over coffee, the two detectives talked candidly. "Let's make a pact, Stonecoat."

"Whatever you say, Harbough."

"Pact to keep each other informed on whatever the other might independently learn about Freeleng and his movements."

Naturally Dave Harbough knew far more than Lucas about his obsession—*Freeleng*. He filled Lucas in on a fact he'd not been aware of, "Our lovely sovereign state of Texas—much as I love 'er—she's footing the bills for Freeleng's rehabilitation on the outside during his probationary period."

"While he's on probation, they're paying his bills?"

"Pro bono legal fees, a shrink, a halfway-house apartment, you name it. He's plugged into the liberal hogwash program that's designed by Yuppies to save his soul. You know how that Jewel song goes? Who will *say-ya-yave* your soul? Most folks think a felon is the state's charge until he's released, but hell, it goes on for as long as the shrink deems it necessary. Galls me to know that my own tax dollars're putting food in that sonofawhore's mouth, clothes on his backside, medicine in his system. Hell, he gets better treatment than a war vet." Harbough took a long swig from his coffee and popped some white pills. Lucas didn't bother to ask about the pills, imagining a man Harbough's age probably took a lot of pills for a lot of aches and pains.

Harbough added, "Rather my tax dollars went toward that boat ramp in the Utah desert I heard the government is paying yearly and dearly for."

"So he's ordered to see a psychiatrist two, three times a week?"

"More regularly than seeing his parole officer."

"Have you talked with his parole officer?"

"Jeff Wallace, good man. But no, not yet. He'd take

offense this soon into the game, but I will be dogging him like I'll be dogging Freeleng. Bet on it."

"And his shrink?"

"Man named Morrissey. That was him in the big white sedan just now, a real jag. And no that jackoff won't be talking to any cop, 'cause the bastard can't or won't divulge word one about a patient."

"Stickler for privilege, civil rights of the convicted murderer, all that, huh?"

"Got that right. I've run into him before. He's kind of a foregone conclusion for most of the nutcases that are set free in this vicinity. Meets 'em as they exit Huntsville, so he can get cozy with 'em from the get-go. Kinda like a pimp hanging out at the bus station." Harbough laughed at the picture this brought into his mind of Dr. Morrissey.

Lucas immediately wondered if and how he might elicit help here from Meredyth Sanger with Freeleng's shrink. Maybe there was some code of conduct, some buddy system in the psychiatric field they might share. She would know the intricacies of the system, and she might know of Morrissey. Shrinks like lawyers, all ran in the same circles. Perhaps one shrink would confide in another more readily than he might to a pair of cops.

Lucas and Harbough vowed to keep a close watch on the activities of Walter Karl Freeleng, and to continue to work together on the Scalper murders.

Harbough finished off a Danish and spoke between swallows. "I have not one . . . scintilla of doubt . . . Freeleng and the Horseman are . . . one and the same. If it weren't so . . . why did the beheadings stop . . . soon as we put the creep behind bars?"

"Sounds like a make to me."

"Every forensics man or woman I've ever spoken to

about this crime says that a man so compelled to mutilate the bodies of his victims, to in effect behead them alive, that such a demon could not simply stop the blood lust one morning and walk away from it."

"Was Leonard Chang on the case?"

"Everready? No . . . before his time."

Lucas had ordered a cinnamon roll with his coffee, but the discussion put him off eating. "It was that aspect of the case that first caught my attention, that he severed their heads while they were still alive," Lucas confided. "Caught the notation you made on the margin."

Harbough nodded. "Heard about the good work you're doing at the Thirty-first with the Cold Room files. Tell you this, Stonecoat, the only reason the Headless Horseman beheadings stopped is we put Freeleng away when we did. Now it's bound to start up again like some bad acid scene or an *X-Files* episode on TV. Only this is the real world, and this creep gets out of our sight, some innocent someone's going to literally lose her head."

"I couldn't agree with you more."

"Bastard always did women. Always the weaker sex and the weakest among them. No woman's safe in Houston this night."

"Like water through stone," Lucas agreed.

Harbough leaned in and asked, "Say what?"

"As you said, this man, Freeleng, will return to his nature."

Harbough considered this aloud, pulling at his chin, "Like water seeping through stone, yeah. His brain returns to its most primitive path."

They each stood, shook hands and parted.

Lucas walked back to his Dodge Intrepid where he sat thinking about what he'd learned of Freeleng this morning. Now, alone with the case file, alone with his thoughts on Freeleng and the Horseman murders, Lucas knew he must ask Meredyth Sanger for a favor. He also knew that she collected on favors, and it would mean he'd have to take on that pet project of hers, the one involving Lucas talking to rookies about how it feels to take another man's life for the first time. She'd been at him to do it for weeks. In a way, she had checkmated him once again.

He yanked his cell phone off its cradle and dialed headquarters, asking for Meredyth but getting Randy Oglesby instead. Randy simply said, "Dr. Sanger's taken a day off, Lucas. Can I help you?"

"No thanks. I'll talk to her soon enough."

"Because if this is about that lecturing job she wants you to do . . ." he fished.

Looking at his dashboard clock, Lucas barely heard Randy. "Talk to you again soon, Rando," he told the computer whiz kid and hung up.

Lucas thought now of putting it off till tomorrow, but he feared Freeleng would not be putting things off. So he again lifted the phone, and this time he dialed Meredyth's private number.

A new boyfriend, someone he only knew as Samuel Spellman, answered. She had finally gotten rid of the Yuppie university PR guy she'd been seeing, which had pleased Lucas; but now she had found this stockbroker, who appeared to be out of work at the moment and prepared to break her of all her funds. At least, this is how it appeared to Lucas. He secretly wanted to go over to her plush high-rise apartment, toss the creep out the window and replace him there in her bed. But she'd never go for the caveman violence, and he knew it. In one of their more heated arguments, he'd once told her, "If you ran your professional life as you do your personal life, you'd be out of a job."

"Agreed," she had snapped back, "but then I don't have a boss over my personal life. And if I did, it wouldn't be you, mister!"

"Yeah, Sam-boy?" he now said into the phone to Spellman, knowing how the man hated being called Sam-boy, "this is—"

"I know who the hell it is, Lucas. Just a second. She's right here."

Meredyth came on line, asking, "Lucas? I thought you'd be in Huntsville by now. What is it, Lucas? And it better be important. I'm supposed to be off today."

"I *am* in Huntsville," he replied. "Off? Are you teasing me?" he asked, taunting her with tone-implied sexual innuendo. "About time you showered for work, isn't it?" he added.

"I have the *day* off!"

"Oh, sorry. I wasn't aware," he lied.

"What is it you want? And where are you calling from? This connection is terrible."

"Other side of Huntsville, nearing the reservation to see my grandfather. You did clear it with Captain Lincoln, didn't you? Earlier you said—"

"Oh, yes, of course." She softened. "How can I help you, Lucas?" Lucas heard an audible groan escape Samboy.

"I want to know if you know of a Dr. Thomas William Morrissey."

"Oh, God, don't tell me he's been found murdered."

"No, but why do you ask?"

"He deals with some of the most psychotic patients in the state, hell in the country. Everyone expects him dead by year's end, and when he makes it through another year. . . . Well, suffice it to say that the winner of the pool makes a bundle."

"Yeah, I understand he deals with the dregs of society."

"I wouldn't even call them that, since they're not part of society to begin with. His patients are seldom people who can function in society. Ninety percent, and he knows this going in, will return to prison or be shot to death, by either a cop like you or someone on the street."

"So, you know a lot about this guy, huh?"

"I've grudgingly admired him, and I've despised the man. He's written books about his specialty, using fictitious names but quite real cases—primarily case studies that he's written about. But why are you interested? Has he been hurt, hospitalized, what?"

"Just because I have an interest in someone, it doesn't mean he's in the hospital." Lucas thought of the irony of his remark, at once realizing that his grandfather was near death and Jack Kirshner lay in a coma in the hospital. "It's a bit of a complicated story. Has to do with one of our Cold Room files, some beheading murders back in the eighties."

"You think Morrissey knows who the Headless Horseman is?"

"Then you know of the case?"

"If you lived in Houston at the time, you knew about the case."

"I know something about it now, and so does Morrissey. He's going to be treating Walter Karl Freeleng. Ring any bells?"

"Yeah, it does. He's the guy they think did the beheadings, but no one could pin the killings on Freeleng."

"Freeleng just took a walk, paroled, and is now under Morrissey's care."

"I'll be damned."

"No, never. Satan wouldn't stand for the competition, Mere."

"Funny. Ha, ha, funny."

"You can fill me in about Morrissey when—"

"You just take care of your grandfather. Stop this delaying business you're doing and go see him!"

"All right . . . all right."

"When you're back, sure, we can talk about Dr. Morrissey."

"What can you tell me about him now?"

"What do you want to know about him, Lucas?" Lucas heard an interested Meredyth shush her beau beside her, and he smiled.

"Will he cooperate?" asked Lucas.

"Cooperate on what?"

"We're looking closely at Freeleng now that he's out. Will Morrissey stand in our way or cooperate?"

"No, Lucas, he won't . . . cooperate, as you put it. Besides, why are you involved? You told me you had too much on your plate as it is, and now—"

Lucas ignored the question, asking his own instead. "Why the hell won't this guy Morrissey cooperate?"

"The man prizes above all things the doctor-patient privilege—as I do."

"But if this guy Freeleng tells him about having killed all those women, wouldn't the man find a way to let us know?"

"No, not this man."

"Isn't there some way to compel him to—"

"To what? Wear a wire? No, there is no compelling a

psychiatrist to rat out a patient if the man does not want to do so. You'll never get anywhere going that route. A man like Morrissey, who has built a reputation on this principle of American law, will never sell out a patient. He'll go to prison himself before doing so. I know him."

"That's madness. Even if he—"

"No, it's not madness, it's called ethics, a principle that must remain untouchable. Possibly—"

"Don't say it, Mere."

"What? Say what?" she demanded.

"Principles, possibly something I should get. Isn't that what you were about to say?"

"God, you can be so paranoid, Lucas. I intended to say that if we didn't have the doctor-patient protections—"

"It's just another rock for the pedophiles and other Gila monsters to hide beneath!"

"Perhaps so, but it's also a civil right that you and I enjoy as well. Imagine some shrink you dealt with going on public-access television to tell the world you are unfit to perform your duties as a police officer on the basis of information you spoke to her in confidence, Lucas."

Lucas realized she was now talking about *their* relationship. She knew enough about his disorders and problems to, if she wished, fill out a departmental form and end his career tomorrow. They both knew this. It colored every conversation they had. He walked along a slippery edge with her every time they disagreed, but she had never used this trump card in all the years they'd known each other. He weighed her point now.

Still, he had to say, "Yeah, but I'm not a rapist, murdering butcher out for jollies."

"All Morrissey can do as Freeleng's doctor is to insist that the man clear his conscience, confess and repent his crime. If he's in fact hiding anything, the doctor's first concern is and must be to his patient and his patient's mental health, stability and well-being."

"If he's hiding anything? Of course he's hiding something. Everybody's hiding something," Lucas insisted over the static from his cell phone.

"Given the lack of evidence brought against him at trial, there's little a doctor in Morrissey's situation can do. He can't do the job of the police, can't do the job of the courts or the penal system. All he can do is his own job, Lucas."

"Sounds like all Freeleng has to do is find the nearest confessional and start all over."

"If Morrissey can talk a criminal into confessing to murder or multiple murders, then he will direct a man to turn himself in—that's also the law. He's actually had some cases that have turned out that way."

"Really? And how many would that be?"

"Not enough, I agree."

"Think I'll try to find a copy of his book."

"*Books*, and I understand he's working on a new one."

"So, you've read them?"

"I have."

"What do you think, honestly, of the man?"

"His writing is obtuse—textbook style, sleep inducing, passive in tone and verb choice—but his theories are, to say the least, strangely eccentric. Unfortunately they have the veneer of the revolutionary, which some people fall for."

"Eccentric how?"

"For one, he believes in confusing his patients with mumbo jumbo or pseudopsychology—much of which he doesn't think is pseudo at all."

"Sue-do what?"

"Bullshit . . . He uses full-blown bullshit and a threatening manner as means to an end, as tools to get to the truth, so he explores nonsense, fiction."

Lucas pondered this for a moment, repeating the word, "Bullshit, bullshit . . . bullshit . . . So, does it work? His bull . . . shit, I mean?"

"It does according to him, according to his case files, his results, but someday someone, a patient most likely, is going to figure out he's full of it, and we're going to be scrapping up the results, so—"

"So, you don't buy into it?" Lucas asked, again checking the clock for the time. He floored the gas pedal and scurried past a semi blocking his view. Behind him the Huntsville city limits sign filled his rearview mirror as he flew past the truck.

"I don't use it. And for Morrissey to use it, well, it represents the ultimate hypocrisy, don't you see?"

"How so?"

"Think about it. The man will die before revealing a word of a patient's private session, because he believes in the principle of full disclosure without fear of redress or that the words will be used to incriminate a patient, yet he gets the patient to open up as a result of a series of lies, one piled upon another, many of which are as ludicrous as a conversation between . . ."

"Between us?"

"Stop putting words in my mouth. God, but you can be infuriating, Lucas. Listen, I was going for as ludicrous as Daffy Duck and Bugs Bunny. In any case, in the end, Dr. Morrissey draws composites of these very people he ministers to, to create his so-called case studies for his book sales. That's a grandiose hypocrisy, so far as I'm concerned."

"Hey, I for one found Bugs Bunny stimulating and enlightening with a rapier wit. As for Daffy, who else entertains the masses more? He deserves his webbed feet in plaster on the Hollywood walk of fame."

"Cute, Lucas."

"As for Morrissey, you're telling me the good doctor doesn't share with the police, but he shares with the public, and you say he gets results?"

"Let's put it this way: *He* thinks he does."

"And most people act on what they think rather than what they know, or what is real. Gotcha."

"It's kind of like that whole *Men Are from Mars, Women Are from Venus,* thing, you know? It only creates more rifts between the sexes to continue to label the other gender as weird and totally, futilely incomprehensible to the other."

"I don't follow you, Mere."

"So, too, with violent behavior. You see, Lucas? Morrissey labels violent behavior and then thinks he has a handle on it. That the offender, being able to apply a name to his societal disease, better understands it, and so can control it. Kinda like the notion of any disease or illness. Once you can apply a name to it, you can begin to heal or at least contemplate your options."

"That's Morrissey's thing in a nutshell, huh?"

"You got it, Lucas."

"Do you agree with it, the therapeutic power of knowing what to call the disease, I mean?"

"Absolutely."

"Then you agree with Morrissey that a rapist and a murderer can be rehabilitated?"

"No, not really."

"You're confusing me, Mere."

"I agree that it helps the patient to know the name of his disease. And to some degree it makes a sociopath or a megalomaniac feel better to be labeled as such, to know the name of his disorder. That does not necessarily mean that a killer will live differently or perceive differently or make good use of knowledge."

"I see," muttered Lucas into the phone as he slowed for a pickup pulling a horse trailer.

Meredyth continued, "In fact, for many, it becomes just another excuse to kill. 'Oh, look at me, I'm a born sociopath, so I can't possibly be anything else, so I will just be what I am, and that means hurting others.' A diabetic it might work for, a full-blown lunatic killer, no."

Lucas thanked her and again apologized for bothering her at home.

"What about the Scalper, Lucas? Have you given it any more thought?" she asked, but she only got a dial tone.

ƑIVE

Snake: wise, defying

Looking out over the depressed reservation landscape, dotted with hovels and dilapidated trailer homes, Lucas saw through his windshield a gathering crowd, made up primarily of dirty-faced children and young teens, all admiring his shiny red Dodge Intrepid as if it were a stallion. The mag wheels alone cost more than most adults on the reservation saw their entire lives. Here, the major currency remained barter; and bartering still remained the highest form of art known to the speaking world.

Lucas climbed from his car, half-wondering who would try to talk him out of the car, or at least into the driver's seat for a drive. The cloud of fine dirt kicked up by the application of his brakes now swirled shroudlike around Lucas, painting him in soft, bright hues. From a distance, he must look like a ghost, he thought. It had been almost a year since he had last visited home. Whenever he met with his grandfather, they did so out on the prairie, away from this place. It had become something of a ritual with them.

Everyone on the reservation knew Lucas, and those who didn't knew of his reputation as a man hunter. He nodded appreciatively to those who'd gathered in greeting, walking toward his grandfather's newly constructed home, the largest home on the reservation. While modest by any standard other than that of the reservation Indian, here it stood out as a palatial cabin. On both sides of the old man's home stood broken-down trailers, their screen doors twisted on hinges, awnings leaning too low, window frames rotting and shutters dangling like Saturday night drunks, swinging and torn.

His grandfather, given a choice, had asked for a Lincoln Log–style home. Lucas had made it so. Naturally the new lifestyle of Grandfather Keeowskowee had drawn the eye and ire of most everyone on the reservation—and it had added to the suspicion that somehow Lucas Stonecoat had been behind the sudden influx of money and building going on here. Lucas had anonymously donated funds he'd pocketed after doing private-eye work for Zachary Roundpoint, payment for having identified Roundpoint's mother's killer in a case dating back to 1948. Roundpoint had been very grateful and generous in the end.

Even as a child growing up on the Coushatta reservation, Lucas had found the place arid, death dealing and stomach turning, but today an added feature colored the red-clay ghetto. He found the entire res strangely quiet, despite the fact it normally buzzed with whatever news came along the moccasin grapevine.

Only a Texas wind whipping through the barren land and the few trees around Keeowskowee's home—trees Lucas had paid to have planted there—spoke to him. Then suddenly Tsalie appeared in the doorway of his grandfather's cabin, looking beautiful and natural and stricken, saying, "I tried to reach you, but you were already gone."

Lucas felt as if his heart had risen into his mouth, so fearful was he of the answer to the question forming on his lips. "Is he . . . Have I come too late?" Even as he said the words, his thoughts filled with her dark beauty: her radiant eyes; full lips; long, braided hair, jet-black still.

"Your stubborn cousin Billy took the old man into Houston."

"Took him to Houston? Why? What do you mean?"

"With tribal funds, they are getting him the best of care, so they say." She placed such emphasis on the two words "tribal funds" that he guessed that by now *everyone* had surmised where the recent tribal funds had come from.

"Who authorized this?"

"Billy took it upon himself. He would not listen to reason, much less his . . . me."

Lucas inwardly grimaced. Tsalie had married Billy Hawk some seven years before. "Was the old man well enough to travel?"

Ignoring the question, she continued, "But to Billy's credit, he loves the old man, and he thinks the white hospital can . . . can save him. That their medicine can save his life." Tears welled up and Lucas caught her as she nearly collapsed in his arms. It felt as if she had never left his arms all these years. As always, she smelled of natural herbs and wildflowers, some concoction she'd created to spray in her hair and on her body.

Lucas swore, swallowing his anger at the same time. "Goddamn that husband of yours," he muttered into her ear.

She defended like a bear, claws slightly extending as she pushed from his embrace. "Billy could not stand it any longer. You were not here, and so—"

"I'm sorry it took me so long, but—"

"You don't know how . . . how difficult it became. Grandfather could not breathe at all, and this went on for hours."

"Why didn't someone call me sooner then?"

"I tried calling you as soon as I realized that Billy meant to do this at whatever cost. When someone told him of the money in the longhouse account, well, that's when he decided to have your father moved by ambulance. He believed, given that you live in the white world now, that you would bless his actions."

"You say my grandfather could not breathe?"

"He has pneumonia, and you know how he has smoked for as long as we've all known him. His lungs have collapsed. His body is in a complete shutdown mode, Lucas."

"Grandfather will not want to be stuck with pins or tubes, and he does not want to be put on a respirator. If Hawk had any sense, if he must take the old man somewhere, why not into those hills?" Lucas pointed to the rolling green hills in the distance. "A white man's hospital is no place for my grandfather."

Lucas collapsed onto the broad wooden steps leading up to the expansive cabin porch. He dropped his head in his hands. She joined him there and placed a comforting arm around his shoulder. He felt as wonderful as he had when they were children, and this brought back images of them playing childish games, dreaming childish dreams right here on this very ground.

Just then two children came running up, shouting at Tsalie, saying, "Mommy! Mommy! Can we go to the swimming hole? Now? Please, please, please!"

Tsalie smiled back at her children and made them step closer to meet Lucas. She introduced him as her oldest and dearest friend. She said to Lucas, "My two daughters. This is Christa, and this is Angeline."

"How beautiful you both are," he replied, sending the two little girls into a paroxysm of blushing and giggles.

"Both born on the reservation in Oklahoma where you and Billy were living?" It was information gleaned from what he had last heard of the couple, along with the fact that Billy had started drinking and had lost his truck driver's license as a result, and so his job. He then went into construction work, mostly lifting and carrying and transporting. Lucas had heard the family had fallen on hard times when Billy suffered an accident that left him unable to work. After hearing this, Lucas had lost track of their whereabouts until now. They had only recently returned to Texas, showing up back at Coushatta, where they had begun.

After the girls acknowledged Lucas, he gave each a silver dollar and a warm smile. Tsalie then directed them with a firm, "Go now, you two! Go play."

"But you promised we could go swimming," complained Angeline.

"Later, after lunch, we will all go to the swimming hole." The idea left Lucas with an image of their mother in a bathing suit. Lucas watched the children scamper off.

"And so, their father is in Houston at what hospital admitting my grandfather?"

"Don't be too angry with Hawk, Lucas. He loves your grandfather even as you do. He could not stand to see him suffering so. . . . So, he looks for hope."

"I've got to get back to Houston then."

"Stay long enough to have lunch with me and the children."

It was an invitation he knew he could not refuse—time

alone, or semi-alone, with her. "They're beautiful," he said, indicating her two girls, thinking, *They ought to be mine.*

As if reading his mind or the expression in his eyes, she replied, "Yes, beautiful reservation children. Some of us chose this life, and we do not regret it, Lucas. Tell me, do you ever regret your choice? Of leaving?"

"Do I regret leaving? I regret leaving you, regret not making you come with me. But no. I had to go. Grandfather foresaw it, I knew it and so did you." He placed his massive hand over her two smaller hands, warmly pressed and asked, "Are you happy? I need to know that you are happy."

"Happy? Oh, yes, in my children, with Hawk reasonably so."

He frowned, repeating, " 'Reasonably so'?"

"Life is always a challenge in the company of your cousin, Lucas, as you should know. But yes, I am well off."

He nodded appreciatively. "That's what I remember most about you."

"What's that?"

"How much you always found something good in just about everyone, and how much you always liked a challenge." He laughed.

She joined in his laughter, adding, "And you, you were the ultimate challenge."

"I've long wanted to call you, to find you, look in on you, see that you were all right."

She smiled at this. "That's kind of you, really, but I have done well with my life, as have you. I'm sorry I could not come to you when you were so horribly hurt in Dallas, Lucas. I learned of it later. We were out of touch, on the road, following work, you see, and—"

"No apologies, Tsalie. It's not necessary."

"I have seen the newspaper reports. Your grandfather would not let us miss them. How you are stomping out crime single-handedly."

He ignored her compliment, asking, "Are you still teaching at reservation schools?"

"When I can find the work, yes. But Billy's work keeps moving us."

"A never-ending battle, no doubt."

"Like stomping out fires that will not stay out, yes."

"How long have you been here in Huntsville?"

"Not long, a few weeks. Was trying to get up the nerve to contact you when your grandfather suddenly needed care. Billy and I, we . . . well, I've been living here, day and night, with your grandfather since he fell ill. There's some food on the table. Come inside." She then called out to her two girls to join them for lunch.

The patient lost all patience, shooting to his feet. He now stood. A lumbering, towering man, hulking huge over the cowering Dr. Thomas W. Morrissey, whose glasses flew in one direction, his notepad in another. Now the boy-son loomed large over Dr. Morrissey, the fanciful man in suspenders with all the answers, all the big words. The doctor who was doing good by providing these sessions so that the system could grind on; just doing it out of the goodness of his wrinkled old heart, so that the patient (all patients had become one patient so far as Thomas Morrissey was concerned) wanted to disembowel the warbling psychobabbling bastard right here and right now. Right where he perched on his leather chair . . .

He wanted it in the worst way, and he meant to have

it. He took the huge hunter's blade with its surreal surface reflecting off the office light straight from beneath the coat where he'd used tape to conceal it. Easily and smoothly and without hesitation, the patient slid the blade into Dr. Thomas W. Morrissey's welcoming, smiling chest. Big, easy target.

Instant relief flooded throughout the patient's body.

Meanwhile, Morrissey might easily have been mistaken for a roasting turkey. The knife carves a path right around the gut, a neat and circular incision, as if the blade has eyes—perhaps even a mind of its own. All the while Morrissey's own eyes bulge wide, popping out in Jim Carrey–cartoon fashion at what he sees. *What's happening to me,* he must wonder now, his mouth filling with blood as the spillover wells up in a crimson tidal wave, up into his throat until he begins choking on his own lifeblood, up in a gurgle and a sputter of rich, red fluid, as if oil has been struck, creating a treble now, sound bytes of death. The death chorus overall, the boy-filled-with-anger, becoming orchestrator and choreographer of this macabre scene, smiles the smile of great release, relief, even sexual pleasure at having destroyed this good-hearted man to capture his spirit and place it among others of his collection.

"What collection? Son? What sort of collection?" asked the dying man.

"Wouldn't you like to know?"

"Yes, I very much would like to know. Tell me. Speak honestlyfreely."

The dead man, the dead doctor, sat up before the patient, still alive, still talking, still asking the patient questions with all-due smug impatience. The patient opened his eyes to see that what he had thought a *fait accompli* was only wish fulfillment. His mind registered the fact that, nothing whatever had come full circle, and nothing of his fantasy to kill Dr. Morrissey had been fulfilled after all. What did Dr. Morrissey call it? *Wish-full-up-ment* gone horribly awry only to *wish-empty-down-ment*?

It had all been just another fantasy, so Morrissey had not stopped living, had not stopped the babbling, professorial nonsense. Morrissey remained so very much of this world that he still sat upright and boardlike only a few feet from his patient. The patient who lied more to himself than anyone else, the same patient who had never left the couch.

The hunting knife remained taped to the inner lining of the coat, which he'd insisted on keeping wrapped about him.

"Our session, I see is up for today, sir," Morrissey said.

" 'Sir' . . . Now that's more like it. Shows respect, old man."

"I'll expect you this time next week, and we are—despite your wish to carve out my entrails for your so-called collection—making considerable progress."

Over lunch, Lucas learned, as coincidence might have it, that his grandfather now resided in the same hospital in Houston as did Jack Kirshner. This happenstance, this serendipitous fact, lent more mystery to Jack's strange preamble to his coma, all that about wanting a death sleep.

Lucas's grandfather had, throughout his lifetime, read the dreams of men and explained them to the uninitiated. In fact, Lucas's grandfather had been the most important shaman in his village. Everyone who knew Keeowskowee had been touched by him, and everyone would mourn his leaving. His being in hospital in Houston explained why the reservation had appeared so empty and silent when Lucas first drove in. According to Tsalie, most everyone on the reservation was now camped out at Houston Memorial, awaiting word on Keeowskowee's condition.

Lucas imagined the hospital under siege, imagined an ancient scene: fires burning, men preparing weapons and praying to their gods for conquest even as they sharpened their primitive tools. That's what it must look like to officials and staff there, he thought. He prayed there would be no confrontational cops on hand.

The children rampaged through their meal and out the door almost as quickly as they'd come in for lunch, leaving the adults alone again in the fresh-wood aroma of the recently built log home. Lucas momentarily wished for the crowded little space of his grandfather's old trailer; it would have brought him and Tsalie closer, at least physically. He missed their past, their togetherness.

She stood and began to gather up dishes. Lucas reached across the table and took her hand, telling her, "I must leave now. I want to be with the old man, whatever comes."

"Of course. It's been good seeing you, Lucas."

"Yes, it has been wonderful to see you." He rose and kissed her; a friend's kiss, followed by a smile. She kissed him back with a long, languid, passionate embrace.

When the embrace ended, she said, "So that you know always what you walked away from."

"I know, Tsalie. I have always known."

Lucas then left, each footstep heavy, kicking up miniature dust clouds about his boots. His departure was marked not only by Tsalie's eyes but also those of every pair of eyes remaining on the reservation, old and young. He drove away to the thumping beat of The Doors on his

CD player, Jim Morrison plaintively trying to get some woman out of his head.

When Lucas arrived at Houston Memorial, he saw first the strobe lights of squad cars and a line of blue-clad men looking on at a milling crowd of Texas Indians wearing Stetson hats, leather boots and blue jeans. It appeared an odd standoff, not unlike a Norman Rockwell depiction of Custer's last stand, both sides preparing for a long vigil.

Lucas climbed from his car and walked among his people, looking out of place among them in his detective's clothes. From the sidelines, he imagined he must look like an Indian don, shaking hands, greeting old friends of both his and his grandfather's. He thought of his connection with the Red Mafioso, Roundpoint, the man whom he had helped in a relentless, obsessive bid to unmask a killer, but no ordinary killer. Lucas had located the man who had murdered and mutilated Roundpoint's mother when Roundpoint was yet a toddler. Roundpoint, a Native American hit man, had promised that anytime Lucas needed a favor, that he was only a phone call away. Lucas had maintained no contact with Roundpoint, fearing any semblance of taint could cost him his detective's shield, but he wondered now if he shouldn't have stayed in touch with the man.

In a sense, the two of them, Lucas and Roundpoint, had much in common. Both he and Roundpoint were outcasts, living between two worlds, the red and the white, each trying to find his own path that was neither red nor white. It had been through Roundpoint's generosity that Lucas had passed along a small fortune to be divvied up by the reservation council, after he'd taken enough out to build his grandfather's new house. If any wind of this were to get back to Captain Lincoln or IAD, Lucas knew his life's work would come to a screeching halt.

The size of the crowd presaged a hell of a wake for Keeowskowee. The Indian chanting presaged one hell of a funeral, as well, Lucas thought. He grasped hands extended to him and shook them warmly with both his own hands cranking, and he thanked all those who had caused the hospital administration a great deal of jitters this day.

Lucas stepped past the police line at the entrance to the hospital from which he imagined the tribe had been ejected. Stepping from the throng, he flashed his badge at white faces he did not know; he got the nod and stepped through the hospital's glass doors where security met him head-on, believing him one of the masses here to cause trouble. Lucas again merely flashed his Houston gold shield and the security man stepped aside. At the desk, Lucas asked for the room number where his grandfather lay dying.

The clerk, eyeballing the commotion outside and then Lucas, finally gave him the room number with the caveat, "But he's not there right now."

"Where is he?"

"They're running tests."

"Who? Who are 'they'?"

"His doctors, of course."

"And who gave them permission to run any tests?"

"His other grandson. The one he came in with. Your brother, I presume."

Lucas bolted for the stairwell and rushed up the four flights to the floor he needed. Once there, he pushed through the stairwell door and searched for room 4224. Inside, he found Billy Hawk, his heavyset cousin, watching the Jets battle the Dolphins when a TV commercial broke in, something about Jimmy Dean's low fat, healthiest sausage ever. Lucas instantly attacked Hawk verbally, saying, "So, now you're acting as the old man's grandson? What gives you the fucking right to put him in this place, and then to OK tests on *my* grandfather!" Lucas had traversed the space between them, yanking Billy from his seat and pinning him to a wall where their eyes met.

"Lucas, there was no time. He would have died, and he is like my grandfather. He has always been my grandfather in practice."

"Then you're prolonging his death? Is that why we're all here, Hawk?"

"He was in pain, suffering! You had to be there."

"He can handle pain, Hawk. What he can't handle is life-support. We have had discussions about what to do if it came to this. The old man does not want any heroic measures taken. Not by any doctors, and certainly not by you."

"But if they can prolong his life, Lucas! Surely, then—"

"Surely what?" Lucas only tightened his grip on Hawk's lapels. "Sure . . . Surely then you still have someone to take all your worries and concerns and fears to? Hawk, it's time you stood on your own damned feet and stopped leaning on others, especially that frail old man. Now, where is he?"

"Oncology lab."

"Fuck, cancer tests? They're running goddamn cancer tests on him, when we all know that he has cancer?"

A doctor, standing at the threshold, nervously cleared his throat, interrupting them and looking as if he was afraid to enter the fray. Still, in a controlled, radio-quality voice, the middle-aged Asian man, clinically stated, "Mr.

Stonecoat, your grandfather's condition is bad, very bad. No one's denying that, but we believe that every aspect of his case ought to be considered, every test run, every possibility exhausted before we place him out on that ice floe you . . . your people are so fond of using."

"And precisely what will your testing show, Doctor? That he has no lungs left? That his liver is damaged, his pancreas is shot? That the cancer is or is not in his bones? That he can't breathe on his own? That he requires round-the-clock attention and a respirator?"

"He asked for it, Lucas," said Hawk.

Lucas glared at his cousin. "What?"

"The old man asked me to bring him here, to seek help."

Lucas shook his head and paced, considering this before erupting with, "You're lying, Billy."

"That's not fair, Lucas."

"Where is he? I want to see my grandfather now!" Lucas shouted at the dumbfounded doctor.

"He should be on his way back up by now," replied the physician. As he spoke, an elevator opened and a prone form, looking more ghostlike than corporeal, came rolling into the room. He lay shrouded in a white sheet, reminding Lucas of cadavers at the police morgue. Dusty, chalk white skin pulled over emaciated, skeletal limbs and features. This was not Lucas's grandfather.

Lucas bent over his grandfather, staring into the eyes of death, feeling death as another shroud around the old man. Lucas felt the depth of grief that Billy, too, must feel. They had both, as boys growing up on the reservation, been raised by this dying man. Now they stood on the outer circle of their own mortality, no buffer between them, their generation, and the great beyond. The bottom rung of grief, overwhelming emotion clouded Lucas's eyes with tears as he grasped hold of the hand that had become bone and vein. "I love you, Grandfather. I'm here with you now."

Lucas's grandfather, doped to the ceiling, could not focus on him. He looked like the proverbial bag of bones beneath the sheet. His legs appeared to be nonexistent, his arms twigs, the hands somehow elongated, monstrously exaggerated fingers in their thin appearance. Optical illusion, Lucas silently wondered. When he touched the bone-hard fingers, Lucas felt his insides turn over; his heart screamed the silent scream brought on by the acid-drip of reality's harshest moment. Lucas felt the acid seep into each valve of his heart, one drip at a time. It required all his reserve of strength to not allow his horror to be reflected on his face, to not allow the old man to see his terror and fear.

"Yes, the old man's time has come, Doctor. It's time everyone recognizes that. Ready the ice floe," Lucas determined aloud. "I want him out of here, tonight."

"You and your brother can work this one out, Mr. Stonecoat. In the meantime, he's been admitted, so he must remain overnight for observation. Hospital rules."

"Your rules don't apply here, Doctor. Trust me."

"But he should be kept under observation, and we have all the facilities to ease his last moments, should it—"

"Observation of what?" Lucas felt his frustration boiling now. He took menacing steps toward the doctor as he spoke, when another, older doctor stepped in to support the first doctor with the platitude, "We are merely concerned about what's best for the patient."

"You must allow us to do our jobs, Mr. Stonecoat," finished the first doctor, condescension dripping from him.

"Besides," added the elder doctor, "we have a number of additional tests we need to run on your grandfather before we can even begin to—"

"For God's sake! Look at this man. You people are talking insanity. There is no reason for any further tests other than to pad your goddamned bills, to collect as much as possible from Medicare, insurance and the patient."

"I resent the implication that—"

Again Lucas cut the doctor off. "If I have an independent medical professional go over my grandfather's records, and he agrees with me that you people are running needless, pointless tests in some scam for . . . for whatever reason you have, be it cash or experimentation, then I will sue this fucking hospital and every fucking doctor who came within ten feet of my grandfather. Is that clear enough for you, Doctors?"

"Quite," replied the older one, while the younger man inched from the room.

"No more tests, and I want you two out of here now. Now!"

Amid grumblings, Lucas forced the older doctor to follow the wiser one from the room. Lucas added, "My *brother* and I have to talk!" But as he closed the door on the doctors, Lucas added, "And tell them at the desk, that if I see one more doctor cross this threshold, I'm going to be arrested for assault, but not before I deck a few doctors. You got that, gentlemen?"

"What the hell are you doing, Lucas?" asked his burly cousin. Rather than answer, Lucas made a phone call while Billy Hawk paced and listened. At the same time, Lucas's grandfather, on oxygen now, fought for every breath.

In moments, Lucas was speaking to a hospice, telling

them what he faced at Memorial, and pleading that they help him get the old man back home. There his grandfather could comfortably and with dignity die in the company of his entire family.

A Pakistani oncologist showed up at the door, asking to speak with Lucas, cajoling Lucas into slowing down and having a cup of coffee with him in the doctors lounge. "I con tell yu somethings ha'bowt your gran-fadder's condission, and where we go from he'ah, Mr. Stonecoat," the little man spoke, his hands clutching a manila envelope.

Lucas's first impulse was indeed to consider assault, but the mild little man seemed such a small target for Lucas's enormous anger. Lucas instead slowly explained the facts to the man. "My grandfather wants no heroic efforts taken to save him. We have had many long conversations about this."

"Oh, but dis not heroic," countered Dr. Hakisa, his name coming from his name tag.

"He's dying. There's nothing you or anyone here can do to prevent that. Prolonging it is not what the patient wishes, nor does his family wish it. It was a mistake to bring him here in the first place, Dr. Hack . . ."

"Hak-ee-sa," the man corrected.

"Besides, Grandfather is—"

"But more tests will only take five more days," countered Hakisa in a profoundly complacent tone. "What measure is five days in a lifetime, Mr. Stonecoat?"

"No, no five days of treating this man like your personal pincushion!"

"To be reasonable in a time of grief, I know, is most difficult, but—"

"Look, you are a man whose people understand the life cycle. You can look at him and see that his time is here, now. This man's in pain, and has been for years. He's fought a long, long battle, years before you ever laid eyes on him, and now . . . Now he can't even properly . . . can't breathe." Lucas's words faltered as he fought back tears. "And there's not a damn thing you or modern medicine can do for him. So please, let it go."

Instead, Hakisa stepped toward the patient to have a look. Lucas put a hand on the man's shoulder and said in a threatening near-whisper, "Step back!"

Again Lucas hustled a doctor from the hospital room. "It's the family now. He needs his family around him, not a lot of doctors, tubes, IVs and machines."

Six

Man: human life

His heart weighty with memories and a mix of anger for the circumstances, Lucas went again to his dying grandfather's side. Staring into the old man's unfocused eyes, he realized that he hadn't begun to deal with the enormous grief balling up inside of himself; he hadn't had the time, what with every damned doctor in the building pleading with him to let them run additional, unwanted, unneeded tests on the old man.

He lifted his grandfather's hand in his and cradled the back of his neck at the same time, saying, "I love you, Grandfather, as I have loved no other man on this planet. You have fought many battles and won them all. But this is one you can lose. It's all right to lose this one. I know your heart, and I will someday again see your soul."

Lucas looked across the bed at Billy Hawk whose name had never fit him. As soft and as pudgy as dough, his ethics were about as pliable as clay, too. Younger than Lucas only by a year and six months, Billy at least cried genuine tears. He did love the old man. He simply hadn't had the powerful tie that bound Lucas and Keeowskowee, in great part because he never listened to the old man, not really, not with his heart. Sure, he loved the old shaman, too, and they had been in daily contact since Billy and Tsalie had moved back from Oklahoma four weeks ago.

Lucas understood Hawk's debilitating depression over the old man's passing, but still he had to press the issue, saying to Billy, "The truth now. Grandfather did not ask to come here. He would not ever have asked to come here. You always told the worst lies, Billy, and that much hasn't changed."

Billy blubbered an attempted reply, but Lucas cut him off before he could form words, adding, "That said, help me to get him back home, Hawk."

Hawk shakily replied, "I will help you any way I can."

"Go down to our reservation brothers. Find who has the best shocks on the best air-riding pickup out there. If the hospice people don't get that ambulance to us in half an hour, we're taking him out over our shoulders and down to that pickup."

A moan of recognition erupted from the old man, his eyes now focusing a little better, settling like a butterfly with flapping wings on Lucas.

"I'm with you, Grandfather," Lucas informed him.

"With me, where? Where the hell am I?" The old man remained completely disorientated, but he grasped on to Lucas's hand. Lucas felt some small impulse yet in his grandfather to yank himself up and out of bed. Instead, he began speaking in some unintelligible gibberish, all in Native tongue.

"You're in a hospital in Houston, Grandfather. The question is, do you want to remain here, or do you want to go home? In either case, you are dying and not expected to live long. What do you say? What do you want to do, Grandfather? Stay here or go home?"

"The white man . . . has no medicine . . . to help me. I go home then. Yes, and there I will die."

"You heard it, Hawk. He'd rather die at home surrounded by family and friends than all alone in this sterile environment. You might've asked him that before you carted him here."

Hawk evenly replied, "I'm sorry. I'll help any way that I can."

Suddenly in the doorway stood the tall, darkly clad figure of Zachary Roundpoint, a former hired assassin, and the man who had killed Houston's Native American mafioso boss to avenge his mother. Or had that simply been his excuse for killing this man, in order to take over the Native American underworld in the city? Lucas might never know the answer to this question.

"Heard about your problem, Stonecoat," he said. "I'm here to help in whatever way I can." He instantly read Stonecoat's reaction, Lucas's eyes and grimace giving way to frustration, making Roundpoint quickly add, "Don't sweat it. No one saw me enter. They will all assume the helicopter I came in is a medical transport, since it is . . . normally. I had 'em put it down on the fucking roof. Medical evac transport . . . belongs to the fire department where I have a few . . . friends like Lieutenant Whalen."

"You always love to drop names, don't you?" Lucas let go of his grandfather, easing him back onto the pillow below his head. He then stepped slowly toward Roundpoint, looking as if he might take a swing at the other man. Billy looked on in confusion.

Lucas and Roundpoint resembled one another in height,

weight, general appearance down to the cheekbones and angles of the face. Where Roundpoint had a Lou Diamond Phillips appearance, Lucas more closely resembled the actor Jimmy Smits. Lucas said, "I really don't think your brand of expertise is exactly what's needed here, Zachary."

Billy's mouth dropped, his confusion now mixed with awe, at the name he'd suspected. Every Native American in the Southwest had, by now, heard of the infamous Zachary Roundpoint's takeover of the Indian and Mexican mafioso in Houston, Texas.

"Billy," said Lucas, "go down to room forty-eight—"

"Room forty-eight?"

"First floor, yes and—"

"What for?"

"Shut up and listen and I'll tell you. Look in on room forty-eight, and let me know how the cop in the bed there is doing. Tell the nurse you're there for information for me. They'll know me. Patient's name is Jack Kirshner."

Roundpoint stepped aside for Billy to pass, but Billy stopped to introduce himself to Roundpoint and to make a point of mentioning that he was Lucas's cousin and very much in need of a job. Lucas fairly shouted, "Not now, Billy."

Billy glared at Lucas and stalked off down the hallway. Lucas's eyes followed Hawk—an emotionally, mentally and spiritually lost man, Lucas determined. Lucas always knew that Hawk held him in high regard, but this also fostered a deviant jealousy that many of his friends and relatives on the res also held for Lucas, directed at Lucas, who felt uncomfortable being the object of anyone's jealousy. Due to this and the pettiness of reservation life, alongside the poverty and sickness there, walking away from res life came easy for Lucas. Obviously it had for Roundpoint as well. No small town in America had any more pettiness, ignorance, human frailty and xenophobia than did a Native American reservation.

To a large degree, it had been such infighting that had caused the downfall of the Five Civilized Tribes—a protectorate of the U.S. government in Oklahoma Territory, once proudly sending ambassadors to U.S. presidents from Andrew Jackson to Abraham Lincoln. The five tribes split up along the Union and Confederate lines during the white man's Civil War, using the white war as an excuse to revisit old wounds and rifts that had existed in the tribes since the time of Removal on the Trail of Tears. The Cherokee had survived the white man's repeated attempts to wipe them from the face of the earth. They had survived disease, genocide, uprooting from their eastern lands, touching on what was now Alabama, Georgia, Florida, Mississippi and North Carolina. But old wounds and family feuds in the Five Tribes led to the demise of political power gained since dealing with the Indian hater, Andrew Jackson, the force behind the Removal Act of 1820, which directly led to the Trail of Tears. Alongside the prejudice, racism and hatred of whites, the tribes had themselves torn asunder any unity built since the Trail of Tears once they declared, in split-state fashion, for the North and the South. The then-president of the Cherokee Nation, and the most influential man among all the Cherokee Seminole, Chickasaw, Creek and Choctaw pleaded for all the Five Civilized Tribes to remain neutral in the coming storm.

With the sights, sounds and odors of the modern day hospital swirling around Lucas, where he stood in the hallway outside his grandfather's room, he recalled how the old man had told him of Keeowskowee's namesake, a.k.a. John Ross, the most powerful and astute man in the Indian Nation by 1860, and how the tribal majority ignored his great and wise council regarding the Civil War. It did no good whatsoever to blame *all* of the woes of *all* of the nations of the Native American on the policies of the U.S. government, no more than it did to blame every current crisis from Bosnia to El Niño on the U.S. government. And while there had been a systematic policy in place to exterminate or neutralize the entire race—and that policy of genocide was now well documented by revisionist historians—Lucas still felt the Indians, given time, would have just as surely exterminated one another, so great were the intertribal wars.

But most Native Americans read history as most white Americans did, putting their own slant to things, failing to deal with human nature in the bargain. Most reservation Indians of the younger generations knew next to nothing about history beyond the costumes worn at Native American festivals. Like most children in America, they'd say, "What's history got to do with me?"

Lucas had had many discussions on the topic with his grandfather and other elder men of the tribe. In the end, they all agreed. Even now, with the current, far more benevolent U.S. policies long years in place, the Native Americans could not live in peace with one another, often failing to take advantage of policies that encouraged growth, development and education, in particular. The men in power preferred looking back to looking forward. And when an occasional man or woman with strong clan roots, such as Chief Ruth Mankiller, stepped up to the political plate, looking forward, she was labeled a "breed."

Whenever the mainstays of the reservation society disagreed with someone, they called him or her a half-breed bastard who had learned the white ways of lining his own pockets with government-allocated dollars. Which, truth be known, was often the case as well. Most Native Americans successful in dealing with the white world happened to be of mixed blood. The money gene, Lucas joked to his grandfather on occasion. "Full bloods don't have it," he'd say.

Lucas returned to his grandfather's side, additional memories and moments together with the old man filling his mind. He recalled how the old man had taken him at his word, and had literally carted him out to the wilderness area of the Devil's Spine, *Diablo Spinata*. There among the rocks and the feral land, he had left Lucas to fend for himself for a week, leaving him with only the bowie knife he'd given him as a birthday present.

During that quest, Lucas had learned exactly who he was, what he was capable of and what he wanted to do with his life. The old man had given him the opportunity to truly see his vision and to listen to his spirit guides. The old man's influence had made Lucas Stonecoat the man he was today.

Again Lucas took up the old shaman's hand in his and tearfully said, "Already, I miss you, old man. But it is time you went to your father. Let your spirit soar."

"The helicopter ride will do that for the old man, Lucas," came Roundpoint's deep, resonant voice beside him, looking down on the dying man.

Lucas pulled away from Roundpoint when the man put a hand on his shoulder. Anyone with a camera who might catch a glimpse of the two of them together could end Lucas's career.

"Don't read anything into the offer more than my wanting to help you, Lucas. I heard of your need through the moccasin grapevine. We can take him out now, no waiting, no fuss, and no one any the wiser."

Lucas sought out sincerity in Zachary's eyes. Even finding it, Lucas feared taking the man's handout, but he looked at his grandfather, knowing that at any moment the old man could be gone. "How did you get a medical helicopter on such short—"

"Bribery, the oldest lesson the whites taught our fathers, remember?" replied Roundpoint before Lucas could finish the question.

"The Trail of Tears was cleared with profiteering and larceny. So . . . all right, let's do it."

"A sound decision."

The old man grumbled something, and Lucas returned to the bedside and bent over the restraining bar, placed his ear to his Keeowskowee's mouth and asked, "What is it, Grandfather?"

"I went away . . . went to your sleeping . . . friend—"

Lucas's eyes widened and he asked, "Jack Kirshner?"

"—Spoke to him."

Lucas wondered at the words. Wondered who else might the old man be referring to, when his grandfather added, "Your friend in trouble. He will be all right, Lucas. He will be well," mumbled the old shaman. "And so will I . . ."

Lucas wondered anew at the connection between Kirshner and himself.

"I've got the orderlies on standby. I've got a helicopter on the roof. Do we airlift him out of here and back to Coushatta or not?" asked Roundpoint.

Lucas's eyes fell, and he shook his head, realizing how

this would look, if he took Roundpoint's hospitable offer. "I won't be owned by you or any man, Zachary."

"I know this, Lucas."

"Then why are you here? Why are you doing this?"

Roundpoint breathed in a deep breath and expelled it, exasperated. Toying with the black fedora hat in his hands, he finally muttered, "As once I told you, Lucas, a man like me, I have no friends."

"What's that got to do with—"

"All I ask is your friendship. Nothing more."

"You're known for taking far more, Zachary."

"I know no one else I . . . respect more than you, Lucas."

The admission touched him, but to cover his emotions, Lucas callously replied, "Yeah, and IAD will buy that, too."

"The helicopter is the safest, surest way to get your grandfather home alive. It's equipped with everything he needs, including two paramedics. Take it, damn you."

Lucas looked from Roundpoint to his grandfather and back again.

"Take the offer."

Lucas took a deep breath and nodded. "All right, let's do it."

"Wheel his bed to the elevator. Punch the roof button. I have two paramedics waiting at the other end. Leave it to them, my friend."

"I have hospice representatives meeting us out at the reservation," Lucas commented as he busied himself with lifting the wheels on the bed and moving it out. He took some childish pleasure in the thought of Billy Hawk's returning to an empty room.

Zachary Roundpoint followed Lucas into the elevator,

and with the old man again asleep, they talked across the ancient shaman's body.

"I'm sorry to see your spirit-father this way," Roundpoint offered.

With the elevator ascending, Lucas focused for a moment on the fact that Roundpoint had killed his own "spirit-father"—Mendoza—but then the man had deserved death. He'd been the antithesis of Keeowskowee. "Thank you, Zachary. Listen, there is something else you can do for me."

"Name it."

"You have an army of men in the Native American community, and you have a foothold in the Chicano community as well."

"You can't believe I control that many—"

"Can you ask your *army* to root out this man the press is calling the Scalper. If he is one of us, I want his head."

"He is *not* one of us," Roundpoint countered.

"How do you know this?"

"As I know the stars only shine at night, I know this, but also, I have already made inquiries. There's nothing on the street that ties any Native to these crimes, despite the fact that I'm sure one of us will be hauled in for them."

The elevator doors opened on the roof, the cab filled with a powerful wind from the helicopter rotor blades threatening to deafen and topple them. Lucas stepped up to Zachary Roundpoint and took his hand and firmly shook it. "Thank you, my brother, for your help."

"He should die in that beautiful home you built for him, Lucas."

Lucas, confident now that his grandfather would see his last moments in familiar surroundings, climbed into the waiting helicopter behind the paramedics who'd secured the old man inside.

Suddenly Lucas felt a tugging at his leg. Looking down from the chopper door, he saw that it was Billy Hawk. He kicked out at his cousin, shouting, "No more room. Besides! You need to bring my car back to the reservation!" He tossed the keys down to his cousin as the whirlybird lifted and disappeared into the cloud-filled night.

In the old days, Keeowskowee might well have been taken to his favorite mountainous area, far into the hills, to die a natural death there. If Lucas thought he had time, he'd take the old man up to the Devil's Spine, that place of rich spectral activity. It would be where the old man's spirit might live an eternity. They had spoken of this possibility, but short of this, the old man wanted to die at home. Short of doing things the old way, hospice and the idea of dying at home, surrounded by loved ones, felt right; it certainly felt better than the white medical establishment's idea of dying with tubes shoved up every orifice.

Still, Hawk felt differently, and when Lucas felt his cousin's firm grasp on his leg, tugging at him. He clearly heard Billy shouting over the sound of the rotors, "What the hell's going on?" Lucas had lost his temper and kicked out at Billy who fell on his back and watched the helicopter ascend over him, blowing his long mane of hair into a thousand swirls of angel-hair spaghetti. Lucas read his cousin's lips as Billy shouted and waved a fist. "He's your blood and he is my blood, my father's brother. I love him, but cannot watch him day and night suffer. You, you are not home, yet you will dump him on the rest of us and step away, and then—"

Lucas thought it strange that he could make out so many of the words of his angry cousin. He thought it strange that the words came so clearly to his ears, despite the sound of the helicopter blades.

Then Lucas woke up in an upright sitting position in a chair here where he had pulled himself to the vigil alongside his dying grandfather.

How much did I say aloud? the patient wondered, but only said, "Yeah, you got that fuckin' right."

"Yes, well, should you ever care to have the tape"— he indicated the recorder on his desk—"played back for your listening pleasure. You know, Stanley, had you told me earlier that mycallingyou 'son' bothered you so, well-I-certainly-wouldn't've continued doing so, and I-won'tnow-hesitate-to-call you as-you-wish, Mr.—ahhh . . ."

Did the doctor say Mr. Garrette or did he say Mr. Early Release Parolee? "Didn't say you had to call me Mr. Anything," the patient replied, agitated as he stepped through the door, the butcher's knife weighty across his own left breast. He wondered if Doc Morrissey had noticed the slight tug on the jacket today. He'd thought himself clever by placing it on the left side for a change. He wondered if the snowy old man had any idea how close he'd actually come to being tomorrow's headline—a corpse for the cops to ponder over, a corpse without entrails.

Stanley Theopolis Garrette and several other of the halfway house clients of Dr. Morrissey had all privately declared a desire to knife the old bastard shrink. "One more time he cusses at me and tosses me outta his office," Wilcox had said, "and I'll carve him up like a Christmas turkey!" Wilcox's dead eyes lit up with the thought, his grin infectious.

"Cut his friggin' head off," countered Wendell.

"Do more'n that," replied Wilcox.

"What else is there?" asked Wilcox.

"The insides, the guts," said Wendell, egging them on.

Their conversation had gone long into the night and followed on the heels of each group session. It grew even more heated after a particularly revealing group session in which they had all met the infamous Walter Karl Freeleng, the suspected Headless Horseman. None of them thought the tall, emaciated Freeleng was all that much to look at, but Morrissey had treated Freeleng like "a goddamn celebrity," as Wendell had put it that night.

Their talks after the group sessions, sharing impressions of Morrissey and his techniques, had become ritual for Garrette, Wilcox and Wendell. Each one displayed his own brand of bravado and daring in word and intent. Each had claimed he would one day kill Morrissey.

They also discussed Morrissey. How the old guy had one foot in the grave already. How someone ought to put him out of his misery, put out his light, stop the babbling brook. The old fool lived in obvious pain from having endured this world too long already, the parolee told himself now.

"I will look forward, sir, to our next visit," chimed the old fool. "It willprove-nodoubt stimulatingly apprehensible and fort-truitous, all to one end, sir. Toyourbetter-health, sir."

Now he's mocking me, thought the patient, with that "sir" crap. Doesn't really feel it. Doesn't believe it when he says it. *Sir, sir, sir shit. Bullshit,* he wanted to reply, his hand patting the coat over the knife, but he let it go and instead watched the contented smile build on Dr. Morrissey's face.

The old man knows everything.

He has the eyes of God, thought the patient.

He creates words out of thin air . . . words that didn't exist before he breathed life into them.

Right out of thin air in midair, midsentence, he did it.

He knew that his every patient stood a broken soul, a fallen angel. He'd already said so.

Perhaps this is why the patient named Stanley always hesitated to kill Dr. Morrissey. Morrissey proved the only one in the so-called normal world who understood him. Perhaps it explained why the doctor's other patients, while threatening to do so, did not kill him either. One thing to think it . . . one thing to say it . . . quite another to do the deed.

Maybe I need this guy more alive than dead, Stanley Garrette decided, staring into the doctor's eyebrows and ice-blue eyes. Maybe I'll just have to content myself with killing someone else instead . . . to feed the demons and dragons skulking deep within.

LATER THAT SAME EVENING

An uncooperative wind whistled past his head, tearing at his backpack and flashlight, everything he carried. Forty plus stories up, the wind was a treacherous enemy.

The night sky was painted in absolute blackness, clouds teeming, covering all sight of moon and stars, cowering all light. Add a strange, lone crow, a raven, or a pigeon—*close enough*—perched nearby and you had all the props in place. Neither Edgar Allan Poe nor H. P. Lovecraft could have painted a better scene, the man in the black jumpsuit thought.

He gave some consideration to the Scalper; the Scalper as portrayed in the feeble press. Everything egged on the Scalper, including the press itself, to play out his fantastic fantasy—a fantasy that could end only in rape and murder. It made him question himself, and he wondered if the horrors wrought by the Scalper could not be improved upon this night. Wondered if he could not do the Scalper one better.

The pigeon standing in for the crow winked at him and keened out a sound that reminded him to focus on the job at hand. He wore black from head to toe, including a black ski mask and gloves and climbing boots. "The bastards think they have something to fear now, but suppose they had something worse than a mere scalping to fear. Wait until they get this package," he told the pigeon.

The man the press called a megalomaniac, the killer with a scalp and hand fetish all balled up into one, opened his black case and uncoiled the thick rope found there. His gloved hands found the nylon rope smooth, exquisite. They hadn't yet connected the dots, and after tonight, they'd be hard-pressed to do so. He would see to that.

He stood atop the skyscraper. Now only the birds and an occasional alley cat might look up and take notice. Each gloved hand worked to lower the thin but durable black nylon rope over the edge of the Houston skyscraper. He worked its length to exactly the window he wanted. "Talk about premeditated," he said aloud. Plans for one Laurel Kensington, living alone in the high-rise, had culminated here and now. He tightened the final cinch on his halter, laced it about his groin, checked the rigging and the tie-off a final time. Finally he lifted himself over the lip of the building and rappelled downward, using his body weight to gain momentum. A bird in flight, he thought. An angel of death on the wing . . .

The exhilaration of the moment flooded all of the killer's heightened senses, the city streets some forty stories below him. He sought his prey from the air like a falcon, maybe an angel, he told himself. "Maybe the press will, after this, call me something respectable, like the Falcon, maybe, huh?" he said to the pigeon as it pirouetted in the sky above him now, curious and cooing dovelike, like an angel's messenger.

"Morrissey was right. We're all easily bored and boredom leads to evil, but what's the alternative. Yes, I'm already bored with being called the Scalper." He couldn't kill Dr. Morrissey, as much as he'd like to. After all, he needed his head doctor. The man represented the only person on this earth he could talk to. So he had to seek out someone else to vent his rage on. Hadn't the good doctor told him that he should find constructive ways to vent his anger? And hadn't the fallen angels been told as much by God?

"Maybe I'll come to be known as the Angel Killer, the Angel of Mercy. I make them beg for mercy, and then I give it," he told himself, amused at the thought, laughing now. He didn't want it to be a simple murder; he wanted something richly fulfilling, something complex, multilayered, grandiose and beautiful in its execution. Execution, now there was a word that even Dr. M couldn't mangle. Executions were already about mangling.

Yes, he would mangle the victim; break the legs and arms and twist them into the position of the swastika for starters, maybe do a zodiac thing for another, really keep the authorities guessing and pissing their pants. He would be king; he would become a presence, a singular power in a city of power-seekers. He would make Ted Bundy look like a Boy Scout by comparison.

To this end the masked killer, who had been an avid mountain climber at one time, the day before had purchased new, state-of-the-art rope and tackle equipment. With it, the Angel of Death meant to show the world how a determined second-story man could, if he liked, break into any fucking where that he wanted to break into . . . whether the place be forty stories or no, gated or no, secure or no. Tonight, no building in the city remained safe. He had the tools and the know-how, and he wanted to show the world.

"No one's life remains safe so long as the Falcon flies or the Death Angel wings its way straight out of nowhere and into Laurel Kensington's life." He again wondered what the press would call him after this particularly clever attack took place.

Nobody, not even the rich and famous, not even the resplendent money changers in the new temples built to the stars in Houston's most exclusive district—no one was safe, no one was beyond his reach. Not even the lovely young Laurel, socialite, stockbroker and daughter of a senator. He had first been told about her and then he had read about her in the society pages of the *Houston Times*. Not even she was safe, not from him, not from death.

She deserved his attention.

He planned to give her a great deal of just that. . . .

In fact, his feet and full weight now rested on her windowpane, his body crouched there at the end of his tether, a modern day gargoyle, staring in through the glass to the darkened interior—Laurel's bedroom. The pane would be impossible to break, the builders having spared no expense against the winds up here. The wind continued to claw at him, trying to pull him from the side of the building as if he were an insect, snatch him off the glass and thrust him out and down. The sound of the wind here proved deafening, the smell of it was invigorating as he swallowed it whole into his lungs. He thought of something Dr. Morrissey had once told the group, that they breathed in and out the same molecules and atoms as did Abraham Lincoln, Albert Einstein, William Shakespeare, Samuel L. Clemens, Winston Churchill, as well as Genghis Khan, Peter the Great, Vlad the Impaler and Hitler. "What you choose to do with those molecules and atoms you inhale, is up to you," Morrissey had chastised them, as if they were all children. But something about breathing the same air as Adolf Hitler appealed to the winged killer.

The architects of this building had also breathed in the same finite air as the killer. Those builders, he believed, would not have felt the need to laser-proof the glass. No one could have imagined that a man armed with a portable laser wand would comb the outside of the building for prey. But then, they didn't count on him, nor could anyone have prophesied his coming.

He found the laser wand he'd purchased for the task, and began cutting a sharply focused edge. Although from his perspective the laser beamed bright and huge, no one forty stories down would notice. It made a hissing noise.

His thoughts wandered to what he intended for young, innocent Laurel. The killer continued the task of cutting, knowing that Laurel Kensington, lovely, tall, willowy, would not be home for at least another hour. "Celebrating that new promotion," he assured himself, recalling how he had learned of it. How he had learned of her comings and goings, her Yuppie high-rise apartment. Strange how easily some people could pick up a wealth of information by just hanging about a neighborhood watering hole, listening in on talk between girlfriends and just being observant. A person like that could prove a fount of information for anyone interested in procuring news.

By the time Laurel unlocked the door and figured out why the apartment felt so cold and how the wind could possibly have come through windows that didn't open, it would be too late. She'd literally be in his web. He'd brought a webbed net to initially subdue her. Should she enter with a friend or companion, it would be too late for him, too. For the thin, lightweight killer's knife will have gone to work, and this time the fantasy would be made real once again, like it surely had been with the two victims that the Scalper had so recently mutilated in Houston. Taking their hands as trophies along with their scalps, nice touch, he thought. "But I think we can do him one better," he muttered to the pigeon again. "I'll give them something more to think about than playing cowboys and Indians. . . ."

The hissing sound of the laser continued winding a path about the windowpane, a hole large enough for him to crawl through. He began to like the sound of the laser as it cut through the glass. *Hiss, listen to it hiss,* he thought.

In a moment, with a slight touch of the hands, the dangling man sent the glass cascading inward, shards and beads of it spraying the lush pile carpeting on the inside. He then swung his body and went—flying—into Laurel Kensington's darkened bedroom.

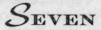

SEVEN

Four ages of man: infant, youth, mid & old age

Lucas and his grandfather Keeowskowee made reservation history when the helicopter touched down on the stony surface outside the old man's log cabin. The ranting, whirring noise of the metal beast had awakened the remaining population of the small village. No one had ever seen a sight such as this; women and children watched from the safety of blankets wrapped about them. Some had to cover their eyes as the great dust cloud enveloped them.

The following night and the next day Lucas spent at his grandfather's bedside. Every effort to create a comfortable death had been made, and Lucas had become the central figure in this effort. He stood, he sat, he paced, he held Keeowskowee's hand and retold old stories that his grandfather had told him when he was a boy, stories of their tribe, and stories that chronicled their family history.

At times, unable to stand the sound of the old man's labored breathing, unable to look on his suffering a moment longer, Lucas stepped away while Tsalie spelled him.

Hawk refused to be present a moment longer. He had wanted the professionals to take over all responsibility, and now they were out of the picture. It fell to the family to be the death-care professionals along with the help of the hospice people who supplied oxygen tanks, a hospital bed, morphine and advice.

Lucas had not come to his temporary home on the reservation entirely empty-handed; along with his toothbrush and a change of clothes, he had brought information. Randy Oglesby had kindly dug up facts on the man known in Houston legal circles as the "early parolee's favorite shrink," often called *Doc Residual* for his ongoing series of books, as well as the "residuals" he received from the state to work with the sociopaths he called *clients*.

Lucas had dipped into the good doctor's books, books pandering to true-crime fans about the morbid, the weird, the deviant, and the gruesome among us. Each story in the volume culled from his case files, Dr. Morrissey changed the names to protect the guilty, but odd to Lucas's way of thinking was a man sworn to keep sacrosanct doctor-patient relations who turned them into profit. A sizeable profit if one went by the number of printings shown on the inside pages of the doctor's first book—which, while by no means a bestseller, must represent a cozy second income. The profit off the patients and the psychoanalysis they'd undergone troubled Lucas, who weighed all that he had learned of Dr. Morrissey in this short span of time.

Lucas paced the narrow avenue of his grandfather's hallway, having made tread marks between living room and kitchen for beer after beer, a bag of pretzels and some cheese. Tossing down the file on Dr. Morrissey that he'd begun, Lucas now stared out the living room window onto reservation life outside. Children played at the nearby, recently created playground where a new school and longhouse had also been constructed with the funds Lucas had anonymously given the Coushatta Reservation Indian Council. It was money given to the councilmen to do with as they liked, so long as it benefited all Cherokees on the res, all of the *First People*. The Indian hit man and now Indian mafia boss, Zachary Roundpoint, had given Lucas the money soon after information Lucas uncovered linked Roundpoint's murdered mother with Roundpoint's mentor, a man who had acted as Zachary's surrogate father. That man, Mendoza, had been the Indian mafia don of Houston, until Zachary Roundpoint siezed that crown by killing Mendoza when he reverted back to the old Cherokee *Law of Blood*. Of course, Mendoza's body, likely somewhere in the desert, never surfaced; and no clues to Mendoza's disappearance had ever been discovered either.

The money came as payment for Lucas's having solved the mystery of Roundpoint's mother's murder, which had occurred in 1948. Mendoza had lived with the memory of the brutal murder on what little remained of his conscience all the years since '48. To ease his conscience, Mendoza had, in fact, fabricated layers of fiction to insulate himself, and perhaps his "son" Zachary, from the truth. Lucas came very near to paying with his life for having peeled back the layers of Mendoza's true character.

Roundpoint's reward money, known to no one but the two of them, raised questions throughout the reservation. Questions about where the money came from had, thus far, never directly found their way back to Lucas's superiors, but apparently every Indian on the res knew by now that he was somehow linked to it, likely due to this damned log home he'd built for his grandfather. Fortunately no one off the res cared a whit for what went on here, and thus far all remained well.

Lucas now watched young Cherokee boys in the dawn sun, run their hands over his red Intrepid, parked just outside. Hawk had driven the car back to the reservation as Lucas had told him. Lucas turned from the window now and stared at the Morrissey file. He wondered whether Morrissey insisted that every patient sign over the rights to "his" story before he would take on a case.

As the day wore on, Lucas learned more about Dr. Thomas W. Morrissey. The more he learned of the man, the more he found him to be a kind of legal system leech, and a sort of linchpin for the criminally insane. He seemed to know every maniac ever released from a Texas asylum or prison. He most definitely appeared a favorite of the court system whenever the legals needed someplace to send a sociopath. Perhaps because he was in a specialized minority, a psychiatrist who courted the most difficult cases. The establishment took full advantage.

Morrissey had most certainly acquired a reputation, and once gained, the courts and the parole system, with few options available, forwarded their problem children on to Morrissey. And, of course, the larger number of lunatics that Morrissey worked with, the more he pocketed. As Meredyth had pointed out, Morrissey used these individuals in his ongoing series of case studies published by the University of North Central Texas and Pentax Publishers in New York as popular paperback psychiatric palaver.

Groundless in the view of many in the field of psychiatry, Lucas guessed, feeling fairly sure that such a hunch would be borne out by a little research.

"So, all the worst cases are forwarded to Morrissey from the Criminal Justice Department," Lucas said to the empty room. Tsalie was upstairs, monitoring Grandfather Keeowskowee. Hawk was either catching a nap at his trailer or at the local watering hole, downing Jack Daniel's and beer chasers again. The two girls were in school.

Lucas knew that few professional men in Morrissey's field understood forensic psychology, and fewer still understood the criminally insane. Raging debates on treatment existed; no one had the answers. Even the most jaded, hardened or seasoned in the profession knew that castration of the genitals much less jail time, would not stop a serial rapist or a child molester. The problem seemed wired or twistedly wired in the cranium, not the groin. Some scientists speculated on the possibility of a missing genetic code that predisposes one to have no sympathy and empathy pains; others spoke of a distinctly present gene that predisposed one to violence, rape and lust-muder; but thus far no such gene had been isolated either way.

Morrissey had started in medicine as a forensic psychologist, usually brought in on a case to help convict a madman. His services had been paid by the district attorney's office in years past. Then something untoward had happened to cause a rift there, something buried in the records of a backdoor confrontation that remained sealed. . . .

According to Morrissey in a rare interview in the *Houston Chronicle*, "Sometime late in a rigged ball game played out countless times, men grow tired and disillusioned with a system that merely locks monsters away without any true rehabilitative efforts in place." The good doctor had turned to the other side, the defense teams, filling in testimony on behalf of serial rapists, spree murderers and serial killers of every ilk, age, sex and stripe. Again, according to Morrissey, he had, "After years of working closely with such fiends as Richard Ramirez, the Vampire Killer and Tony Sibola, the L.A. Cannibal, I formed the opinion that such monsters are creations of modern industrial life—a life that deeply, profoundly alienates men in particular from their own innermost and deepest feelings, exchanging honest emotions for shame, guilt, fetishes, fantasies, phobias and other internal toxic waste."

Finally Morrissey quit private practice altogether and went to work for the State of Texas Rehabilitative Services Division, using his expertise as a psychiatrist with special knowledge of the criminal mind, "To reintegrate and reestablish into mainstream society the very disintegrated and disenfranchised monsters I have gotten to know so well."

Now this retinue of monsters came through him in an effort to start out on new careers, from shoe salesmen to JCPenny clerks, Wal-Mart baggers, night watchmen, desk clerks, security guards and lawnmower men. Morrissey's job? To help the pathetic outsiders—*out-standers* as he called them in his book—blend into the community as smoothly as they could. This meant transition work, opening the convicted and released inmate up to new possibilities and connections, granting hope to those released on parole into Houston society. Hope of change, hope of fitting in, hope of a future. All quite liberal and forward sounding. So Dr. Thomas W. Morrissey nowadays appeared in court on behalf of the kind of people he once helped prosecute, his entire new practice was predicated on what to others might appear an ancient fallacy: Once a man had served his time, he had every right to the full protection of the Constitution and American civil liberties as anyone under the U.S. flag. Whether Morrissey actually believed this remained doubtful, but perhaps he believed that the miniscule percentage that indeed made it back into society as useful members outweighed the horrendous other statistic that sent nearly all sociopaths and psychopaths back to victimizing others, then back to the cell if not to an early grave.

Lucas had gotten hold of a copy of Morrissey's latest book, *Evolunacy: The Evolution of Lunatic Behavior in Organized Society from the Time of Christ to the Present.*

It appeared to be a remarkable compilation, an encyclopedia of madness, mania, maniacs, cults and cultists, murderers and as the title promised, lunatics. No era in the history of man was spared, for in the preface Dr. Morrissey promised a companion piece in the future that would go far back beyond the time of Christ to the dawn of recorded history, to tie man to the demon ape, the same demon ape written about in Robert Ardrey's *The Territorial Imperative* and other books, and hinted at in the research of the evolutionary experts, the Leakys, and more recently in the bestselling *Demonic Male* by Richard Wrangham.

If the reasoning held true, it gave a whole new meaning to the phrases "born to be wild" and "natural-born killers." It also fueled the debate for the true purpose of genetic engineering and makeovers. *Forget cloning sheep,* Lucas thought. All sheep were docile by nature. Who would be the first to clone a Hitler? More intelligent and forward-looking scientists might be seeking the day when the more docile of the male species, say a Byron, a Shelley, a Keats might be cloned. The reasoning behind such books as Morrissey's had it that all males and females of the Homo sapiens species evolved from killer apes, and that the male of the species is/was/and always will be programmed to kill—often senselessly and ruthlessly as on the order of lust-murders. The theory went that if it smells good to an animal, he'll kill and eat it.

This theory had it that humans did not evolve from the fuzzy-whuzzies of Disneyland and Ronald Reagan–Bonzo flicks, but rather the cannibalistic apes that were among the first animals to kill their own, including their own children.

A threatened killer ape. Was that the sum total of a man? Likely a man like Freeleng, yes. Perhaps, in a sense, the holy books around the globe had all along been right. That God pitted the angels among us against the satanic among us, thus creating a war that would last throughout evolution until all such traces of one or the other—good or evil—would be obliterated from the earth. If good should win, perhaps one day mankind, in a distant future, might live outside the shadow of murder. The specter of monsters in the realm might become only fairy tale instead of reality. Oddly enough, this euphoric, utopian belief, that mankind was indeed on a quest for pure thought, pure love, and pure brotherhood remained the cornerstone of every major religion and the lesser known religions as well as the ancient, the occult, the cult and even the more recently evolved metaphysical thought. Certainly a significant number of today's youth believed in a day when peace and purity must conquer chaos and ugliness.

Lucas found it interesting that he agreed with Dr. Morrissey on certain beliefs: that mayhem and chaos in an individual began in the brain at birth, that some people were simply more genetically predisposed or "wired" for violence than others. Morrissey's book did not offer these up as excuses but as observable "facts" from his many years of dealing with society's most disturbed, sociopathic individuals, those missing the *remorse gene*, as Morrissey called it. Still, free will remained. Choice ruled.

It felt overwhelming at the moment, an information overload, and Lucas knew his judgment might be both unfounded and leading him off track. He found the old shaman's favorite chair, the one from his trailer home he had refused to give up.

Lucas didn't know when he dozed off, but suddenly he was no longer in his grandfather's house, but back at the hospital. Someone whispered in his ear as he read Morrissey's book.

"Taking another exam, Lieutenant Stonecoat?" asked Jack Kirshner even as he spit up blood. He'd come out of coma to stare at Lucas's red face and scarred neck.

Lucas saw the book drop toward the floor, but it never hit bottom. "Jack, don't talk. Stay calm. Nurse! Nurse!" Lucas shouted as he simultaneously squeezed the buzzer and called for help. "Don't move a muscle, Jack! You've a bullet lodged near your heart, left ventricle and if you move—"

A pretty brunette nurse pushed through the door, and seeing that Kirshner was among the living, she shouted over her shoulder, "Four-Eight is conscious! Get staff doctors in here, stat!"

Kirshner began pulling at his restraints, cursing and saying, "Lucas! Why in hell they got me tied down like a roped calf?"

"It's for your own good, sir," the nurse replied for Lucas. She'd immediately begun working over Jack, shoving Lucas aside, telling him he'd have to vacate as she checked Kirshner's vital signs, warning Jack and, it seemed, Lucas, in one short staccato order, "Don't move a muscle, Officer." She then asked Jack, "Do you know where you are, sir? How many fingers am I holding up? Can you tell me your name, sir? Who's in the White House, sir? What year is it, sir?"

"Kirshner, three fingers, and I'm in a hospital, and you've got my chart, right? So, you can call me Jack, sweetie."

"Who's in the White House, sir?"

"Alice."

"Alice?"

"Alice and the Mad Hatter."

The nurse ignored his lame joke and asked, "Do you remember what happened to you, sir?"

"Not really, but maybe you can take me there?" He fondled her even with his hands strapped to his sides. Lucas thought it rather absurd. The man had wound up here because of sexual indiscretions, and coming out of coma, he followed his natural instincts the way a killer follows his. He went straight for the pleasure button.

"Officer, you have three bullets roaming around inside you. You must remain perfectly still."

"Three's my lucky number then. Hey, Stonecoat! What're you doing here anyways?"

"Watching out for your sorry behind, Kirshner."

"Nothing like a shooting to bring people together, huh? I finally caught some shut-eye . . . the hard way, I know. Insomnia, now that's a real bitch, right Lucas?"

Lucas managed a smile for Jack, whose boyish good

looks—exactly what had gotten him into this trouble—
had faded to a pale reflection of his usual image. His hair
fell flaxen across his forehead, drenched with perspiration.
His color reminded Lucas of white desert sands. Jack
didn't look nearly as good as he wanted Lucas and the
nurse to think he felt, nor did he likely feel half so brave
as he put on. But after all, this was a dream, right?

Suddenly the room flooded with doctors coming
through the door, each shouting at accompanying nurses
for one thing and another. The scene brought back un-
pleasant memories for Lucas, memories of a time when
he and his former partner, Lafayette Jackson, were
wheeled into an operating room, each in similar condition.
But their wounds had come as result of honest police work
and not a relationship war that had broken out in a squad
room.

Almost in an instant, Jack Kirshner and his bed disappeared before Lucas's eyes as the doctors rushed Jack's
prone body to the operating theater. Now that consciousness had returned, they'd quickly sedated him. The doctors,
also known as *they,* quickly began to work on removing
the bullets still lodged inside the man. The bullets sounded
like so many angry, dormant bees come to life.

Lucas felt a wave of nausea mixed with foreboding.
Something told him that Kirshner would not survive the
multiple operations. He hoped to be proven wrong.

"Call for you, Detective," said Tsalie, looking beautiful
in a nurse's uniform, and now poking him in the ribs in
a teasing fashion. She quickly left by way of the door in
his head, where Lucas stood in a hospital room with an
open sky overhead filled with billowy clouds and a blind-
ingly bright sun. As beautiful as the depiction on the ceiling was, Lucas felt the overwhelming emptiness of this

room, and he smelled the sickening medicinal odors. The room felt more like his grandfather's than Kirshner's.

"You can take the call at the nurses station or here," suggested Tsalie, sticking her head back into the room and pointing from a cloud miles above him. Lucas only now realized that Jack Kirshner's face was missing, replaced by a glowing light, a sign of death, and then the light floated from the room and only Kirshner's face and body remained.

Lucas's dream hand grabbed up the receiver. He waited for the call to be put through. Captain Lincoln came on line, saying, "We've got a mutilation murder not two blocks from the precinct, Lucas. Hell, I can look out the window and see the station house from here. Every-freakin'-body in the city'll be on our asses over this one, senator's daughter . . . mutilated almost beyond recognition. I want you on it, Lucas. Get over to one thousand three hundred four Bloomfield, apartment four thousand twenty-four. Got that?"

"Captain, I'm swamped as it is, and the COMIT—"

"Fuck the old files, Lucas. I need you on this one in the here and now!"

From Lincoln's tone, Lucas knew no argument now would dissuade his captain. "What's so special about this one, Captain?" he asked. "Senator's daughter?"

"You'll see, just as I did, just as Dr. Sanger did, when you get here. Christ, Lucas, hurry."

"Meredyth's with you?"

"Dr. Sanger's here already, Lucas. We're just waiting on you. But be warned, Sanger is too broken up to be of much help. . . . May have to call in someone else on this one. Anyway, get over here, now!"

"Yes sir, Captain."

Fate before, and now even his dreams, appeared to be thrusting Lucas and Meredyth together, whether either of them wanted it or not. From all of Lucas's tribal learning and his reading of Carl Jung and others who'd studied dream states, he knew that while dreams came to the dreamer in symbolic language, dreams were ignored at the risk of the dreamer. He knew that the dream state, the unconscious, didn't lie. It was the one place where a man could in fact *be true to himself*, if only he learned to read the symbolic language of his dreams.

Lucas tried to imagine the horror of a murder scene that would prompt Lincoln to call in a forensic psychiatrist ahead of the detective he wanted on the case and, for that matter, to make Lucas the special detective in charge. Usually such extreme measures came with Ted Bundy–type killers or some maniac like Charles Manson or a newly appointed Jack-the-Ripper. Still, this was only a dream, right?

"Wait a minute," Lucas said to the empty room. "One thousand three hundred four Bloomfield? Apartment four thousand twenty-four? That'd be a high-rise, high-rent district, not far from where Meredyth herself lives in posh comfort. In fact, it's only a few doors down." Forty stories up, the best alarm and protection services in the city, and still a woman is murdered in her own home. The notion assaulted Lucas's every sensibility, yet all his senses were protected by the dream state. Dreams can't hurt you, only the waking state lies, or so Jungian psychotherapy went. What did this dream mean? That he feared for Meredyth, who lived in a high-rise apartment, that he wanted to protect her, to be a shining knight for her?

Lucas rushed from the dream hospital and out to his

waiting car, his mind tumbling over the possibilities of a high-rise home invasion. It happened all the time, actually, but more often than not the high rise stood in a broken down part of the city, on a desolated lot, quite often among the low-income housing population, committed by a nutcase coming in off of a fire escape. But the sleek downtown high-rise district didn't have fire escapes, having passed building codes that substituted for forty- and sixty-story metal ladders. Still, people were killed in all socioeconomic levels, and high-rise, high-rent district murders happened. Usually a lover's quarrel gotten out of hand, or a burglary gone bust.

Lucas allowed his hunter's mind to play over the possibilities of the game. It took his mind off the death that was so close, so personal in nature, the kind stalking his grandfather, the sort stalking Jack Kirshner, or the kind Lucas stalked. So he talked in his dream. "Most likely, the killer knew the victim and was invited in." Lucas continued talking to himself as he drove the ten blocks between the fictitious hospital and the high-rise death scene, his surreal strobe light alerting others to get out of his way. "Perhaps some smooth talker secreted himself inside the building during the day and used a series of moves to invite himself into an apartment, something to do with a sudden electrical failure or water problem in 'his' unit. One of those guys with a line for all occasions, who used the personal pronoun *we* at every turn, in every breath to lull his victim into thinking that *we* had something in common. '*We* got quite a storm out there. . . . *We're* in this together. . . . Some elevator *we* got here. . . . Some world *we* got when *our* own president becomes the stand-in butt for every dumb dirtbag joke, huh?'"

Lucas found the kill scene awash in spectral dream

rain—a silver, gossamer ice. The streets were slick, reflecting city lights and the strobes of a hundred marked police cars. There were barricades to ward off and try to control chaos, photographers and onlookers were rubbernecking and shouting in the sea of colored light and confusion. "What the hell do they need another cop for?" he asked his dream self.

Then he found himself being vigorously shaken, so hard it had to be by the hand of a god. When his eyes opened, he saw the beautiful onyx eyes of Tsalie pinned on him where she stood over him, saying, "You must go. They need you. If you fall back to sleep, you could lose your badge or something."

"What're you talking about, Tsalie?" he grumbled.

"That phone call. I heard every word you said. You told your boss that you'd be there, so now you must be there. Go! Grandfather is calm at the moment. His breathing comes easier."

"It wasn't a . . . I wasn't dreaming that?"

"No, they called. You took down a note. Look." She lifted a notepad from the beside phone, and after attempting to focus and wake himself, his free hand tearing at the sleep in his eyes, he read the note taken in his own shaky handwriting:

1304 Bloomfield, apartment 4024

Lucas gathered up his gun and trench coat and started for the door, all the while wondering about the dream, particularly about Kirshner's part in it, wondering when he had gone from the sky-filled hospital room to the dark death scene, wondering why dreams always got an *F* on transitions. He stopped long enough to telephone the hospital, asking if Kirshner had come out of coma. He was informed that Jack Kirshner had died only moments before.

"Died? How?"

"He came out of coma and began fighting his constraints. We theorize," continued the doctor, "that the bullet lodged near his heart severed an artery and sent him into hemo-shock, but then, that's merely conjecture until an autopsy can be performed."

"Son of a bitch," moaned Lucas. "Autopsy? Hold on any autopsy until and unless one is ordered by the Medical Examiner, Doctor. You got that?"

"But we need to determine the cause of death."

"Goddamn three bullets in him tells a hell of a story, Doc. Besides, he's Jewish—maybe not orthodox, but he is Jewish, and his family might just have some say-so here. Have you talked to them?"

"Well, no, not yet."

"Then do so, and talk to Leonard Chang's office before you go cutting this man open like some damned melon, okay?"

"Your friend at the hospital?" asked Tsalie as Lucas dropped the phone down.

He solemnly nodded. "Gone."

"I'm sorry, Lucas."

"Been a rough couple of days. Are you sure you will be all right here, alone with the old man?"

"Hawk promised to be back within the hour. Go. You must not disappoint your bosses. You'll wind up back here on the res like the rest of us."

He looked deeply into her eyes. "I thought you were happy; you told me you were."

"In my children, yes. In my aspirations? Well, how

many of us live up to our aspirations, Lucas? You are the exception."

He leaned into her, kissed her. Then he apologized for the kiss, explaining, "I'm sorry I did that, but then again . . . I'm not. How does a man help himself? You are . . . were . . . mine and I foolishly lost you."

"Don't Lucas. Don't say any more, please."

He read the pain in her eyes. He rushed out, and she followed to the porch, watching him go. As he made his way to his car, he shouted back over his shoulder, "Call me if there is any change in Grandfather's condition. Anything at all."

He drove with his red light flashing, taking the interstate and pushing the Intrepid to its limit, cursing those who were slow to get out of his way. He looked down at the speedometer, amazed to see the needle twitching at 110 miles per hour. He eased off to ninety and forced himself to use cruise control. He thought of Kirshner and his grandfather's assurance that the man would be all right. Had his grandfather been wrong?

Lucas had thought his shaman grandfather had meant that Jack would come to, be healed and go on to live a whole and fruitful life, but now he wondered if the old man simply meant that Jack would be okay in death.

Kirshner, a young, strong man, gone in the blink of an eye. Lucas feared the same might happen to his grandfather, and that he would not be at Keeowskowee's bedside for his passing. Hawk would find that reason enough to curse Lucas for the rest of his life.

Perhaps he should turn right around and damn Lincoln, the job, the badge and all that he had worked for since his rehabilitation after Dallas. Had his head been clear, had he known the phone call from his captain to be real,

Lucas might have declined Lincoln's order, and rightfully so, explaining the situation. That now appeared no longer an option.

He stomped the gas pedal, returning the Dodge to 100 miles per hour. He watched a huge Exxon tanker that he'd buzzed past disappear behind him like a rolling hill.

$\mathcal{E}$IGHT

Rattlesnake jaw: strong

It rained silver-black and somber in the predawn while Lucas arrived at the scene at 4 A.M. With ominous storm clouds overhead, the sort resembling a roiling, bubbling witches' cauldron, Lucas knew that the city would soon be visited by a Texas prairie downpour. Looking out on the scene, Lucas felt an overwhelming sense of déjà vu. He climbed from his car, locked it with a single beep from his automatic key switch and stepped past the people forming a human wall of curiosity seekers even at this hour, even if old Texas sky gods *were* threatening.

He found the sea of marked police cars and barricades and chaos, photographers and onlookers rubbernecking and shouting, just as in his premonitory dream.

He muttered under his breath, "What the hell does Lincoln need me for?"

"Most likely he thinks you're as good as your press," replied Dave Harbough who waylaid Lucas. The big, burly Harbough, round-faced with less than his usual jovial smile added, "Been waiting for you to show up. This is Freeleng's work, Lucas, pure and simple."

"Have you had a look at the crime scene?"

"Your boss allowed it. Professional courtesy. He knows I'm also working the Scalper Killing, so—"

"This have anything to do with the Scalper?"

"None whatsoever. This is the work of the Beheader— Freeleng."

"Who discovered the body?"

"Called in. A nine-one-one call."

"From whom?"

"Nobody's saying, but my guess is Freeleng."

"Is he that stupid?"

"Crime makes you stupid," he said, grunted and hunched his shoulders. "Voice is disguised, put through some sort of electro-gizmo, but I'd stake my life on it."

"I have some connections with the FBI."

"They any good?"

"If anyone can remove the distortion on the tape and get an identifiable voiceprint, it's those guys. For now, I'd better get upstairs."

"You look like hell, Stonecoat, if you don't mind my saying so."

"Just drove in from Huntsville."

"Yeah, sorry . . . Heard about your grandfather."

"Thanks."

"I'll telephone you, Lucas, later, but someway, somehow, we gotta nail this sonofabitch. He's only going to escalate, you know. I got nothing new on the Scalper. No doubt you don't either."

"No doubt." Lucas struggled past the perimeters and the crowd, found the police guard at the door, flashed his badge and went through. He rode the elevator up to the fortieth floor where the body awaited his inspection.

Along his route, he not only mulled over what Harbough had said regarding the crime scene and his suspicions, but how he said it, how he looked when he said it, how hard he worked for a reaction from Lucas, every inflection and nonverbal cue. Harbough had it bad for Freeleng. Lucas realized that the older cop had demonized Freeleng so as to make him responsible for every murder in the city if it were possible, kind of like making Freeleng the *El Niño* of serial killers, Lucas concluded. He knew he must keep an open mind as he stepped from the elevator and saw the commotion down the hall. He went directly for the death room.

When Lucas stepped into the crime scene, he stopped short of the body lying on the living room floor to take a moment to bless the guardian that had kept him from consuming a heavy meal this black, overcast morning. A chill, rippling wind blew across the scene as if someone had turned the air-conditioning on high. The force of wind that seemed to enter from the bedroom lifted framed photos, rustled a dog-eared paperback lying on the coffee table, and fluttered a nearby tablecloth.

The same wind made it impossible to lay coroner's tags about the body for photos until someone closed the bedroom door. He heard crying coming from the same adjoining room. His eyes fell on Captain Gordon J. Lincoln, but he did not see Meredyth.

Lincoln could offer no words for the moment, allowing Lucas to take in the horror before them. A woman's nude body lay center stage, as if a prop in a staged play, intentionally left before the door, so authorities had to push the door into the body to shove it open and step over her just to get inside. The body had no head, but he could tell the gender from the graceful, sculptured breasts and limbs; he read it from the splayed legs and broken arms, limbs that had been contorted into the shape of the swastika. The body looked the part of a broken doll. The body's broken appearance brought to mind the opening credit artwork on Otto Preminger's film version of Robert Treaver's *Anatomy of a Murder*, which Lucas had seen as a child. Lucas felt a momentary kinship with Jimmy Stewart, the actor who played the lead role in the film version. The utter sense of absolute desolation and confusion that played across Stewart's features must now be playing across his own, Lucas imagined.

As hardened as Lucas had become to the evil men did, he still helplessly wondered how anything called human could do such a horrid thing as this to another living creature. A once lovely, sentient human being had been treated like butcher's meat. Someone had covered the woman's head area with a linen cloth, but the sunken cloth could not disguise the fact that her head was not beneath the cloth. Meanwhile, the cloth had grown a nasty purple stain at one end where the neck once met the head.

Lincoln lifted the cloth, saying, "The bastard thinks he's got a sense of humor, Lucas." Pulling away the cloth, Lincoln revealed that the woman's head had been replaced by a honeydew melon. "Still somewhat cool from being in the fridge," Lincoln informed Lucas.

Lucas did a sudden double-take when he realized the bronze statue on a shelf across the room was not bronze but rather the woman's severed head. The woman's eyes stared wide at Lucas from a mahogany bookshelf lining one wall. A pair of diamond-studded, heart-shaped earrings winked as if filling in for her dead eyes.

Lincoln, watching Lucas's reaction, noted, "Bastard

taped the eyes open with see-through Scotch tape, making sure the effect would be lasting. Obviously robbery was hardly the motive here. Note the earrings? She musta just come off a hot date."

Robbery was *not* the motive here, Lucas thought, shooting a grimace at his boss. The severed head element alone filled Lucas with guilt. It fairly screamed Freeleng. Just as Dave Harbough had said at the prison, they shouldn't have let the bastard out of their sights.

"Freeleng did this, Captain. Freeleng was here," he coldly concluded. "The Headless Horseman is back."

"Yeah, got the same conclusion from Dave Harbough, Lucas, but I wouldn't lock down on any single theory just yet."

Lucas only half heard his superior. Lucas reeled from the realization that he'd somehow been a part of this, somehow let it happen, and his eyes, wherever they went in this blood-soaked apartment gave him no rest from the thought. His Cherokee blood rising, he wanted to hunt down Freeleng and murder him tonight in retaliation for this. For the moment, he just wanted a place to rest his eyes from the horror, but he found none.

Entrails had been strewn across the room, some lying over an otherwise pristine couch, some on the smoke-gray carpet, some on the glass-topped table. Worse still, the enormous hole cut out of the victim's gut, in order to get at the entrails. The killer had refilled the open stomach with wax from a burning candle, a huge, votive candle that had been fixed into the dead woman's stomach to burn there and melt out into the interior of the torso, creating a cementlike green surface. It had been a forest green candle, and the pool it had created appeared black green.

The dead woman's breasts and vaginal area had been sprayed with hot wax that had melted in mounds over each. Tentacles of the green wax showered down the crease at each hip, and at the lower torso, and down the thighs and into the private parts.

Lucas turned from this horror only to be confronted by the severed head again. The severed and bloody-stumped head remained upright between bookends that depicted replicas of ancient gargoyles, items bought at any novelty store or bookshop these days. The killer had also selected two volumes to place with the head, each showing spine out against the bloody head. The spines read: *The Complete Works of Edgar Allan Poe* and *The Complete Works of H. P. Lovecraft*. Lucas surmised from the collection of other books in the home that the two volumes had belonged to the victim, and not the headhunting, disemboweling candlestick maker. This he surmised since all of the other books dealt, in one fashion or another, with occult themes, vampire themes or classic gothic horror tales. The woman had the complete works of the masters of horror, from Robert Bloch and Richard Matheson to Clive Barker, Stephen Robertson's Decoy Series and *Dr. O* by Glenn Hale, a novel with a cult following. Lucas had read *Dr. O* on learning the book held a bizarre scene found nowhere else in all of literature.

The apartment stood stacked with candles and incense burners, and Lucas wondered if the killer had used one of her own candles to burn inside her. It made a difference. If the killer had used one of her candles, it may well have been a random impulse spur-of-the-moment act, whereas if he'd entered with the candle, his candle, then the addition of the candle into the wound was part of the premeditated act. Premeditation went into the break-in, the planning of the kill, the tools a killer carried with him, all nails in the bastard's coffin, if and when the sovereign state of Texas should ever have the opportunity to indict and prosecute this fiend.

Lincoln stepped wide of the body and fluids staining the plush carpeting, coming to Lucas's side. "Listen, Lucas, you'd better go in and speak with Meredyth." Lincoln pointed with his shoulder, indicating the sound of crying in the other room.

"Who's she with?"

"No one. Unfortunately she recognized the victim. She knows her from somewhere. They did aerobics together at some posh gym in the Old Towne district."

"Christ . . ."

"I had no idea when I called her in. Neither did she. The victim moved in only recently. Meredyth didn't really know her that well—certainly didn't know this was her place, not until she saw the head on the bookshelf."

"But the features are mutilated," Lucas countered.

"The earrings. A recent present from the boyfriend. Meredyth admired them only yesterday at the gym. Apparently, there was marriage talk. The woman was showing them off, wearing them everywhere. You'll find a matching ring on her finger. The boyfriend must be loaded."

"He know yet?"

"We're running him down. Seems he's out of town, business trip. Left right after they parted tonight, poor bastard."

"Then you don't like him for this?"

"Not a chance. He didn't even have cold feet according to Meredyth."

"She knows the boyfriend?"

"Met him once at the gym."

Lucas gritted his teeth, his heart thumping soundly in a three-pronged staccato beat for Meredyth's pain. "Damn," he muttered. "How'd the creep get in? No sign of forced entry. That much is clear at the door. So, she must've let him in, must've known—"

"All the forced entry you can handle, you'll find in the bedroom. Came through the window somehow."

"How the hell could he come through the window? We're forty stories up!"

"Some kinda freaking fly-man, Lucas. Bastard cut a fucking hole big enough to climb through, but how he managed outside the window, I couldn't tell you. There's no balcony out there, and it's a sheer drop—forty stories. So the bastard—"

"Came in from nowhere?"

"Flew in. Over the top."

"Military guy, maybe? Using rappelling equipment, I imagine." Lucas tried to focus on anything but the disembodied head on the mantel. "Not even safe in a high-rise in this city anymore. That's gonna be the headline, Captain."

"Quite likely, yes to all you've said, Lucas, but you don't have to be military to learn to use that rappelling stuff these days."

Lucas nodded, bit back a thought and said, "Circus performer, mountain climber, movie stuntman, Indian chief, nutcase, reserve forces, take your pick."

"Go look in on Meredyth and take a look at the entry point. See if you see anything I didn't."

"Will do."

Lincoln, who rivaled Lucas in height, also had forty pounds and six years on Lucas. The captain's voice and demeanor marked him as a leader. He stopped Lucas with a hand to the shoulder. Both men stood over six feet tall, their eyes met in a concentrated stare. "Lucas, whoever this bastard is, he really did a number on the victim. This bastard's a woman hater. He'll continue to prey on the women of this city until we stop him."

"Freeleng hasn't been out of prison for more than what, forty-eight hours, Captain. He was a woman hater and a beheader, remember."

"That was never proven, Lucas."

"It will be . . ."

Lucas now went straight for Meredyth, who appeared soul-weary where she sat perched on the victim's still pristinely made bed. In fact, except for the busted window and the cool rush of wind and rain, nothing in the room proved untoward. The killer had done his bloody business in the outer room, likely grabbing the victim as she entered the door.

Meredyth looked up when he entered. Standing, she reached out to him, bawling his name, "Lucas! Oh, Lucas, the bastard . . . what he did to her . . . Oh, it hurts, so much."

He held her. How long he held her, he did not know, but it felt long and it felt right. When he released Meredyth, she looked deeply into his coal black Indian eyes and vowed, "We have to nail the sick *motherfuckingsonofabitch* that did this to Laurel."

Laurel . . . It was the first he'd heard her name. "We will. I promise you, we will." Lucas helped her back to a sitting position on the bed. He let go of her shoulders, tentatively as if fearful she might fall over. When he felt certain of her steadiness, Lucas went to the window and examined the precision cut along the large refrigerator-sized entryway the killer had provided for himself. Lucas then noted how the laser-cutting action used by the killer had littered the carpet with glass beads, here and there lay large portions of pane that had been pushed through by the killer. The beads sparkled up at him reflecting the moonlight entering through the window, and with the wind still gushing through the gaping hole, the shimmering, wet beads played a game of scatter and bunch, scatter and bunch. Pointing to the result of the killer's entrance, Lucas said, "Looks like fairy dust, don't you think?"

Meredyth only shuddered in response, stood and began pacing on the far side of the room, away from the broken glass.

Studying the huge gash to the fortieth-floor window, Lucas gauged both the level of determination and of know-how in the killer's method of entry. He leaned out and stared at the sheer drop below to where the cars and people continued their small lives. This gave him no sense of dizziness or apprehension; it recalled for him a time when he had worked as just another steel walker in Dallas before he had finished the academy there. He and other Indians in the city found work on the high-rise skeletal rails of buildings in progress. Heights had never given Lucas any problem.

Add steelworkers to the list of possible stuntmen capable of pulling this off, he told himself.

Lucas leaned out even farther to stare up to the sky and the rooftop of this place, hearing Meredyth's soft, cautionary words behind him as he did so. Ignoring her concern, he intently studied the distance to the top of the building, several stories. He saw no unusual or loose dangling ropes, no marks or mars along the side of the building. There was nothing to indicate that anyone had ever been here, nothing but the telltale man-sized hole he now stood leaning through like some aberrant Alice in Wonderland, half in and half out of the looking-glass.

With all the possible windows to come through, why did the killer target this one? Had he targeted Laurel first? Most likely that was an affirmative, Lucas decided.

The mirrored windows of the vertical cliff face looked back in placid and inscrutable darkness, the eyes of giants who, while witness to the event, remained as silent as the face of a mountainside, he thought. Who would be looking for a murderer up here? Who would even pay a cat burglar any attention way up here? If he wore anything smacking of a uniform, anyone viewing him from adjacent buildings would likely sum him up as a worker, just doing a job.

Lucas looked down again without the slightest dizziness at doing so, and he marveled at the sheer cliff face of the skyscraper. "Took some guts to come in this way," he heard himself say.

"Guts hell! The bastard's a coward!" she screamed. "Laurel Kensington didn't stand a chance. To attack a defenseless person half his size and weight and strength. Bloody gutless bastard!"

He didn't know what to say; what words might extend some solace. He imagined no words could. "I take it, you knew her well."

"No, no . . . I didn't know her well, but we were . . . we were getting there. She didn't deserve this, Lucas. No one does, but Laurel, she was a private duty nurse. She cared for people. All she wanted in this life was to help others. We lunched after workouts once or twice. We weren't best of friends, but we might have been. Damn the creature that did this!" She pounded a fist into a bureau drawer, bloodying her knuckle.

Lucas whipped out a handkerchief and pushed it at her, saying, "We don't need any more blood splatters here, Mere. Tie that off." He hadn't meant to sound out the words as an order, but the command seemed actually to somewhat calm her.

She took the neatly folded handkerchief and bull-whipped it open, dropped again to the neatly made bed and asked Lucas to tie the scarf around her hand for her. As he did so, she said, "When Lincoln called, I didn't recognize the address or apartment number. She'd just moved. Said she wanted more safety locks between her and Houston. A lot of good that did."

"Was she into anything, you know, unusual?"

"Unusual? What do you mean, unusual?"

"Kinky, hinky, dangerous."

"Laurel? No, she seemed as normal as the day is long."

"Seemed? You know as well as I do that most people seem fine on the surface."

"She didn't do drugs, didn't hang out in bars, didn't bring home strangers."

"Just looking at her things, her books, she appears interested in the occult. Maybe she hung with a crowd so inclined at an occult theme bar, maybe? We need a lead somewhere to start. Need to take a close look at—"

"At the victim? As if she brought this on herself? God, I hate that, Lucas."

"She may have brought it on herself without realizing it, Mere. You know that's possible. From what I see, she liked bizarre reading material, which could mean she took it a step further. It spilled over into her personal—"

"Hell, so what? She enjoyed a good horror movie, *Werewolf in Paris* was her favorite movie. She loved a good horror novel, although she abhorred Stephen King. Other than that, she was the most normal, middle-of-the road person I know."

"Besides your normal self?" He tried to lighten the moment.

"Yeah, besides my screwed-up self."

"So, I'd better get back in there. See what I can figure out about this creep."

"I've gotta go back in there, too. Do my job," she replied, getting up and going toward the body in the other room.

Lucas intercepted her, placing himself between the door and her. "No way, Mere. You're too close to this, to her."

"Who better to nail the mother that did this to her?"

"Let us . . . you know . . . clean up a bit first."

"No, I have to do this. Kim Desinor would grit her teeth and do this."

Lucas gave a moment's pause to his memory of the FBI psychic detective, wishing that Houston had her on its payroll. He simply replied, "You're not Dr. Desinor, and you don't need to be trying to live up to her standard. Hell, Mere, she's a bona fide psychic. If she were a Cherokee, she'd be a shaman."

"You took her out to the desert her last night in Houston, I understand. Did the two of you . . . have a good time."

"Yes, matter of fact, we did. I took her to *Diablo Spinata,* that place I have told you so much about."

"Where spirits abound?"

"Where I have wanted to take you, but you could never squeeze it in."

"But apparently she did . . . squeeze it in, I mean?"

"It proved a beautiful night, but turns out she's extremely in love with some guy back in Baltimore, Maryland—a cop who she met in New Orleans while working a case there. Not interested in any . . . complications."

"Sorry it didn't work out between you two, Lucas, but she's right about one thing. You are a complication."

"Who me? A complication? But you're right. Never had a chance, nothing to work out."

She took a deep breath and returned to the subject at hand. "Still, I am a forensic psychiatrist and that's what you need on this case. That's why Lincoln called me in, and—"

He took her shoulder firmly in hand and shook his head. "You have got to be the most stubborn person outside myself I know. There are other forensic psychiatrists we can draw on."

"None better than me, and my knowing the victim, even a little bit, it could honestly help."

A knock at the closed door preceded Captain Lincoln, who stepped in and asked them if they were all right, directing his gaze at her.

Meredyth wiped her eyes, cleared her throat and calmly stated, "I'm fine, Captain. Just needed a moment. I can do this."

"Are you sure?" Lincoln exchanged a supplicating look with Lucas who merely frowned and shrugged.

Meredyth didn't respond with words but with action, stepping past them both and into the horror chamber.

NINE

Coyote track

Meredyth Sanger stared at both the victim and the crime scene as a forensic psychiatrist. She had learned much from her training and experience; she had learned much from Dr. Kim Desinor when Desinor had come in on the awful Snatcher case the year before. Meredyth now sized up the scene and told Lincoln and Stonecoat what she thought of the killer, minus the expletives.

"He's a showman, staging the event. It's all a big game to him. No, not a game, more than a game. This is a big production, like a play. He's staging his own goddamn production."

"Gets his rocks off by rubbing it in our faces?" asked Gordon Lincoln.

"More like showing authority, society—*all of us*—that no one is safe from him if he so chooses to . . . to come calling. The placement of the head on the shelf is a metaphor for contempt, a metaphor for the entire event."

"You mean he holds us *all* in contempt," suggested Lucas.

"He's sending messages, not in words but in gestures, like that"—she pointed but did not look again at the severed head—"and . . . and through the candle set to burn inside her gutted stomach, all symbolic of . . . of . . ."

Lincoln verbally nudged her, asking, "Of what?"

"I don't know, just yet, but he is sending a message. Of that much I am sure."

"Even in his mode of entry," agreed Lucas. "He likely exited the way he came, too. I've sent men up to the roof to scour for any clues there, but so far nothing but pigeon droppings."

"You think so, Lucas?" asked Lincoln, rubbing his chin in a mix of confusion and appreciation. "You think the sick sonofabitch is sending a message even in how he enters and exists the crime scene?"

"I once read of a case where the killer routinely did a similar thing with the candle in the stomach, only it was the victim's mouth," recalled Meredyth, her usual composure slowly returning. "And I've read of cases in which the killer cut out the stomach and filled it with something, but I think it was food, food which the killer then feasted on."

Lincoln's stomach growled with the abhorrence this elicited, but Meredyth continued, adding to the unsavory image of a wacko dining out of his victim's stomach. "Everything from the victim's refrigerator wound up in the fucking wound."

"I remember that case," said Lucas. "In fact, it happened in Dallas when I was a rookie there, but they caught the guy."

"Real sicko bastard who worked out some notion in his head that if he ate the sins of the dead—whom he himself had dispatched—he could then save himself from perdition or some such fate because . . . because—"

"Because," Lucas finished for her, "he believed himself
to be some sort of sacrificing angel to come along and
wipe out their sins, taking them onto himself, his soul."

Meredyth recalled the case more clearly and added,
"Thereby showing God his willingness to be like the Son
of God, Jesus, and so . . ."

"Yeah, more dead in the name of Jesus," agreed Lucas.
"After the creep was caught and put away, I never gave
it another thought. For life, I thought."

"Well, our guy here and now is beheading, disemboweling, mutilating the features and hot-waxing the genitals
and burning a candle in the wound," said Lincoln. "So
can we concentrate on the present, people?"

Meredyth, quick-shot fashion, replied, "Like I said.
This deviant is sending a number of messages. He may be
more interested in sending his messages than in taking . . .
than he was in taking Laurel's life."

"You're in charge of this one, Lucas. This one's more
politically charged than that Scalper Killer nut. I've already had a call from Senator Kensington, from aboard
his private jet. He clearly wants you on the case. He's
well aware of your record."

"But what about the mayor's pet project, the Scalper
Killings?"

"Never argue with a man who owns his own plane,
Lucas."

Lucas appreciatively nodded. "Then who's on for the
Scalper?"

"Actually I'd hoped you'd take on both, but I'm not
going to ask you."

"Good."

"We'll put Kaminsky or Hagberg on the case. Neither

one knows much about Native American crime, but—"

"There's little evidence to support the notion that the killer is a Native American, Captain. Your assumptions expose your prejudices, sir." Lucas's fired-up eyes displayed his ire, reinforcing his words.

"What about the scalp-taking and the pictographs cut into the flesh?" protested Meredyth, now fully regained to herself as Dr. M. Sanger. "Doesn't that remind you somewhat of the Minerva Roundpoint killing you investigated last year? That's Plains Indian shit, isn't it, Lucas?"

"Minerva Roundpoint was killed by a jealous lover who happened to be of mixed Indian and Spanish blood. Look, Captain, at least call in a specialist on pictographs, a pictography expert to sort out the messages and meanings of the cuts."

"Damn it, Lucas, nobody knows that kind of shit like you do. Even if this latest yo-yo proves to be not so Native as he'd like us to believe, you *are*. Besides, you already know more about the meaning of Plains Indian marks on a kill than anyone in Houston, including the so-called experts."

"I'll consult on the case then. Won't cost the city an extra penny. I can't do both *and* handle all my COMIT responsibilities."

Lucas turned to the difficult task of evidence gathering and overseeing a team of evidence technicians. Lucas, while officially in charge of the investigation, knew he would lean heavily on Dr. Meredyth Sanger for will and support.

Laurel Kensington's father suddenly filled the doorway, his overcoat like a shroud, billowing out with the wind that poured through the apartment from the bedroom window. He came in shouting for Laurel by name, as if to conjure her back. His scream of pain filled the space like an extended gunshot, until he settled into a keening animalistic chant of the loved one's name, as if it might be a magical mantra to recall her into this life. *Not remotely likely,* Lucas thought, *not with a severed head.* Still, Lucas and the other seasoned cops and professionals on hand knew real suffering when they saw and heard it. Senator Kensington was playing to no cameras here.

Kensington, in Gucci leathers and a London Fog overcoat that he'd quickly pulled on over a pair of hundred-dollar pajamas, collapsed after seeing Laurel's head still on the bookshelf. He collided with the body then, fell to his knees over it and crumpled into the blood and serum and forensic tags, vials and bags. Lincoln helped the man to his feet and ushered him out, a broken spirit. All down the hall, the senator could be heard mumbling, "She was my angel, my precious gift, my gift from God. . . ."

Meredyth joined Lincoln in escorting the dispirited, disturbed father off from the scene. "I flew in from Washington, dropped everything when I heard something had happened," continued the man now in a low, too-controlled tone. "Took the jet, you know?"

Lucas felt pangs of horror for the father. No parent should see his child's life ended in so horrible a fashion. This act was no accident, no mishap, not a fatal error or act of God. It was the premeditated murder of an innocent young woman, a woman likely stalked by her killer for days, weeks, if not months in preparation to torture and kill her. No amount of wealth, no amount of private jets mattered now.

Lucas called out to the senator, asking, "Were you being blackmailed by anyone, sir?"

"No, absolutely not."

"Any ugly or threatening letters?"

"I'm in public office. What do you think?"

"We'll want to have them, all of them, to pore over. Any idea whether your daughter was experiencing anything unusual lately?" asked Lucas, not wishing to lead the senator to his own foregone conclusion. "Any changes in habits, friends, hangouts?" They all stood in the hallway now, at a safe distance from the sight and odor of the body that had been the senator's daughter.

"Sure, we talked all the time about her being careless, but she took my advice this last time and got a great new apartment with a security guard and checks up and down. This place doesn't come cheap."

"We'll need her old address, any new acquaintances," suggested Lucas.

"I'll cooperate in any way I can, but she didn't always confide. Hell, I just learned yesterday that she was . . . planned to . . . be married." He lost it again, visibly crumpling into Meredyth's comforting arms.

"I knew your daughter, Mr. Kensington, and she spoke so highly of you. She loved you very much." Meredyth led him farther away from the smell of death enveloping his little girl and the hallway.

Amazed at Meredyth's show of strength in the face of all this, Lucas found new respect for her; but he had found very little else here, certainly no useful clues. The killer had been thorough, methodical, displaying a neurotic need to tidy up after himself, while leaving the place in the disarray of a sideshow haunted house. Lucas wondered if Freeleng had left such a pattern, if Freeleng did in fact match the killer's modus operandi.

The evidence techs had sifted through and around the apartment like so many automatons, gathering information for the forensic lab and ultimately for Chang. Leonard had loyal, dedicated people on his staff. If anything could be made of the scraps left behind by the killer, Leonard Chang would find them.

As for releasing the body, Lucas saw no need to hold on to it a moment longer; everyone wanted to reconnect the parts, particularly the severed head, something Chang could also do on his slab. Lucas returned to stand near the deceased. He shouted in command fashion, "Wrap it up here, people, and get Ms. Kensington to Chang's capable hands. And thanks, everyone."

Lucas thought how his words sounded like a director wrapping up shooting on a picture, and how it macabrely fit into the killer's MO, if Meredyth were right about his need to stage an event. What could be more unnatural than this ugly scene inside the lush high-rise apartment of a senator's daughter.

After Lucas saw Meredyth home, he grabbed several hours sleep before his phone woke him. On the other end of the line Tsalie sounded as if she'd been crying. Gathering her breath, she said, "It is time you return here. Grandfather is looking for you, and he will soon be gone, Lucas."

He drove back to Huntsville and the Coushatta with his strobe light this time, effected not so much by Tsalie's words as the sound of her voice, like a wounded bird, a small warble in the back of her throat.

With the police strobe light flashing, Lucas made it back out to the reservation in record time, arriving just after 9:30 A.M. Welcomed by Tsalie, they embraced as old friends in the doorway. Billy looked on sourly, beer can in hand. Lucas sensed that they had been fighting, and even in the dim light of the foyer, he saw a welt on her left wrist. He scanned for any sign of violence done to her elsewhere, a growing anger for Billy Hawk welling inside.

"Go to him," she instructed, realizing what he now searched for, her face reddening with shame. Lucas nodded, gave a furtive glance at Billy, who gave a casual hello with a lift of his beer can to his lips, as if to toast Lucas's arrival.

Lucas took the steps to the old man's upstairs bedroom two at a time, wondering as he went what Tsalie and Billy had been arguing over. A natural condition for people living together under stress, Lucas surmised, but he still wondered if it might be something more than the normal tiff. The thought that the other man had harmed her incensed him, yet he knew the line she had drawn with her eyes was quite real. He could only help her if she asked for help. For now, he must concentrate on his grandfather's condition.

He entered the room, the feel of death undeniably close, thick and as cloying as tobacco smoke in the lodge house during a council meeting. Lucas mentally pushed through the smoke of death, realizing only now that his grandfather had by some incredible miracle sat up. He was puffing on a pipe that had lain at his bedside for as long as Lucas had known him. The smoke was real and his grandfather remained alive, breathing his last breaths to the smell and taste of Red Man tobacco.

The old man's eyes glistened with a strange light and a smile creased his features on seeing Lucas. "You're better," Lucas said to him.

"Better . . . life I go . . ."

"How did you get that pipe lit? Where did you find the strength?"

"Billy."

"And I suppose he helped you to sit up?"

"He did."

Lucas knew now what the fight had been about. He couldn't fault Billy. If the old man commanded a thing be done, it must be done. Lucas would have helped him to sit up and smoke as well, had he asked Lucas for such help.

"I wish . . . to die . . . a man, on my . . . terms," he said. His voice was feeble, his breath catching with each word. "I go now." He reached a pair of weak limbs toward Lucas. Obviously the morphine worked wonders, Lucas thought, wondering if he shouldn't get some of the stuff for himself.

No more words between them, Lucas lifted the pipe from the old man's lips and placed it on the bedside table, the aroma rising with curling remnant smoke, a racing ghost. He next held his grandfather in his arms, knowing instinctively the old man wished it so. Lucas held on as the old man's spirit passed through Lucas's body and out and into the next life. Lucas felt the old man's essence move through him like a charging wind. It felt like spectral water, a river of life, running in and out of Lucas's chest for a millisecond, heating his entire body.

Lucas remained holding on to the bony outer husk of the man he loved most in this life until the tears came. Tsalie came to stand behind him. She placed her arms around him, asking him to come away, her own tears staining Lucas's shirt.

"Let me put him to rest first."

Lucas carefully placed his grandfather in a lying position. "He looks at peace," he murmured.

"He does," she quickly agreed.

Both of them stared at the still-curling smoke from the old man's pipe. Both of them felt his presence still in the room but no longer in the husk of his body.

Lucas closed the old man's staring eyes, his hand shaking. "All of us have lost today a great part of our spirit. Where is your husband?"

"Billy ran the moment he saw Grandfather was gone."

"Ran?"

"Out the door. In search of understanding in a bottle."

"You shouldn't be so hard on him," Lucas said.

"Me, hard on him?"

"For having helped Grandfather up to smoke his pipe."

"It's not about a pipe."

"Something you'd care to talk about then?"

"He's crazy. He's taken a job that will get him killed."

Lucas pictured Billy walking a skyscraper skeleton. Then he asked, "Work is a good thing for my cousin."

"Working for that . . . that gangster?"

"Gangster?" Lucas hadn't heard the word in a long time. It sounded quaint. Then it dawned on Lucas what she meant. "You mean Roundpoint?"

"Afraid so."

Lucas breathed deeply and took her in his arms, assuring her with the only words he could find at the moment. "Billy sees an opportunity to make your life easier, he will take it."

"And what happens when he gets killed for his trouble? What does that do for me and his children?"

"A Native American man has few choices in this life, Tsalie."

"You created a new choice, Lucas. You are looked up to by the children on the reservation as someone who escaped the poverty and the suffering. This house . . . all

the renovation to the reserve . . . it's all . . . a monument
to that."

"This is a modest house, Tsalie. Besides, the currency
came by way of Roundpoint's generosity . . . not mine."

"I don't for a moment believe that Zachary Roundpoint
would return a dime to his people, except perhaps to en-
snare them. Lucas, are you ensnared?"

"I do not work for Roundpoint, and I am not being
bribed by him. Does that answer?"

"Anywhere else in this land, yes. But here, no. The
rumors say otherwise."

"Do not listen to false wind. Meanwhile, I'll talk to
Billy."

"It will do no good. His mind is set, and Roundpoint's
lifestyle . . . it appeals to Billy. It's not just the money or
him wanting to take care of us. It's . . . it's the allure of
Roundpoint's world."

"I see." He well imagined it true. He kissed her on the
forehead. She lifted her chin and her lips to his, breathing
him in. Lucas helplessly kissed her full on the lips, imagining the spirit of his grandfather enveloping them and
pushing them together. Had that been his plan all along?
Lucas would not put it past Keeowskowee to create a
reunion between them on the occasion of his death.

She pulled away, pleading, "Oh, dear, Lucas, please . . .
I'm sorry for having . . . having enticed you this way.
Please, forgive me . . . I . . . I . . ."

"No need. No need," he assured her repeatedly. "No
need for apologies or guilt or shame. Certainly you have
no need of my forgiveness."

Gasping for breath, she changed the subject. "I've made
some arrangements about the funeral. Everyone agrees
you must give the eulogy, Lucas."

"Eulogy? Me?" It had not in the least ever occurred to him.

"Naturally. Come along. Leave him for a time. Come down with me. We'll go over the details. We all know how busy you are, and that at any moment we could lose you again to that white world you live in." She managed a smile that eased her words. Coming from Billy they would have been stinging; coming from Tsalie, they were caressing, understanding words.

Lucas left the room with one final look at his mother's father. "I love you, old spirit," he shouted to the room. "Go with your gods."

Lucas remained long enough on the reservation to eulogize his grandfather and bury him. He staved off Lincoln and the rest of the world with a handful of phone calls. Meanwhile, the reservation was abuzz with gossip as to what exactly was going on between Tsalie and Lucas. Uppermost in every mind, the dispensation of the old man's single most important possession: the log cabin.

Lucas's eulogy hammered home one point, that Keeowskowee lived his life as friend to any and every man who needed him or asked anything of him. He had touched many, many lives, and all to the good. Even Billy Hawk's, he had joked. Then he publicly lied, telling everyone and Billy at the same time, "The old man's dying wish was for me to plead with you, Billy, to not take the red path toward death—"

"What do you mean, red path?"

"Live in peace, here on the res with your wife and family. Take the white path of peace," replied Lucas. "That was Grandfather's counsel. Do not go the path of Roundpoint. Grandfather asked that you do not take the job Roundpoint offered you. Instead, he would barter his house."

This news left everyone aghast. Billy's mouth fell open. Tsalie's eyes widened, staring through Lucas, knowing the truth.

"So, give it serious thought, Billy. If you can drop this fascination with Houston life, and the life offered you by joining Roundpoint's Indian mafia, then the house belongs to your wife and your children. Even in death, Grandfather's wish was to help others, and in particular you and your family, my cousin."

The entire congregation, on exiting the wake, buzzed with this news. As they filed past, they paid respects to the family members, many urging Billy to make the right choice. Just as many thanked Lucas for favors he denied: the new books in the schools, the new playground, several newly dug wells and home builders' loans. All this stemmed from the windfall monies that the council had "come across" via an anonymous donor. Lucas was that donor, but anonymous he had not remained. Some of those passing by told Lucas it had been the finest eulogy they had heard in years, and that all he had said about his grandfather had been true.

"I miss Grandpa," whined one of Tsalie's children, the other taking up the cry. They had quickly adopted the kind and spirited old man as their own grandfather, Lucas realized.

"Take them for something to eat in the longhouse," Billy told his wife. Tsalie thanked Lucas and kissed him on the cheek before gathering the children and leaving.

Alone now with Billy, the shorter, stouter man said, "I won't accept charity, Lucas."

"What charity? It—the house—belonged to Grandfather, free and clear. He could and he did deed it over to the one person he most wanted to leave it to, Billy."

"And if I accept this gracious offer? What does it do to our friendship, Lucas? The house rightfully should have gone back into your hands, not mine. We both know that."

"I respect the words of the dying. I respect the final words of my grandfather. All else means nothing, so many sandcastles, Billy. That's what working for Roundpoint will get you in the end, so much piled up . . . sand. Nothing but a desert execution and burial, fodder for Gila monsters."

Billy raised a hand to Lucas and they shook, smiling, a truce and the bargain explicitly set. Lucas felt he might have not only saved Tsalie's marriage but Billy's life. He felt a bit like the old man, Keeowskowee—a positively sly, cunning man.

"Let's go get some of that good chow they've got waiting at the longhouse for everyone, Lucas."

"Indian soul food? Sounds great." A look back at the old man's simple pine coffin, and Lucas felt anxious to finish the fire ceremony the old man had requested. He wanted to go out in smoke, like his forefathers before him, on a burning pyre. No one had done that in this generation, but the old man had insisted. He had all his life harkened back to the old ways, while at the same time keeping a firm eye on the new world; understanding and appreciating the best of both, generally disregarding the worst of either.

Later, after the feast, Keeowskowee's body was carried to the pyre, lifted atop it while still in the pine coffin and the pyre was set ablaze. It proved an amazing sight for both tired old eyes and the eyes of youth. The ritual was performed by the man who would take Keeowskowee's place as village shaman, a fifty-year-old apprentice named Owl Goingback. He was a friend of the family, and while he did an excellent job of masking his excitement at taking on the mantle of shaman, he managed a half smile now as the smoke took the old shaman's spirit skyward.

Goingback shouted at the retreating smoke, "Come back to me as my guide in matters of magic and healing, old teacher, old friend."

All round the roaring fire, men, women and children chanted the old songs to give Keeowskowee the kind of funeral his soul required.

Amid the ceremony, Lucas leaned toward Billy, telling him, "Billy boy, you've got to be the luckiest man on the face of the planet to have Tsalie at your side, two beautiful children and a fine house, the largest on the reservation. Who knows, next year about this time, you might even be on the tribal council if you play your cards right."

"You still love her."

Lucas considered his words carefully. Lying would not suffice. "I will always love her and honor her. You, Billy have shamed her."

"Shamed her?"

"With your actions, yes."

"I only told her to be friendly to you, Lucas. I wasn't exactly acting as her pimp, for God's sake."

"Is that so? She never stooped to your low, Billy. She never will, so you'd better decide to rise to her level."

"Tsalie has you fooled then. She wanted the house as much as I did."

"For her children. I understand that. She needs stability, and so do your girls. They need to light in one place and stay there, to grow up properly. But Tsalie made no sexual overtures, and has remained pure in this sordid business.

I can't say the same for you, Billy, and contingent on keeping the house is that you become sober and remain sober."

"I get the feeling you're making this up as you go, Lucas."

"Good, then you'll always wonder what's coming next. I can be your best friend or your worst enemy, Billy. You know that."

"Then all that business of the old man's leaving the house to me is . . . was a lie?"

"Not exactly. He left it deeded over to your wife, Tsalie. He could not trust you, Billy. Feared you'd get into so much debt that you'd lose the house if it were in your name. It's deeded over to Tsalie." Lucas had arranged with a lawyer to have this done as soon as he could on learning of Tsalie's situation. His grandfather had readily agreed and signed the papers.

Tsalie stood beside them now, her girls hugging each leg. She had overheard Lucas's last words. She exchanged a look of surprise, first with Lucas, then with Billy. "I had no idea, Billy."

Billy smiled wide and shrugged. "It's not a problem." He pursed his lips and raised his eyebrows and shoulders simultaneously. "It's all in the family, right, Lucas?" He pulled Tsalie to him. The gesture of a man claiming a possession.

"A final stipulation made by the old man is that Tsalie never ever deed the home over to anyone during her life-time, and even then only to her children."

"Checkmate, Lucas. You got me. Unless, of course, you *are* making this up as you go."

"One other thing, Billy," replied Lucas, a cold stare fixed on the younger man.

"Go . . . go on," Billy replied.

"If I ever hear that you once, even once, raise a hand to this woman again, I will come back here and personally break your arms and—"

"Break my arms?"

"Your arms, legs, fingers, wrists, whatever it takes to impress upon you that you don't lay a finger on Tsalie or her children."

"You sure you're not on Roundpoint's payroll? That's it, isn't it?"

"Shut up, Billy," ordered Tsalie.

"Isn't that how the longhouse council got the big bucks to fix up this miserable hell?" Billy's voice rose, filling the longhouse, causing the musicians and the chattering to abruptly end.

"That's enough, Billy." Tsalie's face had gone livid with anger.

"I am not in the employ of that assassin, Roundpoint, nor have I ever been," Lucas protested for all to hear. "As tempting as it might be, the certainty of being killed and buried out in the desert, doesn't appeal. But that's precisely where a fuckup like you, Billy, will wind up if—"

Billy attempted to strike Lucas, but the glancing blow and Lucas's boot sent the other man to the floor where he began to blubber his tale of woe—something about the gods being against him all his life.

Lucas, having smelled the booze on Billy's breath, realized that he'd not only been drinking before the wake, but that he'd been drinking shooters here at the wake.

Tsalie rushed to help Billy, now trying to get off the council hall floor, urging him not to retaliate, saying, "You got what you wanted. Leave it alone."

"*We* got what *we* wanted, Tsalie. Tell your old lover that." He pulled away from her. Lucas stormed out.

Lucas packed what few sentimental items he found in the cabin built for his grandfather, a favored knife, a pair of repeater rifles, circa 1869 and 1872, some photographs, a handful of books and some of the old man's own writings—mostly poems, thoughts and anecdotal stories he'd always wished passed down. The old man's hat went into the gunnysack Lucas dragged about the house. He had no interest in the silverware, dishes or bric-a-brac, and the sack remained pitifully deflated. At one point, he stopped in his search for his grandfather in *things*, realizing how futile the attempt actually was. He saw his grandfather's face laughing at him for such foolishness. His grandfather had once said to him, "A man must consider what in his life means the most to him. Each of us holds so many blue chips, so many red and so many white. White chips a man can let go easily and should not cling to, such things as material possessions. Red chips are more valuable, such as special gifts, prized photos, but these too can be replaced. Blue chips are friendships, family, life itself and the life of a loved one. These are the chips you hold on to, Lucas."

The gambling metaphor notwithstanding, Lucas realized the old man had been right.

Tsalie came into the cabin and she, too, stared at him, but she was not laughing, not so much as a trace of a smile. "Why didn't you give me some warning, Lucas, that you were doing this?"

"What, taking a few items from my grandfather's house?"

"You know what I mean! Leaving this place to me and

the children! What do you think everyone on the reservation will think?"

"They will think Grandfather loved you as he always did. Nothing more."

"You know better than that."

"Let them think what they will, let them talk what they will. You and the girls deserve some . . . something from the old man and—"

"From you. It all comes from you. He didn't say a word ever about the house, even when Billy tried grilling him on the subject."

Lucas pictured Billy trying to get a word out of the sly old fox. "And you?"

"I kicked Billy out of Keeowskowee's room. We had a fight over it. He . . . You saw the result when you got here."

"You must promise never to deed the house over to anyone, ever, including Billy. And if ever you are tempted to sell it, you talk to me first."

"I promise."

"Then you accept Grandfather's generous offer." With that, Lucas handed Tsalie a document—the deed to the house. "The old man signed it over to you and your family. The old man's homestead is yours in perpetuity, for as long as you wish to inhabit it with your girls and Billy. As I said, it is in *your* name. Never sign it over to Billy."

"For my girls, yes."

"Good . . . good."

"And you are welcome in . . . our home, anytime, Lucas. You know that."

"Keep Billy away from Roundpoint."

"Leave Billy to me."

"He'd be out of his league in Houston with that crowd. Trust me."

"How well do you know Roundpoint?"

"I followed a 1948 cold case back to the man who murdered his mother. He's been eternally grateful ever since. That is the extent of our relationship. I do not work for him, and I am not a hired assassin for him."

"Rumors fly."

"That's all they are."

"One rumor is true."

"Which is that?"

"That Tsalie still loves Lucas."

He looked deeply into her eyes, seeing tears welling up. "We'd best not take another step down that path. As much as my heart tells me I should, sweet one, my head says otherwise."

"Just once . . . once I would like to hold you again, Lucas. Just once to be with you again."

He recognized the invitation for what it was. "I . . . I'm not far away. I'll call you. If you can get away, we will see one another again, but I won't be back to the res for a long time."

"Call," she said, the word escaping like a breath that'd been locked away in a secret place for a long time.

"I will."

"Promise me that you will."

He hesitated, knowing it impossible. "I . . . I can't promise it, Tsalie."

"Please, Lucas. Promise."

He swallowed hard, considering the ramifications of an affair with her—his cousin's wife. "I'm sorry, Tsalie. I cannot make such a promise."

She dropped her gaze, turned and ran to a back room,

a rumbling, breast-heaving crying trailed in her wake. At the door, Lucas ran into Billy and the two girls. The girls were carrying dolls they'd held tightly all during the wake. They'd been asking question after question about the ritual and the pyre and where Grandfather Keeowskowee's spirit had gone, and how smoke could carry someone so heavy into the next world.

"What's in the sack?" Billy asked Lucas.

"Stuff I wanted from the old man's house."

"Oh, sure, Lucas. Whatever you want, sure, man."

Lucas indicated that Billy should send his children into the living room. As soon as the children were out of earshot and engaged, Lucas stepped close to Billy and said, "You be certain to be a man and take responsibility for those two girls and Tsalie."

"Of course. You can bank on it, Lucas."

"And stay the hell away from the booze, man, and away from Zachary Roundpoint. The man is death walking."

"That's what they say about you, Lucas, but you ain't killed me, yet."

"Just do as I say."

"Sure, sure."

Lucas shook his cousin's hand, carried his bags and the gunnysack out to his car, waved Billy off and took a long, last look at the reservation, realizing a thought too painful to voice: *There's nothing left here for me.* He then caught a glimpse of Tsalie in a back window, staring after him.

Along the route back to Houston from the Huntsville area, Lucas thought about his grandfather and all that the old man had meant to him. He also thought how much the old man had taught him, mostly about survival and tracking skills, but also much to do with human nature. He realized that he owed his present level of education, determination and abilities as a cop to the old man's teachings. Finally he thought of how utterly nonmaterialistic the old man had always been. He had left no will; he was the least materialistic-minded man Lucas had ever known. Perhaps this was why his spirit always soared, for he remained ever free of the material world.

Lucas's earlier talks on the subject of how the house was to be handled fell on deaf ears. The old man kept claiming himself just a tenant, as he was a tenant on the land; that like the trees, the house was permanent only in appearance. "You want to do something with the house, you do it," he'd shouted at Lucas while he still had the strength to talk. When Lucas suggested it be left to Tsalie and her family, the old man thought it a fine idea. He had agreed it must not fall into Billy's hands.

"Sign here, here and here," Lucas had replied, and the old man had complied without a second thought.

Feeling apart from everything, feeling a sense of being without emotion or tactile sensation at all, Lucas returned to the bustling city of Houston. There Lucas threw himself wholeheartedly into the Laurel Kensington case. He alternately stared now from the case file to the ground level window where he sat in the Cold Room, surrounded by the files of the unsolved murders of a city. Alongside Laurel Kensington's murder book, lay those of seven other women, all dating back twenty years, all victims of a killer police believed to be Walter Karl Freeleng, yet the cases remained opened for lack of evidence against Freeleng. In the Kensington case, everything pointed to Freeleng.

In police parlance, Lucas *liked* Freeleng for the Kensington murder.

The Cold Room files reinforced the same theory, that

the man who'd slaughtered Laurel Kensington had the same modus operandi as Walter Karl Freeleng, save for the additional mutilation of the stomach—as if the killer meant to dig out the core of his hatred and ravish it and purify it with the votive candle placed there. But then Freeleng had had a dozen years to embellish his killing fantasies. He'd had time to think and think about the object of his hatred—women in general in his case.

Lucas thought of the number of suspected victims of the original Headless Horseman killings, several having had multiple stab and deep cut wounds as well as being beheaded. Lucas purely hated that Freeleng appeared to have gotten away with those murders, and that, as Harbough had predicted, the maniac had returned to his earlier *calling*. Some seven women had died in this same hideous fashion before Freeleng was put away the first time. Had he begun on seven more with the Kensington woman?

Today's killer, like the Horseman, was methodical and clean. But unlike most copycats he proved to be smarter than his mentor by leaving the severed head at the crime scene rather than bagging it for some obscene purpose. In doing so, he kept no incriminating evidence on his person or in his private sphere.

This gave Lucas pause as he contrasted the Beheader with the Scalper killer still at large. The major obvious contrast between the two killers appeared this notion of one as being a collector while the other was not. The Scalper collected first hands and then scalps, so it stood to reason that somewhere in the bowels of this city, that killer must have a collection of his doings in some refrigerator or freezer chest someplace . . . somewhere. Small comfort, but at least the head guy wasn't taking the heads off with him. Not yet, anyway.

As it happened the original Headless Horseman never displayed the heads at the crime scenes, always taking the severed body part with him. Such a departure from routine did not exactly pin the tail on the donkey, but rather threw up a red flag saying that perhaps Freeleng was not the current murderer.

Still, Harbough had left a message on Lucas's answering machine that he was sitting on Freeleng, watching his every move. "I've dogged his ass from home to store, from store to parole officer, from parole officer to shrink, Lucas. He won't leave my sight until I catch him in the goddamn act," finished Harbough.

After listening to the message, Lucas leaned back in his chair, his back killing him.

He'd been at the grueling research for several hours when Meredyth Sanger had come by to see how he had fared with burying his grandfather. He told her how the ancient ritual of the pyre had made it all worthwhile. "It was good to see his spirit ascend to his real home," Lucas finished, a half smile of acceptance creasing his features.

"I hope you had the support of family," she said.

"Yes, my . . . my cousin, Billy Hawk, and his wife, Tsalie."

"Tsalie . . . what a pretty name."

"She is a beautiful woman, and she gave me much support. I'm afraid her husband is not supportive of anyone but himself."

They parted on good ground, Meredyth offering him a consoling hug and a welcome back. She left him with her psychological profile of the killer. On first perusal, it fit Freeleng to a *T*, Lucas thought.

He breathed only shallowly here in this dust- and mite-ridden dungeon of paper death. He needed out, he felt the walls coming in on him. The place had become less and less quiet and lonely since other men had been assigned to Lucas to help out in computerizing the whole of the ancient files, but it still remained oppressive to his spirit.

On the verge of announcing his departure to the two men working at stations behind him, Hagberg and Kaminsky, Lucas's phone rang. "Stonecoat, Cold Room," said Lucas into the receiver.

"Hey, Lucas, this is Harbough."

"Dave, hello . . . just thinking about you."

"No shit?"

"Got your message." While Lucas had been away for only two days, it felt like a week.

"Wanted again to first be the first . . . offer my condolences . . . regarding your grandad-father." Lucas heard the slurred voice and realized that Harbough had been drinking. A look at his watch told Lucas that it was not yet two in the afternoon. "Wonderful term 'grandfather.' Get it, there's grand in it, grand like great, and *grande* like big in Spanish, like the Rio Grande, and there's father. Great big grande father. What more could a kid ask for than a great-grandie-father, huh? Heard all about it. Tough to lose a loved one. I know. One of Freeleng's victims, pal, she was . . . was a kind woman, a friend, someone I loved, Lucas."

"Goddamn it, Dave, why didn't you pull yourself off the case, if that was true?" Lucas did not appreciate learning this fact so late in the game. The sentiments came spilling out with the sloppiness of drink. He knew that Dave was far too macho for the words spewing forth to ever have used them in his "natural" state. "Dave, you have to get ahold of yourself on this. What've you been up to?"

"Lucas, I've been on Freeleng like hair on an Afghan hound."

"Tailing him?"

"For last forty-eight hours."

"Without sleep?"

"Living on No-Doz pills, coffee and cigarettes, but listen up, Lucas."

"Go ahead, Dave."

"Lucas, I intend to *murder* Freeleng before he can kill again." The bone-chilling words came out as matter-of-factly as if Harbough had said, "I gotta use the john."

"Don't tell me this, Dave."

No answer.

"Dave! Dave!"

"What?" he fairly shouted.

"Have you talked to your partner, Marc, about this?"

"Marc's an asshole. Thinks I'm an asshole. Can't stand the fool. He don't see it same as I do."

"Have you told him you intended killing Freeleng, damn it?"

"No! Figured only one I could trust was you, Injun."

"Damn you, Dave. . . . Why me?"

"I just want someone to understand before I do him. Gotta do what I gotta do."

"Where are you, Dave? Are you at your place?" Lucas realized he didn't even know where Detective Harbough lived.

"You going to try to stop me, Lucas?"

"This is not the answer, Dave! Dave! Don't do this, Dave!" But Dave had hung up, and the two other cops nearby stared across at Lucas.

Lucas immediately called Harbough's 29th Precinct for the man's home address. He met with immediate resistance. "Can't give out personal information on cops no more. New law, Detective. Too many cops getting revenge-attacked at their homes, in their driveways, shit like that. You ought to know. You had Jack Kirshner killed right there in your precinct."

"This is an emergency! Dave's a friend and he's about to . . . to eat his gun," Lucas shouted.

"If he's such a friend, why don't you know his address then?"

The remark, while maddening under the circumstances, gave Lucas pause. He didn't cultivate friends well, and he knew the addresses of few who considered him a friend. "All right then! Put me on with Marc Damon, Harbough's partner, now!"

A moment passed like a week. Finally the desk sergeant came back on and said, "Sorry, Damon's on personal leave—death in the family—Boca Raton."

"Damn it! Then take this one to your goddamn captain, now!" shouted Lucas. "Get me clearance."

"All right, all right, Detective. Just hold your water, man."

Lucas shouted to the men at the other desks who'd continued to stare at him, "Do either of you know Dave Harbough's address?"

Both junior men looked to one another for an answer. Neither knew Harbough. The hold tone was maddening for Lucas, and sitting there waiting while Harbough plotted murder proved equally maddening. He called Kaminsky, the detective behind him to sit on the phone and to contact him by radio as soon as he got Harbough's home address. He then raced upstairs, shouting to the precinct,

"Anyone here know Dave Harbough of the Twenty-ninth? I need the man's home address, now!"

A patrolman in uniform named Stedman shouted back, "I can take you right there, Detective. I live in the same apartment complex, and I'm off duty."

"Ge me there!"

The patrolman and Lucas rushed for a car. The patrolman, looking like a high-school student to Lucas, asked, "What's this all about, sir?"

"You want to save a life, kid? Get me to Harbough's in record time."

Ten

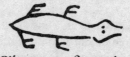

Gila monster: desert signs

Lucas leapt from the squad car, half blinded by the strobe light, as he stared at the building that Patrolman Anthony Stedman had pointed out. Together, they raced for apartment 8-C, Lucas shouting to Stedman, "Locate the super! We've gotta get inside." Stedman did so, and after finding Lucas about to break the door in, the super opened the apartment. All the trouble led to naught, as they learned that Harbough was no longer at home.

"False alarm?" asked Stedman.

"We need an address for Walter Freeleng," Lucas replied.

"Freeleng? The guy Harbough's always talking about?"

"One and the same."

Stedman's eyes narrowed at this, but he said no more. Lucas and Stedman rushed back to the patrol car. Lucas radioed in for an address on the known felon. As soon as dispatch came back with the address, Lucas and Stedman were speeding off again, this time toward Freeleng's place of residence.

Freeleng lived in a halfway house not far from Governor's Square Mall, within close proximity of offices and buildings that Laurel Kensington would have frequented on her lunch breaks. Only a short bus drive separated Freeleng from the aerobics class where she and Meredyth worked out. As they closed in on the area, Lucas realized how easily Freeleng's path might have crossed that of the senator's daughter.

As soon as they came in view of the address given them, Lucas ordered Stedman to drive directly to the front of the place and hit his siren. He wanted to alert Harbough that they were there. Hopefully to shock him into reality—the world of cause and effect, actions and consequences and into a full understanding of what he was about to do, that it meant madness and jail time. Just as Stedman tore to the curb before the halfway house, Walter Freeleng emerged from a nearby grocery store, a bag of groceries in his hands. Lucas surveyed the street, seeing any number of people on both sides, but no Harbough. "Where the hell's Dave?" he muttered to the city noise and traffic.

Freeleng watched the two cops emerge from the cruiser, a great deal amused, a smile creasing his gaunt, aged features. He always looked smug, Lucas thought, as if the smugness were painted on. Lucas shouted to him, "Freeleng! Find cover! We have reason to believe someone has targeted you for murder. Get back inside!"

Freeleng laughed for only a split second before the bullet that suddenly rang out was coursing through his brainpan, pinging around it like a bee. He fell so neatly that the sack in his hands stood balanced on his chest now. A man didn't get any more dead than Freeleng now lay.

Lucas and Stedman dropped to their knees and slid behind the cruiser, fearful the sniper would next fire on them. Stedman shouted, "Is that Harbough out there?"

"I don't know. Get on the horn. Call for backup. We got a sniper and officers penned down."

"You going to report this as possibly Dave's doing, Detective?"

Lucas exchanged a look with Stedman whose eyes never wavered. "If it is Harbough doing the shooting, I hope he had sense enough to not use his standard issue."

Stedman's eyes fixed again on Lucas.

Lucas asked point-blank, "How are you with that?"

"With that? With what?"

"With keeping Harbough's name out of it . . . for now."

Stedman took a deep breath and indicated Freeleng's body, the sack of groceries still sitting atop it. "In Chicago, we used to call it taking out the trash."

"Is that where you're from?" asked Lucas.

"Grew up there. Born in Corpus Christi."

"All right. We were pinned down by random fire while coming to talk to Freeleng over there. Freeleng was caught by a sniper's bullet."

"That's all I know," Stedman agreed.

"Take a few shots at the rooftop. I'll do the same. Call it in. I think the gunfire is over."

Neither man saw the least sign of Dave Harbough. Lucas thought him a remarkable marksman for a drunken cop.

Lucas stepped over to the body and watched Freeleng's blood pooling around his head like a dark halo. From behind him, he heard the call numbers for *officer assistance—shots fired.*

"Maybe now the beheadings will end," Lucas said to Stedman who joined him in standing over the body.

Onlookers gathered about. Workers at the halfway

house pushed past to see Freeleng, their latest rehabilitation case, dead on the street with two cops looking over his body. Lucas thought the crowd—especially those flooding out from the halfway house, many patients of Dr. Thomas Morrissey—particularly ugly. They brought to mind the painting by Hieronymus Bosch of the ugly crowd depicted in his *Christ Carrying the Cross* in which he also depicted the Repentant Thief.

One scrawny man in particular egged on the others standing on the stairwell to the halfway house, shouting obscenities and raising his fist to the sky. Lucas rushed the man whose face blanched white. "You got a name, mister?" Lucas demanded.

"Wendell. My name is Wendell."

"Listen to me, little man! One more word outta you, and you get hauled away. Now shut the fuck up!"

"That's rich! You guys execute poor Freeleng, and we got to keep shut?" the little man replied, but now with the voice of a lawyer, firm and resolute. "Just wait till Dr. Morrissey learns how you set Freeleng up for murder."

"One more word, freak, and your ass is in jail."

The other halfway inmates inched around their little leader, all making menacing gestures. Suddenly the street filled with other police units and everyone calmed down.

A news crew arrived on the scene about the same time as another half dozen police cruisers. The death of Walter Karl Freeleng had gone out over the police airwaves. It was also heralded when a church bell tolled from a few blocks away.

Lucas silently watched as the full machinery of police investigation into murder went to work over the body of Walter Freeleng. A team of evidence technicians scoured the pavement all around, picking through the trash that would have been Freeleng's evening meal, someone having tipped the grocery bag over. A young M.E. named Ken Whitaker had been sent by Chang's office to oversee the techs and to gather information. All this over a known murderer, Lucas thought, imagining the ironies of a thousand other cases in which authorities took less interest, time and manpower to pursue. Someone in a position of power wanted to make this important, Lucas quickly realized. Someone high up did not intend to look the other way with regard to this suspected police execution. It didn't help the shooter to have the name Lucas Stonecoat figuring squarely in the middle of it all. The question had already surfaced: *Just why were you tailing Freeleng when he was shot? What was your motive in being here when no one had assigned this as a case, Detective? Exactly what did you see when you arrived on the scene? How many bullets were fired at the deceased? Where were you and Officer Stedman at the time a single deadly shot came from the sniper-marksman? Do you know that the bullet penetrated Freeleng's brain? From which direction did the bullet come? Did you return fire?*

Standard police tactic separated Lucas from Stedman for separate interrogations to see where they differed in story. They also had to surrender their weapons for ballistic tests against the fatal shot.

From his vantage point, Lucas could not hear Stedman's answers, but they had agreed on the basics before anyone had arrived. A single shot had been fired, laying Freeleng dead in an instant. Lucas and Stedman had returned fire at a rooftop across the street, but no other shots were directed back. The assailant disappeared while Lucas and Stedman had remained on the scene, behind the cruiser, fearful of additional shots. When those shots did not materialize, Lucas rushed the building and did a search with Stedman at his back. They found no one suspicious, as the sniper had planned his getaway well.

"And on the rooftop?" pressed an IAD officer.

"Rooftop?" asked Lucas.

"Where the shots came from, did you investigate the rooftop?"

"Of course."

"And?" He was annoyed now.

"Not so much as a shell casing to look at," replied Lucas. He intended to volunteer nothing.

"Whoever did this knew enough to take the casing with him."

"Whoever did it, he was a consummate professional. Likely hired by someone else. Maybe a long-standing feud or grudge," Lucas suggested, frowning, raising his shoulders and shuffling feet as he did so.

"You don't really give a shit who killed this scumbag, do you, Detective?" the thin, no-lipped IAD officer asked point-blank.

"Why are IAD cops all over this one? No cops are involved. Neither Stedman nor I shot the bastard." Lucas added, pointing to the body as it was carried to a waiting wagon, "Who's taken such an interest?"

"Guy's shrink dropped a dime on a cop named Harbough. His client there claimed harassment and threats."

"I see. . . ." Lucas feigned ignorance.

"You know Dave Harbough, Detective?"

"Met him a short while back, yeah."

"You think he's capable of doing something this stupid?"

Lucas shook his head. "No way. Dave struck me as levelheaded. By the book, you know. You check his records?"

"We have."

"And you found?"

"Yeah, a by-the-book guy . . . like you say, levelheaded. But he's facing retirement, and we all know that does crazy things to cops. . . ."

Lucas frowned and nodded. "Still, I wouldn't judge a man by preconceived notions, Detective—Finally, is it?"

"That's right, Fennelli, Finally Fennelli, they call me."

Lucas smiled. "I can see why." Lucas stared at a man who might have worked as a clerk in a bank or as a notetaker in a college setting. Fennelli was thin, emaciated, pimply, bug-eyed with horn-rimmed glasses, a kind of Bill Gates air about him.

"Seems your week for trouble, Stonecoat. First the Kirshner shoot-out in the squad room, and now this. You always figure in the middle of people getting shot and killed?"

"I must live right."

"And as for Harbough, we both know he had some history with the deceased," finished Fennelli.

"You are pursuing other leads, aren't you? I mean anyone fresh out of the Huntsville pen has gotta have enemies. We both know anyone there with a history can be targeted by someone on the inside, or the outside."

Detective Don Fennelli jotted this down on his notepad, saying, "Sure, sure. We've given that some thought, too, my partner and me."

Fennelli's partner appeared to be through with Officer Stedman. Lucas wondered what the uniformed cop had

had to say, and if Fennelli's partner had shown any more finesse than Fennelli.

"Catch a lift back to the precinct with you, Stedman?" Lucas asked as they moved away from the Internal Affairs Division men. "Men in Black" other cops had termed them—along with many more aspersions. Lucas knew they had a difficult task, policing the police, but no matter how one looked at it, it came down to paid snitches. Still, Lucas sympathized to some degree with the likes of Fennelli, to be an outcast in the profession one had chosen, to have a gift for detection and investigation, only to have that gift utilized in such a way as to incriminate others in the profession. Must be a difficult row to hoe, he realized. What was the alternative? Some state legislature passing laws to create citizen overseers to do the job? Or worse, politicians doing the house cleaning?

Lucas and Stedman discussed the situation on the way back to the 31st. "We got a real situation here, Stonecoat."

"Agreed."

"Maybe we should locate Harbough."

"That'd be the stupidest thing we could do right now," Lucas countered. "It would establish a direct link between us, and pretty soon, you, me and Harbough are in jail for conspiracy to murder Freeleng. No, stay the hell away from Harbough altogether."

"The guy from IAD, the one interrogating me," said Stedman, his voice shaky, "he told me that nobody can account for Dave's whereabouts today. He called in with the flu."

"They're on to him, thanks to that freakin' shrink of Freeleng's. So, just go about your normal duties, and do yourself and me a favor," cautioned Lucas, "and steer clear of the man."

"Will do."

"He'll surface soon enough. Likely contact me. God knows why, but lately, I'm everybody's freakin' friend and sounding board."

"Dave's a good man, a good cop."

"Right now he's a hunted cop. Going down with him isn't something you want to do, Stedman, and it isn't anything you have to do. You had no part in what went on out there, but IAD begins to smell your sweat and to think you're too close to Harbough, they'll drag your ass and mine down with his. Trust me on that. That's what they do. They cast big nets, hoping to drag in as many fish as they can to scale and gut."

"Don't worry. I'll steer clear of Harbough."

"And should he contact you, advise him to come in of his own accord."

"I'll do that."

"And I'll do the same."

Lucas and Stedman shook on it.

Dr. Thomas W. Morrissey stepped from Meredyth Sanger's office just as Lucas arrived. Lucas had come to talk to Meredyth about the Harbough-Freeleng matter, to ask if she had any suggestions on how to deal with Harbough, should the hunted cop contact him. He knew he could trust Meredyth whatever came of the incident. But the matter had to wait once Lucas recognized Dr. Morrissey.

"Oh, Lucas, I'm so glad Randy located you. I hoped you would have the opportunity to meet Dr. Thomas W. Morrissey, whose client list reads like a murderer's row in the serial killers hall of fame."

Lucas stared for a moment at the man, a large, broad-shouldered, white-bearded man who might easily ride

Santa's sleigh in a Christmas float. He appeared too jolly
to be doing the sort of work for which he had become
famous. "So," began Lucas, "you are, or rather were, Walter Freeleng's psychiatric support, Dr. Morrissey. Appears
you've lost one."

"Among others, yes, but never lost one quite this way—
by police execution." Obviously, the grapevine worked
well within the circle of Morrissey's connected friends.
"In any event, I came to offer my full cooperation, so far
as it does not in any way corrupt the doctor-patient privilege, you see."

"Well, I'm afraid all privileges have been terminated
for Walter Freeleng, sir."

"When I first heard that Walter was in some sort of
trouble, my first assumption was that he'd no doubt been
nabbed for some minor infraction against his parole agree-
ment and whisked back to prison. Typical of the way you
people work the system."

Meredyth laughed at this. "You're telling us that we
work end runs around the system? *You*, Dr. Morrissey?"

"Tell me, Detective Stonecoat, exactly how did Freeleng die?"

Lucas assured him, "He was killed by a sniper. Someone likely had a contract out on his life. We suspect the
shooter to be a pro."

"Killed instantly?"

"Yes."

"How . . . how so. I mean precisely how?"

"A bullet to the head."

"The head, exactly as I had heard. Professionals usually
go for the head? Isn't that the surest site for instantaneous
assassination?"

"We only know a sniper shot him through the head

while he walked between a grocery store and his halfway house."

Morrissey's eyes became steely. "You mean he was *executed*, don't you. His executioner aimed for the head. Perhaps the executioner had an agenda all his own?"

"We haven't determined the motive or the killer as yet."

"So, no one in custody, no one responsible?"

"No one at this point." Lucas felt an instant dislike for the shrink and his Aristotelian interrogation. "The shooter got away and left no trace of himself."

"Yet we both know, Detective, who that man must be."

"At this point, we know nothing. IAD has suspicions, thanks to your reporting of Detective David Harbough, but at the moment, they remain merely that—suspicions."

"But you will bring this Harbough character to justice."

"It's not my case or my call, but I'm sure Detective Harbough, having made threats against your patient, a patient now dead, and a patient he had some history with, yes . . . surely, he will be interrogated."

"Freeleng was to have been a chapter in my upcoming book. Now I haven't the benefit of working with the man."

Lucas pushed closer toward the doctor's face. "Is this all a game to you, Doctor? You don't care if your patients are innocent or guilty, alive or dead, so long as they can supply fodder for your books? You learn that Freeleng did in fact do exactly what he was always suspected of, and this adds juice to your chapters, and his victims be damned?"

"I study these monsters! One day my work will be heralded as the cornerstone of understanding the criminal mind, Detective. What you and your system do here is Band-Aid practice. Catch them and put them away, and ignore the fact that more like them are being created every day in this country. My work will open the eyes of law enforcement and criminal psychiatry. We may perhaps step into the twenty-second century with some modicum of understanding of the nature of evil."

"You don't see your own evil part in any of this, do you, Dr. Morrissey?" said Meredyth, standing now alongside Lucas, presenting a united front.

"Mygod what *isit-withyou* people? I came here in the spirit of cooperation. Gave you the names of all my patients, *anyoneofwhom* might . . . That is as much as I can do for you, given the doctor-patient-contract, which I will break for no one. Now, if you will excuse me, I have a group session I wish not to be late for."

Lucas did not move aside for the older man. "Sir, you speak of ethics, but what sort of ethics is it that holds your tongue in matters of murder?"

"I haven't time for a lecture here on how current codes of conduct and so-called ethics and mores fail to take in cultural, socioeconomic and personal concerns, Detective. Now let me pass." He pushed past them.

"Our primary duty, Dr. Morrissey, is to protect the public, not the individual," said Meredyth.

Turning back toward her, Morrissey asked, "Do you plan to bring me up on state censure issues? *Principle* ethics include approaches that focus on the use of rational, objective, universal, and impartial principles in the analysis of ethical dilemmas. This one"—he pointed to Lucas—"he doesn't even know what I have just said. And you, Doctor, you live in a police-state mentality I abhor. *Principle* ethics, my dear, that is how I work, and you know this. Situation by situation, I work."

"I would hope you would not limit your behavior, sir,

to obeying statutes and following ethical standards, but develop a sensitivity to doing what is best not only for your clients, but for the city at large, the *place* in which you practice," suggested Meredyth.

"The basic purpose of practicing ethically is to promote the welfare of the client, not the society he finds himself in," countered Morrisey.

"But the law reflects the minimum standards that society will tolerate," replied Meredyth.

"And your mythical ethical code merely represents the ideal standard set by the profession, as utopian as . . . as Walden Pond."

"There are *mandatory* ethics, Dr. Morrissey. Should you break them, I will have you up on charges."

He looked Lucas squarely in the face now, his own features displaying puzzlement. "Do you see what I must contend with? Imagine it! I can find myself in an ethical quagmire based on competing role expectations—am I the man's doctor, or am I an officer of the court? Only a focus on the best interest of the client, provable either way, will enable me to maintain a clear, ethical position."

Morrissey grew in stature as he puffed himself up, turned and walked away, his expensive Irish cane with a jeweled knob tapping an anthem as he retreated.

"How'd you get the good doctor to come in?" asked Lucas.

"Wasn't easy. Repeated phone calls and threats."

"What did you get from the blowhard?"

"Not much . . . just as he said, his patient list."

"All these possibles for us—in a city of possibles. We don't even know that the Scalper is among them. Did he name Freeleng in the Kensington beheading?"

"No, he claims Freeleng could not possibly have killed

Laurel. He wouldn't release even public records on his
patients but I can get hold of court records on all of them.
We can begin to study them for anything that might
smack of the Scalper and our beheader, such as any
having rappelling as a hobby. Who knows? We might get
lucky. Sorry, but we can't order the man to release his
notes and records on his patients. Only *he* can do that."

"But he is bound by law."

"Bound only if he knows for a certainty that his patient
is a danger to himself or others."

"They're all in Morrissey's care?"

"In group therapy and individual therapy."

"Group therapy? All at his office?"

"At the halfway house, where Freeleng had been resid-
ing."

Lucas asked, "Suppose the patient is a danger to the
therapist himself?"

"We can only hope," replied Meredyth. She turned and
grabbed a piece of paper from her desk.

A note written in scratchy longhand by Dr. Morrissey
had been attached to the list of names. Lucas scanned it
and then said, "Did you read this? Listen to this."

Meredyth had read it, and she now looked on statuelike
as Lucas read the note aloud:

Police are ridiculous in suspecting Walter Freeleng
for the beheading murder of Laurel Kensington. The
man could not have committed the crime. He had
such debilitating arthritis in his hands that he could
not so much as clench his fists, let alone rappel
down a rope and hang outside a forty-story building
while cutting a laser hole into a window. In my
office, he demonstrated quite graphically the pain

caused in simply lifting a chair. His hands were useless, contorted in pain.

Lucas thought of the repercussions this would have for
Dave Harbough, and how he himself had been convinced
that Freeleng murdered Laurel Kensington. Lucas recalled
for a moment the anguish of her father, and he also wondered how Dr. Morrissey had come by so many of the
particulars of the Kensington case. He immediately wondered aloud, "Did you discuss the details of the Kensington case with Morrissey?"

"He came in knowing as much as we do about the case,
Lucas. Why?"

"Has he been in touch with the M.E.'s office? Given
his status in the system, Chang would hardly deny him
access to the records, I suppose. Though Chang would
also have been kept busy by the senator's people, I'm
sure."

"Morrissey said nothing of the kind. Volunteers very
little, actually. What little he did say was just talk, no
substance."

"What *did* he say?"

"Like I said, very little. Kept falling back on doctor-
patient privilege, as you heard in the doorway."

"So, maybe he's simply been told about the situation,
word for word, out of the mouth of the killer himself, one
of the men on his patient list?"

"It begins to feel like Morrissey's playing games with
you, doesn't it, Detective?" asked Meredyth.

"So, what next?" asked Lucas.

"Subpoena all documents on these names."

"Yeah, see what shakes out if we rustle the nut tree."

"Lucas, I want to tell you again how sorry I am about

your grandfather," she said taking his hands in hers. "I know how very close you two were. I wish I could have been there with you through this difficult time."

"It . . . it was hard, but now the old man's spirit is free. He is where he wants to be."

Meredyth opened her arms and pulled him to her, giving Lucas a warm hug. Lucas luxuriated in her hold and touch for as long as she deemed proper. When she pulled away, giving him a bright smile, she said, "I met your cousin today."

"Cousin by marriage?"

"Tsalie . . ."

"When, I mean how?"

"She showed up downstairs in search of you. Said she wanted to check on your progress since the funeral. Sounded quite concerned, Lucas. You were out, and while I offered her the opportunity to wait up here, she seemed in a hurry, nervous even. Maybe you should give her a call."

"Yeah, I'll . . . I'll do that."

"Extremely pretty, Lucas."

"Yes, yes. We grew up together."

"Oh, really? Childhood sweethearts?"

"Something like that."

"But she married your cousin."

"Right . . . right . . . You want to tell me why I'm here?"

"That's been satisfied, Lucas. I wanted you to meet Morrissey, but there's more. Hang on."

Meredyth, knowing Lucas felt uncomfortable speaking of Tsalie, knowing him to be the master of deflecting thorny problems, turned to her desk and shouted into her intercom for her private-duty assistant. "Randy! I need you in here."

Lucas stepped a little away from Meredyth as Randy Oglesby came through the door asking, "Yes?"

She looked at the patient list and extended it to Randy. "Run these names through our files, and get court records on each. After that, run their MOs against the Scalper case and Laura Kensington's killer. After that, draw up a sub-poena request for any of the names that smells and hand deliver it to Judge Rutherford Frye."

"Fry-'em-High Frye, right . . . Right on it," replied Randy who had overheard some of the argumentative confrontation during Morrissey's departure. "I think that old fart, Morrissey, is a real dick."

"Your powers of observation, Randy," replied Meredyth, "never cease to amaze."

Several hours had passed when Randy called Meredyth and Lucas back to his office. Lucas now paced the room pantherlike, while awaiting Meredyth's return. Finally he grabbed the list of names that Randy had whittled down to three possible suspects. It read:

Lester Franklin Wilcox
Jared Oliver Wendell
Stanley Theopolis Garrette

"I could get photos of each of the suspects," Randy added, "but it'll take time."

"Do that, Randy, and get them down to me as quickly as possible," replied Lucas.

"In the meantime I'll get warrants for arrest drawn up for each of them," suggested Meredyth.

"I'm going to Judge Frye anyway. Let me handle the

warrants as well," Randy suggested. "You can both get some much needed rest."

Meredyth clenched her hands together and added, "I hate Morrissey's stand on ethics in our profession. I've had dealings with similar types who abuse their power. A man like Morrissey—so needed by the system—may easily fall into the trap of thinking himself to be an untouchable."

"Above the law, you mean?"

"Above it all."

"Above what all?"

"You, me, society, rules, regs, morals, values, laws, man-made or divine."

"You think that's where Morrissey sits now, today?"

"From what I have observed of the man, on interview shows, and from what I've gleaned from reading his books, and now on meeting him face-to-face, yes."

"Then this whole charade of coming in and handing us his most-likely-to-scalp-or-behead-a-woman list . . . you think he's yanking our collective chain? Toying with law enforcement, playing puppeteer or something to the system?"

"He may genuinely fear these three men himself. He may find it useful for you to concentrate on them, throw a little fear into them. You know, work the system as only Morrissey can," she suggested.

"Use *us*, you mean . . ."

"Precisely."

"I see."

"That's not to say that one or more of the two killers you are looking for, the Beheader and the Scalper aren't among these men. From the records so far, they may well be the best leads you have."

"So, we pick up Wendell's ass for interrogation in the scalping murders or the beheadings or both. Then we proceed from there. See what he knows about these other two."

"Shake that tree," agreed Meredyth, "but why begin with Wendell?"

"I met that little weasel when Freeleng was killed. Guy's going to be easy to turn."

Lucas raised his hands as if caught in a checkmate. "I'll arrange it. Meanwhile, get whatever documents you can out of the courts and from Morrissey's files."

"We're on it," Randy assured Lucas.

Lucas went for the door and waved a perfunctory goodbye. "Thank you for the sympathy on the passing of my grandfather," he said to Meredyth before stepping out. "It means a great deal to me."

Randy exchanged a look of resignation with Meredyth. "He doesn't mean to be so cold. It just comes with the territory. Look at it this way: First he's a stony Indian personality, next the cop veneer is put on and he's got this machismo thing going atop that, so . . . Well, what can we mere mortals expect from him in the way of feelings?"

"He's torn up inside, Randy." She thought of Tsalie, wondering if Lucas were in love with the woman. "That's obvious."

"It is?"

"To me, it is."

"Well, guess that's why you pull down the big bucks, Doc."

ELEVEN

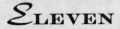

Deer tracks: ample game

Later in the day, Meredyth had called Lucas back to her office where Randy had arranged for Chinese takeout. Together, the three ate and discussed their latest findings.

"This creep Jared Oliver Wendell is a real piece of work," said Lucas. "First rape and murder at age thirteen. Slipped into a neighbor's house, raped and bludgeoned a nine-year-old girl to death. Got out on his twenty-fifth birthday, a changed man—all rehabilitated. Returned for attempted rape at knifepoint a year later. Now out at age thirty—as a model prisoner."

Meredyth flipped through one of the printouts Randy had brought in, and read: "Wilcox, Lester Franklin, age thirty-two, juvenile offender at age eleven, first arrested for decapitating a neighbor's dog after beating the dog senseless with a hammer. He went on from there to burglary, rape, and by the time he was of age to stand trial for adult crimes, he had in fact killed and decapitated a prostitute, taking the head with him. Authorities located the head in his bedroom. He'd been using it as a sex toy since the killing."

"Ugh!" groaned Randy.

"Paroled twenty years later, he is now a rehabilitated man," commented Lucas, scanning a sheet Meredyth had handed him. "Has worked a number of odd jobs, including that of a steelworker, which gives him experience negotiating high-rise construction sites."

"Bingo! That ought to help with getting those warrants," Meredyth replied.

Annoyed, Lucas asked, "What's been the holdup with the paperwork?"

"No Judge Frye. The man suffered a heart attack. In the hospital for now," she said, holding a separate fact sheet on Stanley Theopolis Garrette. From this she read, "Garrette's crimes involved torturing his victims while still alive. He cut off body parts, the genitalia to be exact. Never worked up to the hands. He collected the parts in jars, all found in his basement freezer when authorities finally caught up to him. Released as a model prisoner seven months ago into the care of Dr. Thomas W. Morrissey. On parole for life, he could go back for any infraction." She stopped reading, looked up at Lucas and added, "Garrette has broken parole in Morrissey's presence, carrying a concealed weapon into office visits, but Morrissey says this occurs more often than not with his patients."

"That's reason enough to return them to jail."

"The doctor says he would refuse to press charges for what he calls a patient's security blanket."

"Some security blanket," said Randy, smirking.

Lucas sat up. "Morrissey told you this man, Wendell,

violated his probation? Why didn't you tell me this sooner? It could simplify our righteous-arrest problem. We could fashion a warrant around this, predicate the arrest on the basis of—"

"Can't do it on the basis of what Morrissey has told me, Lucas. It doesn't work that way."

"What the hell are you talking about, Meredyth?"

"What he told me, he told me in confidence. We can't simply arrest Garrette, Wilcox or Wendell on hearsay, and I'm not testifying against a confidence."

"Why not?"

"I'm no Linda Tripp. Besides, Morrissey will deny ever having said it."

"What did he tell you about the other two? Anything that might help out here?"

"Same thing. All three carry some sort of weapon into their sessions as a safety valve, as Morrissey puts it. Morrissey is proud of the fact that he allows it—says it's part of their therapy."

"Then why not simply snatch the bastards coming or going to Morrissey's office, and return them to the pen for weapons violation of parole?"

"Or rather for interrogation first. Throw a scare into the three of them, maybe get 'em talking?" suggested Randy, which made the two police professionals stare for a moment at the civilian staffer.

"It could mean better closure on a case," added Meredyth. "Involve the parole officers. Get the officers to make a spot shakedown on the street outside Morrissey's office. He finds the weapons violation, not us."

"You want to know what makes these guys tick before you send 'em away, huh?" asked Lucas. "Seems a fine line between Morrissey's game and yours, no disrespect intended, Doctor . . ."

"Just throwing one or more of these guys back into prison for the sake of getting them off the street won't guarantee that you have the right man behind bars, Lieutenant," Meredyth defended.

"Dr. Sanger's right, Lucas."

"Yeah, when she's right, she's right." He pushed the container of sweet and sour pork and the chow mein away, snatched open a fortune cookie and read to himself: *An arresting moment in your life is on its way.* . . . It gave Lucas a laugh. He left the opened message behind, chewing on the cookie as he went. He knew the message would be read in his absence, and that Meredyth and Randy would also get a laugh from the prophetic words.

Lucas had three arrests to arrange. Perhaps he could enlist Officer Stedman's aid, along with a few other uniforms. He, too, thought it would be best if someone other than himself did the actual interrogation of the suspects since he could too easily become a target of the litigious Dr. Morrissey at this point. He could think of no better officers than the female detective team of Lynn Blanton and Sandra Offiah for this task. The strongest of the strong and the most arrogant of the arrogant withered before these two lady detectives. Lucas had seen them at work on several occasions.

Lucas went about setting his plan in motion. He'd begin with Jared Oliver Wendell, the bony punk that spewed forth such venom from the relative safety of the halfway house steps when Freeleng had been shot. The scarecrow man would fall apart like straw under intense interrogation, Lucas believed. He would stop Wendell on the street, hoping to discover a knife or other weapon on him, which would allow police to hold him for as long as they deemed necessary.

Returning to his office in the Cold Room, Lucas found a message on his desk, a simple scribble of a telephone number without explanation. He didn't know the number or who had left it. Curious, he dialed.

A gruff voice answered, stating two words, "Recycled Cowboys."

"Recycled who?"

"You got the bar, man. What can I do for you?"

Lucas realized it must be Dave Harbough who had gotten the message to him. "This is Lieutenant Lucas Stonecoat. Is Dave Harbough there?"

"You got it! Dave!" the bartender shouted. "Somebody here for you, name of Stonecoat? You wanna talk to him?"

Harbough came on the line, asking, "Is it true, Lucas?"

"Is what true, Dave?"

"That Freeleng's been cleared on the voiceprint? That he had crippling arthritis in his hands? That the bastard couldn't't'a possibly done Laurel Kensington?"

"Who told you all this, Dave?"

"I ran into Doc Residual."

"Morrissey? Where?"

"He said Leonard Chang would back him on the arthritis. Is it true?"

"Yeah, all true, Dave, but—"

"Then I *kilt* the sonofabitch for . . . for the wrong reasons?"

Lucas hesitated answering. Harbough sounded more drunk than usual. "Freeleng . . . he deserved what he got,

Dave. We both know that, regardless of what Morrissey fed you. How did Morrissey find you, Dave?"

"He didn't find me. I found him!"

For a moment Dave's old fire sounded through the line. "Caught him on his rounds at that damned halfway house. Wanted him to know I did Freeleng. Wanted to rub it in."

"Are you crazy, Dave?"

"Crazy . . . old . . . tired . . . tired of the bullshit system that allows these freaks a revolving door . . ."

"Dave, you gotta turn yourself in to me, Dave."

"You tell them it was me on the roof, Lucas?"

"No, Dave . . . I didn't."

"Thanks, Lucas. That's all I wanted to know."

"Dave, IAD's been turning this town upside down looking for you, you know that? They suspect you, because Morrissey's told them of your threats against Freeleng. Everybody knew you hated the SOB. Was it you on that rooftop?"

"I'll deal with IAD, Lucas. You steer clear . . . of me. They'll think . . . you had nothing to do with it."

"Dave! Listen to me. Best thing you can do at this point is come in. Turn yourself in, Dave . . . Dave!"

But Lucas was now speaking to a dead line.

Lucas dialed for dispatch to locate the address of Recycled Cowboys. Armed with it, he rushed to Harbough's aid, disregarding the advice he'd given Stedman and the advice Harbough had just given him. He couldn't simply sit back and steer clear. He feared Dave would get into a shooting match with IAD should they approach him. The man was on the edge. Maybe he wanted IAD to take him out in a hail of gunfire.

Lucas raced across the city, lights flashing. When he got to the bar, he pulled up onto the curb across the street, leapt from his seat and began crossing when he saw Harbough step from the bar. Two IAD men, Fennelli and Hill, approached Dave with guns raised, considering him armed and dangerous.

Harbough was ordered to assume the position. Instead, he pulled his weapon and swallowed the barrel. Lucas screamed out his name the same instant the blast took Harbough's face away.

Lucas went to his knees, crying out the single, useless wailing, *"Noooooooooo!"*

Lucas, still mourning the death of yet another police friend, stared down at photos of his three most likely perpetrators of the Scalper crimes and the more recent Beheading crime. He still had no warrants as yet. He had decided to take them out one at a time, not Dave Harbough fashion, but quickly and by the book.

He had the halfway house staked out from a safe distance, using a van from the motor pool. When he spotted Jared Oliver Wendell returning from a morning stroll, he approached the little man who panicked. The arrest quickly turned into a circus in front of the halfway house. Lucas and a handful of plainclothes detectives had to bodily lift a raging, kicking Wendell off his feet and put him into the van for questioning downtown. During the scuffle, Wendell's knife fell from its moorings inside his jacket, a six-inch blade rivaling Lucas's own bowie knife.

Wendell kept screaming out, "Dr. Morrissey set this up, didn't he? Dr. Morrissey never liked me! He always picks on me!"

Arriving at the station house, Wendell became belligerent, defiant, his tone completely different than the sniveling, childlike behavior exhibited on the street. "I know my rights. I am a citizen. I have paid my debt to society. I hold you responsible for this travesty of justice, this . . . this rush to judgment against me, Lieutenant!"

"You remember me then?" asked Lucas.

"You were one of the men involved in Freeleng's murder, and now you want to see me murdered. You all want to kill every one of us living in the halfway house. You have some twisted belief that no one can be rehabilitated, but you are wrong, Lieutenant Stonecoat. I am living proof that a man can change."

"Hell, you got that right," replied Lucas, cuffing him and forcing him through the doors of Precinct 31. "You *change* with the wind, little man."

The duty sergeant, seeing Lucas enter with the prisoner, asked, "Stonecoat, whataya got there?"

"Book this for interrogation, Sarge. Parole violation. Carrying a six-inch blade, and we know he knows something about the Scalper case."

"The Scalper case. Wow! Still, he'll have to go to holding, Lieutenant."

"No. No way . . . I need an interrogation of this piece of . . . this suspect—now."

"Did you fill out a 1916-*form-J* for the space?"

"Christ, Sergeant."

"All the rooms are full, Lieutenant."

"Call Captain Lincoln. God . . ."

"Lincoln's out, a fund-raiser the mayor's office is running."

"Christ. Look, Sandra Offiah and Lynn Blanton are set up to interrogate this suspect."

"You shitting me?"

"No, no shit, Sarge."

"Did you arrange it with Lieutenant Offiah?"

"Said they'd be here when I needed them."

"Yeah, some team they are, huh? Like *Cagney and Lacy*, them two."

"That's the buzz."

"I'll buzz 'em, see if they're willing to forego . . ."

"Do that, and thanks."

Just as Offiah and Blanton came from one of the interrogation rooms, Officer Stedman suddenly stood before Lucas, his face twitching. "We managed to get Dave killed, the two of us."

Lucas pulled Stedman aside, shushing him. It proved already too late. The two female interrogators, who were something of a legend in the precinct for getting results, now whispered back and forth with the duty sergeant.

Lucas chastised Stedman loudly, for all to hear, for his reckless words. "The hell with your bullshit, Stedman! We didn't kill Dave Harbough. He fucking killed himself. I was there. He blew himself away after drinking himself into a stupor. We did everything we could to help Harbough."

An agitated Stedman replied, "You told me to steer clear of Harbough and the whole affair. I did, and now he's blown his head off."

"You want IAD to finger you as some sort of accomplice in what he did?"

"He ate his gun, Lieutenant. He ate his gun, and you and me and all his friends, we let it happen."

"We did all we could. I tried to reason with him, but—"

Stedman rushed off without another word.

Lucas leaned against the wall, paralyzed for a moment. "Sonofabitch." He groaned and recalled how Kim Desinor had told him to beware, that death rode like a demonic gargoyle on his shoulder. Maybe she had been right.

"Been to too many funerals lately," he muttered.

"We got your man, Lucas," said Sandra Offiah.

"We'll get to him tomorrow," said Lynn Blanton.

The duty sergeant added, "We can hold your man on the weapons violation for a couple of days, Stonecoat. He ain't going anywhere."

Lucas realized the whole deal was queered by Stedman's untimely remarks. He silently cursed the delay.

THE FOLLOWING DAY IN MEREDYTH SANGER'S OFFICE

Texas Senator Kensington wanted movement in the case. He wanted answers to the questions plaguing him since the day he saw his child's head staring back at him from her mantel. He had been on the phone with the governor's office, the governor went to the mayor, the mayor to the commissioner, and the commissioner to Captain Gordon J. Lincoln. Pressure was on to solve the killing of the senator's little girl, and the rest be damned. Both Lucas and Meredyth Sanger had heard it from Lincoln in a less than pleasing tone. And it came clear on the six o'clock news why Jared Oliver Wendell had been held overnight; it was so that Lincoln could announce that a suspect in the death of the senator's daughter was indeed in custody. It had all been worked out between Lincoln and the booking sergeant, that the first announcement of anyone arrested in connection with the case be held overnight before interrogation. It did not matter who it might be.

Randy stepped into Meredyth Sanger's office with her coffee and an armload of computer printouts, saying, "By the way, not much has come of the matching and cross-referencing on the MO used in the Kensington murder, but bits and pieces of his MO have come up."

"Bits and pieces? As in body parts?" The grim cop humor that Randy didn't expect to hear from his boss gave him pause, but he could think of no reply to it. Instead he replied, "No one killer has ever, you know, done all three at once, that is beheading, gutting and stuffing the victim's stomach with a burning candle."

"But you've had matches . . . in pieces?"

"Of course. Lots of beheadings over the past few years, and plenty of guttings, but only one candle burning in a disemboweled victim. Killer was caught, though, and put away. Name was Gerald Lamar Jessup. Typical profile: white, middle class, married with children."

"Let me see what you have there on this creep."

Randy handed over the information. He had run an intensive search both through the police computer and the FBI's violent offenders file in Washington, D.C. "This includes FBI, state and local records," he added.

Meredyth scanned what Randy had learned about the uncommonly and singular modus operandi belonging to Laurel Kensington's killer. The killer named Jessup and another with similar tastes was a man named Brent Cobb. In the case of Cobb, this was a man who finished off a long night of torturing the victim with knife cuts to the entire body, bleeding the victim into weakness just before finally disemboweling. He always carried a large candle with him, forced it into the open wound at the gut, lit it and watched it burn for hours while he sat staring at his "flaming art" as he later referred to it in official documents.

She read that this occurred in Florida, the Orlando area.

She wondered if it were mere coincidence that the time coincided with what a psychiatrist friend of hers had told her of a similar Scalper case that had occurred at very nearly the same time and vicinity. She had put out a computer request of her own among psychiatrists across the country via a Web site for shrinks.

It felt strangely odd somehow to have both a candle-burner and the Scalper here in her Texas metropolis, as if there must be some sort of connection. Still, both Jessup and Cobb had gotten life without the possibility of parole. Jessup had been knifed in a prison shower where he'd been allowed to bleed to death. Cobb had had a similar fate outside in broad daylight in the prison yard. Such lifers with histories of violence against women seldom lived out their appointed sentences, so hated were they among inmates in the general population. Since both of these men had carved up their victims, their demise seemed fitting ends. Those facts also proved dead ends for Meredyth Sanger in Houston, Texas, today.

"Meanwhile, what else have you learned in the cross-checks on our case?" asked Lucas, his disembodied voice sending a slight shiver through Randy who—staring about the office—replied, "Detective? Where are you?" His eyes lit on the intercom, but he saw no blipping light.

Lucas lifted his head over the black leather sofa where he'd been catching some rest and listening in on the phone conversation between Meredyth and Dr. Richard Ames, and before that she'd been on with Dr. Thomas Morrissey's secretary. Meredyth had requested copies of Morrissey's files on Lester Franklin Wilcox, Jared Oliver Wendell and Stanley Theopolis Garrette. The secretary had refused. Meredyth threatened a court order, but nothing had moved the woman on the other end.

"I didn't know you were here, Lucas," began Randy, confused. "I didn't see you come in."

"Arrived before you this morning," Lucas replied without further explanation.

Meanwhile, Meredyth had stood and come around her desk, extending the Cobb file to Lucas. "Flaming Art Killer," she informed him. "You might just want to have a look at this one."

Randy stood smiling at the two, detective and psychiatrist, as if he wanted to take a picture. When they noticed his attention, he stammered, "Nice to . . . to see you two . . . getting along again. Kind of like old times."

"Randy is overwhelmed, Lucas," Meredyth said, smiling. "He can't recall ever feeling so much peace in this office while you and I have occupied it together. You're likely wondering," she said to Randy, "if we have somehow worked out our differences, right, Randy?"

And the obvious sexual tension between us, Lucas thought but did not say.

Indeed, Randy wondered if they may have consummated their relationship through some intimacy, perhaps last night on the very couch where Lucas still lay; or perhaps it had been the night that she so needed consoling when her friend had been found murdered. His eyes alone voiced these conclusions. "Glad to see you two getting along so well," Randy said matter-of-factly. "Maybe this means my job will be that much easier and securer?"

"Are you sure there's nothing more on the cross-checks?" asked Lucas.

"Anything else of significant interest, Randy?" added Meredyth, both of them now ignoring Randy's curiosity.

"Yeah, one thing did strike me. The Headless Horseman angle, all that, and now this sudden cat-burglar entrance for the Horseman? It doesn't figure. Anyway, searching through all the head-chopping going on around this country, I found nothing significantly similar. Except for our earlier Houston headhunter guy who, according to some, was Freeleng, and according to some was never apprehended. Just suppose . . . I mean, imagine if Freeleng was never the guy!"

"It was Freeleng, all right," Lucas countered, sitting up. "I'd bet my badge on that one."

Meredyth said, "I know you feel some loyalty to Dave Harbough's memory, Lucas, but—"

"He may not have killed Laurel Kensington, but Dave Harbough had him pegged correctly as the Horseman, and he was put away for his last attempted beheading. That much the Cold Room file on the case told me."

Randy and Meredyth exchanged a quick glance. Randy finally said, "Any rate, I also scanned for matches with the Scalper dude, and, man, that's like the rarest of rare. Something back in the early eighties in and around Winter Park, Florida, pursued by a Dr. Dean Grant in a case he had written up about—"

"Winter Park? That's like part of Orlando, and the other guy was also in Orlando?" Meredyth added. "That's the case Richard Ames E-mailed me about. That struck me earlier as odd, the two cases being out of Florida."

"Florida's full of weird," said Lucas.

Randy added, "I didn't know Winter Park was near Orlando, but there was like this series of bloody, nasty scalpings that also included some skinning of the victims. Two killers involved, one a normal-sized guy, but the brains of the outfit turned out to be this weird-assed midget."

"Midget?" asked Lucas, bolting upright, curious.

"They prefer the term Little People," replied Meredyth.

"You got it, a Little People–person turned out to be doing the skinning and scalping. And he wasn't Native American, Lucas," Randy said this last part as if it were about winning a lottery. "Reports say the little guy turned out to be the dominant one of the duo, if you can believe it. The normal-sized guy was killed in pursuit. The little man was believed killed, but his body was never recovered."

"Never recovered?"

"Lost him in an alligator-infested swamp. An autopsy of a gator, believed to have swallowed the midget whole—"

Lucas interrupted with helpless laughter. Randy cleared his throat and went on, "Autopsy only proved they cut open the wrong gator, according to Dr. Grant, medical examiner for Chicago on lease to the Orlando authorities at the time. By the way, the Scalpers in this instance were both male and both white middle-aged men, but a clamor was up that it was likely a Native American. So . . . now we got a repeat going, maybe? Got any midgets in the picture?"

"History repeats herself again," added Lucas. "Whoever came through that window was light, was small in stature, I'd guess. Though no midget—ahhh, Little Person."

"Anything from forensics?" asked Meredyth.

"Nothing useful as yet. Usual hair, fiber evidence. Of course, no match to pin the stuff on the donkey, you know."

"As far as the taking of hands . . . there was this interesting case in Chicago in the same time period or pretty close, the late eighties, that is," said Randy, handing over another file.

"See what you can do about going over the complete list of Dr. Morrissey's current, violent criminal-patients, Randy. See if any of them are from Florida, specifically the Orlando area, and underscore any unusual heights and weights. Maybe this is about weights and measures in some weird sorta way. And thanks," finished Meredyth.

"Sure . . . I'll just leave you two ahhh . . . alone," Randy replied, a half grin creasing his features as he left.

"What do you suppose that was all about?" asked Meredyth of Lucas.

"I think, but don't quote me, he thinks that we, that you and I are . . . well, involved on a deeper level now."

"What?"

"That we're, you know, intimate."

"How? Where did he get that idea?"

"Search me."

"Because you're on my couch before office hours?"

"Don't ask me. I certainly didn't send him any signals."

"Well, neither did I."

Lucas laughed and said, "By noon, he'll have us married if we're not careful."

She only stared in response.

Lucas's laughter now broke into an uncontrolled howl, a sound as wild as that of a wolf. He then stood and waved good-bye to her, disappearing through the door.

After Randy and Lucas had left her office, Meredyth began studying the last file Randy had handed her. In it she found several unusual coincidences between the eighties hand-taking killer of Chicago and their current Houston mutilator. It was a case that her friend and colleague, Dr. Richard Ames, had been a psychiatric consult on. It also involved Dr. Dean Grant, as had the Scalper case in Florida. She immediately again rang Ames in Chicago, telling him of her interest in both cases.

"Yes, well, the Florida Scalper and the Chicago Handyman . . . cases, hmmmm? Why would you be interested in such an odd set of old cases? It's ancient history. . . ." Meredyth Sanger thought Dr. Richard Ames of Chicago sounded angry for being asked to answer questions regarding these cases, and yet he had come to her upon seeing a call she had put out on the World Wide Web about cases involving hand-taking, scalpings and beheadings. But he'd said nothing to her about the hand-taking case.

She had known Richard Ames for many years, and while they were not the best of friends, they were friendly and saw one another frequently at conventions and national conferences on crime.

"You came to me, remember, Richard? Now, what can you tell me about my problem here in Houston? You have any notions why some sick bastard would be interested in scalps and hands?"

"Are you sure you are not simply baiting me, Dr. Sanger?"

What the hell is he talking about? she wondered. "What the hell are you talking about?" she finally chose to say, wondering why he sounded so defensive, as if fending off some ugly rumor or still uglier truth.

Silence answered her.

"Is there a problem, Richard?"

Ames finally admitted, "I still have fucking nightmares about the Handyman case."

"I'm sorry, Richard, I didn't know."

He added, "At the time, Dr. Dean Grant was the

Chicago medical examiner, and he was chiefly responsible. . . . That is . . . he was in charge of the Handyman case."

Why the hell is he talking like Johnnie Cochran? "Grant, of course, Dean Grant. I've read his recently published memoirs—*Life in Death's Shadow*. Remarkable memoir."

"And a remarkable man."

"Agreed."

She heard Ames light up a cigarette at his end and begin puffing. Ames continued, "Well, then . . . if you're familiar with his book, you may want to read his chapter on the Handyman case. It's detailed. Obviously Grant has long since retired. He's touring the country now, speaking of his various cases, promoting his volume two now, taking full advantage of America's love affair with serial killers and the oft macabre world of forensic medicine. And people love him for his own story—that he beat cancer."

"Really? Touring for his book, you say?"

"Fact is, he recently visited your city of Houston just—"

"Really? When?"

"Only months ago, maybe four. Was well publicized, Meredyth."

Meredyth now recalled having heard of Grant's appearance before a crowd of hundreds at a medical convention at the Hyatt Regency. Ames filled in the particulars of Dr. Dean Grant's visit.

She replied with a weak, "Oh, yes, I recall now, but I failed to make it."

"Too bad. He puts on quite a one-man show."

"I was embroiled you might say with the James Renquist affair."

"Renquist? Local business?"

"Could say that. Fellow was a cop, killed his wife and two kiddies, boiled them in water in a huge vat in his basement, cut them into chunks and served them as appetizer and main course at a function to raise money for the retired police fund here in Houston. Took a while before anyone knew they were consuming human flesh."

"Eeeek," replied Ames. "Think I did hear something of that mischief."

"Said Renquist was the best fund-raiser they ever had when all was said and done. He netted several thousand that same day. Anyway, since I was called into the psychiatric evalution, I missed seeing Grant's . . . ahhh—"

"Performance, show? You can call it what you will, but Meredyth, perhaps someone else did succeed in making the circus that day. . . . Or rather, from a loser's point of view, did not fail to make it."

"Meaning?"

"Dean Grant's been speaking out about the Handyman case and the Scalper case in some detail. These were, after all, two of his most high-profile cases. You are calling me regarding the murders there in Houston, asking about the Handyman case, and you mentioned the Scalper case in Florida, so I am assuming victims have had their hands and scalps removed? But that's not the way the Handyman worked. He scalped no one."

"He? Is he still alive?"

"Still in maximum security, state penitentiary for the criminally insane. One reason Saylor, the Handyman, remains alive today is that he is legitimately insane. So he's not in a prison yard where other inmates can get at him."

"I see."

Ames continued, puffing on his cigarette between

pauses. "I did a study on the man. Name was Morgan Saylor. As balmy as they come."

"I see . . ."

"Do you? I'm saying that perhaps your killer had a front row seat at one of Grant's . . . performances."

"You sound a bit disdainful of Grant."

Ames sighed heavily into the phone. "We were once good friends, worked closely on a number of cases. Just seems a sideshow, this thing he's doing now. Dean does a lot of grisly show-and-tell . . . if you know what I mean. . . ."

"You mean he uses a lot of props?"

"Props, instruments, reenactments, simulations, you name it. Attracts all sorts of weirdos."

"I see, of course. . . ."

Ames further suggested, "You might want to get any surveillance tapes made at that speech, have a close scrutiny done."

"Brilliant deduction. So, our killer is in the audience listening to Dean Grant's most spectacular case files, and the crazy decides it might be fun to mimic these earlier grisly cases of Grant's? Is that what you're saying?"

"It's only a guess, an educated one, but a guess nonetheless. Still, it stands to reason . . ."

She quickly agreed, setting Ames somewhat at ease. "Makes some logical sense, Richard."

"Indeed, since two of the chief components of your killer's MO are items found in earlier cases belonging to Chicago's chief medical examiner, who coincidentally visited his little circus of horrors on your town recently."

"Don't misunderstand, Richard, we have two separate killers, using two separate MOs. You see, one is scalping and claiming hands, the other is lopping off heads."

"I see."

"Tell me, do you know the work of Dr. Thomas William Morrissey, Richard?"

"Who doesn't? He's almost as well known in the profession as M. Scott Peck, 'cept he's weird. . . ."

"Can you picture him studying Dr. Dean Grant's cases and then feeding such information to a psychotic patient, a killer?" asked Meredyth.

"I wouldn't put it past the man, no. In his mind, it would be homework."

"Homework?"

"You know, after sessions . . . Give the patient busywork, something to do physically to work on his problems."

"Homework," she repeated. "Homework for a sociopath . . ."

"He tries to get the patient to look closely—nose in the dirt—at the very thing he is . . . You see, to stare into the abyss of himself, so to speak."

"To look unerringly at the mutilations and lust-murders committed by other socios?"

"You got it."

Meredyth had kept such a vile suspicion to herself until now, but she knew that Ames could keep a confidence. "We're looking at Morrissey's patient list as our most likely suspects," she explained. "You see, we have something even more unusual going on here, and there might be a tenuous link."

"I see. Tell me about it."

She did so, bringing Ames up to speed on the Beheader and the Scalper.

Ames agreed with her theory, after some long thought,

saying, "There is indeed something strange in the cases, strangely coincidental. Not only the fact that both are occurring at the same juncture, but that each killer's MO is such a complex ritual."

"It screams of two distinct killers at ease with themselves. Two killers who had perfected a ritual so well that boredom may have set in, causing a need for a new high, a new ripple-effect in the pond where this scum resides. Just strange to have two such practiced serial killers at work at the same time in the same localized vicinity. Wouldn't you agree?"

"Something odd indeed, something . . ." he jokingly said, "I can't quite put my hands precisely on, but it makes my throat hurt, my wrists hurt and my scalp tingle."

"Me, too, if it's any consolation."

"You have a maniac who is taking scalps and hands on the one hand—no pun intended—heads, disemboweling and burning candles in the cavity of the stomach on the other hand. Quite a mix."

"We think so."

"Two separate, distinct serial killers working simultaneously in the same territory. Unusual . . . at least in my admittedly limited experience. But this dual kill spree could work in your favor once you get a fix on the perpetrators. Have you asked yourself whether the two know of each other?"

"It has occurred to me, yes, that they might even share the same shrink—Morrissey."

"That might explain a great deal. Imagine if you will, two killers trying to outdo one another on the horror scale, or the FBI's torture scale of one to ten."

"These SOBs want things confused, which means both

are not only intelligent, but they are enjoying themselves as they read about confused city officials and authorities running about with no leads. These same men must be highly dangerous, as they're reaching for new repertoire as they go, shuffling the cards, remixing the ingredients of their crimes."

"Are you aware, Meredyth, that you speak of them as if they *know* one another, possibly as competitors?"

"It has occurred to me. What if they are trying to out-distance one another, like . . . like they want to be the best known of all serial killers for all time, like . . . like Jack the Ripper."

"Or Charlie Manson . . ."

"What if each is getting his jollies this way, competing to best the other?"

Ames grunted as if changing position in his chair. "We may well be onto something here, Meredyth. I would ex-plore that possibility, absolutely . . . yes."

"I will, along with the possibility of our killer or killers being in audience at Grant's sideshow as you call it."

"Never repeat that, please. Besides, it's more like a freak show." Ames's booming, James-Earl-Jones laugh filled her ear.

"You know all our discussions stay between us, Rich-ard."

"Thank you. Now, additionally about your Beheader guy who is coming in from the rooftops. I imagine no one is self-taught in such antics. He may possibly have a military background. Check for these qualities in Morris-sey's patient list."

"We have a list he's deemed to share with us that we've reduced to his three most volatile patients."

"Volatile according to what standard?"

"The crimes they were arrested for. At any rate, we are checking out their backgrounds, military and otherwise."

"Has he provided his files on these men?"

"We're still struggling to get them. He's not exactly forthcoming."

"Careful even after you believe you have full disclosure with a man like Morrissey. Full disclosure is not something a man like him will readily accept."

"Understood."

"One day, the man will himself be a headline."

"Agreed."

"Wish I could be of more help."

"But you have been, Richard."

"Well, I can offer you my services, but if you can get Grant down there, you'd probably do well to get Grant. He is topflight, you know, despite his showmanship. And, of course, he likes to run the show. Still, if he is unable to assist you, perhaps I could fill in, help you with the profile and the headwork on these guys."

"I'd like you here, yes, whether Grant comes aboard or not."

"I worked alongside Dean on the Handyman killing spree. Saylor, this maniac killer got it in his head that he needed to sew a pair of human hands onto his wooden dummy."

"My God . . ."

"There's more: problem came in that he could never quite get the perfect matchup between dummy and hands, you see, so—"

She gasped. "Perfect matchup?"

"Saylor kept going back to the well for more hands, but in the end, it turned out that he had a goddamn basement full of wooden dummies to place hands on, but in his head . . . in his brain, there's only one dummy. He talks to the dummy, and the dummy talks back, you see, demanding a better fit." Nervous laughter erupted from Ames. "Said at his trial, 'We'—meaning he and his dummy—'We were looking for the perfect pair of hands to use in our act.' "

"Our act?"

"Guy was a small-time nightclub magician, you see, and well, I'm sure you have read up on the case if you've gotten this far."

"Only the outcome. I apparently need to read about the main event. What about the other case? The one involving the scalping business in Florida?"

"Not being a principal player on the case, I know less about it. Dean was asked to come in on the case, but I was not. Dean worked with people there in Florida. I did not."

She thought his tone was now laced with an edgy bitterness, but Meredyth had more important considerations than assuaging old hurts, rightly or wrongly perceived by Ames. "It all seems too pat, Richard."

"How's that?"

Meredyth thought carefully about her next words. "Can this be coincidence only? Or might there be some connection between Dr. Dean Grant—or his infamous cases—and the current monsters—two of them—roaming Houston streets and climbing into windows?"

"As far as the Handyman case," added Ames, she thought with a bit of hesitancy in his usually driving voice, "for a time, I . . . I myself became a suspect and so, I am not altogether objective in that—"

"Suspect? You?"

"Never officially, of course, but unofficially even

among people I had counted my friends, including Dean to a lesser degree. Still, he stood by me in the end."

She didn't know what to say. She settled for "Really?" and felt foolish saying it.

"I had some difficulty dealing with the case, you see, the hands being chopped off, you see. Something about the taking of people's hands—severing a man's hands—well, suffice it to say ... it ... it simply disturbed me to the core, far more so than any beheading murder I'd ever been associated with. 'Fraid my own phobias got the best of me. Couldn't function for the better part of the case. Dean ... at least Dean was ... tried to be understanding about it."

"Still, your behavior had him and others wondering?"

"Guessing, suspicious, yes. I mean everyone felt shaken and disturbed by the sight of the bodies, but we'd all seen worse mutilations—far worse. Battlefield worst-case scenarios, all of us. I just ... I don't know ... overreacted. Started seeing a psychiatrist myself afterward. Turns out I had this traumatic experience as a child that involved my hands. I won't bore you with the details."

"Not at all, Richard. Anytime you wish to speak of it, you know I am a friend and an admirer. Loved your last book *Evil Instinct*—"

"*Evil Intent*," he gently corrected her on the title.

"Either way, it made all the sense in the world, Richard, your definition of evil, how to recognize it, deal with it when encountering it in the practice of psychiatry. Great stuff."

"Thank you. I put a great deal of effort into it."

"So, if there is a connection between Dean Grant and our killers here, could it be a pair of former maniacs that Grant may have put away at some earlier time?"

"Possibly. We need to check on all his cases for that possibility. I can do that best from here, checking with the Chicago police records. Still, another possibility is that you could have someone who was once in a position to know about Dean's cases long before Dean showed up in Houston to talk about them."

"Or did our Houston Scalper/hand-taker and the be-header/carver guy simply hear of the cases or read of them in Grant's memoirs? Independent of one another? Or should we assume the two have a mutual connection, some tenuous connection, yet a connection, no doubt. And might that connection be Dr. Thomas Morrissey?"

"Any number of possibilities. We must keep an open mind to all theories at this point."

"Any help from Chicago will be appreciated, Richard. And I meant it about talking to me. We should stay in more contact, my friend."

"Absolutely, and I will forward along any information I deem useful to you, Meredyth."

They hung up and Meredyth tried to picture a shocked, disturbed Dr. Richard Ames, but the unflappable, steel-up-the-backbone black man she knew simply could not be viewed as frightened or out of control. The Handyman case must surely have touched some deep-seated phobia hidden below layers and bands of self-confidence. It made her wonder just how useful self-confidence and assurance were in the face of uncontrollable horrors.

It made her think of the series of victims left with their stomachs turned out, candles burning in place of hearts, hands removed, scalps removed, heads removed. The victims must surely have lost all sense of safety from without and within, all sense of their own selves, self-worth, self-strength, self-awareness stripped from them. All taken from them by monsters, one of which might now be crawling through a forty-story window somewhere in this mammoth city, while the other sought a new scalp for his collection, along with a new set of human hands—but why? Could it be some complicated psychological and sociopathic maze created of not one but two fevered brains, two minds set on murder of the most heinous nature? Or might it be as simple as Dr. Richard Ames had suggested: two maniacs vying for the most shock value for their acts, competing for attention, newspaper headlines—attempting to outdo one another and relishing the effort?

What kind of a world do we live in, she wondered, in which newspapers, TV, radio, film, books and other media glamorized serial killings and serial killers, creating an environment in which bubble-gum cards and T-shirts featured the likes of Richard Speck and John Wayne Gacey, a world in which kids found murder and mutilation "cool" and an answer to their schoolyard pressures, their daily stress, and/or their worst fear—boredom.

In any case, she had a job to do. She must somehow learn when and where the next Scalper attack and the next beheading would occur. How does one stop such creatures of the night?

$\mathcal{T}$WELVE

Crossed arrows: friendship

The following day, Randy Oglesby managed to dig up more rare information on the Florida Scalper of the eighties. He also located more information on the old Chicago, Illinois, case involving a killer who took his victims hands, the case referred to by the press as the Handyman Killings, also in the early eighties. Meredyth Sanger hadn't the heart to tell him that she'd already been put onto the Handyman case via human networking.

Meanwhile, Dr. Dean Grant proved unavailable for anything but phone consults, as he was involved in the filming of a movie on his life—in which William Shatner would play Grant. So Meredyth put the wheels in motion to have Dr. Richard Ames flown from Chicago to Houston.

Still, Grant, now retired and living in Orange County, California, like the Houston authorities, saw too much coincidence in the current butchery with the two cases of the past for any of it to be dismissed. Over the phone Grant cautioned, "Your killer has to be familiar with the earlier cases, but that doesn't mean he was in my audience in Houston."

"Either way, we are interested in obtaining any video-tapes of your session here. And I would like to know if you had any dealings with a Dr. Thomas William Mor-rissey while you were—"

"Morrissey . . . Morrissey . . . Can't say that I have, but I meet so many people when touring. . . . Is he a suspect?"

"Not at this time."

"Well, your killer may just as well have had some deal-ings with our office, or else he may well have studied the cases for some reason, possibly in a police-science class."

"Oh, really?"

"They're classic cases. They have been written up for several textbooks, but nowadays, with information access so simple, he may just as well have read about these cases on w-w-w-dot-com-dot-home-grown autopsy or what-ever." Grant paused to see if he'd engendered a laugh from her. When he got none, he continued, "I maintain my own Web site nowadays, a kind of Murderer's Row, if you will, of my former cases—many of them quite bi-zarre. All these cases sound like crime-detection history, and any browsing of true-crime books at Amazon-dot-com, on-line bookstores or a judicious reading of the works of Colin Wilson or Ann Rule would likely get you the same results."

"You sound familiar with the criminal mind and the nature of murder, Dr. Grant," she replied.

"In my case, it was either understand the rage and why a man turns to murder—understand it and combat it—or become a murderer myself. Long story I won't bore you with. Suffice it to say, I have dissected the killing impulse along with literally thousands of cadavers."

"Thank you, I think . . ."

"Not so quickly. We have someone specialized in searching the Web, who may be of help to you."

"So do I, sir."

"Then you are fortunate. Not every law-enforcement team does."

"All the same, if you could get us a list of attendees at the Houston show, along with the tapes—"

"No such list exists, but I will search my archives for any such tape. I suggest you talk to the people who put the show together, Instinct Ink Productions."

"I'll check with them on the tape," she said, penciling the name on a notepad. "Meantime, any orderlies, nurses or assistants you ever worked with. That might be a helpful start toward pinpointing our killers here," she said, tapping nervously at her desk with the pencil.

"What's that woodpecker sound?" he asked.

She immediately stopped tapping on the desk. "Oh, that, nothing."

"Sounds like you could use a little R and R, Dr. Sanger. Retirement's fun. You should try it. Listen, I have a new boat with extra berths that I've been dying to try out, but I hate to sail alone so—"

"Thanks, but not ready for retirement just yet." She thought him a bit overly friendly. "So, what about info on people who worked on your teams over the years co-inciding with the Scalping and hand-taking murders."

"That can be arranged, but it might take some time. I'll fax it to you as soon as I can lay my hands on it. I'll have to contact Dr. Sybil Shanley in Chicago, who has my old job there."

"Good, but don't take too much time."

"Time, my dear, is to me like water to a water buffalo.

I'm most aware of its preciousness. I'll call into the office, see if I can get my old friend and replacement, Dr. Shanley, to go over the records for anything unusual or anyone on the payroll at the time who was terminated, that sort of thing. Still, I can't make any promises, you realize. In point of fact, it was an associate, a Dr. Howard Black who first brought the Handyman case to my attention."

"And where is Black today?"

"Long dead, I'm afraid."

"I see. All right, I understand it will take time to get this information to us, but you will look into it, right, Dr. Grant?"

"Understood."

"And thanks for all the help and anything—anything— you can throw our way." God she hated cow-towing to the so-called giants in the police-science field. She broke the connection, realizing that if there were a pair of competing psychos copycatting every horrid crime in the encyclopedia of crime, that the similarities between the ongoing slaughters in Houston to crimes in the past might well prove endless.

The thought came accompanying terror.

An eerie night passed without a killing in Houston, Texas. Even the TV newscasters felt a sense of relief and exhaustion having anticipated the latest in gangland shootings, break-in shootings, knifings, poisonings, rapes, rape-murders, abductions or disappearances, but nothing came in from the various precincts other than bar fights and neighborhood disturbances. It was as if death had taken a holiday; it was as if the violent among the population had become mute—or at least curiously stopped and poised, waiting along with everyone else for the Beheader or the Scalper to strike once more.

But dawn broke and no horrifying discoveries materialized anywhere in the city. The city went on with its business, and Precinct 31 did likewise.

Most people stepped livelier, relieved to hear no news of a scalping murder, a corpse less its hands or head. The collective sigh of relief that spread over the city felt like a wave at a sporting event.

By 10 A.M. the first pot of coffee of the day in Meredyth's sector had disappeared, only to be replaced with another. The aroma filled both the outer and the inner offices where Randy Oglesby and Meredyth Sanger respectively worked.

Meredyth had long since buried herself once more in the files surrounding the strange cases of Dr. Dean Grant, the Handyman case and the Florida Scalper case. She'd shared her interest in these cases with Lucas, who had come upstairs to read some of the paperwork on them as well. Unlike her, he hadn't gotten much sleep the night before. . . . Something about a visit from his dead grandfather, he'd told her, but Lucas hadn't wished to go into detail.

She imagined he'd spent the night on peyote—enough to bring anyone's grandfather back from the dead.

"Dr. Sanger?" came a voice at the outer office door and in stepped a tall, handsome black man with hands the size of the Texas Panhandle. Lucas thought him an ex–basketball star who'd somehow lost his way, perhaps a former Rockets player; but Lucas didn't recognize the features, and he could not place the man's face.

"Richard! So glad to welcome you to Houston," Meredyth replied, coming from behind her desk and extending a hand.

"Dr. Ames," he said by way of introduction, after hugging Meredyth and extending a hand to Lucas. "Richard Ames, from Chicago."

Lucas felt a bit put out by the way that Meredyth had pushed past him to get to Ames, taking the man's hand in hers, shaking firmly, their eyes dancing while the tall black man hugged her to him.

Lucas introduced himself to Ames, wondering if the black man had ever been an Olympic basketball player. Ames's size and build were daunting. Meredyth had told him about Ames coming, but she hadn't prepared him for how handsome and virile this shrink was—so far from the egghead stereotype. Lucas felt a twinge of anger spiced with a pinch of jealousy as the two psychiatrists talked of third parties and old times of which he had no knowledge.

"Can you bring me up to date?" Ames asked, suddenly all business. "Crime-scene photos, any additional information forthcoming, all that?"

"Absolutely," she replied, guiding him deeper into her office. "Lucas?" she called over her shoulder. Standing beside Ames, Lucas felt short, as if standing beside a flagpole.

"Well, we just received this in from the FBI field lab," said Lucas, slapping down a manila file folder he held in his left hand.

"What's this?" asked Meredyth.

"Voiceprint on the call-in on Laurel Kensington, which we'd hoped to match up to Freeleng."

"Negative?" she asked.

" 'Fraid so."

Meredyth sighed and nodded in Lucas's direction, sorry

that the evidence had not borne out Dave Harbough's suspicions. With a shake of her head, she told Ames, "Just
another lead that didn't pan out on the Beheader case."

"So, let's see what else you have," suggested Ames,
moving on. Together, the two psychiatrists and Lucas
pored over the information that had became available to
them. Randy had passed it along as he had retrieved it.

Lucas flatly said, "First looked over the records for the
clients of Dr. Morrissey, those three we deemed his most
troublesome and dangerous cases. Morrissey's rogues,
door number one, two or three: Lester Franklin Wilcox,
Jared Oliver Wendell, or Stanley Theopolis Garrette?
Take your pick."

Meredyth explained to Ames, "Dr. Morrissey did confide that all three have, on occasion, in one fashion or
another, threatened his life and have spoken about taking
out their pent-up aggressions on society."

"Doesn't make them any different from a lot of us,"
joked Ames. His amiable face and smile looked like that
of a young Morgan Freeman, Lucas thought. Lucas felt
keenly aware of Meredyth's obvious pleasure at having
Ames in on the case.

Ames and Meredyth began working together over the
documents amassed on each of the three names provided
them by Morrissey. If one or the other of the killers were
among these names, Lucas imagined the two psychiatrists,
putting heads together, could find some answers. He saw
that they had completely forgotten that he stood nearby,
so rapt had their combined attention become on the pro-
filing work they had entered into.

"Well, I have one of our bad boys in custody downstairs," began Lucas.

"Oh, and who would that be?" asked Ames.

"Jared Oliver Wendell. He's been held overnight for forty-eight hours on charges of breaking his parole. Meantime, he's being questioned on the killings."

"Which killings?"

"Right now, either or. Think I'll go see if the grilling has had any effect so far."

Ames said nothing in response, his mind and eyes pinned to the pages before him. Meredyth muttered, "Yeah, think that would be best, Lucas. Later . . ."

Ames looked up to say a word to Lucas as well, but too late. Lucas had disappeared, and Ames wondered how long between the last word the detective had said and his response. He had lost track of time. His intense focus had become instantly all encompassing on the new killings. That and a flood of bad memories had blotted out not only Lucas Stonecoat's presence but that of Meredyth, although she remained in the room.

"You okay, Richard?" Meredyth asked, realizing how glazed his stare had become.

"Yes, yes . . . fine . . . just a little . . . shaken. Awful business you have going on here."

"I've given a great deal of thought to your suggestion that the killers could well be in a competition to outdo each other. I've discussed it with Lucas, and he agrees it may hold merit. And we're both like you. We're weirded out by this hand-taking business more than any of the other atrocities."

"Hand-taking will certainly do that. Something primitive is touched when we see someone's hands severed, even more so than the severing of a head. Don't ask me why."

"Perhaps we ought to go downstairs, see what progress,

if any, has come of the interrogation being run on Wendell."

"If we can find a cup of coffee along the way," he
replied.

"That can certainly be arranged."

Together, they exited her office, located the coffee urn
Randy kept freshly filled all day long and poured two cups
of steaming, black coffee. They then found the elevator
and took it down to the squad room to find Lucas and the
interrogation team.

After two nights now in custody, time added on for striking a guard, Jared Oliver Wendell was, for the third time,
questioned about what he knew of the other men in the
halfway house, about Dr. Morrissey's practices, and what
he may or may not know about the Scalper and the Beheader.

The interrogation had thus far proven fruitless. Try as
they might, the team of Lynn Blanton and Sandra Offiah,
could not break through the wall of madness and schizo-
phrenia Wendell presented at his interrogation. In a show
of complete insanity or teasing, one personality informed
on the other, but so too did the other personality inform
on the original, and then a third informed on them both,
making none of the three "confessions" useful when they
finally came. All three, by the time Blanton and Offiah
were through with Wendell, confessed to the same crimes,
or any crime that was put to them.

Born in Pickyune, Mississippi, Sandra Offiah, a small,
round black woman with a quick, intelligent smile and
eyes that shone bright and clear, stood four-foot-six, a
perfect foil to her Paintersville, Kentucky, tall and thin

white partner, Lynn Blanton, whose stern eyes burned into Wendell as angry as hot lasers.

The obvious insanity of the man in the box called for a psychiatric consult to be present. Lucas called upstairs to Randy to ask that Meredyth come down. When she arrived, she did so in the company of Ames, each with a warm cup of coffee in hand.

"You get my message?" asked Lucas.

"What message?"

"What took you so long getting down here?"

Meredyth frowned and asked, "What do you mean?"

"Forget it. Just listen in on the madness. Not a word of it is useful." Lucas turned on the sound box. Together they listened in on the final segment.

"So, Wendell," said Lynn Blanton, her eyes boring a hole through the man once more, "now you're saying Stuart did it?"

"I'm not saying he did it. Damn it, he did do it. Stuart's a fiend. He'll do anything for a laugh, anything."

"Including?" pressed Sandra Offiah. "Yes, go on." She smiled wide like a madwoman while pleading for the added information, ingratiating herself with the maniac, pretending to be his twisted sister, his dark counterpart.

Wendell looked as if he were seeing what he described. A wide smile spread unevenly across his pockmarked, prune-pinched face. His jagged mouth gave him a jack-o'-lantern appearance, making his interrogators stare as he spoke. "Including cutting off pieces of a person while they're still alive," he finished, and giggled.

"What sort of pieces, Wendell?" pressed Offiah.

"Why're you asking him that shit. He doesn't know dick. Ask me," came an annoyed, deeper voice out of

Wendell. The man's features changed with the voice, as if possessed.

"Who are you?" asked Blanton. "Are you Stuart?"

"Stuart? Stuart's a wimp. I'm Wendell's manhood, babe, and if you want some—"

"I want to know who killed Laurel Kensington!"

"It was me," he replied in a gruff voice.

"It's not *me*, it is *I* . . . was I," boomed a third voice from the man. "Don't even know proper grammar, Sedgewick."

"Cut the crap! Who are you?" shouted Blanton.

"Sedgewick. I am Sedgewick, Sedgewick am I . . ."

"Sedgewick, huh?" asked Offiah, her lips pursed as she nodded repeatedly and said, "Uh-huh, uh-huh, uh-huh," still smiling when she finished.

The interrogation continued for hours until Dr. Morrissey showed up with a lawyer and an affidavit stating that Wendell had not violated his parole by carrying a knife— that Morrissey had, in fact, given the man the knife as part of his rehabilitation plan, claiming that, without the knife, Wendell felt completely impotent and inconsequential.

"Since the knife is part of my client's therapy," said the lawyer, "approved by his court-appointed psychiatrist, I suggest that you either charge my client or release him now."

Lucas went into a huddle with Meredyth. "We don't have enough evidence to hold him on murder charges," she said.

"Yeah, and besides we'll learn a lot more by watching him on the outside than by locking him up now."

In the end they agreed to let the creep walk.

Lucas stormed out saying, "I have to get some air."

Meredyth, with Ames following, caught Lucas as he stepped through the precinct door. On the old field-stone stairway of Precinct 31, they spoke.

"I don't think Wendell is capable of murder of this sort," said Meredyth.

"Nor do I," agreed Ames.

"How can you be sure of that? What about his other personalities? Isn't one or the other of them capable of it?" Lucas demanded.

"Not likely. They seemed too familiar with one another, as if they actually, despite the language, were out to please one another, or take the heat for one another."

Ames tried to explain. "Despite the obvious fragmentation of the personalities he presents, Wendell is fundamentally in control, allowing the interplay to go only so far. He seems as aware of the other two personalities as he is of his core personality. This makes him less of a risk."

"You got all that from fifteen fucking minutes? Why didn't Morrissey come to the same conclusion?"

"One or more of the man's personalities threatened Morrissey directly," countered Meredyth. "Makes a therapist a little less than objective."

"All right, so we focus now on the other two on the list. Wilcox and Garrette."

Lucas rotated his head to get the kinks out. His back and shoulders, his feet and legs were killing him as well. He'd forgotten to take any painkillers earlier. The old haunting aches deep within now scratched at him mercilessly like dead branches in a midnight wood. He saw that Meredyth had sized up his situation—saw it in her eyes. She was careful to say nothing about his condition, but rather said, "Any notions how we'll proceed, Lucas? Ar-

resting either will likely prove as fruitless as placing Wendell in the interrogation box."

"You think the other two will be harder to crack?"

"They'll use different strategies, perhaps, but yes. They
have had a lifetime of evading questions put to them by
every kind of official, from police to psychiatrists."

"I say we put them under surveillance. Did Randy get
us an order for surveillance of the other two?"

"He's working on it. Frye's heart condition's really hurt
our chances."

"Tell Lincoln to tell the mayor to tell the governor then.
Damn it all. How're we to conduct an investigation with
our hands tied behind our backs? Tell Randy to contact
me the moment he has the paperwork in hand." With that
Lucas started off.

"Where are you going?" she called after him.

"For a drink and for some . . . sleep."

With the death of Harbough fresh in her thoughts, Meredyth Sanger met privately with Dr. Morrissey at his plush
downtown office. She had checked on his habits and
methods. She learned that he also maintained an office at
the halfway house where his clients resided—the same
halfway house that had witnessed Walter Karl Freeleng's
execution at Harbough's hands. Morrissey agreed to meet
with her, he said, out of curiosity.

"I understand and the city is putting together some sort
of block party on the street where my boys live. Some
public relations Band-Aid going on there, Dr. Sanger?"

"I wouldn't know. Not my department really."

"About the festivities on the street out front of my . . .
the county's halfway house, will there be dancing bears
or perhaps you, Dr. Sanger, will dance?"

"Dr. Morrissey, I have nothing to do with any block party."

"So, why are you here?"

"I understand you saw to it that Detective Dave Harbough got it between the eyes with respect to Freeleng's proving not to be the Beheader. Leonard Chang told you, you told Harbough. Do you think that was wise, given Harbough's condition?"

"What condition? The man literally executed Freeleng. Is Harbough's demise the reason you're taking up my time, Doctor?"

"Look, we've both lost a man, you Freeleng, me Harbough. It's not easy being a police shrink, Doctor."

"I can well imagine."

"May I presume that you do not wish to see another person killed in this affair?"

"Neither of us want to see anyone else lose hold of this precious life, agreed."

"We are looking closely at three of the men you singled out."

"They must not know that I cooperated with you in the slightest. They certainly can't know about that list, as we agreed behind closed doors, Doctor. That's truer now than ever."

"That explains why you broke up Wendell's interrogation. You don't want them suspecting."

"You people fucked up royally, holding the man for three days and two nights! They all know of his arrest. I had to act. Do your people, this Stonecoat fellow, any of you, know what a strain I am laboring under?"

"We appreciate your situation, Doctor."

"Haaa! That's a laugh. Have you made any headway on the Scalper case? Any at all?"

"Some, yes."

"What precisely?"

"I am not at liberty to say, sir."

"And the Beheader case?"

"A little movement forward, yes."

"Damnably slow is what you are. The whole system moves like a sloth."

"I brought a little something for your . . . your consumption, Dr. Morrissey," she said now, opening a manila envelope and spreading out the crime-scene photos. "Two distinctly different victim types, wouldn't you agree, Doctor?"

He shakily stared at the mutilated bodies. "Yes, quite . . . quite . . ."

"We are not dealing with the usual serial killer here, but possibly two."

"It's an interesting theory. What will you have me do with it?"

"I want you to reveal any taped interviews you may have had with anyone you feel capable of this sort of mutilation lust-murder, Doctor." She pointed to the top photo of the beheaded woman's remains. "Who among your flock enjoys high crimes and high drama such as this, staging the body, staging the head?"

"I cannot say."

"You have a professional as well as a moral obligation to do so, not to mention your own safety, sir."

"I have no evidence against any of my clients. The best I can do is again point to the list you have. Keep a watch on the three you have already fingered."

"Did you tell your patients about the Scalper case and the Handyman Case discussed by Dr. Dean Grant at a recent symposium on crime at the Hyatt downtown, sir?"

He flinched but controlled his voice. "I deny telling any of my patients any such thing, Scalper or Handyman. Of course, Freeleng talked about his beheadings at our group meetings, but that's what we do at our group meetings. I encourage them to get it out in the open, what they did in the past, to confront it."

"Then Freeleng was the Headless Horseman after all?"

"Again, doctor-patient client prevents me from saying any more on the subject."

"Your patient is dead, sir."

"The privacy issue follows him to the grave."

"You didn't know Laurel Kensington, Doctor, but she lived within walking distance to the Hyatt Regency. As a private duty nurse, she had clients in the same high-rent district. Look at her *before* picture here, Doctor, and tell me if you chanced to see her at the Hyatt that day you went to hear Dr. Grant speak. She may well have even attended the same session as you."

He stared at it but shook his head vehemently. "Sorry, no. I did not see this woman there or anywhere."

"Did you take anyone to Dr. Grant's session with you?"

"No."

"You wouldn't have taken one or more of your patients, Doctor? Say as an experiment?"

"That's nonsense, no!" He vainly told her, "I have cured those once capable of such crimes from acting on their morbid fantasies."

His visions of godhood filtered through his speech and the content of his words. He told her, "My work contributes greatly to the path mankind has taken toward purity of thought, the evolution of mind and body toward a harmonious nirvana, a kind of perfection in mankind that precludes any violence whatsoever."

After politely listening to this, Meredyth laughed in his face and told him, "Any one of your patients is capable of murder thrice over." As she lifted the pictures and put them away, thinking how little effect they'd had on the man, she ticked off the similarities between the high-rise killer's methods and some of the same methods used by Morrissey's clients in the past. As she did so, it once again dawned on her that the killer might be killers—more than one working in tandem, possibly even a threesome.

"No point in wasting my breath, Doctor," she added, her jaw firmly set. "We could argue the merits of the law on confidentiality all day and never agree."

She stormed out, a bitter taste in her mouth, wishing only ill for Morrissey. Her last words to him were a warning, "You could easily be the next victim of this madman or madmen, and no deal with NBC or ABC or the Fox television network is worth one's life."

LATER THE SAME DAY

First Freeleng and then Morrissey laugh in Lucas's face during the interrogations that have been arranged in Hades, where Freeleng explains to a demonic judge and a saliva-dripping, body-rotting jury that he could not have committed the crime. "How so?" asks the judge with an evil grin, as if he knows the answer already.

"Since my prison stay, I have contracted such debilitating arthritis in the hands that I can't so much as clench my fists, let alone rappel down a rope and hang outside a forty-story building while cutting a laser hole into a window."

He next demonstrates being unable to wrap his hands

around a rappelling rope, and he careens down into the
lowest depths of this place, squealing with delight the entire way. This illicits horrid laughter from the gallery of
ghouls sitting in the jury box. Next, Freeleng, somehow
back from the depths into which he'd fallen, at the insis-
tence of his psychiatrist, Morrissey, attempts to hold on
to a glowing, brightly burning torch, which he drops,
screaming in pain, causing jury and judge to go giddy
with laughter once again.

Freeleng now holds both hands high, each limb resembling a Bonsai tree, each painfully contorted, fingers like
dead roots.

Lucas shouts over the cacophony of devils and the
crackling of fire, saying, "It's all a game, an ugly play."

"What do you want, Detective?" shouts Morrissey,
jumping to his feet, his white beard now aflame, his eyes
jutting madness, and somehow Morrissey and the devil
judge meld into one creature.

"I want medical proof of the condition brought to this
courtroom!" shouts Dave Harbough suddenly at Lucas's
shoulder, his face half blown away.

Lucas awoke in a cold, clammy sweat. "Damn," he
muttered to the empty room. His empty bed felt enormous
without someone beside him. He thought of Tsalie, and
he reached for more peyote.

THE SAME NIGHT

Dr. Meredyth Sanger, seeking out help from others in her
profession, sat in a posh Houston restaurant—Anthony's—
across from the very forensic psychiatrist who worked on
the infamous Handyman Case in Chicago, Dr. Richard

Ames. They'd been friendly for many years now, encountering one another at annual and biannual psychiatric
and forensic symposiums and conferences across the
country. She looked now across at the tall, handsome
black professional as Ames's voice seemed to fill the
room. "Your Lieutenant Stonecoat doesn't appear too
happy to have me on the case."

"Oh, Lucas? No. Why do you say that, Richard?"

"Isn't it obvious? Tell me. Is there something, you
know, personal between the two of you?"

She laughed in nervous response. "Nothing in the least.
We admire one another only in a professional sense. Just
as you and I do."

"But I've always admired you, Meredyth, in more than
a professional manner."

She breathed deeply at this, taken by surprise. "Richard,
I . . . I'm sorry, I didn't know, but—"

"It's one reason I've chosen to subject myself to this
new Handyman Case of yours. I can tell you, it is not
easy for me."

"I really had no idea, Richard. This comes as a . . . quite
a shot in the dark for me."

Ames sat erect, proud, unflappable. She had never
known him to be anything but resolute, like a granite
monolith, but she'd never guessed he had any interest in
her in any but a professional sense. Now the man's voice
dropped to a whisper and he said, "I have always tried to
imagine what it would be like, to be alone with you, to
have you in my—"

"Richard, stop right there." She blushed red. "I am seeing someone at the moment, someone I have sworn to
have a monogamous relationship with, so I don't see this
going anywhere."

"All right, but I thought I must tell you this time. Each time I see you, it becomes, became, a larger . . . issue with me."

"I see." She didn't know what to say. "Shall we order?"

He sipped at his wine, and she did likewise, each staring over the glass at the other. "Is it Stonecoat?"

"Is what Stonecoat?"

"The man you are seeing."

"No . . . no . . ."

"Got some strong vibes off him. I think he cares a great deal about you."

"We've worked a long time together. That's all."

He tipped his wineglass and touched hers with it again. The chime sounded to her like a tolling bell.

$\mathcal{T}$HIRTEEN

Teepee: temporary home

The call came at 8:52 P.M., sending Lucas to a fashionable high-rise district called Salem, an ancient word meaning peace. When Lucas entered the crime scene, he found Dr. Ames, Meredyth, Medical Examiner Chang, and an evidence technician in deep conversation. All but Dr. Richard Ames were, for the moment, ignoring the headless corpse and the burning candle in the empty gut. Only a head on a mantel was missing. Lucas wondered if it had been stashed already by the evidence-gathering techie.

"Where's the head?" he asked Meredyth.

"Killer left only the scalp," she replied, indicating a bloody splotch of skin and hair beside the torso of what appeared a woman in her mid to late twenties. "Heather Balmoral is her name."

"Scalped . . . Why scalped? I mean on top of beheading her?"

"I would say that this guy likes teasing us, the authorities, that is," suggested Ames, whose color had blanched to an ashen gray.

Meredyth, who lifted a handkerchief to her nose, added, "This time, the bastard has done it all: head, hands, the gutting and candle thing, and the goddamn scalp. So, now what are we to make of all of it?"

Chang stepped up to Lucas, the bloody scalp now in a plastic, see-through bag, which he held toward Lucas's eyes. "You an Indian, Stonecoat, what you think?" Chang bit his lower lip.

"I think it's barbaric is what I think."

"Until now, in Houston, thought to be thing of the past, but now no longer archaic," replied Chang, waving the bloody baggy before Lucas's eyes.

Lucas snatched the bag and shook it back in Chang's face, saying, "I didn't say archaic, I said barbaric. There's a difference, Dr. Chang."

"Why you not call me Leonard?" Chang replied, that small perpetual smile of the Asian now widening in a grim grin. "Randy Oglesby tell me there a case of serial scalping since before . . ."

"Since before?" asked Lucas. "Yeah, I know, in Orlando, Florida, back in the eighties."

"That not archaic?"

"No. In both cases, it was barbaric."

"I'll look it up."

"Do that." Lucas turned his attention to the corpse staring now at the empty shell of Heather Balmoral. The odor here was of blood, bile and sandlewood. It made a nauseating odor, reminding Lucas of the last time he'd gone to a wake where the tremendously overwhelming stench of sweet flowers had sent him scurrying from the place. He again felt glad that his grandfather had not been buried in the white man's way.

"This was a long-burning candle, four, maybe five hour.

My guess, she a long-time dead before he lit fuse . . . I mean wick . . ." said Chang.

"So, what's your best estimate on time of death?"

"Hard to say, but my guess be somewhere between midnight and two A.M. last."

"Same mode of entry?" he asked.

"Bedroom window, yes."

"Laser cut from the outside," added Captain Lincoln, stepping in from the back room.

"So, it appears our Beheader is also our Scalper," Lucas answered.

"Or . . . our Scalper is our Beheader," countered Meredyth.

Ames added, "Excellent deduction."

Captain Lincoln, looking agitated, escorted Lucas away from the others to say, "Glad you're here, Lucas. We've got to get a fix on this bastard and end this thing immediately, before someone else ends up a fucking candlestick. Christ, look at this." Lincoln pointed shakily at the body.

Save for the missing head, the scene looked disturbingly familiar. "Appears he has changed his fantasy a tad," said Lucas. "Taking the head off with him. Suggest anything to you, Doctors?" Lucas looked from Ames to Meredyth and back again.

Ames bluntly replied, "It would appear, yes."

Chang stepped between them. "I've been considering possibility this one be a copycatter."

"Copycatter?"

Meredyth joined them. "Chang means in the sense that our murderer is copycatting famous cases. Chang and I have discussed it at length, as have Richard and I. This maniac . . . he's into imitative killing."

"Imitative?" asked Lincoln.

"Doing the MO of another killer," added Ames, a pinched look souring his features, "perhaps two."

"Two? The guy's imitating two other serial killers?"

"Two, three, maybe four even," added Ames.

Meredyth interjected with, "Now we have the element of scalping, gutting, beheading, the candle thing, and the taking of the victim's head and hands away, all in one corpse. Yes, could be a copycatting of a number of previously well-known but forgotten serial killers."

"But we have to keep an open mind," cautioned Ames.

Lucas returned to the disfigured body, its limbs broken once again in the form of a swastika. He kneeled down like a man in prayer, studying the horror left by the killer.

Meredyth took up the word slack, "It's as if he's building up to doing his victims in a manner that harkens back to other, famous crimes, Captain Lincoln."

Lucas further explained, saying, "Our profile shows him more likely to add another dimension to his fantasy than most serial killers who feel safe following the same pattern over and over. This guy may well be one killer who simply likes diversity."

"What does that tell us about him?" asked Lincoln.

"That he's not bound by any one, single, unifying fantasy, which will make him far more difficult to track, yet it also sets up his Achilles' heel," Meredyth replied.

"Meaning?" asked Lincoln, curious now.

"Meaning," said Lucas, a hand reaching out to Lincoln who helped Lucas to his feet, "he believes this acceleration of violence will lead us in the wrong direction, after someone foaming at the mouth, someone with a long history of mental illness, when in fact, we don't know this."

Meredyth, her hands in the air, as if attempting to hold

that which could not be held on to, added, "His safety is in feeling he *can* mix it up. Do it differently each time, until police believe it's yet another, separate killer. But he will stumble. He must."

"He already has," replied Lucas, making all the others stare at him. "Don't you see. We're onto him now. The Beheader is the Scalper is the Handyman."

"One guy?" asked Lincoln. "Are you telling me that this, all of this, has been the work of one sick sonofabitch and not two?"

"One guy, Lucas?" asked Meredyth, equally surprised that Lucas had come to this conclusion independent of her and Ames's considerations along the same line.

"Yes, one guy with an escalating lust-murder fantasy that keeps on evolving until *we* end it."

Ames raised his shoulders and asked, "How can you be so sure that there's only one man behind this?"

"I can't be absolutely certain. This is all craziness," said Lucas, his hands raised. "Still, it feels like one mind at work here. One controlling force."

"I confess, I've had the same thoughts," replied Ames. "If it's not two men with one competing idea, you see."

Meredyth took in a deep breath, considering Lucas's point and adding, "If Lucas is right, if it's the work of only one man, think of the logistics of it all, Lucas. How one man, one monster could wreak so much havoc so quickly and surely on Houston."

"I'll grant you that much. He's certainly been busy. It's his game and has been all along. Now we at least have picked up our game piece." With that, Lucas shouted, "Somebody send out for coffee. . . . We're going to be here for a long time."

ACROSS TOWN, THE SAME NIGHT

Dr. Thomas W. Morrissey stared around the circle of men gathered in the communal room at the halfway house. Here the psychiatrist practiced his peculiar brand of therapy on not one but seven men. Seven whose rehabilitation lay in his hands. All seven faces stared back in sullen resignation. They knew what day it was, and they knew what time it was—time for Dr. Morrissey's lecture. They joked that Morrissey was the Jerry Springer of the psychiatric world.

"So, here we are again, gentlemen, to unburden ourselves. This will mark our twenty-fifth get-together, something of a milestone anniversary, wouldn't you agree?"

Except for the habitual, steady *tap-tap-tapping* of Stanley Theopolis Garrette's pencil—Garrette kept copious but questionable notes on all the sessions—the response came out as the dull sounds of acquiescence. Mere ramblings, one man ciphering in his head, trying to match what he knew with the number twenty-five. Another toying about with his shoelace, his eyes and mind riveted to his untied shoe, so occupied as to have no idea what Dr. Morrissey had said. A third sat searching. His eyes scanned the interior of an old fedora hat he carried at all times. He doubtfully searched for confirmation of Morrissey's judgment there: the fact it had been twenty-five sessions already. This one spoke to the hat as if it were a pet. His eyes caressed the interior, a man in a completely other world, quietly murmuring to some soul inside the hat, a soul that spoke to him alone.

Dr. Morrissey had discovered that this man, a fellow named Abel Allandale—a spree killer who had walked

into a White Castle restaurant in Cleveland, Ohio, and
opened fire, killing four and maiming two before he was
wrestled to the ground and taken into custody—had somehow slipped through the cracks. *A model prisoner,* he'd
been called when granted parole at the advanced age of
seventy-two. White-haired and harmless to look at, nondescript to beyond nondescript throughout his miserable
life, Allandale had, as a boy, aspired to become a chemist
at one time. But everything he touched turned to mold
and all attempts turned to failure until one day he took it
out on the world.

Morrissey knew what *model prisoner* meant these days.
Space in a cell, a prison bed. It was a euphemism for "We
can't do any more with this man," and they were right.

So, naturally, they turn him over to me, Morrissey
thought as he gazed at the man who made love to his hat.
Morrissey had only recently discovered that Allandale
kept a photo of his dead mother in the hat, cut into the
shape of a circle to fit the bottom of the hat.

Garrette's hand seemed to possess a life of its own, as
it continued to play with the pencil, beating out an un-
gainly anthem. *Tap . . . tap . . . tap-ping . . .*

Add to these madmen, four who were, despite their own
strangeness, closer to reality. Shabaz Hiraq, a swarthy
Pakistani who mumbled, "Death to all tyrants and their
legions" in his native tongue; Jared Oliver Wendell, a self-
confessed schizophrenic, who in his own self-confession,
acknowledged his other selves.

Tap . . . tap . . . tap-ping . . .

Dr. Morrissey had as yet to be fully convinced that
Wendell was a true schizoid rather than a clever actor.
Lester Wilcox, a man easily controlled, easily led like his
counterpart, Stanley Theopolis Garrette. All three of these

last were murderers and rapists, but they had a bead on reality, and William Morrissey meant to shake them up, return them to the reality, he believed, they must endure, that of society and societal constraints on behavior such as they had exhibited in the past. It would take a miracle worker to do that, and he believed himself to be one.

Tap . . . tap . . . ta-tap . . . ta-tap-ping . . .

These seven deviants always made for an interesting evening group session, but Dr. Morrissey feared only three of them possibly dangerous, any one of whom might prove useful characters in his new book. The three who frightened him had begun to make verbal threats in the form of not too veiled innuendo. The scrawniest of the three, Wendell did it through his more masterful splinter self he called Sedgewick.

Tap . . . tap . . . tap . . . Tap . . . tap . . . tap-ping . . .

Most likely just talk, like the blades these three carried about with them, one in his boot, one taped to the inner lining of his jacket, the other around a chain, hung backward between his shoulder blades, nestled in the T-shirt.

"So, who will begin the discussion tonight?" asked Dr. Morrissey. "Who among us has the balls to speak up?"

This was met with the usual dumb silence, making Garrette's tapping pencil thunderous now, also making Dr. Morrissey frown, stand and pace until he stood behind one of his patients: Wendell. He slapped Wendell on the back of the head, shouting, "Cat got your tongue? Tell us about your day, Wendell. What've you been up to? Tell everybody how you went for a stroll with the police today. Why do you suppose they think you have something to do with the Scalper or the Beheader, Wendell?"

"*Stupidassity* is all."

"Stupid what?"

"*Assity, stupid-assity!* The cops are full of it, and the system runs on it." Wendell's voice had changed dramatically.

"Am I speaking now to *Wendell* or to *Sedgewick*?"

"Sedgewick, of course. Wendell is a mere vessel. You certainly ought to know that by now. You with all your degrees and experience, really . . ." Wendell had found a handkerchief and held it up to his nose in the manner of a fancy.

"Why're you picking on him?" asked Wilcox. "Leave him alone. He don't know shit . . . not a fucking thing."

"Who? Which one doesn't know shit? *Wendell* or *Sedgewick?*"

"I don't know, not neither of them." Wilcox, a small man, sat hunched in his chair like a two-ton gargoyle, stocky and thick-necked. His eyes always seethed with anger and a set of bad teeth had created a perpetual snarl on the left side of his face.

"Oh, and what about you, Wilcox? What do you know about the rash of killings plaguing the realm?"

"What realm? Whataya talking about now, Doc?"

"The city. Houston. What do you know about the Scalper and the Beheader? What's the word on the street, Wilcox? What have you heard?"

"Not a damn thing. Same as Wendell. Hell, I thought Freeleng was doing the headhunting. So, what the hell do I know?"

"But you like to get the daily paper to read about the killings, don't you?"

Stanley Theopolis Garrette interrupted, shouting, "You taught us to do exactly that, Doctor. Part of your plan for us, remember? Wallow in the *depravamania*, the *luna-*

lustiness, as you say. Rub our noses in our own *depra-vamanity*, that it's part of being human, part of humanity. We're supposed to swallow your swill and grovel in our own *swine-nosity* until we're sick to death of it, and then maybe we'll give up the *obfixation*? Isn't that your message?"

"You are still so full of hatred for me, Stanley. Why is that? Are you still filled with hatred for anyone and anything to do with society at large? I had thought we'd made some *progressamation* here, but obviously not."

"*Progressamation, stupidassity,* there're no such goddamn words in existence, but you got us thinking we can be cured on the basis of make-believe words and you make up your therapy as you go, don't you, Doc? *Doc Residual.*"

"Don't fucking call me that, Stanley!"

"You're the one lives in a make-believe world, Thomas William."

"I am Dr. Morrissey to you!"

"All right, son, if you want to be called doctor, if you have a need to be called by your *label!*"

"That's it, Mr. Garrette!"

"What's it? What's to say what it is? It could be anything . . . the White House, a poem, and what's to say, Dr. Morrissey, that you're not it?"

"It? Whatever are you talking about, Garrette?"

"That you are not it—the Scalper, the Beheader, both!"

"That's preposterous."

The others watched the verbal battle, all eyes alight with anticipation of each new word. Garrette's insistent tapping had been replaced by allegations, Morrissey realized. He knew he must choose his next words carefully.

Each man held the other in his eye now. Dr. Morrissey

said, "You wouldn't be projecting now, would you, Stanley? Unloading yourself indirectly. By pointing the finger at me, you in essence unburden yourself so that you may—"

"Bullshit! More psychobabble bullshit! Answer the question, Doctor. Are you into scalps or heads? Which do you prefer? Hands, entrails?"

"The question is misdirected, Stanley!" Morrissey's face had grown red, the veins in his neck bulging ropelike. "Hold up a mirror!"

Garrette, calm and determined replied, "Maybe you've been around people like me and the others so long that you *are* the mirror, William."

"Damn you, do not refer to me as William." The answer came out in a spray of spittle.

"Been with our kind so long that you want to know what it's like to be one of us, isn't that it, Willie? Gotten so close to people like us, that you want to know what it feels like to do the things we do, huh, Willie? To be or not to be . . . to find oneness with the universal evil. I understand your wanting to know what if feels like to fucking cut off somebody's head, to hold it in your hands."

"This session is over! Go back to your fucking cages, every damn one of you, now!" Morrissey, with a faint nod of the head, alerted the men he had termed "guardians"—halfway house graduates he trusted—to see each of the seven psychos back to their rooms immediately.

"Cops got nothing on any of us, and they're just stupid," came Wendell's last remark as they were marched off. "Barking up the wrong damn tree. Look what they did to Freeleng!"

Wilcox only muttered under his breath, something sounding like a curse or a threat.

Stanley Garrette stopped at the entryway to the big room and declared in a coldly incisive voice, "I don't know shit about those murders. Maybe it's been ol' Sedgewick all along."

Laughter filled the hallway as the men, hearing this, joined Garrette for a thunderous belly laugh.

AT THE 2 A.M. HOUR THAT SAME NIGHT

The killing, slow and deliberate, created suffering in the victim until she again passed out. Now the final, climactic moment, and death comes to Elena Proust as he cuts her throat and allows her blood to paint the rich gray carpet. The neck is carefully cut now all the way around, the serrated knife digging deeply through the flesh until meeting the thin neck bone. Once completed, the killer snaps the head forward, back, side to side and wrests it free from the cord of the neck bone. The feel of it, the weight in his hands, the basketball-ness of it, fills him with a sense of power.

It feels wonderful to take life, but even more so to hold the end result of death in his hands.

He'd rappelled down the side of the woman's building, selecting just the right window. There he had cut his way in as he had at the Kensington woman's apartment, the Balmoral apartment and others. Again it had been an easy matter to lay in wait for Elena. She was his from the instant he wrapped his hands about her throat and mouth. She'd struggled. This had only heightened his excitement. She'd pleaded. This had given him a sensual arousal that came to him only in moments of intense suffering—the intense suffering of the victim, like a helpless yew with its head caught in a fence.

She'd begged for her life. He liked that. He had once fantasized a woman whom he could do this to over and over, but death always stepped in to end it—as was the case now.

"Damned hard to sustain," he told the corpse. "Fucking women . . . You're all alike."

The face, even in death, appeared so beautiful. He wondered how he should stage it to best effect for the authorities. Then he wondered if he shouldn't keep it, at least for a little while, watch it decay before him, perhaps use it to pleasure himself with at a later time by defiling it—Elena's eyes, nose, mouth, her flowing, blood-caked red hair.

"Yes, we can party again," he told the dead features, "but I gotta leave a little something of you for the authorities." With that said, he began an incision at the forehead and worked to part a large portion of the victim's scalp from her head.

"Now, that's something." He spoke to the dead woman's head. He then stuffed the head into his plastic-lined tool bag.

Returning to the body, he placed the scalp atop her blood pool, where her neck and head had once been. He next began dissecting the stomach, opening it wide and removing the slippery contents he found there. The intestines squirmed out of his hands and coiled alongside the body with the sound of a mildly hissing nest of snakes. He liked the feel of them and the sound they made in his head. As a boy, he'd loved snakes, devouring books about the various species from rattlesnakes to coral snakes. The serpentine intestines seemed to have eyes, and they seemed to be following him with their eyes.

He lifted a large, fat green candle, one he had picked up at a local Target store, jammed it between the ribs to hold it in place. Next he lit the candle. He sat back and watched the flame burn bright, flicker, come alive again and glow. He breathed in the aromatic odor of the candle as it mixed with the smell of death.

He chanted, *"Ariso, ariso, domino, ariso domino,"* over the flame and the headless body. Words he had learned as a boy in the Catholic church he had infrequently attended.

A few hours later, having fully relished the room he had filled with death, the killer severed and bagged each hand alongside the head. He then stood, took in a final deep breath, looked at the clock on the table beside the bloodied sofa, found it ticking toward 5 A.M., making him wonder where the time had gone. Killing made time stand still for him; he lost all track of it while in the process of murder and the rituals he'd established after the kill. Killing also made him hungry, as it made him wakeful, fully alive, his senses replenished, the way "normal" men felt after good sex, Dr. Morrissey had told the group one night.

He sighed, feeling a deep well of sadness overtake him; it was a familiar letdown feeling, a feeling of grim disappointment to have to face the fact that it was over, and him left with enormous grief—not guilt, but simple grief.

He thought of the first person he had ever murdered. It had been a little neighbor girl, an easy victim for a twelve-year-old boy filled with venom and hatred for his father.

He now went to his tool bag, replaced all the tools into the deep impressions made for them by the manufacturer.

He slung the bag with head and hands—a Hefty bag he'd
brought with him—over one shoulder and clipped his tool
pack to his belt. In a moment, he swung out into the night,
playing Batman again. His gruesome prizes intact, he disappeared up the side of the building, returning the way
he had come.

If anyone had seen him crawl up the side of the building and over the lip of the roof, they'd have imagined him
a gargoyle or a gremlin, he believed.

The evidence gathering at Heather Balmoral's apartment
had continued through the morning hours, and with dawn
approaching and everyone finally preparing to leave the
scene of the atrocious crime, a voice broke the stillness.
"We got another one!" called out a uniformed cop from
the doorway to Captain Lincoln and Lucas Stonecoat.

"Another what?" asked Lincoln.

All eyes were on the uniformed patrolman.

" 'Nother call about a headless corpse, only a few
blocks over."

"Goddamn this villian!" shouted Lincoln.

"He's increased quota big time. Stepped up his time
line," added Lucas.

"Else someone trying to pass a murder off as belonging
to this guy," countered a more cautious Meredyth.

"Give the information to the detectives," Lincoln told
the officer. Lucas thought, *Fuck, but I'm really going to
need another notepad.*

Another victim of the head-taker, again in a luxury
high-rise apartment, the same mode of entry only too obvious . . . and so it went in Lucas Stonecoat's notepad as
he jotted down the salient points of the newest death

room. Once again, while the victim had suffered a beheading, the victim's scalp remained the only portion of the head left behind. Large patches of skin had been removed from the back and torso as well, a new ripple. So, while the killer this time had walked off a second time with the head, he'd also again taken the victim's hands.

"It's got to be the same guy. All along, it's been the same killer," said Lucas, staring at the carnage before him. "The Scalper and the Beheader are one and the same."

Meredyth, seeming to have steeled herself against the horror of the mutilations she'd now witnessed, calmly said, "The question the evidence begs is twofold, Lucas."

"And how's that?" replied Lincoln, confused.

Ames stood mute, rubbing each of his wrists in succession, reliving old nightmares, Meredyth realized. She grasped his arm and wrapped herself to him, giving him support. Then she answered Lincoln and Lucas's questioning eyes. "Is it a copycatting of the Orlando Scalper murders and the Chicago Handyman murders of the early eighties, two cases Randy earlier pulled information on, or—the other question hangs in the balance."

"Which is?"

"Is the murder of Elena Proust a feint to throw authorities off, someone such as a jilted boyfriend covering his tracks by using what he's read in the newspapers?"

"No, no way," countered Lucas.

"How can you be so sure?" asked Lincoln.

Lucas stared across at Meredyth and added, "The striking similarities between the crime scene at Heather Balmoral's place and here . . . It's downright overwhelming, down to the taking of the head and hands, down to the scalp being left behind, none of which had been reported as tandem incidents at a single crime scene to the press."

Lincoln turned to Meredyth and said, "He's right. No one would copycat a killer and add to the MO reported in the press."

A detective from the Two-Five, taking over for Dave Harbough, a crass and pencil-thin fellow with pasty black hair named Gwinn, joked, "Hey, Stonecoat, I think this is for you," as he held up the scalp at the end of a pair of tweezers, blood caking it so badly it looked like roadkill.

Lucas ignored Gwinn, as he might an annoying gnat, and went to the bedroom. There he found all the evidence he needed to confirm that their killer had murdered not one but two people this night. The glass beads on the carpeting in the bedroom were telling. The spray exploded inward—the correct direction. Additional evidence proved that they were dealing with the same killer, and that he entered from outside the high-rise window. A small drop of blood and shred of skin stuck to the window where the killer had exited. "Bag this," Lucas ordered Chang's technician who had followed him into the room. "It could prove important later."

The size of the laser-cut hole through the window proved the same, down to measurements. Meanwhile, Chang's people found the cuts to the body, the candle and the scalp remnant, were all identical. Including the serrations on the knife.

Lucas returned to Lincoln after an hour of browsing the death scene, speaking with the technicians and Chang. "It's got to be our boy working overtime." He only spoke that which everyone in the room already contemplated. "I'm ready to believe it has all been the work of one man."

They closed out the scene with everyone exhausted and angry.

"I'm damned frustrated at having to do this twice in the same night," muttered Lucas into Meredyth's ear.

"Worse than frustration, Lucas, is the fear. I'm fearful it will not be the last such scene we're called out to, and I'm still not convinced it isn't the work of two men now working in tandem."

"We've got to get surveillance teams on Wilcox and Garrette. What's taking so long with those surveillance warrants?"

"Randy believes they will be in our hands by 9 A.M. today."

"It's almost that now."

Ames, his black face ashen, came to join them. "It's horrible. As if it were like yesterday . . . the same . . . the hands severed . . ."

"It's not just about their damned hands, Ames," said Lucas, losing his calm. "Their heads, their scalps, their insides are cut out and replaced with a fucking burning candle. What do you make of that, Dr. Ames? What's going through this bastard's brain while he's unraveling their intestines?"

Lucas stalked off from the two psychiatrists, unable to say another word, not wishing to hear a futile reply.

However, Leonard Chang chased Lucas down and pulled him into the kitchnette where he said, "I not so sure this not work of two different killer, Lucas."

"Whataya mean, Leonard?"

"This time severed hands cut off *after* she dead already, my professional 'pinion."

Lucas took in a great breath of air, shaking his head, stalking off, returning, pacing, his hands raising and lowering until he finally stopped stone cold and asked Chang,

"One killer, two killers . . . Goddamn it, Chang, which is it?"

Chang shook his head in response, saying, "I sorry, Lucas . . . but I not know. Sorry to, like they say, burst your bubble gum, Lucas."

Randy Oglesby telephoned for Lucas to meet him in Dr. Sanger's office, saying, "We have video on Dean Grant's lecture when he was here in Houston, and I have vital information concerning Morrissey's patients, names, ages, histories, records of criminal activity, past employment— all of it on all of them. One of them . . . Garrette . . . had training in rappelling in the military as luck would have it. Thought you two would like to comb through it."

"Any of them have experience as a steelworker?"

"Actually, yes."

"Wendell?"

"No, Wilcox."

"I'll be right up." Lucas closed the murder book he had been going over, the first victim in the string of high-rise murders. Examining it alongside the first scalping murders, he found the mode of entry into the victim's apartments strikingly similar. In both cases, the killer used a laser glass cutter. The significant difference came in the high-rise dangling act the killer now used. He had perfected it out of a sense of boredom, Lucas believed, after finding it too easy to kill victims on the first or even second story of a building.

By now Judge Jerome Patterson's edict to OK a surveillance of Wilcox and Garrette had been put into place, and teams were on both suspects.

When he reached Meredyth's office, Lucas's red eyes met her red eyes. He saw that Dr. Ames sat hunched over

Meredyth's seminar table, poring over files and writing a great deal onto a notepad. Together, they now combed the files for any connection with Grant, Florida, Chicago, crime labs, police departments, anything touching on the Scalper murders or the Handyman case.

The detective and the two psychiatrists continued to focus on the two remaining files on patients Morrissey had pointed to—Lester Franklin Wilcox, and Stanley Theopolis Garrette, both of whom had had rappelling experience, Garrette in the military and Wilcox as a hobby in his youth.

Randy had also secured computer printout photos on each of the two suspects. Lucas studied the two distinct faces and wondered at the innate madness in each pair of eyes.

Meredyth put on the tape sent to them by Dean Grant. He'd secured the tape, he said, from the promoters of the show in an attempt to hurry things along for the HPD. With the lights turned off, the three of them, with Randy looking in from time to time, scanned the crowd whenever the cameras panned the audience, for any sign of their suspects. Wendell came into view, but the other two were not present.

"That bastard," muttered Lucas. "It's him."

"Go slowly, Lucas. This doesn't mean he killed those women. It merely proves he was there to hear of Grant's most notorious cases."

"And in a group therapy session, he may well have told the others about it," suggested Ames.

"Why was he there? How'd he know about Grant's appearance in the first place?" asked Lucas.

"There," said Meredyth, "it's Dr. Morrissey, only a few seats behind Wendell."

"No Wilcox, no Garrette so far as I can see," added Lucas.

"Perhaps this was part of Wendell's therapy, to hear of others like himself," suggested Ames. "We know that Morrissey conducts group sessions for these sociopaths so they can see that they are not the only monsters on the block. He believes in introducing them to one another, but also in introducing each to the kinds of crimes the others have committed."

Meredyth agreed, nodding and saying, "I've read about his group therapy sessions in his books, Lucas. Dr. Ames is right."

Lucas thought for a moment and said, "I wonder at the madness that releases such men back into society to begin with. Now, with each released on society, each one of these devils fits the profile of the high-rise lust-murderer or murderers."

He listened as Ames recounted for them the facts concerning their two likeliest suspects. "Lester Franklin Wilcox, now supposedly cured of his mental disorder and penchant for murder, did disembowel his victims after death. He made love to them in that state, an avowed necrophiliac. . . ."

"Ugggh!" groaned Randy.

Ames continued, saying, "And Garrette—still not ruled out as the killer—did in fact use hot wax from candles to taunt and torment his victims before ending their suffering with a severing of the jugular."

Randy protested, "None of them scalped anyone or removed hands!"

Ames disagreed, saying, "Such horrid fantasies as theirs can, and often do, evolve into greater horrors with the passage of time. If Morrissey has unwittingly fed these fantasies, there is little telling . . ."

This left the room in a long silence.

Meredyth broke the silence with, "Imagine that Laurel Kensington might well have been seen in or around the Hyatt Regency while Dean Grant was there with his traveling forensics show. That she was seen there by her killer, or at least by Wendell."

"What makes you think so?" asked Lucas.

"Laurel's workplace was within walking distance, and she had a number of clients in the vicinity. Laurel was a private duty nurse, and she had big money clients in that area."

"Balmoral worked in real estate, in downtown properties, mortgages, and the like," Lucas added. "She'd be seen in that same area. Any number of reasons for her to be in the vicinity of the Hyatt then."

They continued to explore this idea, going to a map of the city and drawing a line between the office building where Laurel Kensington worked, where she lived and the Hyatt downtown. They did the same with Balmoral. The two overlapping, small triangles created by the red marker told an interesting story. Lucas solemnly imagined the possibility that Laurel Kensington had not been a random selection, when he stated, "Suppose these were targeted women, women stalked for some time before the killer knew their exact locations in the high-rises where they had, in the end, died."

"If that's the case, our killer is interested in a certain type of victim," suggested Ames. "How has Laurel Kensington similarities to the other victims? She and Balmoral, for instance, are as different as night and day. What sort of victim profile have we?"

"That's just it. They've all differed in the extreme," Lucas added, pacing now as he gave thought to this. "Some have been heavier, muscular women, actually, large-framed, broad-shouldered women." He stopped his pacing to check some details in two of the files on Meredyth's desk. "Two with red hair were the larger women, the three brunettes were frail, far thinner, with smaller mass."

Meredyth, now staring out her window at the endless sea of high-rise buildings in Houston, added, "All have been within the age bracket of twenty-five to thirty-two, and all have lived quiet, uneventful lives that should not have led to violent death. All of them thought themselves well protected, living in safe havens. None were into drugs, alcohol or prostitution, none of them courted this kind of end."

"It's a puzzle," said Lucas, "but some of the pieces appear to be coming together."

"You have taken the evidence left at the crime scene to indicate that the work of the Scalper and the Beheader, since both make the same entrance from atop a building, rappelling downward to the targeted window, to be the work of one man," said Ames. "But suppose . . . just for a moment . . . suppose that we actually have two killers, possibly more, on our hands. That the idea of the Scalper and the Beheader being one killer who is sending the message that he is two, is in fact *bogus*. Suppose, that they *are* two separate killers, who in fact are aware of each other, possibly even know one another, and are trying to outdo one another?"

Ames allowed this suggestion to sink in deeply. Both Lucas and Meredyth considered the idea in silence. Ames continued, his voice spilling out to the outer room where

Randy Oglesby could hear. "They kill and read about one another in the press, possibly even contact one another, having had prior knowledge of one another, either in prison or in some other context—"

"Say a group psychiatric session conducted by none other than Dr. Thomas Morrissey," suggested Meredyth.

"Exactly," agreed Ames.

"Now we're putting this thing together. We've got a twenty-four-hour surveillance on Stanley Theopolis Garrette and Lester Franklin Wilcox."

"Can we get a judge to order up a search warrant of the halfway house where they live?" asked Meredyth.

"Do we have enough supposition to convince a judge?" asked Lucas. "Not bloody likely."

"In another reality, I always wanted to be a second-story man, myself," said Ames with a wry grin.

"Are you suggesting, Dr. Ames, that we break in and examine the halfway house rooms belonging to our suspects?"

"Whatever you find, it will be fruit of the forbidden tree in a court of law," warned Meredyth.

"Still, should we discover anything, we'll know once and for all, if we're on the right track with Morrissey's patients, or if this entire time, we have had the wrong direction," said Lucas, recalling how wrong Dave Harbough had been about Freeleng.

"There's a block party going on tonight on the street where the halfway house is located. That'll cause a lot of distraction, and perhaps we could add to the distraction, say with a little imagination," suggested Meredyth.

"Block party?"

"Arranged by the police, for community service. Lots

of free hot dogs, hamburgers, drinks and games," said Meredyth.

Lucas looked from Meredyth to Ames and back again, saying now with eyes wide, "You two have had this planned for some time, haven't you?"

"We cooked it up a few days ago when Richard made the first suggestion that our killer might be our *killers* in competition with one another. It took time to organize the block party."

"I see."

"And with your penchant for getting in and out of places without being seen, Lucas . . . Well, I naturally thought . . ."

"Gotcha," he said, letting her off the hook. "My natural catlike grace, my innate Indian ability at stealth, like the time I was almost brought up on charges by my captain for infiltrating a crime scene that had been strictly off limits to me?"

"It led to good results, remember?" she replied.

"This could be a dead end. I can't imagine these psychotics squirreling away body parts in their halfway house rooms," said Ames.

"No, I would find paperwork on a storage facility, a key to a locker, a safe-deposit box that might lead to a diary, any number of things."

"Point taken."

"All right, so what diversions did you have in mind?"

"A street brawl will break out amid the festivities," she replied. "I've already arranged it with some uniforms."

"You know I could lose my badge if anything goes wrong."

"I'll stand with you if it comes to that."

Lucas shook his head and smiled. "I believe you would."

"Are we agreed?"

"Into the lion's den I go."

"It may be the only way," she replied.

"We don't have a lot of options left," Lucas agreed. "And letting time pass is an invitation to another kill."

$\mathcal{F}$OURTEEN

Morning stars: to direct, guide

Lucas, Meredyth and Ames put their plan into motion. The street out front of the halfway house where Walter Freeleng had been killed by a sniper bullet only a week before, was now filled with people all partaking of the benevolence of the Houston Police Department in conjunction with the Chamber of Commerce, all to promote better relations between the police and the policed. A carnival atmosphere prevailed: There were helium balloons, game booths lining the cordoned-off street, food vendors giving away free food and drink—all courtesy of the City of Houston.

Lucas, dressed in black, moved among the crowd, amazed at how quickly and efficiently Meredyth had put together the ruse. She had explained that the block party concept was one easily grasped by the city fathers for promoting harmony in troubled precincts. The block party had been scheduled for July with the upcoming Independence Day city-wide activities. It had not been difficult to move the event up a few weeks with the help of officials she had known for years when she explained the need as one of an imperative nature. It was necessary for this neighborhood to have some relief *now*, she'd told the city fathers, explaining that, with the sniper shooting of Walter Freeleng, the area had become a hotbed of psychological unrest, citing several daylight robberies, bar fights and other eruptions.

Now Lucas made his way toward the rear of the half-way house, a several-stories high redbrick building that looked like an old government building, its Romanesque windows like those of any Federal building. Few people in the neighborhood had been aware that the place housed released murderers and rapists, until the Freeleng shooting had brought the halfway house attention from the press. Now protests had been conducted to move the inhabitants somewhere else, somewhere far from here.

Lucas tested a loose, clapboard window shutter from where he crouched in shadow behind the halfway house. The shutter came off in his hand. The sister shutter swung open, creaking on a rusted-out hinge, making a mini-banshee scream. The windowpane itself reflected only blackness, dim with grime and dirt, so caked with it, in fact, that nothing on the interior could report back. The window was locked or, more certainly, nailed closed. He doubted that he could break it, or that he could even squeeze in since the window frame was nailed shut and would not budge.

Lucas wondered whether he should just abort this so-called plan for another that might prove more fruitful in the long run.

Lucas was at total critical mass, about to explode. If he lost it, rushed into Morrissey's office and took the man out back and beat him to a pulp, he knew he would lose his detective rank, likely his career. Still, it was something that he really, really wanted to do.

He could call in a favor from Roundpoint. Roundpoint had the wherewithal to snatch the good doctor from his home. Were they to do so, then a masked Lucas could enter the room where Morrissey was deposited. Then Lucas could conduct a serious and productive interrogation.

But Lucas's fantasy did not stop with Morrissey. He could also have the three suspects, Morrissey's most dangerous clients, picked up as well. He could conduct the interrogation he wanted. No lawyers in the way, no system in the way. Roundpoint was fully behind Lucas, both hated what the high-rise killer had done to strike fear into the heart of the city.

The interrogation of Doc Residual could net them a great deal. It might come to light that Morrissey indeed encouraged one or more of his charges to indulge in their killing fantasies. To thine own self be true, his books encouraged, to "be one's self" and give into the urges that beset a man, from lust to rape to murder. The doctor's thinking was that if the killing instinct were fed in a fantasy fashion in overdose amounts, then the killer would be fulfilled by the thoughts alone. He need not act on his *agressivitals*, as Morrissey termed such urges embedded deep within the mind. Morrissey was likely not the puppet master he thought he was, and if so, how misconstrued might his instructions to his patients be?

Lucas chuckled at the thought of a meeting between Roundpoint and Morrissey. He imagined a frightened Dr. Morrissey rushing to retire after facing Roundpoint's brand of interrogation.

Lucas now made his way into the backyard and stared up at a series of wooden platforms and stairs leading to each level. On each level were more windows. He'd see if any presented easy access. Armed with information Meredyth had procured for the exact mailing addresses of his two targets, which showed their room numbers here at the halfway house, Lucas stealthily made his way forward, when he saw that a basement door stood ajar. The doorway led directly into the very basement where the window would have led him. He slipped through and, with a flashlight, glanced about the basement room. It held four washers and six dryers for laundry. In the rear, he located a series of small cages with locks on them, private storage for the residents, he realized. Each metal cage was tagged with the corresponding room number. Lucas located numbers 1306 and 2202, each corresponding to Lester Franklin Wilcox and Stanley Theopolis Garrette, respectively. Lucas's light beam sluiced about each cage. In one, Lucas saw a small, portable refrigerator. He felt instantly curious of the contents of the icebox as it hummed, alive with electrical current.

Lucas had brought a set of fine burglar's tools, but the locks on the cages were ancient, huge, and rusty. The instruments were useless here, unless he spent a half hour on the job. He decided instead to search the place for a crowbar, a hacksaw or a lock cutter but no such tools presented themselves. He stared up at the sides of the cages. They ended just shy of the ceiling, no room to squeeze through. He searched for any sort of tool or metal object with which to force the locks. He didn't want to fire his weapon in here, knowing the resounding echo would send people running to inspect the basement. Instead, he gave up the refrigerator for the moment, and went back to seeking a way into the building—and the two rooms he so wanted to investigate.

He returned to the rear of the building and the stairwell going up. He believed nonchalance the best approach to such circumstances, so he nonchalantly tried the back door. It opened at his touch.

This felt too easy.

Something in the back of his mind and something else in his gut told him to go lightly and to be wary. He stepped through the door and it pinched his ears with a rusty metal cry from each hinge.

The interior felt as dark as it looked. In fact, he felt as if he'd just stepped back in time to perhaps the year 1950 or earlier, when such buildings as this existed in plenty. The hallways were as dark as caverns. Dark paneling and ancient paisley print wallpaper greeted him as he found the stairwell that would take him to the second floor. He might as well begin with 2202, he surmised. *Take the plunge.*

He eased his way up the stairs, passing an ancient painting and an even older man talking to his hat and paying Lucas no attention whatsoever. On the second landing, he quickly located 2202 from the series of doors on each side of the corridor. He pushed the door inward but it stood firm, locked. To this he responded with his burglar's tools, opening his pack and locating the needle he wanted, a skeletal key that he played the lock with, and in a moment, it clicked. He turned the knob and waltzed into Stanley Theopolis Garrette's private room. He thought it ironic that the cages in the basement were more secure than the rooms.

The place stank of beer and dirty clothes, and it appeared a full-blown pigsty. Amid the trash, the dirty clothes and filth of closets, he searched for any sign of rope, rappelling equipment, a laser glass cutter, a bowling bag for the missing heads, a hatchet or machete as Chang had indicated were used in the taking of the hands and heads, but he found nothing of the sort. He silently cursed the stench and his ill luck all at once.

Lucas concluded then that the killer must be downstairs in room 1306, and that he must be Wilcox. He left the room as quietly as he had come. No one had seen him go in or come out.

Lucas made his way back to the stairwell and maneuvered his way past a pair of drunks arguing over a shoe one had pulled from his own feet. Lucas passed a room where chairs sat in a circle, a group session room. He passed a small office, presumably used by Morrissey when he came here for his group sessions with the men of this place.

Lucas then located a wing of rooms on this floor, and soon stood before 1306. He grasped the doorknob and found it turning in his hand. Again, too easy. *A set up?* he wondered.

He cautiously stepped through and into the darkness of the interior. The room was immaculate, nothing out of place. It appeared cleaned by a maid. Was Wilcox obsessively clean? That would account for his having left nothing at the scene of the crimes.

Lucas began searching the room, tearing open drawer after drawer, checking below mattress and box spring, searching high and low in the closet, but he found nothing more incriminating than *Hustler* magazines anywhere. He sought out any key that might open Wilcox's cage in the basement, but he could find none.

Frustrated, checking the time, Lucas feared he must leave here with not a shred more information than he had coming in. The refrigeration unit in the basement preyed on his mind. Why was it in a locked cage in the basement? If you wanted a late-night snack, why not the room for the refrigerator?

Lucas stepped from Wilcox's room, thinking himself in the clear when Wendell stepped from the shadows, a crazed grin on his mad face. "Looking for something, Lieutenant Stonecoat?"

Lucas wheeled on the little creep, bringing his gun up instinctively to meet the man's eyes. Wendell went un-fazed, adding, "Why don't you search my room? I tell you, all of this killing . . . this butchery . . . it's . . . it's Sedgewick's doing."

"Christ, why aren't you at the street party with every-one else, Wendell?"

"Don't worry. I won't tell Dr. Morrissey about your late-night visit."

"Tell him what?"

"That you're snooping around here without a search warrant in violation of the civil rights of the two men whose rooms you've ransacked."

Lucas was struck by Wendell's clarity on matters of the law; his demeanor and calm seemed at odds with his per-formance on the day of his interrogation. "What does Wil-cox have in his refrigerator, Wendell?"

"Refrigerator?"

"Downstairs in the basement."

"No appliances of any kind allowed in the rooms, you know. As for the basement door being ajar . . . Who do you suppose left it open for you, Lieutenant? I left it open for you to wander in, just as I did the back door. I saw you coming, sneaky as the Indian you are. I spy on every-body, you see. Gotta stay ahead, on top, you know. Place like this? If you wanna stay alive . . . I mean, you should see what I got living next door to me! And look what happened to poor ol' Freeleng!" He cackled the last words.

Lucas heard some of the madness creeping back into the little man's voice now. He allowed him to continue. "I have a telescope in my room. Saw you two blocks away."

"Really? How wise of you, Wendell. Which one's your room, Wendell?"

"Top floor, five floors up. You want to search my place? We can take the elevator."

Lucas wanted to smack the smart little creep, when he realized just how savvy the so-called schizoid was being. He had Lucas on charges of breaking and entering—he had made that clear despite his reassurances. He had invited Lucas to look into his own room as well, knowing Lucas would decline after having seen Wendell's performance at the station house—after convincing one and all that he was too much the maniac to serve as the cool, calculating Scalper or Beheader.

Yet Lucas noted a glint in the man's eye. He had come armed with Wendell's picture, a photo of Wendell sitting at the Dean Grant lecture at the Hyatt. He held it up to Wendell now and asked point-blank, "What were you doing here, Wendell? Spying on Dr. Morrissey?"

Wendell flinched only slightly, but enough to tell Lucas that he'd surprised the skinny madman. Without a moment's more hesitation, Lucas grabbed him by the throat and pushed him through Wilcox's door. There Lucas slapped him so hard that Wendell went to his knees, blubbering.

"*You* know what's going on around here. You know who comes and goes and when and how. You're going to share that with me now, little man, and we're not going by any rules but mine."

"I didn't kill anyone! Sedgewick did it."

Lucas slapped him hard again, sending Wendell to a prostrate position. Blood ran from Wendell's nose and lip where Lucas's huge hand had made contact. Lucas put his gun to Wendell's head. "You want me to put an end to your miserable life and to Sedgewick's here and now?"

"Go ahead, fire, you gutless wonder." It came out as another voice, the sound of Sedgewick, Lucas realized, who recalled having heard it during the interrogation.

"This wimp doesn't know dick. I told those bitches that at your precinct, and now I'm telling you."

"Then you tell me what I want to hear, or you and the wimp both die, here and now."

"Bullshit."

Lucas struck Wendell with the gun, a red gash now trailed across his creased forehead. Sedgewick wailed in pain. "Goddamn you!"

Lucas struck out with his boot, catching Wendell's ribs with his right foot. Wendell doubled over in pain now. "Please, stop," he begged. "I'll take you to Dr. Morrissey. *He* . . . he can explain . . . *everything*."

"Morrissey? He's here, now? How can he explain the murders?"

"He knows about them."

"He does? Has he *known* all along?"

"You could say that. You could say he figured it all out in the end."

"He wasn't in his office."

"No, he isn't there."

"Take me to him now."

"He's in the group room. That's where they told him what they'd been doing."

"*They?*"

"I overheard. If they knew that I know, they'd kill me. You gotta promise me protection. Put me into that thing you do, that protective custody thing." Lucas realized that Wendell the Wimp was back in control of his body and mind, but he wondered at the ease with which Wendell went in and out of his other personalities.

"Take me to Morrissey."

"All right! All right! But I will not be responsible for . . . for your safety or your life, Lieutenant."

Lucas forced the weasel to his feet and pushed him toward the door. "Keep talking the entire way, like we're old friends, just visiting. Now go."

The two of them emerged into the dark hallway and made their way back to the group therapy room. Lucas pushed Wendell ahead of him, and now he pushed him into the group therapy room. Lucas himself stepped into the room behind Wendell.

No Dr. Morrissey.

"Well, where is he?"

"Gone home, I suppose, but not without bruises."

"What're you talking about, bruises?"

Wendell gave him a conspiratorial half smile and said, "He was attacked by . . . by some of the men. When I last saw him, he was curled up in the fetal position in *that* corner." He pointed to emphasize his words. "Morrissey was beaten pretty badly, but the phones were ripped out. No way to call nine-one-one, you know, and the SOB is as good as his word, he told the house guardians—that's what they're called nowadays—to do nothing, to stand down, that he was all right, and they were to report this incident to *no one*. He was bleeding from his forehead, nose, lip. Everybody got a *kick* out of it, so to speak." The little madman gave a quick and furtive glance to an overhead chandelier.

Lucas looked up to the ceiling and imagined Morrissey dangling from the ancient chandelier, his hands tied behind his back, his throat snapped from having been hung. But where was Morrissey now, and was he still in danger?

"And what about you, Wendell? What part did you play in this attack on Morrissey?"

"Everybody was trying to get a shot at him, but only the two of them, Wilcox and Garrette, threatened him with a knifing."

"Wilcox and Garrette?"

"That's right."

"*Did* they knife him?"

"Nah, no balls, all show. Flash and dash is all. No matter how much they were urged on. They chickened."

"Some of you wanted to hang him by that chandelier you were staring at," suggested Lucas, "and maybe cut his throat, watch him slowly bleed to death like a swine at slaugher? Right? Am I right, Wendell?" Lucas turned face-to-face with the smaller man, his angry breath lifting Wendell's eyelids.

"Some of them did, yeah. You're good, Detective. Sure you're not psychic or something?"

"So, some of the men wanted to murder Morrissey right here on the premises? Sedgewick included?"

"Sedgewick just talks a big game. He can't stand the sight of blood. Faints right out. All talk."

"What about your other self . . . ahhh . . . Stuart, or even you, Wendell?"

"I . . . some of us . . . we may have egged them on, but

only those two actually participated in the beating of that poor old man. Hell, I like Dr. Morrissey, always have. He treated me real good. Took me on as one of his most interesting cases. Wrote about me in his new manuscript."

"But you, or some part of you, enjoyed seeing him beaten, didn't you, Wendell?"

"Maybe . . ."

"Is that true of the other killings, too. Is that why your room is filled with newspaper clippings about the other killings?" bluffed Lucas.

"True of the other killings, too?" Wendell asked, considering this as if it were a calculus question. "Newspaper clippings? Since when is it a crime to follow a crime in the press? Lots of people do that."

Again Lucas saw something flit across the madman's cornea as if some shadow creature lurked deep within him. Something deep within Lucas told him that Wendell was not completely innocent in these crimes. Perhaps he knew more than just the comings and goings of the other inmates in this asylum; perhaps he was central and integral to the crimes. Perhaps he was the mastermind, the single variable, the one unchanging linchpin in this whole ugly, bloody trail.

Lucas grabbed Wendell and dragged him to the window, tearing his collar in the bargain. At the window, Lucas cut a length of rope from the 1940s-style sash. With rope and tassel, Lucas tied Wendell by the neck, noose-fashion. Wendell blubbered and begged to be left alone, but Lucas only led him back to the chandelier, where he hoisted the other man's skinny frame to the winking fake crystal. Lucas hung Wendell there like a bug on a string.

Wendell cried out for help while Lucas cursed him. "You sonofabitch. Your little weaselly act is over!"

Already choking, Wendell dangled by his neck and struggled to deal with his weight and gravity and the pull on his throat.

Hearing Wendell's bobcatlike cry, the cry of a shrieking woman, house guardians in white uniforms appeared at two different doorways. House guardians were the favored men of the halfway house, those who most strikingly had returned to a relatively normal life after prison. They, too, had been in prison, but here they were the model citizens, given some modicum of power over the others to enforce such things as curfews—and obviously doing a poor job of it.

Several guardians approached Lucas menacingly to the backdrop of Wendell's screams and choking. Lucas announced himself, flashing his badge, telling them to halt and stay back. One of them shouted, "I'm going for the cops!" and raced off.

Lucas knew his time with Wendell would be short. He tugged at the little man and spun him by his legs. The chandelier spun with him, sending eerie shadows all across the big hall where the group therapy sessions for this house of murderers were held by Dr. Morrissey.

"How were you involved, Wendell, in the Scalper murders?"

"I was never . . ." His words were choked off.

"The taking of the hands. Was that your idea? You get those notions from Dr. Grant's lecture? You pass along those notions to the real killers, Wilcox and Garrette?"

"No, I never . . ." He gasped for air, clawed at the chandelier, trying to heave his weight up, desperate for relief.

"You're going to die now, Wendell, unless you begin to tell me the truth. *Now!*"

One of the guardians lunged at Lucas, but Lucas

brought his gun up squarely to meet the man's huge eyes. The guardian backed off to where he had been at the doorway, joining his comrades there. Lucas continued his unorthodox interrogation. "OK, all right, Wendell . . . What part did you play in the taking of the heads? And will I find them in the basement, in that freezer I saw?"

Barely able to breathe out the words, Wendell cried, "All right!" He gurgled and managed another choked, "All right! I . . ."

Lucas grabbed his legs and raised him from the torturous stranglehold the chandelier had on Wendell. "Give me a hand, here!" he ordered the guardians, who reacted as they might to any voice of authority. They lowered Wendell, his neck beet red from the choking he'd endured.

"Now, little man, talk to me, or I'll put you back where I had you, *now!*"

Wendell sputtered, tried to catch his breath. One of the guardians grabbed Lucas in an attempt to pull him away. Lucas wheeled around and brought his fist-wrapped gun into the man's cowlike face, sending him to the floor, his nose bleeding profusely. The remaining two guardians fell in line when Lucas shouted, "Back off!" He then returned his attention to Wendell and continued his interrogation.

"Now, Wendell, compose yourself. Tell you what we'll do. Since death by hanging appears so repugnant to you, we're going to take a walk, upstairs to the roof. By the time we get there, if you haven't told me the truth about your part in all of this, then you're going to find out how death by flying feels."

"Fly—flying?" he managed to sputter as Lucas snatched him to his feet.

"March for the stairwell. We'll just see if the Beheader can defy gravity. I always wanted to see a chicken fly.

Some folks say a chicken can't fly, Wendell, too domesticated, but I've seen some cocks go a pretty good distance, haven't you? You a cock or a chicken, Wendell?"

With each word, they took another step. The two remaining house gaurdians stood at the foot of the stairs, unable to do anything but watch. Behind him, Lucas heard Meredyth Sanger shouting his name, her tone angry.

Lucas forced Wendell ahead to the next landing.

"Lucas! This has gone too far!" cried Meredyth. "Let it drop here and now before it goes any further."

Lucas glanced down to see Meredyth's anguished face beside that of a confused Dr. Richard Ames. Several uniformed cops poured in around them.

Lucas stepped up his interrogation and his march to the rooftop. "Now, little man, again, you tell me what part you played in the death of Laurel Kensington and the others. We know that you scoped out where she lived. That you fingered her for death, Wendell, you or some goddamn part of you."

"I never did no such thing."

"You acted as a pimp for Wilcox or Garrette or both, Wendell. We know that much. You were downtown at the same time Laurel Kensington sat in an audience to hear Dr. Dean Grant speak about his more gruesome cases. She was into that, read all the true-crime books, and when she heard Grant was speaking, naturally she had to be there. Dr. Morrissey knew of your interest in Grant's cases, and he got you in. He befriended you, Wendell. He liked you."

"Morrissey's a moron, a stupid motherfucker."

They were on the rooftop now.

Wendell added, "But then you already know that much."

"You like being smarter than other people, don't you, Wendell?"

"I don't *like* it. I just am."

"All this stupidity you display, and all these personalities you display, they're all part of your goddamned act, aren't they, Wendell."

Lucas had forced him to the edge of the building now, shoving him to look at his fate. "Can you walk on water, Wendell? Can you walk on air? Can you fly? You better hope so."

"Only them other two were actually involved. I . . . I gave them ideas, suggestions, but I never was involved, not even in the room. No jury can convict me of doing a thing. I didn't lift a finger to harm any of those people, Lieutenant. Not a thing."

"You gave them ideas, huh? Suggestions?" Lucas wrenched the man's arm behind his back; he wanted to break the little man's neck for him. He wanted to send him sailing out over the edge of the building, watch him make a splat on the pavement below. Only a few stories but enough to break every bone in his body. But Lucas needed him alive and talking. "Did you also procure victims for them?"

"Never."

"But you were the only one who saw Laurel Kensington at the downtown Hyatt where Dean Grant spoke. She was a fan of Grant's books. She took the day off to be there and, for some morbid reason, Dr. Morrissey took you down there to hear about Dean Grant's most bizarre cases. You crossed paths with her, and you somehow got free of Morrissey and followed her to learn where she lived."

"It was Sedgewick."

"No, it was Wendell."

"No, it was Stuart. You don't know how many evil thoughts Stuart can have."

Wendell fell into the internal and infernal business of shunting off responsibility to his other personalities again.

"What am I going to find if I break into the refrigerators, Wendell?"

"Just what you might expect."

"What, goddamn you!"

"Hands one level, scalps on another."

"Where are they now? Wilcox and Garrette?"

"They're out . . ."

"Out where?"

"Out . . . on the hunt."

"Where, you bastard, *where*?" Lucas brought his gun up to slam it against Wendell's skull again when he suddenly found himself surrounded by men, all the men in blue uniform, all pointing guns at him.

Meredyth raced across the tarmac rooftop to stand before Lucas, making herself a target, shouting for everyone to lower their weapons. Some of the cops knew her from her work at the 31st Precinct, others recognized Lucas from his picture in the papers on past cases.

Wendell began muttering to himself, talking to his other personalities, "Fellas, we gotta stick together on this."

"Oh, shit," muttered Lucas.

"I never . . . *we* . . . *we* never had a hand in it. . . ." Wendell continued to quietly plead with the *others* within. "Fellas, we gotta be smart about this, fellas. This here guy is psychic for Christ's sake, a psychic cop. He knows we all had a hand in it. He wants to send us all back to prison, *all of us!* Are we going to let him do that?"

"Goddamn little weasel is reverting back to talking to

all of his selves!" Lucas shouted. "He's ready to crack, and he's the only one who can give up the other two, and they're out there tonight—hunting—Meredyth." Lucas pointed to the rooftops of Houston with one hand and held on to Wendell by the sash still around his neck.

Meredyth looked from Lucas to the blubbering Wendell and back at the uniformed officers and Dr. Ames who stared on. She shouted, "We let Lieutenant Stonecoat complete his interrogation here and now, gentlemen. It could save a life or lives. Whataya say?"

Lucas didn't wait for the ensuing quibbling debate. He simply lifted Wendell over his head, extending his arms to the fullest, like a man about to pitch a hay bale onto a truck, but this hay bale was a human being and instead of a truck there was only a concrete chasm. Wendell screamed repeatedly.

"Tell me what I want to know! Give me the address and names of tonight's victims, Wendell, and you live to tell it to a judge. Otherwise, you die here, now, in that gutter down there!"

Dangling in midair with only the crazed cop's hands between him and death, Wendell cried out, "All right! All right!"

"All right, what? A name, an address!"

"Her name's Atchinson, Katherine Atchinson, one thousand two hundred Arlington, apartment one thousand seven hundred three."

"And the other one?"

"Morrissey."

"Forget Morrissey."

"Dr. Morrissey, five hundred forty-four Groveland, Jackson Heights."

"Morrissey, you've targeted Morrissey? Sure, makes

sense that after the attack on him, you'd have to do him."

"*They . . . they* talked about doing him. It wasn't *me*. I got nothing to do with killing."

"Morrissey reports any one of you, and you go back to the pen, and your three-way fun and games are over."

Lucas again felt the urge to throw the garbage out over the edge. Somehow Meredyth sensed this, and placed a restraining hand on him. Once again, guns were pointed at Lucas.

"Let him down, Lucas. Come back off that ledge. Come on, now. We have information to work with. We've got Wendell in custody. Let's go after the other two."

Lucas nodded and lowered Wendell to the tarmac. The uniformed men rushed in to take Wendell into custody, sniveling all the while that he'd been coerced into confession.

FIFTEEN

Lasso: captivity

"They've targeted two for murder and mutilation tonight, and one of them is Morrissey." Lucas brought Ames and Meredyth up to speed as they made their way out of the halfway house.

Pushing their way through the block-party crowd, Lucas located his Intrepid. "I'll put it on the wire for the closest units to race for one thousand two hundred Arlington, apartment one thousand seven hundred three, while you two get to Morrissey to warn that sonofabitch of his imminent death at the hands of Garrette or Wilcox."

Lucas wasted no more time, tearing off from the curb and radioing dispatch for help. A female dispatch voice that Lucas recognized as belonging to Henrietta Lewis, a hefty, wide-grinning black woman, came on, asking, "How can HPD dispatch help you, Officer . . . Ahh, Lieutenant Stonecoat, is that you?" She knew his call numbers.

"You got me, Henri. I'm in pursuit of a suspect, and I need backup. Actually I'm some miles away, and I would like to send the closest unit to twelve hundred Arlington, something going down in apartment seventeen hundred and three."

"Got it."

"Possibly prevent a homicide if we act fast."

"Just a minute."

Don't have a minute, Lucas thought but said nothing. In a moment Henri's melodic voice returned, saying, "Lucas, I got bad news for you."

"Whataya mean?"

"What with the mayor's detail being so large tonight, giving that ball downtown, and two block parties being covered, you, my friend, are the closest unit to twelve hundred Arlington at the moment."

"Then I'm it. Request backup. Likely on the trail of the Beheader."

"Ho, oh. Oh my God, Lucas. I'll get some units over there ASAP, I swear, honey."

"Good, you do that, sweetheart."

"Be careful now."

"Gotcha."

He was on his own. And unless Meredyth and Ames had been smart enough to grab some of the uniforms on hand at the block party, they, too, were finding help scarce. He cursed their luck, but then he thought it just another wily move made by the puppet master, Jared Oliver Sedgewick Stuart Wendell. Of course he would plan this double murder to coincide with a scarcity of law enforcement.

Lucas pushed the gas pedal to the floor and careened through a red light, his siren blipping out repeated warnings. He heard the crunch of metal behind him, some fool had failed to heed his siren and lights. The other car caught his rear passenger side, just inches, but enough to spin him around. He did a full 180-degree turn, never slowing, going straight the moment the car found itself righted. He continued racing for the apartment at 1200 Arlington, praying he wasn't too late, wondering what kind of woman lived there, the sort to Garrette's liking, or the sort to Wilcox's liking. He wondered which of the two creatures preferred the frail and demure women, and which preferred the heftier, more robust victim.

He hoped to soon find out.

Meredyth and Ames had meanwhile made it to Dr. Morrissey's house, a plush little mansion of creamy white standing back from the street, surrounded by gardens, bushes, trees and fence. A police car, its lights still flashing stood in the driveway, but no officers were in sight. The lone unit was the only one in the vicinity, and while Meredyth had given orders to await their arrival, apparently, the officers saw fit to scale the fence and enter the premises. Apparently no one had buzzed the gate to allow them entry.

"It's already a crime in progress," muttered Ames, taking in the situation.

"A murder in progress, you mean."

"I'll try to raise Officers Haley and Prentice," she replied, working through dispatch.

A male dispatcher's voice came back decisively. "Neither officer is responding to his radio. This doesn't bode well. Suggest you wait for additional backup."

"How long will that be?"

"Five minutes, six tops."

"All right, someone will be here waiting." She slipped her .38 Smith & Wesson from her purse and checked the safety mechanism.

"What're you doing, Meredyth?" asked Ames.

"I'm going in there now. You wait here for the backup units."

"I can't let you go in there alone."

"What kind of man would you be?" she replied. "Come on, Richard. You don't want to pull that macho shit with me. Besides, do you know how to use a thirty-eight?"

"Do you?"

"Thanks to Lucas, yes." She didn't wait for any further discussion, but rather climbed from her car and onto the police unit's top, from there she scaled the fence. The cruiser had obviously been pulled up to the fence for this purpose.

Inside the gate, she turned to face Ames who put a hand through to her, taking hers. "Be careful, and come back with all your parts intact."

"Get on the radio. Get that backup here, Richard. I'll be careful."

Ahead of her, she heard nothing, saw nothing, but a side door, a large window, in fact, stood open to the night breeze lifting the sheer curtains. She slipped into the darkened home, assuming that was where the two police had entered. She knew she had to be careful to not get shot by them.

She guessed that Morrissey was either asleep in bed or incapacitated, since he had not answered the police at the gate. Again she paused, listening for footfalls, murmurings, any sound at all that might be coming from the two policemen who'd entered ahead of her. Were they, too, incapacitated? If not, why hadn't they answered their radios? And if they were down, wounded or dead, it meant that their attacker, Garrette or Wilcox, had quietly allowed them to step into his trap. Was he doing the same with her?

She concentrated on all that Lucas had taught her about holding and firing a weapon. All those extra hours put in on the firing range with Lucas cuddling up to her, showing her how to caress, squeeze and hold the weapon, as he'd phrased it, always with the innuendo that using a gun was a sexual experience. Her training with a firearm, such as it was, must pay off here and now, tonight.

She thought of how delectable it would be to kill the man who had murdered Laurel Kensington. . . .

Richard Ames had been assured that other police units were on their way, but where in hell were they, he wondered. He sat in the driver's seat of the police unit, not at all happy with Meredyth's decision to breach the gate and enter the home alone. Something kept crowding him out here in the unit; he kept bumping his elbow on the hard metal of an upright shotgun tethered in place by a thick leather belt with a lock on it.

He glanced at the powerful weapon, a twelve-gauge pump-action beauty. Like a cannon, he felt certain, in the right hands—not his. He'd never fired such a weapon in his life. Still, it represented firepower, and maybe . . . Suppose it was needed inside? Suppose Meredyth got herself killed here tonight. He'd have to explain to people how he had sat out here and allowed her to go inside alone. He'd have to explain that to Lucas Stonecoat.

He dug into his pants pocket for his Swiss Army knife, which he carried with him at all times. He began slicing through the thick leather holding the gun in place, but it was tough and difficult going. It would take time, precious time.

No sirens. No lights in sight. He kept cutting away at the leather girdle that hugged the gun stock, the metal barrel tip practically kissing the unit's interior rooftop. Even if he could successfully cut clear through the leather girdle, he wondered if he'd be able to tear the big cannon from its moorings, given the angle.

"Damn it, just do it!" he cursed himself and continued to work at freeing the gun.

He remembered someone telling him about the kick of such weapons, how they could dislocate a man's shoulder or break a man's collarbone if not held snugly against the shoulder when fired. He tried desperately to concentrate on getting the gun free, telling himself to worry about other problems as they arose.

Still, the leather girdle tenaciously fought to remain intact, frustrating Dr. Richard Ames's efforts.

Even if I can get the damn thing free, will it be in time? he wondered.

Meredyth could make out the sound of laughter—nasty, maniacal laughter. She inched toward it, hearing a male voice in desperate plea, asking for another chance, for mercy. Then a strange silence fell over the place, like a heavy blanket.

Then the eerie silence of the mansion shattered with one sudden command, a powerful voice shouting, "Play the tape! Play it!"

A tape recording began to play, a recording of Morrissey, speaking to a group of patients. He bombarded them with his anger, shouting, "How dare any of you for a moment think me capable of copycatting your crimes!"

This was followed by the voices of other men, men confessing to the Scalper and Beheader murders.

Then suddenly even the tape was hushed by a god-awful sound, a noise that Meredyth Sanger found impossible to place. *Whomp-chuck!* followed by a second, duplicate, *Whomp-chuck!*

She raced toward the sound, her gun at the ready, barging through a stout wooden door and falling over the uniformed body of one of the cops, her gun leaping from her hand, her eyes meeting those of the second dead officer there on the floor. She lay in a thick goo of blood, while the taped voices laughed and screamed for blood—Morrissey's blood.

Meredyth looked up to see Morrissey's eyes, wide with horror. The man remained alive, breathing erratically, lashed to his desk chair. His tree-limb arms were extended, with no hands at their ends. In the darkness, Meredyth felt before she saw the movement of a massive shadow float from the dark corner to the creeping light coming in from somewhere behind Morrissey's unmoving but whimpering form. It seemed as if she were getting Morrissey's whimpers in stereo. He was crying in pain on the tape as well as here in the flesh.

She searched the dark, blood-spattered floor for her gun but could not see it. Meanwhile, the menacing black shape circled the room, and the angry voices on the tape shouted obscenities.

Her eyes adjusting to the light, Meredyth saw that each of Morrissey's hands lay on his desk before him, severed, the fingers pointing clawlike, the razor-sharp machete still embedded in his desk, two, in fact, one at each wrist. Morrissey's slight shift in weight had brought his severed wrists loose from each blade. He'd weakly lifted each stump to his eyes, a madness shining now in his dark pupils as the scream escaped him, drowning out the distress on the tape that continued to play.

During that scream in which Morrissey sounded his profound anguish and horror, the killer pointed a thin camping hatchet at Meredyth, raised it over his head and stood with feet firmly planted, about to release the hatchet with all his might and body weight behind it. She rolled over the body beside her and the hatchet ate into the dead cop, missing her by inches. Even as she rolled over the dead man, she searched for his weapon, but found none.

She clamored to her knees, the smell of blood all around her, her hair caked with it, her face and limbs smeared in it. Fearful of the next hatchet blow, she realized that the killer was toying with her. They both knew she could gain no foothold in the slick blood on the tiled floor. She could gain no footing and with each slip back into the dead body that had given up so much blood, the killer laughed uproariously.

When she did find her hands and knees firmly planted, she saw Wilcox's face clearly now, his maniacal grin wide with success as the hatchet came down a second time.

Again she tried to avoid the blow, anticipating, rolling to her left. At the same instant, a blast from a powerful weapon hit Wilcox square in the chest, sending him back-peddling and careening through the window behind him.

Meredyth looked up to find Dr. Richard Ames, shaken but firmly holding on to a huge shotgun. "Found it strapped in the unit, had to cut through the leather tie-down to get it out. Key must be on one of them." He pointed to the two dead cops, each with a bullet hole through the head.

"Thank God you came in behind me," she muttered. Taking a deep breath, she clawed to her feet by holding on to the wooden desk to steady herself. She went to Morrissey, whose anguish was complete and utter.

A light, lilting breeze played at the curtains, and soft moonlight filtered through the shattered window—strange counterpoint to the horror before Meredyth. Morrissey's forehead reflected back a bloody circle where he had been scalped. His bloody scalp lay on the desk like a heap of discarded, blood-soaked gauze for him to contemplate along with the two lifeless hands.

The tape continued to play, and now the unmistakable voice of Jared Oliver Wendell was telling Garrette, Wilcox and the others what to do, shouting, "Bloody the bastard. Do it! Do it! Do it! We don't need him any longer. You're obsolete, Dr. Morrissey. Do you hear that? Unlike us, Garrette, Wilcox and I . . . we provide a service to society. Society has to have someone to fear, so we created the Scalper and the Beheader, didn't we, fellas?"

Cheers followed this outburst.

"No, we no longer need you, Doctor," continued Wendell. "The three of us, we have each other, and I'll keep feeding the little fish for my friends to devour." He then cackled with laughter and the tape ended.

"Christ, he looks like he's been lobotomized," Ames muttered in her ear.

Morrissey choked on his own blood now. "It was . . . little one, Wen-dell, orchestra . . . ting whole ugly thing. Wilcox—said so . . ." Dr. Morrissey managed to sputter on. "It's corroborated by the tape," his words comingling with his last death rattle. The shock of having been carved with various knives to incapacitate him, the horror of having been scalped alive, and the final shock of having his hands severed drove him into a trauma from which few could recover.

"We have Wendell in custody, Wilcox is dead, and Stonecoat is onto Garrette, Dr. Morrissey," she gave him assurances as he passed from life, her last words going unheard.

She then looked up into Ames's horrified eyes, seeing that Richard now focused on the severed hands and the scalp.

"You heard what Morrissey said. Wilcox confided that Wendell masterminded the killings, and you heard what Wendell said on the tape. We have to secure the tape as evidence. It was Morrissey's last wish. Nothing can happen to it. You're my witness, Richard. I'm confiscating it here and now."

Ames made no reply, frozen before the sight of the severed hands, his own hands absently massaging each other and each wrist.

Meredyth went to Ames, walked him away from the carnage and shook him, shouting, "Richard!"

"What?" he shouted in return.

"You heard what Morrissey said about Wendell having orchestrated the killings, didn't you?"

"I . . . I think I heard that, yes, but shouldn't you leave the tape for the police?"

"I'm securing the tape," she firmly said, going about doing so, working around Morrissey's corpse. "Placing it in my possession, and you are witness to it. Richard. Richard, in a court of law, they don't want to hear what we *think* we heard."

He hesitated, still shaken.

"Damn it, Richard. He said Wilcox told him as much! That madman Morrissey had to know at some point, but he waited too long to make the call."

"We should confiscate all his notes, every scrap of paper, go through it all with a fine-tooth comb. If he knew, then he will have corroborated it in writing somewhere. He was a writer, after all . . . when he had hands, that is."

She breathed easier seeing that Richard had returned to himself. Her bloodied shoe hit something hard and metallic. Stooping, she found her gun and held tightly to it.

"Sorry," he said. "But it's the hands. The hands always bother me. Bothered me in Chicago with the Handyman Case, bothers me now with this madness."

"I understand, and hey, thanks for saving my life."

"The man left me no choice. Still, first time I ever, you know, took a life."

"You saved other lives in the bargain, Richard. He would have gone on killing."

"Yeah, right. Of course."

A banshee screech erupted at the window: Wilcox rose up like a demon from Hades, his mad eyes fixed on Meredyth as he dove for her. A single shot to the heart sent him pirouetting, clawing at thick burgundy drapery and finally stumbling back into the hell from which he'd climbed, dead again.

They heard the noise of policemen entering the home now. "In here," she called. "Someone want to turn on some damn lights?"

Richard Ames found the light switch and flicked it on. Instantly he wished he hadn't done so. The carnage done to Morrissey proved awful in the light, freezing Richard anew.

Several of the charging policemen also froze at the sight of two of their own dead amid the bloody tiles, and on taking in the sight of the scalpless, handless Dr. Morrissey.

One of the cops had spied Meredyth's attempt to conceal the tape in her hands, and said in a thick, authoritarian voice, "I'll have your weapon, Dr. Sanger and whatever it is you're hiding there."

She sighed and handed over both her .38 and the tape, saying, "Irreplaceable evidence, so tag it and bag it. This tape proves the identity of the Scalper and the Beheader. Do you understand how important that is, Officer Stedman?" She recognized Stedman from the 31st; he'd sat in on sessions dealing with the taking of a life on the street.

He nodded. "It will follow the chain of custody to the letter. You have my word on it."

She returned his nod, realizing this had become personal for the young officer as with them all. She looked at Richard's face which had gone stark. "Richard, let's go find Lucas. We'll need backup, Stedman. This isn't over yet."

"I'll back you, Doctor. We'll get twenty cars behind you if need be."

"You want to sit the next one out, Richard?" she asked the granite-faced Ames.

Ames, steeling himself, replied, "No, I want to see this through . . . to the end. There'll be untold questioning, and I won't leave you alone, not now."

She smiled into his eyes, and they held on to one another as more police poured in around them. Meredyth saw hardened veterans crossing themselves and asking, "My God, what went on here?"

Sixteen

Crossing paths

Lucas Stonecoat hadn't given up on dispatch. He'd called Henrietta back even as he pulled up to the curb before 1200 Arlington, asking, "What about a chopper, Henrietta? Think we can get a bird over this area to shine a light on the seventeenth floor?"

"We can, we can! I'll get on it. Have to pull one from someplace. Give me time, honey."

"I'm out of time, sweetie." Lucas raced from his car and toward the doorman to whom he flashed his badge and announced himself. "Stonecoat, Lieutenant, Thirty-First Precinct. I need full cooperation."

"Yes, sir . . . anything I can do, sir."

The man was well trained or well practiced, Lucas thought, searching his name tag for information. "Nicholas, mind if I call you Nick?"

"Everybody does."

"Listen, Nick, I have to get into room seventeen hundred three, and I need to get in there *now*. It could be a matter of life and death."

"Just like in the movies, huh?"

"Just like, yeah. Can you get me in? Do you have a passkey?"

"Night man. I'm in charge. I got all the keys back of the register, locked up tight."

"We have no time to waste, Nick."

"I gotcha." With that the doorman rushed through the revolving doors and for the locked keys. "You don't have a passkey that'll open the door?"

"They done away with that. Had a problem with the last doorman. Creep was sneaking into people's apartments, sifting through the ladies' underwear."

"Really?"

"Takes all kinds."

"Who lives in seventeen hundred three, Nick?"

"That'd be that nice young lady Miss Atchinson."

"Atchinson?"

"Katie Debra Atchinson, just moved here about six months ago from San Atonio."

The information matched what the toady Wendell had coughed up. "Do you know whether or not she's home?"

"Fact is, I don't recall seeing her tonight, but then she might've come in before my shift. Couldn't say for certain."

"I gotta get up there, Nick."

"What's this all about?" Nicholas unlocked the door to a closeted area behind the register. Lucas shifted nervously on his feet while the stout doorman hummed a tune and searched for the exact key, finally announcing, "Here she is."

"There're more police on the way. Guide them through and up as soon as they arrive, Nick. And thanks for this!" Lucas snatched the key from him.

"What's this all about?" Nicholas repeated as Lucas boarded the elevator. As the door closed, Lucas said, "Could be about the Scalper, could be about the Beheader, could be a false alarm."

The elevator doors closed on Nicholas's blanched face.

Lucas's heart pounded in his chest as the elevator rose at what seemed to be a snail's pace. Anxiety rode on both shoulders as he tried to catch his breath. At this moment, the Beheader could well be perched over his victim, making the final cut, or worse, he may have come and gone. That felt unlikely, as Chang had indicated the bastard took his time with his victims, appearing to have lounged about the death scene for some time after.

Lucas wondered if he'd find Wilcox or Garrette. He had no way of knowing. He wondered if the intended victim were even home yet, in which case, Lucas might be taken for the victim. Then again, Lucas could find Garrette or Wilcox dangling from a rappelling line outside the bedroom window, still working to get inside. The possibilities and suppositions proved endless.

Finally Lucas stepped off the elevator at the seventeenth floor. He moved along the corridor, searching for 1703, locating it immediately. It hugged the elevator shaft, and no doubt if the killer stood behind the door, he'd heard the elevator rise and stop on this floor.

Using the passkey, Lucas turned the lock and opened the door. He pushed the door out before him like a ghost on hinges. His thankful eyes reported back a tidy room with no blood and no decapitated body propped for anyone to discover on entering. *Good sign, good omen,* he thought.

Still, the madman could be poised and ready for him.

He knew he could not let his guard down. Wendell the weasel must have Katie Atchinson's Saturday night routine down cold, the killer knowing just when to ambush her, timing it just right. As the thought occurred to Lucas, he heard the shattering of glass in the next room, the bedroom, he guessed, where the killer had only now just entered.

Lucas pulled his gun and went for the bedroom door, fully prepared to put the bastard down if he showed the least sign of resistance, when he stumbled over a potted plant at his feet. Cursing, he barged through the door only to see a hole and a dangling rappelling harness tied to the bedpost before he was blindsided with a blow to the head. The shock stunned him and sent his gun into the dark interior of the bedroom.

Lucas didn't go down, but rather struggled to hold on to his attacker who now pummeled him repeatedly about the head and shoulders, using both his fists and all his power. Lucas caught sight of something like a hammer about to come down on him. He grabbed the arm holding the hammer—which turned out to be a camping hatchet— as it came down at him. He gripped the other man's wrists tightly, forcing him against the bed where both men bounced and found the floor.

They grappled with one another, each fearing for his life now. Lucas heard the hatchet thud to the floor, and reached to the small of his back where he always carried his bowie knife. He brought it up to the other man's eyes and found himself staring at Stanley Theopolis Garrette.

Suddenly Lucas felt a crushing blow to his temple and saw black. He went limp and fell over. He groaned and rolled about the shattered glass there on the carpet for a moment before opening his eyes to see the other man now holding both his bowie knife and the hatchet. Garrette's arms went overhead as he prepared to bring the blades to bear on Lucas.

Lucas brought up both legs and kicked the man with all of his strength, sending Garrette, screaming, through the window. His scream seemed cut short by the fierce wind coming through the gaping hole there.

Lucas saw that the weight of the killer had somehow pulled the rappelling equipment loose. Both it and Garrette dangled just outside the window. Garrette had escaped death by grabbing on to the harness. The monster now clawed his way upward in an attempt to escape back into the night from whence he had come.

Lucas, blood running down his face, the dim light distorting his features into a mask of rage, struggled to his feet, but he slipped on a baseball bat that Garrette had undoubtably found alongside the bed and used on Lucas. Garrette's bag of instruments of torture lay discarded in one corner.

Lucas searched the dark for his gun but could not locate it. He looked up to see that Garrette's feet proved all that remained as the other man scurried up the rappelling harness, tugging his weight hand over hand. Lucas spied his bowie knife across the floor, reflected in the dim light streaming through the broken window. He crawled to it, his pain intensifying, threatening to send him into a blackout. He fought with every fiber to remain conscious. His hand found the hefty knife, and he concentrated on lifting it and placing it back into its sheath at the small of his back. The exercise helped him remain focused and awake.

Angry at his attacker, angry for all the victims who hadn't survived his attacks, feeling as if all the monster's victims had found residence in him, and all came now welling up from within, Lucas let out an anguished cry. A second cry, this time a wild war cry escaped Lucas, who then backed up, took a running jump and leapt out the window, grasping ahold of the harness.

He found himself dangling seventeen stories up. Overhead, he saw Garrette struggling to hold on after the impact of Lucas striking the tether. Further overhead, Lucas saw that 1200 Arlington was being added on to, that a maze of skeletal metal beams, the beginnings of additional floors, awaited Garrette.

Lucas struggled first to simply hold on and acclimate to the conditions there, the bitter and strong wind, in particular. As he did so, he asked himself why he had been such a fool, why he had not simply taken the elevator up. He could have been comfortably awaiting his prey when the bastard came up over the lip of the building. Lucas realized that he'd been so dazed by the beating that such logic had not computed at the time most needed. Now, here he was. Rather, here he dangled.

He tried to swing the rappelling line in close, to attempt to slip back inside, to put the safer, alternative plan into motion. It proved impossible to do so against the other man's weight. While these considerations wormed their way through his aching head, Lucas looked up to see that the other man was trying to draw a bead on him, not with a gun but with his portable laser cutter, which he'd fired up.

Lucas dodged and knew this was an end game unless . . . unless . . . He calculated the distance and reached up and tugged on the end of the laser wand. The now misdirected laser cut into the side of the building. Both men held on to the tether with one hand each. They struggled for possession of the weapon until Lucas, another war cry emanating from deep within, tore it from Garrette's grasp. The sudden freeing of the slender wand sent it careening down the side of the building.

Lucas felt a deep gash at his collarbone; he felt the well of spewing blood as well. He reached up to tear away the screwdriver the other man had just jammed into him.

"Sonofabitch!" he cried out. Weak from the shock, Lucas still somehow managed to hold on to the tether with one hand and remove the bowie knife with the other. In a daze now that threatened to send him into darkness and down seventeen flights to his death, Lucas heard his grandfather's voice bolster him, saying, "Don't close your eyes. Focus on your prey. Fire the weapon with your eyes open."

Lucas had no weapon save the bowie knife, which he could not reach, his pain was so great, and the screwdriver easily, like liquid, had slipped from his grasp, winking at him like some evil porcelain doll as it plummeted away.

Garrette continued upward, making some headway, feeling secure that he had slowed Lucas sufficiently. Lucas stared up to see him pulling away while the wind continued to rip at them both, and while a lone pigeon watched from its perch on the nineteenth floor across from Lucas.

At the same instant, Nicholas the doorman led the backup unit police to apartment 1703, the current resident, Miss Katie Atchinson, alongside them asking what was going on. When they got to the door, they found it standing open, a cold wind blowing through the condo and sending its chill into the hallway.

Nicholas consoled the petite Miss Atchinson, the uniformed policemen drew their weapons and ordered the civilians to stand back. The two police officers entered the dark interior, turning on lights as they went from room to room. When they got to the bedroom, they both heard and felt the source of the cold. In a moment they could see the gaping hole in the window—large enough for a man to climb through. In the half-moon sky, they also saw the rappelling rope dangling there.

One of them switched on the light, and they saw blood on the ruffled, white bedspread and on the carpeting.

"Hell of a bill she's looking at," commented one of the cops just as Katherine Debra Atchinson looked in.

"I tried to keep her out," pleaded the doorman.

"How hard did you try?" asked the taller of the two policemen.

The shorter, stockier policeman inched out the window cautiously, as if he expected to be pulled through if caught off guard, as if he suspected the intruder here a fly on the sleek granite wall outside. "It's him all right. Gotta be," he said.

"Him? Him who?" asked the woman tenant even as her eyes played over the destruction of her bedroom.

"The Beheader guy, the guy who takes their heads."

"Could be the Scalper," countered the other officer. "Guy who takes their hands. We don't know for sure." This one began to rummage about the floor, finding Lucas's 9mm Glock and Garrette's camping hatchet.

His partner pointed out the tool bag propped in one corner. "Don't touch nothing until we get a forensic team down here, Louie. Got that? And no souvenirs."

"Whataya think I am, Joe, some kinda ghoul?"

"I don't get it," said the doorman, scratching his ear. "Where's the lieutenant?"

"That's likely his blood all over the place, and this side of the building faces the street we didn't come in on, so he's likely a pile of mush and blood on the pavement," speculated Louie.

Joe leaned out the window and stared up at the sky and the direction from which the rappelling tether dangled, just in time to see someone's legs and feet dangling near the top ledge. "Damn, the guy's still here. On the roof, Louie, now! And find out where the hell's our backup!"

Meredyth Sanger stood behind them now, Ames and Stedman beside her. She shouted, "Where's Stonecoat?"

"We believe he's been killed. Who are you?"

"Killed? When? How?" She could not believe the notion. The idea fought for survival in her mind but could not take shape. The formless possibility simply could not gel, and she could not accept it as a truth, yet her heart felt ripped from her chest on hearing this from the men who had summed up the crime scene. Ames helped support her. Stedman grit his teeth.

Again, the taller of the two uniformed officers asked her, "Who are you? Are you HPD?"

"Sanger, Doctor."

"Doctor?"

"Pyschiatric consult with the Thirty-First Precinct." She did not know the two officers, but Stedman intervened, saying, "Louie, let's get an evidence technician team in here to do a sweep."

"We suspect the Beheader or the Scalper, is on the roof right about now, Stedman."

"We were heading that way just now. Send backup our

way," the shorter of the two officers shouted, pushing past Meredyth.

"We are your backup," countered Stedman.

"We're going up with you," added Meredyth.

Ames said, "Have to see this thing through. And it's most certainly the Beheader up there and not the Scalper."

"How do you know this?" asked the skeptical officer.

Merdyth replied, "We've already put the Scalper out of his misery. Let's do the same for the other one."

"*All right*, Doctor! We're with you."

They raced for the elevator and the rooftop.

Lucas reached up over the lip of the building where construction had halted, grabbed hold of the Beheader's ankle and tripped him where he had stood on the rooftop. Bringing his bowie knife from its sheath, Lucas cut hard into the man's Achilles tendon. Garrette let out a banshee wail in response to the pain and blood Lucas had caused, but the maniac, determined to run, kicked out at Lucas and brought a machete up and over his prone head. The killer brought the machete down on Lucas. Lucas swerved to avoid the long knife, losing his grip on the building's edge, his body and the rappelling harness cascading outward. Now Garrette began slicing through the rappelling harness in an effort to send Lucas flying off on a seventeen-story plunge.

Something caught Garrette's ear from behind. He ceased cutting, but he'd bitten into the leather enough to cause considerable damage. The tear grew wider with gravity, Lucas's weight and each passing second.

Garrette, hearing the approach of others on an elevator behind him, stood now, spat on Lucas and hobbled off, his injured leg slowing him.

The tear in the harness widened. Lucas grabbed the brickwork ledge with both hands as the harness cascaded downward, taking only a moment to slap his left foot and the idle pigeon cooped there.

Lucas was holding on as best he could when he felt himself being hauled upward. Overhead, he saw two uniformed officers hauling him up while Meredyth and Richard Ames looked on. Meredyth had tears staining her face, Ames was cheering the cops on. A third uniformed cop searched the perimeter of the building for the now-invisible Stanley Garrette.

"Where's Garrette?" he said between puffs of air, his bruises and pain enfolding him.

"He was nowhere in sight when we arrived," Meredyth replied.

Lucas fought to get to his feet over her objections. He started searching the adjacent rooftops. Several buildings were joined here, and the killer must surely have gone to his left. "He's somewhere nearby. Let go of me!" he ordered.

Everyone stood apart from Lucas whose bloody appearance and anger-filled eyes frightened Meredyth. He looked like the leftovers of a human sacrifice, she thought.

Lucas struggled with both mind and body to continue the chase after Garrette. He stumbled, then found his feet, turned on the others and said, "Get on your radio. Throw up a perimeter around this entire block, now! He's getting away!"

Meredyth shouted to Lucas, telling him that they had them all on tape, confessing to Morrissey. "Wilcox is dead, thanks to Ames, and your instruction on how to shoot straight, Lucas. Wendell is in custody, and Garrette can't get far. You're hurt badly. Come away with me, and let's get you some medical attention."

He again pulled away from her. "I'm still in pursuit of a suspect, Mere. I'm going after Garrette. He can't have gotten far. He's wounded, too, and his only weapon is a machete."

"You're covered in blood, Lucas, and you're in no condition to—"

He snatched himself from her, driven now.

"But Lucas!" Meredyth caught a glimpse of savagery in Lucas—standing there, bowie knife in hand.

Lucas rushed away, in pursuit of Garrette, his bowie knife extended. The look in his eye clearly said that the knife was the only weapon Garrette deserved.

Meredyth, frustrated, stared after the stubborn Cherokee detective, whose long mane of black hair trailed after him like a cape. Stedman had gone out of sight of them, searching rooftops when suddenly they heard him scream.

Lucas jumped the small space between buildings. He now stood on a building connected by the metalwork overhead. Both buildings had been converted to condominium apartment dwellings by the same owner, obviously with the plan to connect the two buildings above the seventeenth floor. Overhead metal beams created a grid of interlocking avenues.

Lucas kneeled now over the decapitated body of Patrolman Anthony Stedman, the officer's head a few feet from his feet now. Stedman's eyes stared wide at Lucas, as if in supplication. Lucas feared for a moment the weakness that had placed him here over Stedman's body, in such a vulnerable position himself, just below a metal shed. It appeared that the blow killing Stedman had come from that direction. But no sight of Garrette remained behind.

Lucas looked up to see Meredyth and Ames staring over him and Stedman. Lucas cursed fate and Garrette. "Damn you! Damn you to hell!"

Again Lucas raced ahead of the others. He located the door to the stairwell and elevator here on this side, but found it locked. Had Garrette locked it from the inside on his way down, or had it been locked to Garrette as well? He looked around the dark rooftop and found several places where Garrette might hide with his bloody, deadly matchete.

Lucas approached each in succession, prepared to pounce on the man once he located him. But at each heating unit or outcropping here, he found no one.

He cursed the minutes lost that had allowed Garrette escape. A citywide manhunt could take days, and if Garrette were smart, he'd find a way to escape Houston altogether. Lucas wanted closure on the case, and he wanted it tonight.

He pondered these thoughts, feeling absolutely alone there atop the city, its sounds pulsating up to him in softened hews, a kind of beautiful noise here, like the sound of a whispering woman in an adjoining room.

He felt the first raindrop on his wrist. It had been threatening to rain for hours. *But what a time for it, and now it comes,* he thought. A second drop hit in exactly the same spot on his wrist, making him wonder at such a coincidence. At the same time, he wondered at the heaviness of the two raindrops, and in the next instant, he realized it was a blood rain.

He looked up to see where Garrette had hidden in plain sight amid the girders of the new construction overhead.

Garrette, unable to go through the locked stairwell leading downward, had taken a calculated risk, going upward instead.

Lucas now started up the girder closest to him, going for the weakened prey. Garrette inched his way toward the far, cold edge of the construction steel. There he found a steel-reinforced ladder that would take him the additional seven floors up. Lucas drew on his earlier years as a steelworker, calmly walking the beams toward Garrette, a fire in his eyes. He followed Garrette's retreat, ending when the man threatened, "I'll jump if you come a step closer."

"Oh, really?" Lucas took an additional step, saying, "You mean, like this?"

Garrette responded by throwing the matchete at Lucas's head, the long blade striking the steel girder alongside Lucas's left eye, metal splinters burning into his retina.

"I'll see you in hell, Garrette!" he screamed his response.

A helicopter suddenly came up over the edge of the building, shining a blinding beacon on the scene, frightening Garrette who almost lost his footing. Lucas took another menacing step toward him as a policeman on the chopper ordered them both down.

Garrette shouted over the noise of the helicopter, the bullhorn voice and the wind, crying out, "One more step, and I jump."

"Go ahead, Stanley. Be my guest." Lucas stepped closer.

Garrette backed to the outside edge of the beam he stood on, looking out over at the street below. "I tell you, I'll fly away, you come one more step."

"You don't have the guts, Stanley. You're as pathetic as Wendell. You never had the guts to think for yourself, and you sure don't now. Wendell told you when to put your fly up, and now he's singing about how you forced him to work for you, Stanley. That means you fry for his lies."

"Fuck you," shouted Garrette.

"Lucas! Come down. Let the SWAT team handle it now. Please!" Lucas half turned to look down at Meredyth, giving Garrette a glance. She watched the bulge of Lucas's bowie knife glint under the helicopter spotlight.

"Lucas!" Meredyth's voice continued to rival the wind. "Let the others take it from here!"

Lucas saw the prize in Garrette's eye, that he had his mind on gaining the bowie knife to once again attack Lucas. "You want this, Stanley?" he asked, holding the blade up. "Here. Catch!"

Lucas threw the blade into the air just out of Garrette's grasp. He had gauged the man's desperate eyes accurately. The madman reached for it, losing his footing and pirouetting on the beam for a moment with the bowie blade doing a dance on his fingertips. In a moment, both blade and Garrette held their places in midair, defying gravity, but only for a millisecond and then they began sailing downward.

Lucas called out, "Have a nice flight and landing," as he watched the Beheader, wingless now, find his way to the concrete below. "Hopefully the fall will behead and gut you as well as kill you, you bastard thing." This Lucas followed with a war whoop not lost on those onlookers aboard the helicopter or Meredyth on the rooftop below.

$\mathcal{S}$EVENTEEN

Ward off evil spirits

The ambulance careened into the Houston Memorial emergency bay. "You'll get all the painkillers you want here, Lucas," Meredyth told him.

But Lucas had passed out, and he lay now in eerie silence. She feared he might be hurt more on the inside than the outside, that some internal hemorrhaging might be slowly killing him. She shouted at the medics, "Be certain that the doctors check for any signs of internal bleeding, low blood pressure, any unseen wounds."

They wheeled Lucas away from Meredyth, her heart wrenching at the sight of him in so weakened a condition. She recalled how Jack Kirshner had gone from this life, but as far as the medics could tell, Lucas had not been the victim of any gunshots.

Meredyth had held Lucas up as they made their way down the elevator, back to the street. She had insisted on riding with him in back of the ambulance, where she learned from paramedics that Lucas's wounds were extensive. The nasty wound to the neck particularly troublesome, rivaling the blow he'd suffered to the head. He required stitches, antibiotics and painkillers.

Lucas was in and out of consciousness. He saw Meredyth shouting at paramedics to give him the best of care, saw her rush alongside as he was whisked to a waiting ambulance, and he heard her order the paramedics to get him to the closest trauma facility and the best care money could buy. He recalled having seen her climb into the wagon. He vaguely saw her in a fog there in the ambulance as they rode to the hospital, but there was no mistaking her touch. She held his hand the entire way.

"You look like hell," she told him.

"So do you," he replied, realizing her hair was caked with blood. "Things went all right at Morrissey's?" he asked.

"Morrissey lost his scalp and his hands before we could get there. Died of the trauma. Wilcox was shot to death, shot twice, once with a shotgun blast from Richard, and I put a thirty-eight slug into his heart after he got back up and attempted to kill me again. He made three attempts at me with a hatchet. It was close, Lucas. I'm lucky to be alive, thanks to Richard."

"It appears so. You're covered in blood."

"Wilcox killed two patrolmen who'd gotten there ahead of us. The blood is from them."

"We got all three of the bastards, didn't we," he said.

She nodded. "Two dead, the third in custody, and with this tape." She held up Morrissey's tape, retrieved from Stedman's patrol car by Ames. "Wendell will be behind bars for well over three hundred years, I can assure you."

Lucas closed his eyes at the thought. . . .

•　•　•

Lucas's bodily injuries and wounds had started healing while he lay in his hospital room. Tsalie came in the night, long after everyone else had gone. He had been asleep and came awake under her caress. She'd shed all her clothing.

Tsalie remained the entire night curled in his arms. They made fervent love there, Lucas knowing it must be for this one moment only, that he must never touch her again afterward. Their heated passion finally subsided, and she lay now in the crook of his arm. He believed the lovemaking like a potion, able to allow him to forget his pain for a time.

"How did you get away? Where is Billy tonight?" he now asked.

"Gone . . ."

"Gone where?"

"On a job . . . Something he said he could tell me nothing about, a job for your cursed friend Roundpoint."

"Damn that Billy. I told him to steer clear of Zachary Roundpoint."

"Work for hire, he calls it." She sniffed back a tear for Billy.

"This work can only end in ruin, possibly death."

"Billy seems beat on showing you up, Lucas, to be more successful than you."

"Do you want me to talk to Roundpoint? To Billy? Put an end to this?"

"No, no . . . Billy is not your fat little cousin anymore, Lucas. He has chosen this path, this glamorous lifestyle of the Houston underworld. Besides . . . he will only believe you or me when we agree with him."

"He needs a swift kick in the ass."

"How do the whites say it? He's made his bed, now he can sleep in it. I am so tired of fighting."

"He's sleeping with serpents."

"When he is bitten, I will be free of him. Will you have me then?"

Lucas felt a wave of confusion mingling with uncertainty wash over him. "I . . . I can't say how I . . . will feel in such a case."

"Then tell me tonight meant nothing to you."

"It meant a great deal, Tsalie."

Just then the door opened, and Lucas put a finger to Tsalie's lips. Anyone might come through the door, he thought, but guessed it most likely the night nurse. Still, with no locks on the doors here, Billy could step through, or Captain Lincoln, or Meredyth Sanger. He wondered which would be easiest to face with his cousin's wife in bed with him.

"Lucas?" It was Meredyth's whisper. "My insomnia got the better of me. Thought I'd keep you company. How're we—"

Meredyth pulled up short on seeing Lucas had a woman in his darkened hospital bed, and not just any woman, but the beautiful, dark-featured Indian Meredyth knew only as Tsalie.

Lucas had mentioned how much help his former lover and now sister-in-law had been to him during his grandfather's illness, death and subsequent funeral. Now Meredyth knew exactly what Lucas had meant.

She turned on her heels and made a beeline for the door to Lucas's repeated shouts, "Meredyth! Meredyth!" But it proved no use.

"Meredyth," said Tsalie. "She is the psychiatrist? The one you work with?"

"Yes."

"She is . . . beautiful."

"Yes . . . yes, she is."

Tsalie kissed him passionately in response. Then she said, "It should have always been you and me, Moon Wolf—not you and her, and not Billy and me. We have a chance to fix it right now. It would not take too much to fix. . . ."

He stared up at her, seeing the gleam of hope in her eyes that had taken on the look of greed now. For the first time, he realized what she had been suggesting all along. "Are you asking me to drop a dime on Billy? Ask Round-point to do me a *small* favor?"

"With a single word from you, Lucas, we could have it all back—you, me, the children, all together. You could give up this life that is no life, this profession that leaves you in death's grasp, and we could be happy . . . eternally happy."

Lucas stared at a woman he did not recognize, seeing for the first time how much Tsalie had aged, how the crowsfeet had created a delta around each eye, how the gray had crept into her hair—and her thinking. "Happiness is highly overrated, Tsalie, when the price is murder."

"Murder? Who's talking about murder? We don't have to do a thing. Billy will, in time, get himself killed."

"And when you become bored with me?"

"That will never happen, Lucas."

He shook his head to this, bit his lip and pulled himself upright in the bed, despite the pain it caused.

She reached for him, caressing his face. He pulled away. "You can't know what it is like, living with that drunk all these years. Boredom doesn't begin to describe it."

"I myself am an addict, Tsalie, addicted to painkillers— peyote. So, how soon do you become tired of me?"

"You're in constant pain, Lucas. You use drugs to control the pain. Everyone knows that. Billy is simply weak."

"And what's another body discovered dead in the city, huh?"

"We don't *need* to be a part of it. Time will take care of it, time alone."

"But we are a part of it. We already are."

"What're you saying?"

"You're speaking to a police detective about conspiracy to commit murder, Tsalie, and it does not become you."

"I have not said the word, not once. You have, Lucas!" she defended, perched on her knees now, her breasts dangling, looking now like a cat discovering its claws.

Lucas calmly said, "Billy tried to tell me about you . . . that you were the one ambitious to get control of the old man's house and property. I see now that he was right."

"I am innocent of such remarks. Billy is a liar. You know him to be one."

"You are cunning, far more so than you are innocent."

"Cunning? Me? I have never been called cunning by anyone. The People do not call me cunning."

"No one sees true cunning until it is too late. Grandfather taught me that. He was too weak at the end to see it in you, and I suppose I was as well."

"Damn you, Lucas. We could have a wonderful life together."

"I guess I always knew that you were calculating, Tsalie. I simply didn't want to believe it of you. Now my eyes are open."

She felt the coldness emanating from him now. She lifted off the bed, dressed and prepared to leave. "I hope your recovery is speedy, Lucas, and I hope you will think about my . . . proposal."

"I have already thought about it, Tsalie, and it has poisoned this night."

"I thought of all the men I know, Lucas, that you would have the heart and head to free me of Billy Hawk. Apparently, I was wrong."

"Tsalie . . ." His tone stopped her at the door. "If anything should happen to Billy, I will have to arrest you. That would mean separation from your children, and if you have anything to do with his death, a long separation."

"So, I am in the box I sought to free myself from, only now the lid is tighter."

"Something like that . . ."

The hospital door closed silently in her wake. "Damn," Lucas cursed under his breath. "Damn this life . . ." None of his wounds, none of his old hurts and lifelong injuries compared to this . . . this . . . "Betrayal," he said aloud.

$\mathcal{E}$PILOGUE

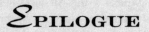

Thunderbird track: bright prospect

TWO MONTHS LATER

Life had returned to normal in Lieutenant Lucas Stone-coat's world, and in the mainstream of Houston. Lucas had returned to his Cold Room files, dedicating himself to the task of making COMIT work. He wanted none of the publicity surrounding the Scalper/Beheader case that had been masterminded by Wendell and operated by Wilcox and Garrette. Still, he would have to be at the trial to do his part, to testify about all that he had seen and heard and done. But he must be cunning in his choice of words, so as to not have the case thrown out on some legal technicality, which is what Wendell's lawyer now counted on.

Lucas had gone over his testimony countless times with Captain Lincoln and the DA's office. This had brought him into limited contact with Meredyth, but she had made it clear that outside their professional life, she wanted nothing more to do with him.

Meantime, Lucas would be facing a hotshot lawyer who

had taken on Wendell's case in order to make a name for himself. The lawyer, a man named Sessoms, had been snooping about Lucas's life. In fact, Sessoms had been dogging Lucas's footsteps since his hospital stay. He had also dug up information about Lucas's unfortunate reversal of fortune with the Dallas PD, the entire episode in which his partner was killed and the departmental investigation had ruled Lucas and his partner too drunk to be serving the public.

Sessoms had been working day and night to dirty Lucas's reputation. The man could not find the dots connecting Wendell to the Scalper and the Beheader, he said, claiming he would do all in his power to suppress information illegally obtained. He claimed that even the tape found at the murder scene at Morrissey's home would be ruled inadmissible due to how police were led there via a coerced confession from his client. However, Sessoms had a weakness in his own case: He could find no one to corroborate Wendell's story that he had been coerced through bodily harm and danger into giving up Wilcox and Garrette and implicating himself in the bargain.

On Lucas's side stood Captain Lincoln, and behind him the mayor's office, the governor and Senator Kensington. Lincoln pointed to the recorded daylong interrogations conducted by Offiah and Blanton as evidence of Wendell's schizophrenic nature, which led to suspicions. He pointed to the legally obtained arrest warrant for Wendell, the legally obtained surveillance of the halfway collective, and from this what police observed of the three suspects handed to them on a list provided by Dr. Thomas Morrissey, who had rightfully feared for his life. Finally Lucas had been invited into the halfway home by the then smugsure defendant. Evidence obtained from Wilcox's refrigerator in the basement included human hands, scalps and one head. Wilcox had shared his icebox with Garrette.

It appeared a tough row ahead, but Lucas felt confident that Wendell would be placed behind bars without chance of parole for the rest of his life.

No one was certain how long or how hard Lucas's side of the story would hold, but it appeared the best for public consumption to date. Aside from the female victims killed, three cops had been slain as a result of Jared Oliver Wendell's *game*. So police across the city had united behind Lucas and against Wendell, who appeared to be the most hated man since Gerald Stano and Jeffrey Dahmer.

Lucas received cards and letters of thanks from strangers all across the city, claiming that now, thanks to him, they could again sleep peacefully in the sanctuary of their high-rise apartments. Lucas also had had a phone call from Zachary Roundpoint, congratulating him on a job well done—and once again telling him that if he ever needed a job to simply call.

"You already have my cousin working for you. I asked you to not allow that," he'd shouted at Roundpoint.

"Your cousin is a big boy, Lucas. Cut the tie. He's working out just fine. Who knows, in time, perhaps he'll have his own territory."

"You're making a shambles of my family, Roundpoint."

"There's nothing left between Billy Hawk and Tsalie, Lucas. You can reach out and take her anytime you wish."

"Sonofabitch," he had muttered in return, realizing just how much planning had gone into Tsalie's deception.

Lucas tried to contact Meredyth, but she remained adamant about not seeing him outside a professional need. He simply kept trying, hoping to wear her down—as he

was doing now in the lobby of her apartment building,
having bribed his way past the doorman with a show of
his badge and a fifty-dollar bill.

Lucas had spent sleepless nights thinking about Meredyth and all that they had been through. He also had sat
up nights wondering about all the madness that had escaped from the psyche of three killers—all supposed to
be living and working toward rehabilitation with the same
shrink in that damnable halfway beehive. He wondered if
Morrissey would agree with him now that such negative
energy infected other people and infested places. He ru-
minated about petty evil and larger evil, and he knew that
he would face a great deal more of the same in the future,
from the pettiness of his cousin Billy—now in the employ
of Zachary Roundpoint—to the enormous evil of the
Scalper/Beheader killers.

Lucas rang the bell at Meredyth's door. He had learned
through Randy Oglesby that she had dumped her boyfriend. Lucas envisioned an evening meal, good wine,
crisp conversation—after an explanation about Tsalie—
and soon they would both be in a mood to get a buzz on.
She'd ask Lucas back here to her place.

Wish-full-up-ment, Dr. Morrissey would have called it,
he told himself. "Yeah, why not," he added, feeling the
promise hanging in the air—a will-o'-the-wisp, just out
of reach. Then the door opened and closed in his face.

"How did you get up here to my door?" she demanded
through the barrier between them.

"Hey, I'm the master of stealth, remember? And I dare
not reveal my secrets."

"What do you want, Lucas?"

"A chance . . . just a chance."

"A chance at what?"

"At you."

She snatched the door open and stared at him. "You have some nerve, Lucas. What about the love of your life—Tsalie?"

"She has my heart no longer. Besides, all I want is an opportunity to take you to dinner. No obligations, no problems."

"Dinner? I don't think so. Why aren't you having dinner with her?"

"Tsalie was my first love, and because of that, she will always be . . . remain a fantasy. I wanted to remember her as the sweet and unblemished creature of our youth, but . . ."

"Go on, but?"

He took a deep breath. "She's no longer the child I loved, no more than I am the boy she loved. Today . . . now . . . you know far more who I am than she. Don't you see? We—you and I—have far more in common, and I know who you are."

"And Tsalie?"

He shook his head and gritted his teeth. "I am no longer at ease with her. I certainly no longer love her."

Meredyth sighed deeply. "I see. That's more words from you than I've heard all year."

This made him laugh. She joined him in laughter. "Come in . . . let me get myself together, and we'll go eat and talk some more."

"Women . . . you love to talk."

"You'll have to put up with it."

"Know of a good place nearby?" he asked.

"Italian, down the street."

"Good wine?"

"The best."

"Let's do it then. Grab your keys, your purse, whatever you need, and we're off."

She went about the apartment, picking up what she needed, combing through her blond hair. He watched her graceful movements from the foyer. "I've missed you, Mere."

She turned and stared into his eyes. "I think you might mean that."

"I do mean that."

"Really?"

"Missed our friendship, our closeness."

"I guess I should be flattered."

"I'm talking a hundred percent here," he added.

She stepped into him and passionately kissed him. He returned her kiss, sending a probing tongue into her mouth. She gasped and said, "Maybe we should order in?"

"I'd like that . . . like it very much."